"Nearly ten years. I've waited long enough to finish what I started on the Blue River Ranch. This time, no one will be there to save you. This time, you will die."

Gabriel cursed. "You got this message, and you still came here?"

Jodi shrugged, tried to make it seem as if this didn't have her in knots.

"This proves my father's innocent," she said.

"No. A copycat could have written it. Or your father could have paid someone to do it."

"But I have to believe it wasn't a copycat. It's either that or accept that my father murdered both of your parents, attacked me and then left me for dead." She paused, shook her head. "Of course, no one in your family had trouble believing it."

"Neither did a jury," Gabriel pointed out.

"My father was convicted on circumstantial evidence," Jodi said, though she was preaching to the choir. Because as the sheriff and the son of the murdered couple, Gabriel knew the case better than everyone else.

Ever

"Maybe you will. I've waited long enough to think what I started so the time I've―" [illegible]. "This time, no one will be there to save you. This time, you will die."

[illegible speech] "You're still a teenage and you still carry a―"

[illegible] gaze [illegible] came to rest, as if the wait had just ended.

"This one was... still innocent," she said. [illegible] his eyes closed and knees sank to the [illegible] could be a real soul, for us to be.

Still [illegible] to believe it tried to capture. Then [illegible] a split into a grin. Then sudden look in the [illegible] for all. It looked like... the car that killed his wife. A cracker behind the [illegible]. The car he once told me he'd trade anything to drive again.

[illegible] but a grin. A third [illegible] out.

[illegible] was, "Good luck?" for [illegible] my figure. "And you get. He was probably it," [illegible] it, like us told me and the son of me. [illegible] a crash. [illegible] my word of case, isn't that everyone else."

ALWAYS A
LAWMAN

BY
DELORES FOSSEN

MILLS &
BOON®

First Published in Great Britain 2017
By Mills & Boon, an imprint of HarperCollins*Publishers*
1 London Bridge Street, London, SE1 9GF

© 2017 Delores Fossen

ISBN: 978-0-263-92938-6

46-1217

MIX
Paper from
responsible sources
FSC™ C007454

www.fsc.org

This book is produced from independently certified FSC™ paper to ensure responsible forest management.

For more information visit: www.harpercollins.co.uk/green

Printed and bound in Spain
by CPI, Barcelona

Delores Fossen, a *USA TODAY* bestselling author, has sold over fifty novels with millions of copies of her books in print worldwide. She's received a Booksellers' Best Award and an RT Reviewers' Choice Best Book Award. She was also a finalist for a prestigious RITA® Award. You can contact the author through her website at www.deloresfossen.com.

Chapter One

She had died here. Temporarily, anyway.

But she was alive now, and Jodi Canton could feel the nerves just beneath the surface of her skin. With the Smith & Wesson gripped in her hand, she inched closer to the dump site where *he* had left her for dead.

There were no signs of the site now. Nearly ten years had passed, and the thick Texas woods had reclaimed the ground. It didn't look nearly so sinister dotted with wildflowers and a honeysuckle vine coiling over it. No drag marks.

No blood.

The years had washed it all away, but Jodi could see it, smell it and even taste it as if it were that sweltering July night when a killer had come within a breath of ending her life.

The nearby house had succumbed to time and the elements, too. It'd been a home then. Now, the white paint was blistered, and several of the windows on the bottom floor were closed off with boards that had grayed with age. Of course, she hadn't expected this place to ever feel like anything but the crime scene that it had once been.

Considering that two people had been murdered inside.

Jodi adjusted the grip on the gun when she heard the

footsteps. They weren't hurried, but her visitor wasn't trying to sneak up on her, either. Jodi had been listening for that. Listening for everything that could get her killed.

Permanently this time.

Just in case she was wrong about who this might be, Jodi pivoted and took aim at him.

"You shouldn't have come here," he said. His voice was husky and deep, part lawman's growl, part Texas drawl.

The man was exactly who she thought it might be. Sheriff Gabriel Beckett. No surprise that he had arrived since this was Beckett land, and she'd parked in plain sight on the side of the road that led to the house. Even though the Becketts no longer lived here, Gabriel would have likely used the road to get to his current house.

"*You* came," Jodi answered, and she lowered her gun.

Muttering some profanity with that husky drawl, Gabriel walked to her side, his attention on the same area where hers was fixed. Or at least it was until he looked at her the same exact moment that she looked at him.

Their gazes connected.

And now it was Jodi who wanted to curse. *Really?* After all this time that punch of attraction was still there? She had huge reasons for the attraction to go away and not a single reason for it to stay.

Yet it remained.

At least on her part anyway. That wasn't heat she saw in Gabriel's eyes. Not attraction heat anyway. He was riled to the bone that she was back at the scene of the crime.

Gabriel hadn't changed much over the years. He was as lanky as he had been a decade ago. His dark brown hair was shorter now, but he still had those sizzling blue eyes. Still had the face that could make most women do a triple take. Simply put, he was one hot cowboy cop.

"Is it true?" Gabriel asked. "Are you actually remembering more details from the night of the attack?"

She'd expected the question and heard the skepticism in his voice. Skepticism that she deserved. Because her remembering anything else was a lie. "No. I told the press that because I thought it would draw out the real killer."

He gave her a look that could have frozen the hottest parts of hell. "That's not only stupid, it's dangerous. You made yourself a target."

"I'm already a target," she mumbled under her breath. And because she thought they needed a change of subject, Jodi tipped her head to the house. "I'm surprised it's still standing. Why haven't you bulldozed it?"

A muscle tightened in his jaw. "There's a difference of opinion about that in the family."

Yes, Jodi had heard about some of those *opinions*. One of his sisters had wanted the place to remain standing, though Jodi had no idea why. She couldn't imagine any of them wanting to live in the house again. Still, maybe it was hard to demolish a childhood home even when that place was now a reminder of the nightmare.

"It's not a good time to be out here," he growled as if delivering an order that she would jump to obey. "And not just because you put out that lie to the press."

Jodi stayed put, and she darn sure didn't jump. "I was hoping if I saw the place again, it actually would help me remember, that what I told the press would no longer be a lie."

He aimed a scowl at her. Then, another scowl at the house and the spot where he'd found her bleeding and dying nearly a decade ago. "Why the heck would you want to remember that?"

He had a point. But so did Jodi. It wasn't a point that would likely make sense to Gabriel.

"I want to see his face." She shook her head. "I want to *remember* his face."

Ironically, it was one of the few things about that night that she couldn't recall. That particular detail was lost in the tangle of memories in her head. She could feel the slice of the knife as it cut into her body.

The pain.

Jodi could remember the blood draining from her. But she couldn't see the man who'd been responsible for turning her life on a dime.

"Why come back now?" Gabriel demanded. "Why tell the press that you're remembering after all this time?"

Good questions. And she had good answers.

"I got an email." Jodi figured that would get his attention, and it did.

Gabriel turned those lethal blue eyes on her. "What kind of email?"

She took out the printed copy from the front pocket of her jeans and handed it to him. Jodi didn't need to see what was written there. She'd memorized every word.

Nearly ten years. I've waited long enough to finish what I started on the Blue River Ranch. This time, no one will be there to save you. This time, you will die.

Gabriel cursed again. "You got this, and you still came here?"

Jodi shrugged, tried to make it seem as if this message didn't have her in knots. It did. But then, she'd been in knots for a long time now. For ten painful years. In some sick way, maybe this meant there'd be a showdown, and the knots would finally loosen.

"This proves my father's innocent," she said and waited for Gabriel to blast that to smithereens.

It didn't take long before he attempted that blast. "No. A copycat could have written it. Or your father could have paid someone to do it."

Both could be true, and she acknowledged that with a slight sound of agreement. "But I have to believe it wasn't a copycat. It's either that or accept that my father murdered both of your parents, attacked me and then left me for dead." She paused, shook her head. "Of course, no one in your family had trouble believing it."

"Neither did a jury," Gabriel pointed out.

It was true. A jury had indeed convicted her father, Travis, of two counts of murder and also of her own attack, and the jurors had given him two consecutive life sentences without the possibility of parole. He was rotting away in a jail cell, exactly where the Becketts wanted him. Of course, it could have been worse. Travis could have gotten the death penalty, but thankfully the DA had backed off on that because of some weaknesses in the case.

No eye witness to put Travis at the scene, and the fact that her father couldn't recall what'd gone on that night.

"My father was convicted on circumstantial evidence," Jodi said, though she was preaching to the choir. Because as the sheriff and the son of the murdered couple, Gabriel knew the case better than everyone else.

Everyone but the real killer, that is.

"My father didn't have the murder weapon on him

when the cops found him," she went on. Yes, Gabriel knew that, too, but she wanted to remind him. "And the wounds to your parents and to me were made with a unique knife."

"A skinning knife with a crescent-shaped blade. Is this going somewhere?" he continued without hesitating. "Because it doesn't matter that your father claimed he didn't own a knife like that—"

"He didn't," she interrupted. "I was the one who cleaned the house. Cleaned his room. The barn. You name it, I cleaned it, and I never saw a blade that resembled anything like a crescent."

It wasn't easy for her to talk about the knife. But even when she didn't talk about it, the image of it was still clear in her head. Not from that night, though. Jodi hadn't actually seen it, but the FBI had shown her photos of a skinning knife. And they were certain that's what had been used on her because the tip of it had broken off during the attack. The surgeon had removed it from what'd been left of her spleen.

"That doesn't mean Travis didn't have that knife hidden away," Gabriel countered. "And I don't care if he says he didn't. Nor do I care that he claims he can't remember anything from that night because he had three times more than the legal limit of alcohol. The bottom line is that he had motive, and my father's blood on his shirt."

Blood that someone could have planted there when Travis was passed out drunk by the Blue River, where the deputies had found him hours after the murders and her own attack.

Jodi couldn't have argued that her alcoholic father hadn't been in any shape to murder two people, one of them sheriff at the time. That's because the DA had successfully argued that Travis could have gotten drunk afterward.

And yes, her father did have motive.

Bad blood between him and the Becketts. Feuds over land and water rights that had been going on before Jodi was born. It had created the perfect trifecta for law enforcement. Her father had had the means, motive and opportunity to butcher two people and then turn that knife on Jodi when he thought maybe she'd witnessed what he had done.

She hadn't.

Because of the blasted tears she'd been crying over Gabriel's rejection, she hadn't seen anything. She'd barely had time to hear the footsteps before her attacker had clubbed her on the head and started stabbing her.

"Have you considered the reason you don't remember your attacker's face is because you blocked it out?" Gabriel asked a moment later. "Because it was too traumatic for you to see the face of the man that you thought loved you?"

Jodi had to take a moment to try to tamp down the panic rising inside her. No way could she believe that.

"My father never confessed to the murders," she pointed out.

"That doesn't mean he didn't do it," he countered and then huffed. No doubt signaling an end to an argument they'd been having for a decade. He looked at the email again. "You gave a copy of this to the FBI?"

She nodded, annoyed that it was a question. "Of course I gave it to them since they're the ones who handled this investigation. With you and your brother's help, of course."

In fact, Gabriel's brother, Jameson, had pretty much spearheaded the case in the beginning. Not that anyone had been dragging their feet. No. Everyone seemed to be racing toward any evidence that would result in her father's conviction. But Jameson had been a key player in getting that guilty verdict.

"I just wanted to make sure you didn't withhold anything from the FBI," Gabriel added. "Because they need to see any and all threats, so they can put a stop to them."

Jodi's annoyance went up a notch. Gabriel was talking down to her. Talking to her as if she was a criminal. Or an idiot. "I know you don't think much of what I do for a living, but I'd have no reason to keep something like that to myself."

He handed her back the email, his gaze connecting with hers again, and she got another dose of his doubt.

Gabriel definitely didn't think much of what she did. Consultant for Sentry, a private security firm. Many cops thought that Sentry toed the line when it came to investigations.

And sometimes they did.

"I don't wear one of these," she said, tapping his badge, "but that doesn't mean I'm not out for justice just like you, Jameson and your deputies."

"Justice at any price," he argued.

She shrugged, trying to make sure she didn't look as if that'd stung a little. "Repeating my boss's motto—the law isn't always justice."

"Hector March." Gabriel said her boss's name as if it were profanity. To him, it was. "Is he out of jail yet?"

That was another jab. And another sting. "Yes. And for the record, what Hector did was definitely justice. The illegal video surveillance he set up eventually led to the arrest of a pimp who was known for beating up his girls. He used his fists to do whatever he wanted, and now he's been stopped."

There was too much emotion in her voice now. Too much emotion inside her, as well. It was hard to rein in the feelings of being powerless against a much stronger attacker, but Jodi had had a lot of practice doing just that.

"The pimp would have gone to jail eventually through legal means," Gabriel growled.

It was probably the truth. Probably. But Hector had made it happen a little sooner than the cops could have managed it.

"If I can save one woman from getting beaten or killed, I'll do it," Jodi insisted. "And yes, I'm overidentifying."

She waved off any other part of this discussion that might happen because she'd admitted that. It was obvious Gabriel and she were never going to agree when it came to Sentry, Hector or her job. Jodi also didn't want to keep talking about something that couldn't change. She'd nearly died. Had the scars to prove it. Nothing was going to undo that.

"You blame me for what happened to you." Gabriel threw that out there like a gauntlet.

She turned toward him so fast that her neck popped. Jodi wanted to say no, that she didn't. Better yet, she wanted to believe it. But she didn't. Not completely anyway.

"I know in here it wasn't your fault." She touched her fingers to her head. "But everything that happened that night has gotten all rolled into one tangled mess inside me. A mess that involves you, me…and the killer. I don't want to include you in that nightmare, but it did begin with you, and I can't just forget that."

"Yeah," he said and looked away. Gabriel always looked away whenever the subject of attraction or sex came up between them. And despite her near murder not actually being about sex, it was sex that had started it all.

Or rather, lack of sex.

"You were nineteen," he reminded her. "Too young to be with me."

Obviously, his mind had hitched a ride on the exact train of thought as hers. "I was an adult."

"Barely. You were also one of my kid sister's best friends. And I was five years older than you. There's a world of difference between a nineteen-year-old college student and a twenty-four-year-old deputy sheriff. Legally, you weren't jailbait, but that still didn't make being with you right."

It was his old argument that she knew all too well since it was the same one he'd used the night of the attack. She'd been staying in the Beckett house, a guest of Gabriel's sister Ivy, who at the time was also her college roommate. Around 10:00 p.m., Jodi had walked the less than a quarter of a mile distance between the Becketts' and Gabriel's place, the house left to him by his grandparents. And Jodi had done that for the sole purpose of seducing Gabriel.

It hadn't worked.

"You turned me down," she said under her breath. Thankfully, it didn't sound as if she still carried a decade of hurt. But it had certainly hurt then. Simply put, Gabriel Beckett was the only man she'd ever wanted. It was ironic, though, that after the night of the attack she'd never wanted him or another man again.

She silently cursed. That was a partial lie. A lie she could feel now that she was standing so close to Gabriel. Much to her disgust, she still wanted him.

"Sex is a commitment," she mumbled. "That's what you told me when you turned me away," Jodi huffed. "Which wasn't the truth since you had sex with half the women in town, and you didn't *commit* to any of them."

He said something under his breath that she didn't catch. Then, something she did catch. Bad profanity. "Why did you really come here? Because I'm not buying it that you're here just to remember. Are you trying to draw out the person who sent you the email?"

She didn't deny it. Jodi did indeed want to draw him out in the open and put an end to this once and for all.

"He could just shoot you," Gabriel reminded her.

"I don't think so. I think he wants his hands on me again." Just saying it nearly made her gag. "I won't be the victim for the rest of my life."

"Then start by not being here." Gabriel paused and glanced around. The kind of glance that a lawman made as if checking to make sure no one else was there. "You're not the only one who got a threatening email."

Everything inside her went still. "Who else? *You?*"

Gabriel nodded. "All three of my siblings, too. Jameson, Ivy and Lauren."

Jodi hadn't needed their names. She'd grown up next to the Becketts and knew them well enough to know their birthdays. Now, of course, they were her enemies. Enemies who'd apparently gotten death threats.

"What'd the emails say?" she asked.

Gabriel drew in a weary breath. "Almost the same as yours. Except for mine. The threat was, well, more explicit. Probably because I'm the sheriff now."

Jodi tried to process that. "What possible reason would my father have to send threats like this?"

"I've given up trying to figure out why killers do what they do." He hesitated again. "But I'm leaning more toward a copycat. There are a lot of sick people out there, and the story got plenty of press. With the tenth anniversary coming up in three months, I believe it's bringing out the lunatics."

"So, you think the emails are empty threats?" Jodi hated to sound disappointed. Hated even more that she was disappointed that it might be true. It sickened her to think the truth had already played out.

And that her father had left her for dead.

"Copycat threats aren't always empty," Gabriel corrected. "That's why I don't want you out here. Not alone anyway. If you want to try to jog your memory again, call me, and I'll have someone meet you."

Jodi probably should be insulted because she was an expert marksman and trained in hand-to-hand combat. She could protect herself.

Probably.

And it was the fact that the *probably* was not a certainty that kept her up at night.

She turned, ready to head back to her car, but something caught her eye. Some movement in one of the second-floor windows. Gabriel must have seen it, too, because he stepped in front of her.

And he drew his gun.

Jodi pulled her weapon, too. "Should there be anyone in the house?" she asked.

"No." That time he absolutely didn't hesitate, and Gabriel started toward the porch. "Before you jump to conclusions, it's probably just a teenager out for a stupid thrill. Or maybe a reporter. Either way, you should go to your car now."

"Just in case it turns out to be something more than a teen or a reporter, I can back you up if you're going inside."

Which he apparently was.

Gabriel didn't turn down her offer of backup. Didn't order her to her car again, either. Maybe because he figured she could be attacked while heading to the road. It was obvious he was thinking this was more than just a false alarm. Of course, after those threatening emails, Jodi doubted there was anything false about it, either.

Mercy. Was the killer here?

That sent her heartbeat racing, the sound of it throbbing in her ears. The memories came. Too many of them too fast. She had to force them back into that little box she'd built in her mind. This was no time for a panic attack. Not in front of a killer.

Not in front of Gabriel, either.

He took slow, cautious steps, his gaze firing not just to the window but all around them. "I'm Sheriff Gabriel Beckett," he called out. "You're trespassing. Come out with your hands in the air."

Nothing.

It was hard to hear because of her racing pulse and the breeze rattling through the live oaks, but Jodi thought she heard someone moving around inside. There were plenty of windows on the back part of the house that the intruder could use to escape. But maybe he didn't have escape in mind.

Maybe this would turn into another attempt to murder her.

If so, she was ready.

"Stay behind me," Gabriel insisted. "And watch our backs."

She did, and Jodi continued to keep an eye out as they made their way up the steps to the porch. But as soon as Gabriel reached the top step, he stopped.

Then, he froze.

Jodi was near enough to him to sense the muscles tensing in his body. And she soon realized why.

Her heart jumped to her throat. "Oh, mercy." Jodi shook her head and inched closer. Not that she needed to be closer to realize what she was seeing.

A knife.

With a crescent-shaped blade. The tip was missing. And there was blood on it.

Chapter Two

Even before he saw the knife. Gabriel had already had a bad feeling. He'd gotten it the moment he laid eyes on Jodi because she should be nowhere near this place. Now, that bad feeling turned to something much worse.

Hell.

Just to be sure his eyes weren't playing tricks on him, he took another look at what someone had left on the porch just about two feet to the left side of the door. No tricks. It was the knife all right. Or rather, *a* knife.

"That blood on it isn't dry," Jodi pointed out. Her voice was trembling just a little, but Gabriel had to hand it to her because she was holding herself together.

On the outside anyway.

On the inside, he figured it was a whole different story. If it was indeed the knife that had killed his parents, then it was the same one the killer had used on Jodi.

"It could be fake blood," Gabriel reminded her.

There was no way he would touch it to find out, though. Since the tip was missing, this was either the actual weapon that had killed his parents or else someone had broken off the end of the blade so that it would resemble it.

But there was a problem with that.

The missing tip that the surgeon had removed from Jodi's body hadn't been mentioned in any of the police reports. Nor was the fact that the killer had taken his father's watch and his mother's necklace. Those were just a few of the little details that the FBI had left out in case some nutjob tried to confess to the crime. So, either someone had hacked into those actual reports, or...

Gabriel didn't want to speculate about an *or* just yet.

While keeping his attention on their surroundings, Gabriel took his phone from his pocket and texted Jameson. He told him that he needed his help and for him to call a CSI to come and take custody of this knife. Jameson was at his house and could be there in a couple of minutes.

Bringing in his brother was better than waiting for the deputies to come in from the sheriff's office. Besides, Jameson was a Texas Ranger and the best backup Gabriel could have. Once Jameson arrived, maybe they could keep Jodi out of this. Of course, the problem was that she was here and therefore already in the middle of it.

Whatever *it* was.

This could still be a prank, and Gabriel was holding on to that hope. Over the years the house had become a magnet for daredevil kids, ghost hunters and pretty much anyone warped enough to want to see an old crime scene. That's how the windows had gotten broken and the boards sprayed with graffiti.

Gabriel tested the doorknob. Locked, just as it should be, and he used his key to open it. He pushed open the door, had a look around and got an instant punch of the musty smell and the dust. An instant punch of the memories, too.

He hated this place.

Hated that it still felt like an open, raw wound. A cut so deep that it would never heal. It was no doubt the same for Jodi. Even though she hadn't lost her parents that day, it had been just as costly for her.

In plenty of ways, she'd lost herself.

For just a moment he got a flash of another memory. Of the smiling nineteen-year-old who'd shown up at his house that night. She'd been wearing cutoff denim shorts, a snug red top and had looked far better than a girl had a right to look.

He pushed that memory aside, too. He'd lost himself that night, as well. Because he hadn't protected her. He hadn't saved his parents, and while Jodi had lived, he darn sure hadn't saved her, either.

Gabriel didn't see anyone in either of the two rooms just off the entry. Nor did he hear anyone. He ducked under the crisscross of boards, his back scraping against the rough wood. He moved just far enough inside for Jodi to step in behind him. Even though she didn't say anything, he could hear her breathing. Which was too fast.

There were no signs of an intruder here. No footprints in the dust on the hardwood floors.

The furniture in the living and dining rooms was still draped with the sheets that his sisters had put on them years earlier. It hadn't felt right to move anything after the CSIs had finished with it, so they'd covered everything, locked and boarded it up. Now, it was like some kind of sick time capsule.

"Anyone up there?" Gabriel called out.

He didn't expect a response and didn't get one. But what he did hear was something he didn't want to hear.

A footstep.

Yeah, someone was definitely upstairs. And judging from the weight of the step, it wasn't a raccoon or some other animal.

Jodi moved as if ready to barge right up there, but Gabriel leaned in front of her and shot her a scowl. "We'll wait here for Jameson. Once he arrives, I'll go upstairs. Alone."

She huffed, clearly not pleased about that. Maybe because she wanted to confront the person who'd left the knife. Of course, she thought it was the same person who had attacked her, but Gabriel was sticking to his guns that her father had been responsible for that.

"We should at least check the back door," she suggested. "That might be how he got in."

Yes, either that or a window. The place wasn't exactly a fortress, though the doors and windows should have at least all been locked. That wouldn't have stopped someone from breaking one of the panes and getting inside, though.

Gabriel went to the center of the foyer, and he volleyed his attention around the rooms and the stairs. He still didn't see anyone or anything out of place. Definitely no more blood to go along with what was on that knife, and if he had seen so much as a drop, he would have stopped and gotten out of there since this could potentially be a crime scene.

Again.

But thankfully there was nothing other than the bad feeling that continued to snake down his spine.

"Stay here," he warned Jodi.

Whether she would or not was anyone's guess, but Gabriel went into the adjacent family room so he could peer through to the kitchen. No one was there, but the rear door was open. The wind was causing it to sway just enough to make this whole ordeal even creepier than it already was.

Gabriel was about to lose patience with himself and whoever the hell had broken in, and he probably would have just charged upstairs if he hadn't heard a sound that he actually wanted to hear.

"What the hell?" someone asked and then added a string of profanity.

Jameson.

He'd probably seen the knife. Or maybe the cussing was for Jodi. Not that Jameson had anything in particular against Jodi, but he would have known it wasn't a good idea for her to be here.

"Someone's upstairs," Jodi said to his brother.

With his gun already drawn, Jameson came into the house, stepping around her, and his attention went straight to Gabriel. "Did the intruder leave the knife?"

"I'm not sure." But Gabriel was about to find out. "Stay here with Jodi."

"The CSIs are on the way," Jameson told him as Gabriel started up the stairs. "I called Cameron, too."

Cameron Doran. A deputy and family friend. Cameron would have been at his own house on the ranch grounds, and while Gabriel appreciated the double backup, he hoped it wouldn't be necessary.

With his gun aimed, Gabriel went up the stairs, pausing after each step to listen for any footsteps or movement. He didn't hear anything other than that damn creaky door downstairs.

At first anyway.

Then, there were definitely footsteps, and they appeared to be coming from his parents' bedroom. No more pausing for him. Gabriel hurried up the stairs and to the landing so he could pivot in that direction.

No one was in the hall, so he went toward the bedroom, passing several others along the way. He kept watch around him. The doors were all closed, but that didn't mean someone wouldn't open one of them and start shooting. Or running anyway. He was still hoping this would turn out to be nothing.

By the time Gabriel made it the forty or so feet to his parents' room, he'd worked up a sweat. And it wasn't helping his temper. This was not how he wanted to spend his afternoon.

He kicked open the door, and he nearly fired when he saw the movement. But it was just the white gauzy curtains fluttering in the breeze.

"He's out back, and he's getting away!" Jodi shouted.

Hell.

Gabriel hurried to the window to look out, and the first thing he spotted was the ladder propped up against the back of the house. But there were no signs of the person who'd put it there.

However, there were signs of Jodi and Jameson.

He saw them run into the yard, such that it was. Once it'd been a manicured lawn, but now it was overgrown with weeds and underbrush.

"Stop or I'll shoot," Jameson called out.

Gabriel saw the guy then. He was dressed all in black, like some kind of ninja, and he was running into the woods. There were plenty of places to hide there and even some old ranch trails where the guy could have stashed a vehicle. Gabriel wanted to stop him because he had some answering to do about that knife.

Jameson and Jodi went after him, and that sent Gabriel hurrying, as well. He didn't go down the ladder because that would have made him an easy target in case the intruder was armed. Instead, he barreled down the hall and stairs and hurried out the back door.

Jameson and Jodi had gotten way ahead of him by now and had disappeared into the woods. With any luck, they were on the intruder's heels. Well, hopefully Jameson was. Gabriel didn't like it that a civilian was in the mix of things. Especially *this* civilian. Despite Jodi's attempt at trying to keep her composure when she saw the knife, Gabriel knew it caused her to have a slam of bad memories.

Once he was in the backyard, he had to hurdle over some of the underbrush, and it took him several long moments of hard running before he spotted Jameson and Jodi again. He'd hardly gotten a glimpse of them before Gabriel heard something else that caused his heart to jump into overdrive.

A cracking sound.

A shot being fired through a silencer.

Gabriel cursed again because neither Jodi's nor Jameson's guns were rigged that way. That meant the shot had come from the intruder. Well, that blew his theory that this was all some kind of sick prank. If the idiot had come here armed, then he meant business.

But what kind of business exactly?

If he'd wanted to kill them, he could have done that when Jodi and he had been talking earlier.

Jameson and Jodi thankfully ducked behind some trees, and using massive oaks as cover, Gabriel darted behind them as he made his way to Jodi. Jameson was only several yards away, and both of them had their guns and attention directed at a thick cluster of bushes and weeds.

Jodi was breathing through her mouth, but other than that, she was holding it together. And she looked like the trained security specialist that she was.

"Did you get a look at his face?" Gabriel wanted to know.

She shook her head and spared him a glance. Gabriel saw it then. The fear. But he also saw the determination to get her hands on this guy.

"Do you see him?" Jameson asked.

Gabriel peered around the tree for a glance. But he didn't get much of a look. That's because a bullet smacked into the bark just inches from his head. A second shot quickly followed.

He cursed and pulled Jodi to the ground. Gabriel hadn't intended to land on her, but that's what happened. The front of his body right on her back. They'd never been lovers, but being pressed against her gave Gabriel a jolt of attraction. A jolt he quickly shoved aside so he could adjust his position in case he got a chance to return fire.

The intruder fired again, and Gabriel tried to pinpoint the shot. Hard to do with the silencer, but he was pretty sure he knew the guy's general area.

"Stop shooting and come out with your hands up," Gabriel shouted out to him.

He didn't expect the intruder to do that.

And was stunned when he did.

"I'm coming out," the man said.

Jodi went stiff and practically shoved Gabriel off her so that she could get to her feet. Gabriel did the same, and he muscled her behind him just in case this was some kind of trick.

But it wasn't.

The man stood, his hands raised in the air. In addition to the black clothes, he was also wearing a ski mask and gloves.

"Where's your gun?" Gabriel snapped.

"On the ground near my feet."

Gabriel didn't want it anywhere near this fool. "Walk toward us. Slowly. Don't make any sudden moves, and remember that part about keeping your hands in the air."

The guy gave a shaky nod, and he started toward them. Jameson came out from cover, his gun trained on the guy. Gabriel and Jodi did the same, and the moment he was close enough to Jameson, his brother hurried to the man, put him facedown on the ground and frisked him.

"Keep watch around us," Gabriel told Jodi.

Her eyes widened a moment, and she must have realized that this man might have brought a *friend* or two with him.

Gabriel went closer to the guy, too, and handed Jameson a pair of plastic cuffs that he took from his pocket. Jameson immediately put them on him.

"Who the hell are you?" Gabriel asked the man.

Gabriel stooped down and yanked off the ski mask. His head was shaved, and there were several homemade tattoos on his forehead and neck. Definitely not someone Gabriel recognized, and judging from the way Jameson shook his head, neither did his brother.

"I'm not saying nothing until I talk to my lawyer," the guy answered. He sounded pretty defiant for someone who'd just surrendered.

But Jodi had some defiance of her own. She got right in the guy's face. "Where did you get that knife?"

He smiled. A sick kind of smile that had Gabriel's insides twisting. He wasn't sure what the heck this was all about, but he intended to find out.

"I'll take him to the sheriff's office," Gabriel said. "He can call his lawyer, and I'll question him." Then, he turned to the guy and hoped he could change his mind about clamming up. "Just so you know, you're looking at three counts of attempted murder."

The guy smiled again. Gabriel sure didn't. He silently cursed. Because they could be dealing with someone who was mentally unstable. If so, they might never get answers. But Jodi clearly wasn't giving up on that just yet.

She was right at the goon's side as Jameson started leading him back to the house. "Tell me where you got the knife."

Gabriel doubted the guy was about to blurt out anything, but just in case, he went ahead and read him his rights. Jodi waited, the impatience all over her face, and the moment Gabriel finished, she repeated her demand.

Nothing. Well, she got nothing other than the smile that Gabriel wished he could knock off the idiot's face.

"He's too young to have been part of your attack," Gabriel reminded Jodi. This guy was barely twenty, maybe still in his teens. He would have been just a kid a decade ago.

"He could still know something about it," she pointed out just as quickly.

"Yeah," Gabriel admitted. "That's why I'll handle this. You should go home, and I'll let you know if he says anything."

That earned him a glare. He'd expected it. She wasn't about to back away from this, but Gabriel had to keep her at bay because he didn't want her compromising his investigation.

"Need some help?" someone called out.

Cameron. The deputy was hurrying around the side of the house toward them. He, too, had his weapon drawn.

"Did you come here in your cruiser?" Gabriel asked him.

Cameron nodded. "Who is this guy? And why is the knife on the porch?"

Good questions. "I'm hoping he'll tell me once we've booked him." Gabriel tipped his head to the woods. "This clown left a gun out there. Keep an eye on it until the CSIs get here to collect it, and then I'll need Jameson and you to drive him to the sheriff's office. I'll be right behind you as soon as I've talked to the CSIs."

And after he'd had a look around.

Something more than the obvious wasn't right.

Jameson headed to the cruiser with the prisoner, and Cameron started for the woods. Jodi didn't budge.

"I want to be there when you question him," she insisted.

"No." And he wasn't going to compromise on that. At best he would allow her to watch from the observation room, but Gabriel was sure even that wasn't a good idea.

Gabriel looked at her, and that's when he saw that she was trembling. Jodi realized he'd noticed, too, and she cursed under her breath.

"I'm fine," she snapped. Her blond hair was damp with sweat, and she pushed it from her face. Her face was beaded with sweat, as well.

They stared at each other, until Jodi glanced away. "Sometimes, I have panic attacks," she said.

He figured she had to be close to one now to admit something like that. It didn't go well with her tough Sentry employee image.

"The water is still on in the house since it comes from a well. I wouldn't drink it because there might be rust in the pipes, but it might help if you splash some on your face."

But the moment he made the offer, it occurred to him why he still had that niggling feeling in his gut. Gabriel's attention zoomed to the back door.

"What?" Jodi asked when she followed his gaze.

"The ladder's there, but the back door was open when I went into the house."

She made a sound to indicate she was giving that some thought. "Well, the guy used the ladder to escape. Jameson and I saw him running from it when we got to the backyard."

Yeah. So, maybe the open back door had nothing to do with their perp. Still, Gabriel intended to check it out. When he'd run through the house to go in pursuit, he hadn't looked around to see if anything else had been...disturbed.

Gabriel started toward the porch with Jodi following along behind him. Part of him wanted to tell her to stay put while he checked it out, but it might not be safe for her to be out here alone. Of course, she would believe she could take care of herself, but if that idiot had indeed brought help, there could be more gunfire.

He didn't slow down until he reached the back door, and then Gabriel paused just to take in the room. The gray tile didn't show the dust, which meant it didn't show any footprints, either. That didn't mean some weren't there, though, so he used his elbow to open the door as wide as it would go, and he stepped to the side.

Jodi stayed in the doorway, but they seemed to spot something at the same time. She made a slight gasping sound.

Because the thing they spotted appeared to be drops of blood.

Gabriel reminded himself that it could be fake. Just like the blood on the knife. But that didn't stop the tightness in his chest.

"Come inside but stay back," he told her. He definitely didn't want her following what appeared to be a trail of blood drops. Drops that led right to the pantry.

The door to the pantry was ajar but not open enough for Gabriel to see if there was anyone or anything inside. With his gun ready, he went closer, and behind him he could hear Jodi shifting her position, as well. No doubt getting ready in case they were about to be attacked again.

As soon as he was close enough, Gabriel gave the door a kick with the toe of his boot. He took aim.

Then he cursed.

Hell.

There was more blood here, pooled on the floor amid the toppled cans. And in the middle of all that blood was what appeared to be a dead body.

Chapter Three

Breathe.

Jodi kept repeating that reminder to herself.

She couldn't keep taking in those short bursts of air that could cause her to hyperventilate. She needed normal breaths because that was her best bet right now at staving off a panic attack.

Gabriel certainly wasn't doing anything to put her at ease. He was seated at his desk at the sheriff's office building on Main Street in Blue River, and he was on his umpteenth phone call since they'd arrived two hours earlier. Jameson and Cameron were in the squad room, and they were doing the same thing.

Obviously there was lots to do now that this was a murder investigation. In addition to the calls and fielding questions from his deputies, Gabriel also kept glancing up at her.

Not that he had to glance far.

Jodi was pacing across his office while she tried to keep herself together.

What Gabriel wasn't doing was questioning their suspect. The bald kid who'd fired shots at them. Maybe a kid who had committed the murder, too. And had also left the knife on the porch. But Gabriel wouldn't have a chance of confirming any of that until the kid's lawyer arrived. Whenever that would be.

Gabriel finally finished his latest call, and immediately started making some notes on his computer. "You should go home," he said. And since Jodi was the only other person in the room, that order was obviously meant for her. "I can have one of the reserve deputies drive you and stay with you until this is all sorted out."

"I'm staying here," she insisted.

Then, she huffed, a little insulted that Gabriel had thought she couldn't take care of herself and needed a deputy. His doubt about her abilities probably had to do with that look that kept crossing her face, the one indicating she was about to have a panic attack. Jodi hated that it was there. Hated that it felt as if she might lose it at any moment, but that wouldn't stop her from defending herself if someone came after her again.

"What did the ME have to say about the body?" she asked.

His eyebrow came up, maybe to show her that he was surprised that she'd known he was talking to the ME. She hadn't heard anything the ME said, but she had been able to tell from Gabriel's questions who'd been on the other end of the phone line.

"He's a white male in his mid-to late thirties," Gabriel answered after a short hesitation. "There was no ID on him. Cause of death appears to be exsanguination from multiple stab wounds to the torso."

Breathe.

That felt like a punch to the chest. Because just hearing the words caused the memories to come. Memories of her own blood loss from stab wounds.

Mercy.

She'd lost so much blood that night that her heart had stopped for a couple of seconds. The medics had brought her back, but it could have gone either way. She could have ended up like the dead man in the Becketts' house. Or like Gabriel's parents who had died on their kitchen floor.

"Is this never going to end?" Jodi said before she could stop herself.

Gabriel cursed, got up from his desk and took hold of her arm. Good thing, too, because she suddenly wasn't too steady on her feet. He put her in the chair and got her a bottle of water from the small fridge in the corner.

"This is why you shouldn't be here," he insisted. "This is too much for you."

"It's too much for all of us."

He certainly didn't argue with that, but he did sit on the armrest and stare down at her. She saw it all in his eyes. His own battle with the nightmarish memories. His unease at her being there.

Except it was more than unease.

Oh, no. It was that attraction again. Anytime they were within breathing distance of each other, the heat returned. Thankfully, they were both in a place to shove it away. It wouldn't stay gone. But for now, they could keep it at bay.

"How do you think he got the knife?" Jodi pressed.

Gabriel lifted his shoulder. "Maybe he found it. I would say it's a duplicate, but there's the problem with only a handful of people knowing about the broken tip. Of course, a handful is more than enough for the info to leak and get to the wrong person. If so, he could be just some nutjob copycat."

All of that made sense, but it didn't exactly soothe her

raw nerves. Too bad Gabriel didn't have a theory that would clear her father's name.

Gabriel gave a heavy sigh. "Look, I don't know what happened, but if this guy confesses to sending the threatening emails and committing the murder, then maybe this will put an end to it." He added another shrug when she stared at him. "Well, for everyone but your father."

Yes. Her father would get a different kind of ending. This wouldn't do a thing to get Travis out of jail.

Jodi looked away from him at the exact moment she felt Gabriel's hand on her shoulder. She didn't jump out of her skin as she usually did from an unexpected touch. In fact, it felt far more comforting than it should.

And that's the reason she stood and moved away from him.

That got his attention. Something she hadn't particularly wanted to get right now. Gabriel was giving her the once-over with those lawman's eyes, and he was obviously waiting for an explanation.

"I just have trouble being touched sometimes," she settled for saying.

A lie. She had trouble with it *all the time*.

He drew his eyebrows together. "Uh, have you gotten help for it?"

She nodded. That wasn't a lie. She'd attempted to get help by seeing a string of therapists. "In my case, help didn't work."

He kept staring at her, clearly still wanting more. She'd already told him far more than she'd spilled to anyone else, and Jodi didn't want to get any deeper into it. He probably wouldn't understand that the only thing that eased the demons was the knowledge that she could now defend herself.

Thankfully, she didn't have to add more because there was movement in the doorway. Jodi automatically reached for her gun, but it was just Cameron.

Cameron had lawman's eyes, too, and he slid a glance between Gabriel and her. The corner of his mouth lifted a fraction and for just a second. A dimple flashed in his cheek.

"You two always did have a thing for each other," he drawled.

Heaven knew what Cameron had seen or sensed to make him say that or to make him give that half smile, but it caused Gabriel to scowl. Unlike most people, Cameron didn't seem to be affected by that particular expression from the king of scowls. Probably because he'd had a lifetime of scowls tossed at him. After all, Gabriel wasn't just his boss, but they'd been friends since childhood.

"Do you have a reason to be here?" Gabriel snapped.

Cameron gave them that lazy smile again, and he handed her a cup of coffee and a small white bag. "It's some doughnuts from the diner. Thought you might need a sugar fix right about now."

She wasn't hungry in the least. In fact, Jodi wasn't sure she'd be able to hold anything down, but Cameron's gesture touched her. "You remembered I have a sweet tooth," she said.

"Hard to forget it. I remember having to wrestle some chocolate cake away from you once when we were kids."

Jodi nodded. "And I had to wrestle them from Lauren and your sister, Gilly."

She caught the slight change in Cameron's expression and knew she'd hit a nerve. Two of them, actually. From what Jodi had heard, Gilly had died during childbirth, and Cameron was raising her child. Since that'd happened only a few months earlier, the grief still had to be raw.

However, there was another rawness, too. One that might never go away, as well. Once, Cameron had been in love with Lauren. And vice versa. But again, those feelings of young love had all been shattered the night of the murders because Cameron had been a deputy then, and Lauren had blamed him for not preventing her parents' deaths. It probably wasn't logical for Lauren to feel that way, but those sorts of raw feelings weren't always logical.

"Yes," Cameron said as if he knew what she was thinking.

His smile stayed in place a moment longer before his attention shifted to Gabriel. "The CSIs are processing the knife right away. We should know soon if the blood belongs to the victim and if there are prints that match our suspect.

"Sorry," Cameron added to Jodi. "This kind of talk doesn't exactly go well with coffee and doughnuts."

"It's all right. I want to know what's happening with the case. Has the kid said anything?" she asked. "Or has his lawyer arrived yet?"

Cameron shook his head to both of her questions. "Nothing from him, but you do have a visitor, and he's demanding to see you. It's your boss, Hector March."

Gabriel shot her a glance, one that seemed like an accusation. "I didn't call him," Jodi insisted. And she looked to Cameron for answers. "The murder is already on the news?"

The deputy nodded.

Good grief. That hadn't taken long at all, but then,

she hadn't expected it to stay quiet. Still, she hadn't wanted to deal with Hector when her nerves were this close to the surface.

Jodi stood, trying to steel herself up by taking some deep breaths and flexing her hands. "Where is he?"

Cameron hitched his thumb toward the squad room. "I had him wait out there. Something he's not very happy about. Apparently, he's not the waiting-around sort."

No, he wasn't. But if Jodi tried to put Hector off, that would only make him dig in his heels even more. She reminded herself that Hector had been the one to help her get back on her feet when she'd been just nineteen and devastated from the knife attack. He'd been the one to offer her a job and train her. She would probably be in a psych ward somewhere if it weren't for him.

She put the coffee and doughnut bag on Gabriel's desk and went out in the hall and toward Reception. Gabriel was right behind her, of course. And Hector was exactly where Cameron had said he would be. Her boss was dressed in his usual black cargo pants and black T-shirt. He'd once been special ops in the Marines, and he still looked as if he were in uniform.

Hector immediately went to her, ignoring Gabriel's scowl. Heck, Cameron was scowling now, too. Apparently, neither approved of Hector's shades-of-gray approach to his business and justice.

Hector didn't touch her. He hadn't in years, since she usually went board stiff when someone put their hands on her. But he did get close enough to whisper, "Are you all right?"

She managed a nod. "Neither of us were hit, and Gabriel has a suspect in custody."

Hector turned to Gabriel then and extended his hand. "I'm Hector March, owner of Sentry Security."

Gabriel didn't shake his hand. "I know who you are."

Hector gave a crisp nod. "And I know who you are, too, Sheriff. Why the hell would you let Jodi get anywhere near that house after we got those threatening emails?"

That grabbed Gabriel's attention. "*We?* You got an email, too?"

"Yes." Hector frowned as if annoyed that he would have to take the time to address this. "It came this morning. But Jodi got hers the day before yesterday, right after she told a reporter that she was remembering some more details of her attack. I'm sure she explained that to you, and that's why you shouldn't have let her go to the house."

"I didn't let Jodi do anything." Gabriel's voice was as crisp as Hector's nod had been. "When I saw her car, I stopped to see what she was doing. She trespassed onto private property and then stumbled onto a crime scene."

Suddenly, all eyes were on her. Even the emergency dispatcher at the reception desk and the other deputies were looking at her. Maybe they were waiting for some kind of logic from her that they would understand. But it wasn't something they'd be able to grasp. Because they'd never been left for dead in a shallow grave.

"I wanted to see if being at the old house would trigger any other memories of the night of my attack," she admitted. Best not to tell them she had also wanted to draw out the snake who'd knifed her.

Hector pulled back his shoulders, clearly not approving of that. "And did it? Are you actually remembering new details?"

"No." In fact, the only thing it had accomplished was nearly getting Gabriel, Jameson and her killed along with giving her a new set of nightmarish memories.

All that blood on the pantry floor.

Mercy, another dead body.

She prayed the man wasn't dead because of her, but Jodi had to accept that he could be.

"Did you give the FBI the email you got?" Gabriel asked Hector at the same moment that Hector asked him, "Is Jodi free to go? I can drive her to her apartment in San Antonio."

"I don't want to go home," she insisted. "I want to listen when Gabriel talks to the suspect."

Hector's mouth tightened. It was yet something else he didn't approve of. Tough. She was staying put.

"And yes, I gave the FBI the email," Hector answered Gabriel, but he kept his attention on her. "Apparently, it's not traceable since the person who sent it bounced it around through several foreign internet providers."

Not a surprise. Jodi hadn't figured it would be so easy to find out who was doing this. But then maybe their suspect would spill it all. Not just about the emails but about the person who'd hired him.

"You think the guy in custody is the one who attacked you ten years ago?" Hector asked.

She didn't jump to answer. Because she wasn't sure how much Gabriel wanted to reveal about this investigation.

"No," Gabriel finally said. "He's too young. Plus, I believe the man who attacked her has already been caught and is in prison."

Hector made a quick sound of agreement. He always did when it came to her father. It was the one thing he had in common with the Becketts—they thought her father was guilty.

"Several other people got threats," Hector went on. "Apparently, all of you did." He glanced at Gabriel, Jameson and then her. "But so did Russell Laney and August Canton."

Judging from the soft grunt of agreement Gabriel made, he was already aware of those last two. Jodi certainly wasn't, and she looked at Gabriel for him to provide some details.

"There are probably others who got the emails, too," Gabriel said as Cameron stepped away to take a call. "The FBI figures some folks just deleted them as a hoax. But, yes, I suspect anyone connected to the initial investigation was on the receiving end of the threats. Russell and August got theirs the same day I did."

Jodi knew both Russell and August, of course. Both had been suspects in the Beckett murders and her attack.

Them, and Jodi's own brother, Theo.

It was public knowledge that the police and then the FBI had questioned all three. Theo, because he'd been a hothead at the time and had a run-in that day with Gabriel's father, Sherman, over some horses that'd broken fence. Russell had gotten caught up in it simply because Jodi had ended her short relationship with him the week before the attack. August was her dad's half brother and had been just as much of a hothead as Theo.

And the cops excluded them all as suspects.

After they'd found her father passed out drunk with Gabriel's father's blood on him.

"August thinks the threatening emails prove that Travis is innocent," Hector went on. "In fact, he's already taking all of this to Travis's lawyers in the hopes that it'll help with his last-ditch appeal."

August was probably the only other person in Texas who believed her father was innocent. Despite that, it never had felt as if August and she were on the same side. That's because August had never approved of her friendship with the Becketts. It didn't matter that the friendship had ended the night of the attack. It was a drop in the bucket, though, to what August held against Jameson. Because Jameson had been the most vocal of the Becketts in professing her father's guilt.

"Theo might have gotten a threatening email, too. Have you been in touch with him?" Hector asked her.

"No. I haven't spoken to him in over a year. I don't even have a phone number for him."

Nor did she know who to contact to get one. As a DEA agent, Theo spent a lot of time on deep-cover assignments, and if the copycat/killer had managed to send Theo an email, then he or she was well connected with insider Justice Department information.

Not exactly a comforting thought if it was true.

"We have an ID on our young suspect," Cameron announced as soon as he finished his latest call. "We got a match on his prints because he's a missing person. His name is Billy Coleman."

Jodi repeated that a couple of times to see if she recognized it. She didn't.

"He's a runaway," Cameron continued. "His parents filed a missing person report about a year ago. Not for the first time, either. He's run away at least two other times. He's seventeen, and judging from his juvie record, he's paranoid schizophrenic. My guess is he's probably off his meds."

Gabriel cursed. And Jodi knew why. Billy was no doubt going to plead mental incompetence, and they might never get answers as to why he'd committed this horrible crime.

But something about that didn't sound right.

"Billy called a lawyer," Jodi pointed out.

"Yeah," Gabriel agreed, and he cursed again. "And he had the name and phone number of the attorney when he got here to the sheriff's office. Not something a runaway teen would necessarily have."

"Especially since he's not from a wealthy family," Cameron supplied. "His parents both work at blue-collar jobs."

So, that confirmed that someone had likely put Billy up to doing this, and if so, that meant he was just another victim of this tangled mess.

"What about the dead guy?" Gabriel asked Cameron. "Any ID on him yet?"

"No. His prints weren't in the system, so we'll have to try to get an ID by searching through missing person reports and getting his picture out to the press."

That might take a while. Especially if the man was homeless and no one was looking for him.

"I really think you should let me take you home," Hector said, turning back to her. "Gabriel can fill you in on anything that happens, including whatever the suspect says in the interview."

She was shaking her head before Hector even finished. "I'm staying here." And she didn't leave any room for argument in her tone.

Hector gave a heavy sigh and looked at Gabriel as if he expected him to force her to leave. "I'm not sure it's a good idea for Jodi to be out anywhere right now," Gabriel answered. "She'll be safer here."

Jodi was more than a little surprised that Gabriel had backed her up. Then she realized why he'd done that. Because she was almost certainly in danger from the person who was manipulating Billy. Gabriel probably didn't want to be a part of another attack that could leave her dead.

"Just go," Jodi told Hector. "I'll be fine."

He obviously knew that "fine" part was a lie. Was also obviously not happy about being dismissed. But he didn't get a chance to voice that unhappiness. That's because Jameson finished his phone call, and he got up from his desk, making a beeline toward them.

"There were prints on the knife," Jameson said, "and the CSIs got an immediate hit." He snapped toward Jodi, and that definitely wasn't a friendly expression he was sporting. "Is there something you want to tell us?" he demanded.

Jodi shook her head, not understanding why Gabriel's brother looked ready to blast her to smithereens.

But she soon found out.

Jameson turned to his brother to finish delivering the news. "It's Jodi's prints on the knife."

Chapter Four

Gabriel had hoped there wouldn't be any more surprises today, but this was a huge one. Since Billy had been wearing gloves, Gabriel hadn't expected there to be any prints at all on the knife.

Especially not Jodi's.

Judging from the stunned look on her face, Jodi hadn't expected it, either. Her attention slashed from Jameson to Gabriel, and she shook her head. She also opened her mouth as if ready to blurt out some kind of denial, but the denial and anything else she might have said died on her lips because she groaned and sank down into the nearest chair.

"Jodi was obviously set up," Hector jumped to say.

Gabriel hated to give the man even a slight benefit of doubt, but Hector could be right. Of course, there was another possibility. One that wasn't going to help ease that stark expression on Jodi's already too pale face.

Gabriel moved closer to her, lifting her chin so they could make eye contact. Like the other time he'd touched her, she tensed, making him wonder just how many "scars" she had from the attack a decade ago. Probably plenty that she wouldn't want to discuss with him.

"Do you remember ever touching the knife?" Gabriel

asked. He'd chosen his words carefully. No need to say aloud that he wanted to know if she'd taken hold of the handle when her attacker had been trying to end her life.

Jodi ran her hand through her hair and shook her head. "I honestly don't know." She shifted her attention to Jameson, and even though the paleness and nerves were still there, she straightened her posture and took a deep breath. "Is the fingerprint pattern consistent with me having grabbed it while I was being stabbed?"

Jameson lifted his shoulder. "There are two clear prints. Your right index finger and thumb. The other prints are smeared."

"That means nothing. Her attacker could have been wearing gloves." Hector again.

It riled Gabriel that Jodi's boss had taken on the role of defending her. Then again, plenty of things riled him about Hector. Including the fact that Jodi had turned to him and not Gabriel after the nightmare ten years ago. Hector considered himself some kind of victim's recovery advocate and had come to visit Jodi in the hospital shortly after the attack. She'd allowed him into her life—while excluding Gabriel.

"Does Jodi need a lawyer?" Hector asked, glancing at both Jameson and Gabriel. "Are you accusing her of something? Because it certainly seems to me that's what you're doing."

Well, it hadn't been certain to Jodi. Her eyes widened, and she shook her head again.

"I know you didn't stab yourself," Gabriel said before she could speak. But that was only the tip of the iceberg. There was another component to this situation.

The most recent murder.

Jodi seemed to understand that even before Gabriel

could bring it up. "I also didn't kill that man and plant the knife on the doorstep so I could clear my father's name." Jodi's voice was stronger now, and she got to her feet to face him. She repeated the part about not killing the man.

Gabriel believed her. Yeah, it was stupid to take her word at face value, especially since he'd hardly seen her in years. He wasn't sure of the woman she'd become. But he seriously doubted that Jodi had become a killer.

"The FBI wants to talk to you," Jameson told her. "They're sending an agent from their San Antonio office."

Which meant the agent would be there soon, since San Antonio was less than an hour's drive away. That might not be enough time, though, for Gabriel to get answers from their suspect. He hoped that didn't mean the agent would take her into custody.

"If this is a copycat killing," Gabriel volunteered, "then the FBI doesn't have jurisdiction. I do." That was splitting legal hairs, but it might stop Jodi from being whisked away and put through what would no doubt be grueling interrogations.

Hell.

Gabriel frowned, then silently cursed himself. He wasn't thinking with his head now. He was thinking like the twenty-four-year-old deputy who had turned Jodi away that night.

He was also thinking like a man.

One who was still attracted to a woman who shouldn't be on his attraction radar. But she was. And there didn't seem to be anything he could do about it.

"I'll get you a lawyer," Hector told her, already taking out his phone.

"No, don't. Not yet anyway." She turned back to Gabriel. "Any idea when Billy's attorney will be here?"

Gabriel had to shake his head. "But it should be soon. We've already bagged his clothes and tested his hands for gunshot residue. There's residue, by the way, and coupled with the fact that he attacked us, that'll be enough to charge him. Well, at least it's enough to charge him for shooting at us."

Jodi continued to stare at him. "You doubt that he killed that man in the house?"

Gabriel really didn't want to get into the specifics of what he thought or didn't think. Not with Hector right there. Not before he'd had a chance to try to work it all out in his head.

But there was a problem.

And Gabriel didn't believe it was his imagination that Jodi wanted to keep Hector out of this, too. Partially out of it anyway, since she'd refused to go with him and had even asked her boss to leave.

"Come with me a minute," Gabriel told her. He motioned for Jodi to follow him and headed toward the hall. He wanted her in the observation room next to where they were holding Billy.

However, Jodi didn't get far because Hector stepped in front of her, blocking her path. "You're not questioning her," Hector snapped, his glare on Gabriel.

The man knew how to test every rileable bone in Gabriel's body. "I can and I will." He tapped his badge in case Hector had forgotten that he was the one in charge here. Of course, Gabriel didn't have an interrogation in mind, but he didn't intend to tell Hector that.

"I'll be all right," Jodi told the man, and she stepped around him.

That put some fire in Hector's eyes. "It's not a good idea for you to talk to the sheriff without your lawyer present. He's abusing your childhood friendship. Hell, you might not even be able to trust him. Remember, he's the one who helped convict your father."

That stopped Jodi, and for several moments Gabriel thought she might change her mind about going with him. She took in more of those deep breaths. The kind a person took while trying to fight off a panic attack. Or a fit of temper.

"Go home," Jodi finally said to Hector. Her voice was as tight as the muscles in her face. "I'll call you when I'm done."

Oh, that didn't please Hector. That fire in his eyes turned to a full blaze. "I'm not going anywhere. I'll be waiting right here when you're finished."

In addition to being a pain, the guy was also mule-headed. Normally, Gabriel would have been pleased that Jodi had someone like that on her side, but this wasn't a normal situation. And Hector wasn't just an ordinary boss. He was someone who cut legal corners to suit his needs.

"Sorry about that," Jodi mumbled as Gabriel ushered her into the observation room.

There was a two-way mirror, and Gabriel immediately spotted Billy seated at the table in the interview room. He appeared to be asleep, his head resting on his folded arms.

Gabriel shut the door just in case Hector decided to follow them. Of course, Jameson and Cameron likely wouldn't allow that to happen. They both knew about Gabriel's low opinion of the man, and they had equally low opinions of Jodi's boss.

"Hector's protective of me," Jodi volunteered.

"Yeah, I can see that." He hadn't intended to make that sound like some kind of question, but it did. And that question was—why?

"I owe Hector," she said, answering that unspoken question. "He was there for me after, well, after."

"Only because you didn't let any of us be there for you," Gabriel pointed out.

She didn't disagree with that. Couldn't. Because she'd refused to see him, Jameson or his sisters, Ivy or Lauren, when she was home from the hospital. After that, she'd disappeared and hadn't resurfaced until eight months later at her father's trial. By then, she'd already started her association with Hector. Just how deep that association went, Gabriel didn't know.

It was possible they were or had been lovers.

Jodi didn't look away. She met his gaze head-on. "I'm stating the obvious here, but when I was recovering from my injuries, my father was charged with murdering your parents. For a while, my brother was a suspect as well, and you and Jameson were looking to put someone— *anyone*—behind bars for what happened. It didn't seem like a good idea to see you and cry on your shoulder. Plus, you had your hands full with the investigation."

"So, you cried on Hector's instead." Gabriel didn't bother cursing himself that time, but it was definitely something he shouldn't have thrown out there. He hadn't brought her in here to dig up the past, but they were certainly doing just that.

"I cried but not on anyone's shoulder," she informed him. "Wait. You're not thinking I turned to Hector because of some romantic feelings?" She cursed, made a face and didn't wait for him to respond. "It's not like that between Hector and me. Or any other man."

Her mouth tightened as if she also had said too much. Now, she looked away, dodging his gaze, and everything in her body language signaled to him that this part of the conversation was over.

Good. It was time to move on, and he tipped his head toward Billy. "There was no blood on his clothes. Nor any visible on any part of his body."

It didn't take her long to process that. "That's why you don't believe he killed the man."

Gabriel nodded. "There was blood everywhere in that pantry, and the guy had been stabbed multiple times. An organized killer could have possibly avoided spatter, but I'm not sure Billy's anywhere near organized."

She stared at the teenager on the other side of the glass. "He could have changed his clothes and cleaned himself up after the murder." But Jodi quickly waved that off. She huffed, but it wasn't exactly a sound of frustration. There was something else mixed with it, too. "You really do know that I wouldn't do something like kill a man, don't you?"

"I know." There was something else mixed with his response, too. Empathy. Hell. More than that. Sympathy. Something that she darn sure wouldn't want him to feel. "And you do know if I'd had any suspicions ten years ago about what was going to happen, I wouldn't have let you leave my house?"

She nodded, sighed. Jodi looked up, their gazes connecting, and for just a split second, it seemed as if the last decade melted away. He caught a glimpse of the girl. The very one who'd had a thing for him. That *thing* was still there; Gabriel could feel it, but it was buried beneath the scars and the pain.

He got another flood of memories then. The heat in his own body. He'd never told Jodi that he'd wanted her that night. Wouldn't tell her, either. Because it wouldn't help. In fact, it could make things worse with them going through the "what could have been" scenarios.

Their eye contact continued, and Gabriel could feel that old attraction becoming a simmer again. Thankfully, the simmer turned chilly when he heard voices in the hall.

"I need to see the sheriff and my client now," a woman demanded. It wasn't a shout but close enough so that Gabriel had no trouble hearing her.

She was no doubt Billy's attorney. Good. That meant Gabriel could get on with the interrogation.

Gabriel threw open the door and came face-to-face with Cameron and a brunette who was dressed to the nines. She had a briefcase on the floor next to her pricey shoes. She certainly didn't look like someone who worked cheap, and that piqued his interest, and suspicions, even more. There was no way Billy could pay someone like this.

So, who was footing this bill?

"I'm Mara Rayburn," she said. Her voice had lowered a couple of notches, but she didn't sound very happy about this visit. "You're Sheriff Beckett?"

Gabriel nodded, but before he could say anything, she took his hand and slapped some papers in his palm. "That's a court order to transfer my client to a psychiatric facility where he belongs."

Heck, that was pretty fast for a court order, so Gabriel looked through it.

"It's legit," Cameron provided, sounding as suspicious about all of this as Gabriel felt. Jodi, too, because she hurried to Gabriel's side to look over the document, as well.

"How'd you get this?" Gabriel demanded. "And who's paying you?"

Mara gave him a blank stare. "I got the court order through normal channels, and as your deputy just pointed out, it's *legit*. As for who's paying me, I'm not required to divulge that information. However, you are required to comply with that court order and release my client. There's a marshal waiting outside to escort Billy to the facility, and I don't want to waste any time. Billy's a very sick young man."

"How so?" Gabriel pressed, though he already knew at least part of the answer.

Mara whipped out yet more papers from the briefcase and handed them to him. "That's a report from the psychiatrist. Billy is paranoid schizophrenic. He not only needs medication, but he also needs to be under medical supervision since he's a danger to himself."

"And others," Gabriel quickly provided.

"He fired shots at us," Jodi added. "And it's possible he killed a man."

Mara's only reaction to that was an eye roll. "Please don't tell me you're going to fight this court order. Because it won't work. Billy will get the help he needs whether you stonewall us or not."

Gabriel hitched his thumb toward Billy. "I've got a dead body, and your client is the only person who can give me answers about that."

"That's your problem, not mine, Sheriff," Mara snapped.

She motioned for someone, and a few moments later, the marshal walked up behind her. Gabriel knew him. Dallas Walker. He was a good marshal, definitely not someone who would be on the take, but he would follow through on his job. And his job would be to make sure that court order was carried out.

"Sorry about this," Dallas mumbled to Gabriel.

"No need to apologize." Mara, again. "Just get my client out of here." She turned as if to leave but then stopped and snared Gabriel's attention. "Anything my client might have said to you isn't admissible because he isn't mentally competent."

Maybe, but the jury was still out on that. "You're not doing Billy any favors by covering for the person who's manipulating him," Gabriel told the woman. "Because the person manipulating him is likely a killer. A killer who's got you on his payroll."

If she had a reaction to that, Gabriel didn't see it, because this time when she turned, she walked away. "Bring my client to the car," she added over her shoulder to the marshal.

Dallas issued another apology, and Cameron led him to the interview room. It didn't take long before the marshal was escorting him out.

Billy had a reaction all right. He smiled. "You two should be real careful," he said like a threat.

Gabriel had to rein in his temper. After all, this idiot could have killed them when they were chasing him. Plus, there was no telling what would go on in that psychiatric facility. Billy could end up not doing any time whatsoever.

"The lawyer didn't ask who I was," Jodi said under her breath.

Yeah. Gabriel had noticed that. Maybe because Mara

hadn't cared enough to ask, but it could be because she already knew every single player in this. Whatever the heck *this* was.

"I'll make some calls," Cameron told them as they watched Dallas whisk Billy away. "We might be able to question him while he's at the facility."

It was a long shot, but at the moment it was all Gabriel had. Especially since they didn't even have an ID on the dead guy.

"Find out all you can about the lawyer," Gabriel told Cameron.

The deputy nodded, left to no doubt get started on that, but as Cameron was walking away, Hector was coming toward Jodi and him.

"My people just sent me a preliminary report on Mara Rayburn." Hector had his phone in his hand and appeared to be reading something on the screen. "She's thirty-two and works for a law firm in San Antonio. A reputable one."

"That doesn't mean she's reputable," Gabriel argued.

Hector made a sound of agreement and handed Gabriel his phone. Gabriel scrolled through the report, though he wouldn't take anything there at face value.

"There are no red flags," Hector concluded. "But I might be able to get financials on her."

"No." Gabriel didn't have to think about that, either. There was no legal way for them to get something like that since they didn't have probable cause on Mara. He darn sure didn't want Hector cutting corners on this and therefore compromising the entire investigation.

Jodi moved closer to Gabriel, her arm up against his as she leaned in to read the report, too. It was thorough for something classified as *preliminary*. Mara's address, phone number, educational background and even the cases she'd tried in court. As detailed as it was, Gabriel had to agree with the no red flags part. There had to be one, though, somewhere.

"Now that Billy's gone, are you ready to go home?" Hector asked her.

Gabriel looked up from the report and realized that Hector was scowling. And the man had his attention nailed to the arm-to-arm contact between Jodi and him. Jodi had said it "wasn't like that" between Hector and her, but clearly her boss had a different notion about that. Because that was pure jealousy in Hector's eyes.

Jodi noticed the jealousy, too, and the scowl. She eased away from Gabriel. "I want to stay here a little longer and see what we're able to find out."

That didn't ease Hector's expression. "You can use the resources in the office to learn anything that the sheriff can."

She lifted her shoulder, stayed put. However, Hector stayed put as well, and Gabriel thought he might have to order the man to leave. He didn't get a chance to do that, though, because he heard yet another voice.

One that he recognized this time.

Jodi did, too, and she groaned, stepping out into the hall with Gabriel right behind her. "August," she muttered like profanity.

It was indeed August Canton, her father's half brother, and he wasn't a stranger to the sheriff's office. Nope. August deemed himself as his half brother's champion of justice and was doing everything possible to get Travis out of jail. Gabriel had his own label for August— pain in the neck.

August wasn't a typical-looking uncle. For one thing,

he was only a few years older than Gabriel. He was the offspring of his father's second marriage, and when his parents had been killed in a car crash when he was twelve, Travis had raised him. More or less. Travis hadn't been much of a parent to either August or Jodi, but that hadn't stopped August from standing by his brother.

And riling Jodi.

Gabriel had only heard August's side of the story on this, but according to him, Jodi wasn't doing nearly enough to clear her father's name. August apparently wanted a lot more from her. August had money, a trust fund left to him by his mother's family, and he was using a lot of his cash to pay for private investigators to dig for anything they could find. Rumor had it that it rankled him that Jodi wasn't putting in as much time and money as he was. But Jodi didn't have a trust fund. Probably didn't have the time, either, because of her job.

"What do you want?" Hector snarled at the man. Apparently, Hector knew Jodi's uncle, as well. And evidently there also wasn't any love lost between them because August's eyes narrowed to slits when he looked at Hector.

August ignored Hector's question, put his hands on his hips and studied Jodi a moment. "I heard somebody tried to kill you. You okay?"

"I'm fine." That had to be a lie, but no one challenged it. "Why are you here?" Jodi asked.

A muscle flickered in August's jaw, and he slid a glance at Hector. "I'm here because of him. Because of your boss." Definitely no friendly vibe coming from August. That tone and glance was all venom.

"Because of me?" Hector challenged.

"Yeah," August verified. "I know you're the one who nearly killed Gabriel and Jodi today."

Chapter Five

Jodi groaned. She was so used to hearing August make stupid accusations that she didn't even consider taking that one seriously.

But judging from his expression, Gabriel did.

Of course, the reason he might be doing that was because Gabriel despised her boss. However, August hadn't shown much disapproval of Hector in the past so she couldn't understand why her uncle had just accused Hector of a serious crime.

Attempted murder—of Gabriel and her, no less.

Hector stepped forward. So did Gabriel, and Jodi got in between the three of them. Not easy to do since all three were obviously primed for a fight. She was as well, but Jodi didn't think it would do any good to aim any suspicion at Hector.

"What the hell are you talking about?" Hector demanded.

Gabriel didn't say anything, but his glare should have been enough to prompt August to get talking.

"We're all in danger because of him." August tipped his head to Hector. "He's been having us watched. Followed," he added. "And he's doing that because he's afraid Jodi's remembering the truth that would blow all of this wide-open."

"What truth?" Hector spat out. Jodi wanted to know the same thing.

"The truth that will set Travis free, and if he's free, that means somebody else did those crimes. Somebody you're protecting. Don't you dare say you don't have friends or criminal informants you're trying to protect. Friends who could have killed Gabriel's folks and tried to kill Jodi."

It was so far-fetched that Jodi wanted to laugh.

"It isn't just you, me and Gabriel," August went on ranting. "Hector's had Russell tailed, too. He's on his way here now to make Hector stop."

Jodi scrubbed her hand over her face. She definitely didn't want her ex-boyfriend in on this, especially since this was all some paranoia on August's part. She turned to Hector to get him to assure August that he would never do anything like that.

Hector folded his arms over his chest and aimed a defiant stare at August. "I didn't have anything to do with the murders, and I'm not trying to protect anyone who would have done them."

What Hector didn't do was deny the other part of August's accusation, and it felt as if someone had dissolved the floor and ground beneath her feet.

No.

Hector couldn't have done that.

Gabriel cursed. "You're having us followed?" he snarled.

It took Hector several long moments to answer. "Not you. I figured you'd spot a tail right off, but I've had men on Jodi, Russell and August."

"You what?" That was all Jodi could get out because her breath suddenly got very thin.

"It was for your own safety." Hector took his hands from his hips and reached for her, but Jodi stepped back.

"Explain that," she said, and she thought her glare might match the ones August and Gabriel were giving her boss.

Hector huffed. "The person sending those threatening emails is dangerous. The murder today proves that. I figured the violence would escalate, so I wanted to keep an eye on not just you but on the most likely suspect—August."

August charged at Hector, but he didn't land the punch that he threw because Gabriel caught on to August and put him against the wall.

"Why follow Russell?" Gabriel asked Hector.

"Because he's been getting threats, too, and I thought August or someone he'd hired would go after him. You have to admit that killing Russell would be a way to shed some doubt on Travis's guilt. And August might have an easier time killing Russell than his own niece."

"I didn't try to kill anyone," August fired back. "I just want everyone to know the truth, and that truth is my brother is innocent."

Gabriel ignored August and turned to her. "Did you know anything about Hector's spying?"

"No. Of course not. And if I had, I would have put an end to it. You had no right," she added, aiming her index finger at Hector.

She wasn't sure what riled her more—that Hector had had her followed or that she hadn't spotted the person he'd hired to do that.

"Have you forgotten that you nearly died?" Hector

said. "Not just ten years ago but today, too. You're in danger, and it's not very smart to rely on the local sheriff to make sure you're safe."

Jodi stared at him. "I'm not relying on the sheriff *or you* for that. I can take care of myself. Now, call off your dogs. Not just the ones following me but the ones on August and Russell, too."

"That's not wise," Hector warned her.

"Do it!" Jodi snapped.

Hector hesitated several long moments, but he finally took out his phone to make the call. However, Gabriel stopped him.

"Did you have a tail on Jodi today?" Gabriel demanded. He didn't continue until Hector nodded. "Then ask him or her if they saw anyone go into my old family home. Anyone besides Jodi, me and a teenager wearing a ski mask."

"He didn't see anyone," Hector assured him. "I had one of my best men on Jodi. Frank," he added to her.

Frank Mendoza, former black ops. He was indeed one of Sentry's best, and it explained why she hadn't noticed him.

"Frank was positioned up the road from where Jodi parked," Hector added, "and he said he didn't see anyone go into the house except Jodi and you."

That meant the killer was there before she arrived. Watching them. Maybe committing the murder while Gabriel and she were just yards away. So much for her stellar training. She hadn't been able to sense something like that practically under her nose.

"I'll call my people now," Hector said.

"How did you find out Hector was having you followed?" Gabriel asked August the moment Hector stepped into an interview room to make his call.

"One of the PIs that I'd hired noticed it. I have security cameras everywhere—in my home, my office. Even in my car. When the PI reported to me that it appeared I was being followed, I told him to run a check on the guy and find out who he was. Imagine my surprise when I learned the tail, Rusty Millington, worked for Hector."

Of course, Jodi knew Rusty, too. He wasn't as good as Frank, but the PI must have been top-notch to detect Rusty.

"Did you report this Rusty and Hector to the cops or the FBI?" Gabriel continued.

August frowned. "I'm reporting it now, to you, and I want you to do something about it."

"I will…if there's anything to be done. It's not a crime to follow someone, and Hector could just say he was looking out for your safety."

"Right." August didn't bother to hide the sarcasm, either. "Hector would like me out of the way so that he has Jodi completely isolated and all to himself."

Jodi was so surprised by that accusation that she flinched.

"You know it's true," August went on. "Hector's in love with you."

She shook her head. "I don't know that at all because it's not true." At least she hoped it wasn't. Hector had certainly done a lot for her, and she wanted to think it was because she did a good job for him, but she had to admit that Hector wanted more than just to be her boss. That said, she doubted he'd go to these extremes to get it.

"Am I interrupting anything?" someone asked.

Jodi had been so deep in thought that she hadn't heard

the footsteps. But Gabriel clearly had because he'd already stepped in front of her. Now, he put his hand over his weapon in his side holster. But it wasn't the threat that Gabriel was gearing up for.

It was Russell.

It'd been at least six years since Jodi had seen him, but he hadn't changed much. Same blond hair and muscled body. In college, everyone had called him the golden boy because of his looks and because he excelled at sports. A city boy. The opposite of Gabriel, the cowboy cop.

But there was a different edge to Russell than there had been back in college. She knew he'd spent three years in the army, and it seemed to have hardened him a little. Put some more muscles on him, too.

"Jodi," Russell said when his attention landed on her. He went to her, his arms already reaching for her, but she motioned for him to stop.

"Uh, I don't hug," she said.

Of course, it sounded rude, but maybe Russell would get it, especially since he'd seen her in the hospital shortly after the attack. She'd had trouble with even the doctors and nurses touching her then, and in fact, Russell had been there for her first panic attack.

Plenty more had followed. And touching and hugging were triggers that she'd learned to avoid.

"Sorry," Russell said. He shook hands with August and then Gabriel. "August told you about Hector having us followed?" he asked Gabriel.

Gabriel nodded. "I also understand you got a threatening email?"

"I did, and I gave it to the FBI." Russell's forehead bunched up. "What I don't understand is why would a copycat or even Travis include me in this? Jodi and I weren't even together when your parents were killed and she was attacked."

"Lots of people are getting the threats," Jodi explained. "Who knows why? Maybe the killer thinks I told you something that could reveal his identity."

Russell glanced at Gabriel, then back at her. "So, you still think your father's innocent?"

"He is," August interrupted.

Jodi wasn't nearly as enthusiastic about that as her uncle was, but she did make a sound of agreement.

What she didn't do was offer up any details about the recent murder, about maybe it being tied to what had happened to her and Gabriel's parents. But if that knife did prove to be the murder weapon, then maybe there was some kind of DNA evidence on it to give them a suspect other than her father.

Russell kept his attention on her. "How are you? I'm guessing what happened today shook you up?"

"Some. I'm okay," Jodi lied. "How about you? I understand you got married?"

Russell flashed that golden-boy smile that had first attracted her to him, but there was no trace of that attraction now. She thought that was mutual, too. "I married a wonderful woman four years ago. I met her not long after I left the army. And I'm a dad. Our son is six months old." The smile faded. "My wife and son are the reason I'm so upset about that threatening email. I don't want anyone going after them because of what went on between us."

Jodi heard the anger just beneath the surface. Anger maybe aimed at her because if he hadn't gone on three dates with her, then none of this would be happening right now. But the anger was warranted because Russell was no doubt concerned about this monster going after his wife and child.

"San Antonio police know about the threat," Russell continued, "and August encouraged me to beef up security. I did. I had a new security system installed, and I've told my wife not to go out of the house without me." The muscles in his face got tight. "Obviously, I don't want to have to live like this much longer, so just how close are you to catching this dirtbag?" He directed that question to Gabriel.

Gabriel shrugged. "There is a suspect. Once I'm able to question him, I'll know more."

"I want to talk to him," Russell said, and it was a demand. August nodded in agreement.

Now it was Gabriel's jaw muscles that got tight. "Not a chance. Unless you two become law enforcement officers, you're not getting anywhere near him. I don't want anything to compromise this investigation. Because if that happens, this guy could be guilty as sin and still walk."

August opened his mouth, probably to argue with that, but he didn't have time to say anything before Hector came out of the interview room.

"I've called off the surveillance for all of you," Hector said, "but there's a problem." He paused. "Someone broke into Jodi's apartment."

Her breath froze, and she felt the instant slam of fear. "When?"

"I'm not sure, but he sent me this." Hector handed her his phone, and she saw the photo on the screen.

It was a selfie from the looks of it. A sick one. Because the person was wearing a ski mask identical to the one their teenage suspect had on when they'd found him. In the background, she could see her bedroom. The clothes that she'd left on the bed. The coffee cup on the dresser. She could also see something else.

The knife the man was holding up in his left hand.

It was a crescent blade with a broken tip.

She choked back a gasp just in time, and if Hector hadn't taken the phone from her, she might have dropped it. Gabriel snatched the phone from Hector, looked at it and cursed.

"When's the last time you were home?" Gabriel asked.

It took her a moment to gather her breath and her composure. Jodi felt the panic fade, replaced by the anger of having someone do this. "Early this morning. He must have gotten in after I left for work."

Russell and August looked at the picture, too. "Or maybe this creep was in your place ages ago," August pointed out.

Jodi had to shake her head. "No, those are the clothes that I put there this morning, and that's the coffee mug I used."

"The FBI is headed to your place," Hector explained. "They'll process the crime scene. And this photo."

Yes, because sometimes there were bits of hidden data in digital pictures. Maybe they'd get lucky. But she doubted this intruder had been sloppy enough to leave a trace of himself behind.

Gabriel glanced at Hector, then Jodi. "How the hell did he get past your security system?"

Good question. Because she had a good system. The best, as a matter of fact—complete with motion detectors and cameras. And she looked at Hector to see if he had an answer for that since he'd been the one to install it.

"Any chance your hired spy gave the intruder the code so he could waltz right into Jodi's apartment?" August asked Hector.

Hector's eyes were narrowed to slits when he turned to August. "No. Any chance your PIs could have found the code and given it to him?"

Oh, no. This was about to get ugly.

"Or maybe you gave that thug the code," August added, and yes, he aimed that accusation at Hector.

"Why the hell would I do that?" Hector snapped.

"To send Jodi running to you. To make her believe that you're the one who can protect her."

That went back to August's theory of Hector trying to isolate her from everyone but him, but obviously it was a theory that ticked off Hector. Since she didn't want punches thrown, she stepped between them again. However, that didn't stop Hector. He just charged right past her, and it might have come to blows if Gabriel hadn't taken hold of Hector. Russell did the same to August.

"I'm not going to stand here and have this moron accuse me of junk like that." Hector's voice was past the anger stage now, and the veins in his neck were bulging. Jodi had never seen him like this, but then August was a pro at pressing hot buttons.

"You," Gabriel said, pointing to August. "Leave now. You two, as well," he added to Hector and Russell.

Russell gladly obliged. In fact, he looked plenty sorry that he'd even made this trip. August, however, didn't go so easily. He spat out some profanities, looking at Jodi as if he wanted her to intervene on his behalf.

She wouldn't.

"You need to go," she told him.

That didn't please August, and it earned her a few

choice curse words from him, but her uncle finally stormed out. It didn't surprise her, though, when Hector stayed put.

"You can't go back to your apartment," he said.

Of course, Jodi knew that, but there'd been so much info for her to process that it took her a couple of moments to realize the next thing Hector was about to point out—that she had to go somewhere safe.

But where?

She'd been trained to fight and shoot, but that wouldn't stop someone from gunning her down. Or worse. It wouldn't stop a monster from killing Gabriel, Russell or someone else just to prove a point. Exactly what point, she didn't know, but anyone who'd gotten a threatening email was at risk. She couldn't protect them all. Neither could Hector or Gabriel.

"I want you to come to my house," Hector insisted. "Or to the office. I can have both guarded 24/7."

Jodi was shaking her head before he even finished. Maybe the unease she was feeling was because Hector had had her followed without telling her. Or maybe nearly being killed had created this edgier-than-usual feeling inside her. Either way, she wasn't going with him.

"Thanks, but no thanks," she answered.

If this snake had managed to get someone into her apartment, he could get to her anywhere. Including the fortress that Hector called home.

Hector's stare turned to a glare that he shifted from her to Gabriel. It was the exact reaction she expected. Some anger mixed with disappointment. Hector wasn't stupid, and he had to have known she was picking sides. A side that would help her get to the bottom of this while not being killed.

And that *side* was with Gabriel.

Hector turned to leave but then stopped. "Gabriel didn't save you ten years ago. Just remember that," Hector said like a warning before he walked out.

Jodi waited to see if Gabriel was going to respond to that. He didn't. He just stood there, hands on his hips, watching as Hector went out of the building.

"I didn't tell Hector that I went to your house that night ten years ago," she explained. "He didn't know I'd come on to you and that you'd turned me down."

Jodi didn't want Gabriel to think she had poured her heart out to Hector. She hadn't. She hadn't poured out her heart to anyone.

Gabriel's silence continued for several more moments before he looked at her. "How exactly did you meet Hector?"

She'd expected questions, just not that one, and she didn't miss that he'd used his lawman's tone to ask it.

"He came to the hospital about a week after the stabbing." It wasn't hard to recall that meeting. In fact, those days, and the physical pain, were as fresh as if it'd just happened. "He said he'd read about the attack, and he wanted to offer me help getting back on my feet."

Gabriel made a sound of sarcastic disapproval, probably because she hadn't accepted any assistance from him, his sisters or her friends. Including Russell, who'd told her he would be there for her in any way he could. But Hector had offered her something no one else had.

"Hector said he could train me in self-defense, that he could teach me to use a firearm. A knife," Jodi softly added. "Everyone but the FBI was skirting around my attack, but Hector talked about it head-on. He said once

I was trained that I could work for him, and that no one would be able to hurt me like that again."

There it was in a nutshell. Jodi would have trusted almost anyone who'd made her believe that she could not only recover but that she would also never again be a victim.

She wouldn't be, either.

The next person who tried to put their hands on her was going to pay.

"And you didn't believe it was suspicious that a stranger would show up and make an offer like that?" Again, he sounded like a lawman, one who had his own doubts.

"What are you asking?"

"If you think Hector could have orchestrated this," Gabriel answered without hesitation.

"No. He didn't know me before the original attack—"

"You're positive?" he snapped.

Well, she had been until now. After giving it some thought, she had to shake her head again. "Hector's not connected to your parents…is he?"

"Not that I know of, but you can bet I'll be checking to see." He looked at her again. "Someone must have given the intruder the code to get past your security system. I'm not saying Hector did that," he quickly added, "but it could have been one of his employees. Someone who's close to both Hector and you."

A person who might have tried to kill them today.

And that someone might have murdered his parents.

"I know you've gone over every case file your father had worked on," she reminded him. "Were you able to exclude everyone connected to his investigations?"

"No." He cursed and rubbed the back of his neck.

"There was a file with notes about Hattie Osmond that didn't make sense."

"Hattie?" she asked. Jodi knew the woman. Or rather, had known her. Hattie was a widow and had owned a big ranch not far from Gabriel's. She'd stayed pretty much to herself until she'd passed away a couple of years ago.

"My dad thought Hattie was being swindled or else blackmailed," Gabriel explained. "She was selling off her livestock and was making weekly trips to the bank."

Yes, that would have been out of the ordinary for her. "Maybe she was sick or wanted to spend her money on her family."

"That's just it. She didn't have a family. I'm talking no heirs except for some distant cousins who didn't even know her. Anyway, when she died, her estate was valued at a fraction of what everyone thought she had, and she'd destroyed a lot of records that people normally keep."

Jodi tried to figure out where he was going with this. "You think Hector was involved in that?"

"Maybe. But your father could have been, too. Or August. Hell. Anybody could have been. It might not even be connected to anything. It's just a loose end, and right now loose ends are all I've got to figure this out."

"Yes," she softly agreed. "And it might be hours or days before you can get in to see Billy Coleman."

Hours that she could be using to find out who'd gotten into her apartment and if Hector did indeed have any old ties that she should know about. While she was at it, she could maybe sneak in to see Billy.

"Do you still have a break room here in the sheriff's office?" she asked. "Because my nerves are a little shot, and I could use some rest."

Gabriel stared at her as if trying to figure out if that was the truth. It wasn't.

"I need my meds," she added, since it was obvious he wasn't going to buy anything other than the truth. Jodi went with a half lie. "I came really close to a panic attack earlier, and the meds are the only thing that'll help. Unfortunately, they sometimes make me drowsy."

More staring, then he nodded and tipped his head to the left side of the building. "The break room is still there. I'll let you know if I hear anything about Billy or the knife."

The knife. She certainly hadn't forgotten about that. Especially since her prints were on it. But that was yet another reason for her to get the heck out of there. The FBI might try to take her into custody while they got that all sorted out. No way did she want to spend hours waiting in an interview room.

Jodi made her way through the building, one that she knew like the back of her hand. That's because she'd come here often enough with Ivy. First, just because Ivy's dad would give them money for ice cream. Then, later, Jodi came so she could flirt with Gabriel.

Not that he'd flirted back.

But she hadn't given up. Not until that night ten years ago anyway.

The break room was just as it had been the last time she was there. Same old leather sofa. Same fridge from the looks of it. Judging from the smells in the air, some-one had recently eaten pizza and had coffee.

There were two ways out—the emergency exit and a window. The door had an alarm on it. It was nothing fancy—just something to alert the lawmen if it opened. Since Jodi didn't want to do that, she checked out the window. No obvious wires or sensors to indicate it was connected to the security system, so she unlocked it and lifted it a fraction.

No alarm.

If it had gone off, she could have told Gabriel she just needed some fresh air. At least now she wouldn't need to lie to his face.

Jodi lifted the window the rest of the way up, pushed out the screen and shimmied outside. She started running the moment her feet landed on the ground.

She didn't get far. The moment she rounded the corner, she smacked right into someone.

Gabriel.

"Back inside," he snarled. Before she had a chance to protest, he took hold of her arm, his grip hard. "You're under arrest."

Chapter Six

This was the first time that Gabriel had brought someone in his custody to his family's ranch. Of course, it was also possibly the first time he'd arrested someone because he was pissed off at them.

It'd been stupid—along with being dangerous—for Jodi to try to run from him, but he'd known from the moment she said she needed a nap that she was going to try to sneak out of the sheriff's office. And if he'd let her out of his sight, she would have tried it again. That's why he'd arrested her, so he could hold her as a witness in his criminal investigation.

Even though Gabriel wouldn't want to have to explain himself to a judge, he was on solid legal ground. As the sheriff, he had a right to compel someone to give a statement if they'd witnessed a crime. He could do that by detaining them, and while detention and protective custody might keep Jodi alive, it wasn't winning him any brownie points with her.

Not that he wanted points, that is.

Gabriel would settle for her just not glaring at him. And for her being safe. God, he needed for her to be safe.

If he'd trusted Hector, that might be the best place for her, but there were too many questions about the man.

Taking Jodi there could be walking her right into the lion's den. Although Gabriel wasn't doing much better by her. He was taking her back to the scene of the crime.

Less than a quarter of a mile from it anyway.

"I shouldn't be here," she said the moment he pulled to a stop in front of his house. It didn't help that it was late, and the muggy heat was practically smothering them. Conditions that were almost identical to that night when she'd been left for dead.

From his truck window, she looked up at the bright moon. Yet another thing that had been in place during the attack. Too bad it hadn't given her enough light to have seen her attacker's face. If she had, then she might be convinced that her father was a killer. Of course, that wouldn't help them with a copycat, but now that Billy was locked up, at least they didn't have to worry about him.

He hoped.

"It's just for tonight," Gabriel assured her. "I can make other arrangements for you tomorrow." Along with having one of the deputies get her car. Right now, it was still parked on the road near the old house. He definitely didn't want to go there tonight.

"*I* can make other arrangements," she insisted.

"Yeah, I'm sure you can, but I didn't think you'd want to be alone."

Jodi didn't argue with that, though that's likely what she wanted to do. After all, she could have reminded him that she lived alone and had for the past decade. But this wasn't an ordinary night.

"I know you don't want anyone to realize that you see-ing the knife and the dead body shook you to the core," he went on. "That's probably because you think I'll take it as a sign of weakness. I wouldn't," he assured her.

"Yet you felt I was weak enough to bring me here," she huffed, pushing her hair from her face. "And I was weak enough to let you do it."

Now, Gabriel huffed. Definitely no brownie points. "Come on in. You can grab a shower, rest or eat. Whatever you want. I'll call and see if there's an update on the knife."

Some of the anger eased in her eyes when she looked at him. "Thank you."

Well, it was a start, and Gabriel took that as a green flag to get her moving out of the truck and onto the porch. Every step had to be a trip down memory lane for her. That's why he hurried and got her inside. There shouldn't be any of those memories of that night in the house since they'd had their short conversation on the porch.

The conversation where he'd turned her down.

He looked at her just as she looked at him, and he saw that she was reliving that little chat, too. And judging from the way her eyebrow lifted, she was maybe waiting for him to say something about it. But what he could say? Nothing that would make this better, that's for sure.

"I thought I was doing the right thing that night," he finally admitted. "I thought I was doing you a favor."

She laughed. Not from humor. Because there wasn't anything funny about what he was saying. Ironic that doing what he thought was the right thing had nearly gotten her killed.

Gabriel wouldn't be able to forget that. Ever.

Jodi went past him and into the living room. She glanced around, maybe noticing that he'd had the place redecorated. It was more him now and not just the house he'd inherited from his grandparents.

"Is the downstairs guest room still where it used to be?" she asked.

He nodded, and she immediately headed up the hall toward it. Only then did Gabriel release the breath he'd been holding. She was staying, for now, but just in case she decided to climb out the window, he set the security system. All the windows and doors were wired to sound the alarm if someone opened any of them. However, the only sound he heard was when she turned on the shower.

Gabriel went into the kitchen, put some sandwiches together and got started on checking for updates.

Nothing.

Well, nothing good anyway. Billy had been checked into the facility and wouldn't be evaluated by the psychiatrist until tomorrow morning. Heaven knew how long it would be before Gabriel could see him after that. Maybe not at all if the shrink deemed him incompetent.

That left Billy's lawyer and the knife.

There was no proof yet as to who was paying the attorney, and the knife was just as much of a puzzle as it had been when Gabriel had seen it on the doorstep of the old house. Jodi's prints combined with the dead guy's blood. Definitely not a good combination.

The broken tip appeared to be a match for the weapon used to kill both his parents and the man they found, but the lab would have to test both to be certain. Maybe during that testing, the techs could confirm whether Jodi's prints had been left there that night or if they'd been planted on it later. And he was certain if it was the latter that someone had indeed planted them. Because Jodi wasn't a killer.

Gabriel had just taken a bite of his sandwich when he heard a strange sound. A gasp, maybe. Definitely not something he wanted to hear. He ran to the guest room, praying that nothing was wrong. He knocked and tested the knob to find it locked. He was just on edge enough to break it down, but that wasn't necessary because Jodi opened it.

The lights were off in the bedroom, the shower still running in the adjoining bathroom, but Jodi was there. She hadn't run away after all, though she certainly looked ready to bolt.

Along with only being partly dressed.

Her jeans were on the bed, no doubt where she'd tossed them before taking her shower. Even though her top was long enough to cover her panties, Gabriel still noticed plenty of her bare legs. Jodi didn't seem to notice since her attention was on the other side of the room. Judging from her stark expression, something had spooked her.

"I thought I saw someone." She had a firm grip on her gun, but she took him by the hand and practically dragged him to the window. Not that she had to work hard to do that. Gabriel headed there while drawing his own weapon.

She didn't go directly in front of the window but instead stood to the side and peered out. Gabriel did the same.

And he cursed.

He rarely went in this room and hadn't realized it had a view of the old house. The moonlight was glinting off the tin roof of the place. It was like a beacon in the night and looked more than a little creepy.

"It might have just been a shadow," she said, her voice a breathy whisper. A whisper that was filled with nerves.

Gabriel tried to pick through the darkness and see if he could spot anyone. There used to be plenty of shrubs that lined the path between his place and the house. He'd had a lot of them cut down after that night because Jodi's attacker had used them to sneak up on her. He hadn't liked the idea of keeping something like that around. But over the years, some cedars had popped up. They were full and bushy, making them a perfect place for someone to hide.

"I don't suppose Ivy, Lauren or Jameson would be out there at this time of night?" Jodi asked.

"No. Jameson built a big log cabin by the river." It was a good half mile from here, and besides, he was still at work. "Ivy left the week after our parents were killed and hasn't been back to the ranch. Lauren didn't come back after she went off to college." He paused. "I figured you knew about Ivy since you two were so close."

Jodi's shoulders stiffened. "No. I haven't seen or heard from her."

Too bad. "Other than the occasional Christmas card and email, she hasn't stayed in touch with anyone. She left around the time that she and your brother broke up."

"Yes," she said under her breath. "They were in love. Or at least they thought they were. Theo blamed Ivy for not believing he was innocent of the murders. He thought she'd put you up to bringing him in for questioning."

Ivy hadn't, but then she hadn't exactly jumped to defend Theo, either. Gabriel wasn't sure why, but in the end Theo's name had been cleared, and he'd gone on to be a DEA agent. All had worked out as well as it could for those two. But Gabriel knew his sister was still bro-

ken in some ways. Maybe clinging to the past, too, since
Ivy had been the one to insist they not tear down the old
house. Of course, she'd insisted that years ago, so maybe
it was time to revisit that issue. He didn't like having
the nightmare staring him right in the face every day
when he drove past it.

His folks would hate that he hadn't been able to keep
the family together. Would hate even more that Gabriel
hadn't tried too hard to bring his sisters back home. But
in the moments when it ate away at him, he rationalized
that they had their own lives. Maybe not especially good
ones since both Ivy and Lauren had lost their partners.

Yeah, his dad and mom wouldn't care for him not
stepping up to the parent role. But Gabriel hadn't seen
any reason to drag them back to a place where the memories might be more than his kid sisters could handle.
Hell. Sometimes, it was too much for him to handle.

Gabriel continued to look around, also glancing at
Jodi to make sure she wasn't about to go into panic attack mode. She wasn't. But her attention kept going back
to that section of the trail where she'd nearly died.

"I remember so many things about that night," Jodi
said, breaking the silence. "Except for his face."

He remembered plenty of things, too, even though
there were times when he wished he didn't. Gabriel certainly remembered finding Jodi. Later he'd had to piece
together what had happened to her when she'd left his
house that night.

After her attacker had cut her up, he'd dragged her
just off the trail and put her in a makeshift "grave" that
he'd dug out with his own hands. It really was just a
couple of inches of topsoil that the person had scraped

away, and then he'd tried to cover her body with some dirt and leaves.

It'd been a miracle that Gabriel had even seen her, especially since by then he'd gotten the frantic call from Ivy to let him know that something "bad" had gone on at the house. After hearing Ivy say that, his focus had been on getting to the house.

Fast.

Gabriel had started running immediately after Ivy's call, and if he hadn't looked down at the exact moment he did, he might not have seen the blood on the ground. He might not have even looked at the grave where the killer had put Jodi.

She could have died right there in that spot.

"I guess it was a false alarm," she added several moments later. "I don't see anyone out there."

Neither did he, but he didn't budge. Jodi did, though. She went into the bathroom to finish getting dressed, but as soon as she'd done that, she hurried straight back to the window.

"Did you get any new info on the investigation?" she asked.

"Not yet. Maybe by morning we'll have something, though." He paused. "You should know that I'll be investigating Hector, to see if he had any connection to our dead guy. Any connection to Hattie, as well."

Jodi didn't seem to have any objections to that. Maybe because she was still upset at her boss having her followed. "August knew her, too, of course."

True. Hattie had lived just up the road from Jodi's family. Gabriel had looked for anything obvious to link August, and anyone else, to Hattie. Now, he needed to dig even deeper because, so far, he hadn't found anything.

"You think August could have killed your father because he was investigating him," she said. It wasn't a question, but if it had been, the answer would have been—it was possible.

"At the time of the murders, August was twenty-eight, broke," Gabriel explained. "He didn't get his trust fund until he was thirty, two years later. He could have milked money from Hattie to pay for all those things he couldn't afford. August always had expensive tastes in cars, women and clothes."

All of that was purely circumstantial, though, and it didn't mean Travis was innocent. Travis could have still murdered Gabriel's parents, and August could have been an accessory.

It could have even been August who'd attacked Jodi.

She tipped her head to the bathroom, probably to say that it was time to put an end to this impromptu surveillance and finish getting cleaned up, but she didn't speak. Something had caught her eye. Just as it'd caught Gabriel's.

There was some movement on the road in front of the old house.

Not a shadow. It was either a deer or a person. The knot in Gabriel's stomach told him it wasn't a deer.

"Wait here," he told her. "I'll get some binoculars."

He didn't remind her to stay back from the glass because Jodi was already doing that. But he did hurry. Whatever he'd seen wasn't coming their direction, but that could change. He didn't have any night goggles and made a mental note to bring a pair to the house, but he had the standard ones that his dad had used for hunting.

Gabriel brought them back to the window and had a look at the spot where he'd seen the movement.

"Nothing," he relayed to Jodi, and he handed her the binoculars so she could check it out for herself. Several moments later she made a sound of agreement. That sound was coupled with some relief, too.

Gabriel took out his phone. "I'll have one of the deputies go by the place just in case."

Even though the CSIs had already processed the pantry and kitchen, he didn't want any thrill seekers trying to get a look at the crime scene. He also didn't want to leave Jodi alone so he could do it himself.

"Wait. It's a man," Jodi said, quickly passing him back the binoculars. No relief now. There was an edge and an urgency in her voice. "He's by the cluster of trees just up the road from your parents' house. He's wearing a ski mask."

That knot in his stomach had been warranted after all, and he had a look for himself. Yeah, he saw someone all right. And the person was on the move. Not leaving, either. The guy was coming in the direction of Gabriel's place.

He handed Jodi the binoculars so he could text Cameron, and he warned the deputy to approach with caution. Since this clown had on a ski mask, this might not be a prank situation after all. It could be the person who'd put Billy up to killing a man and then attacking Jodi and him.

"He's got a gun," Jodi blurted out.

Gabriel had just finished the text, and he pushed her away from the window and against the wall. She automatically pushed back and brought up both her knee and hand as if to fight him. Gabriel eased away from her, hoping it would lessen the panic he suddenly felt in her. The panic hadn't come from the guy with the gun, though. It had come because he'd touched her.

Now, Gabriel had a whole new reason to hate her father. Or whoever the hell it was who'd gone after her with that knife. The attack had left her this way, and after all these years, it might be permanent.

"I just didn't want you in this guy's line of sight," he reminded her.

She nodded and lowered both her knee and her hand. At least she hadn't tried to shoot him. With her training and skills, she might have managed to get off a shot before he could stop her.

Gabriel went back to the window, only glancing at Cameron's text response that he was on the way. It took him a moment to spot the guy again. He was definitely coming toward the house, and he was running now. It would be only a couple of minutes before he got there.

He weighed his options and doubted he'd be able to convince Jodi to hide in the bathroom. That meant Gabriel just had to protect her as best he could.

"Go in the living room and disarm the security system," he told her and rattled off the code. "Otherwise, when I open this window, the alarm will go off, and I won't be able to hear."

Gabriel especially needed to hear if this guy had brought a partner in crime with him. One that was even closer to the house than this one.

Jodi didn't question his order. She ran out of the room, and Gabriel didn't take his attention off the thug. The moment Jodi made it back, he threw open the window and took aim. He waited a couple more seconds, until the man was plenty close enough.

"Stop and put your hands in the air," Gabriel shouted.

Judging from the way the guy snapped back his shoulders, Gabriel had surprised him. What the idiot didn't do was put up his hands. Nor did he stop. He started running, not toward the house but to his right. There were thick woods back there, and Gabriel didn't want him getting away.

"Stay here," he told Jodi.

He didn't figure she would, and she didn't. She was right on his heels and followed him to the door. Gabriel opened it, looking out to make sure he wasn't about to be ambushed. When he didn't see anyone, he hurried to the side of the porch that would give him the best view of the trespasser.

"Stop or I'll shoot," Gabriel called out.

The guy did stop, but he didn't look up at Gabriel. Instead he glanced in the direction of the road in front of the old house. Specifically, he glanced at Jodi's car that was still parked there.

That bad feeling in Gabriel's gut went up a huge notch. His gut was right. Because Jodi's car exploded into a ball of flames.

Chapter Seven

Jodi had hoped a long shower would help loosen her tense muscles. No such luck, though. Sleep hadn't helped, either. Too many dreams. Too many nightmarish images. She had the nightmares so often that they were part of what she now considered normal, but sometimes it was next to impossible to deal with her "normal."

Being around Gabriel wasn't helping with those memories, but even with that weighing her down, Jodi had to admit there was something comforting about having him nearby. Which, of course, only put her on edge even more. She'd learned the hard way that when you let down your guard, you got hurt. That's why she needed to make arrangements for a safe place to stay.

Clearly, that wasn't the ranch.

Though Gabriel had disagreed with that. He'd talked her into staying the night mainly because of the bomber still being out there. He had beefed up security by having two reserve deputies patrol the area, and Gabriel had stayed in the guest room with her. Guarding her.

From the floor.

That's where he'd put his makeshift bed, but Jodi doubted he'd gotten much sleep. She certainly hadn't.

She dressed in the loaner clothes Gabriel had left for

her in the bathroom. Jeans and a loose gray top. She hoped these were things that Ivy had left behind because she didn't like the idea of wearing something from one of his ex-girlfriends.

Or maybe he even had a current girlfriend.

Gabriel hadn't mentioned one, but it was possible that his "normal" included things like dating and relationships. A life. Something she hadn't quite managed to get since she'd been put in that shallow grave.

After she combed her hair, Jodi made her way to the kitchen, where she'd left Gabriel. He was still there but not alone. Jameson and Cameron were seated with him at the breakfast table. She didn't catch what they were saying, and they hushed when they spotted her.

"What's wrong?" she asked. Because judging from their expressions, there'd been either another murder or a serious hitch in the investigation.

Gabriel got up, poured her a cup of coffee and motioned for her to sit. Jodi took the coffee, but she stood. She'd found that pacing usually worked a lot better than being seated if she was about to have to take another mental punch.

"There's been no sign of the bomber," Gabriel said.

Not good but it was something she'd expected. Gabriel and Jameson had searched for several hours after leaving Cameron at the house to watch her. They'd found nothing and called it a night. Now that the sun had been up for several hours, she'd hoped they would find some evidence that would lead them to him. Apparently not.

"There was a security camera in your car," Gabriel added.

With everything going on, she'd forgotten about that.

"It's motion activated, and the feed goes to a storage cloud. Please tell me you saw the guy on there."

Gabriel shook his head. "The bomber managed to jam the feed."

She took a long sip of coffee, her grip too tight on the cup, but at least it stopped her from gasping, trembling or doing something else to make them think she was losing it. But this was critical. Jamming a camera like that would take some expertise and the right equipment. It meant this hadn't been done by some amateur thrill seeker.

"Billy's still locked up and didn't have any computer or phone access," Jameson explained. "That means he's probably not the one who sent this thug."

"His lawyer could have," she quickly pointed out. "Or the person who hired the lawyer for him."

Jameson nodded. "We're looking into it." He didn't sound very hopeful they'd come up with that, but at least it was a lead. Maybe the only one they had right now.

"Why would anyone blow up my car?" she threw out there. "It was obvious I wasn't in it, hadn't been in it for hours. So, if he wasn't trying to kill me, what was the point?"

"To scare you," Gabriel readily answered. "To send you into a panic so that you did something dangerous like run outside so you could be shot."

Jodi heard the disapproval in Gabriel's voice. Disapproval since she had indeed gone outside, but she hadn't panicked. Now, she sat down in the chair next to him and tried to piece her thoughts together.

"If this is a copycat, he'll want to re-create what happened that night," she suggested. "Not just by coming after me but also by killing someone else in the house."

No one at the table disagreed with that. It wasn't exactly a settling thought to have three lawmen admit that someone could want to slice her up again. But there was something in Gabriel's eyes that told her there was more to this than a simple copycat crime.

"We got some of the lab results on the knife," Gabriel continued a moment later. "It's the same one used to murder my parents and attack you. The broken tip was a perfect match to it."

That caused the skin to crawl on the back of her neck. Since she was fighting to tamp down the flashbacks, Jodi was sorry she'd sat down, but she couldn't stand back up. Her legs suddenly felt wobbly.

"And the blood and prints on the knife?" she asked.

"The blood belongs to the guy we found in the pantry." Gabriel looked at her again. "The only prints on it are yours. The lab said they look like defensive prints."

In other words, she had managed to grab the knife that night. That meant she must have seen her attacker's face. Of course, she'd known all along that was possible, but hearing it spelled out made her want to remember even more. If she could just see his face, then it could prove her father hadn't been the one to try to kill her.

Maybe.

And it just might confirm his guilt. But at least she would know. *Her father* would know, since he'd been too drunk to recall much of what'd gone on that night.

"The obvious question is—where has the knife been this whole time?" Jameson asked. "It didn't show any signs of being out in the elements. Or buried."

Jameson glanced at her, maybe to make sure those two words hadn't been too much for her to handle. After all, she'd been buried. But Jodi was pushing away the memories and the panic so she could concentrate on what this new information might mean.

"The killer—or his accomplice," she quickly amended, "could have had it hidden all this time. Then, when I leaked it to the press that I was remembering details of the attack, maybe he freaked out and decided to try to scare me off."

"Or someone could have found the knife shortly after the attacks, kept it and decided to use it to play a sick game with you," Gabriel commented.

Yes, and that led her right back to August. Even if he hadn't been an accomplice or the killer, August might have found the knife near the scene and kept it, believing that it would incriminate her father. Ironic that it only had her prints and not the person responsible for this nightmarish crime.

Cameron finished his cup of coffee and stood. "I'll head to the sheriff's office and see if I can come up with anything on Billy's lawyer."

Jameson stood as well, and looked at Gabriel. "And I'll drive into San Antonio and find out who I can press to get one of us an interview with Billy."

Gabriel thanked them both. Cameron left, but Jameson lingered behind and aimed some glances at both Jodi and him. "You're both welcome to stay at my place. That way, you won't have to be so close to the old house. I suspect the CSIs will be all over it and the grounds."

They would be, but she had to shake her head. "Thanks for the offer, but I have some places in mind where I can go."

Jodi didn't, not yet anyway, but she would. She'd kept money in her apartment and car, but since she couldn't get to either of those, she would need to go to a bank.

Once she had some cash, she could check into a hotel under a fake name and then figure out what her next step was. She didn't want to be tucked away where she couldn't investigate this, but she couldn't allow herself to be an easy target, either.

Jameson made a "suit yourself" sound and walked out. Gabriel got up, too, and followed him. So he could set the security system, Jodi realized. She hadn't needed a reminder of the danger, but that did it. So did Gabriel's expression. It was somehow wired and weary at the same time, and he coupled it with a huff.

"What places?" Gabriel asked, coming back into the kitchen. He went straight to the coffeepot and poured himself another cup.

It took her a moment to realize he was asking her where she had in mind to go. "A friend's house," she lied. "Not Hector's," she quickly added. That wasn't a lie. She had no intention of going there.

Gabriel huffed again, and it was louder than his earlier one. "You have nightmares," he said. "I heard you talking in your sleep, so don't deny it. You've admitted you have panic attacks. Someone tried to kill you, then broke into your apartment and blew up your car. I'm thinking *a friend's house* isn't the place you should be going."

He was right, of course. Even if she had any close friends, she couldn't bring the danger to their doorstep. Besides, judging from Gabriel's tone, he was thinking *friend* meant *lover*.

"You can't believe it's a good idea for me to stay here." But as soon as she said it, Jodi realized something. Maybe it was a good idea.

If she wanted a final confrontation with this monster.

And she did.

Everything happening seemed to be leading back to this place. To the scene of the original crime. Maybe her attacker wanted to finish what he'd started here. Well, she wanted to finish it, too, but with a totally different ending than this sick piece of slime had planned. This time, she wanted to be the one to end his life and put a stop to the danger once and for all.

"Fine," she amended. "I'll stay here."

Gabriel lifted his eyebrow, stared at her. Obviously, he knew what she was doing. But there was no way he could turn her down. Not this time. In fact, after what'd happened ten years ago, he might never turn her down again. Maybe Jodi could use that to bring all of this to a close.

He got in her face. So close that she had no trouble seeing all those flecks of silver in his blue eyes. "You might think you're ready to face down a killer, but it can't go past the thinking stage. Got that?" His jaw was tight. His words spoken through clenched teeth. "I don't want you outside on your own. And I don't want you on the trail that leads between here and my parents' house. I especially don't want you doing anything stupid like making yourself bait."

She shook her head and didn't dodge his intense stare. "You have to admit I'm the ultimate bait. I'm the one he wants."

Gabriel cursed. "You don't know that. Whoever killed that man could be trying to free your father by going after me or my brother. Especially if it's August."

True, and Jodi hated that she didn't know the reason behind all of this. Hated even more that her own kin could be responsible.

And that wasn't all that was causing her nerves to go into overdrive.

There was one more facet to this, especially if she did indeed stay here for another night or two. The attraction. She looked at Gabriel to see if that had occurred to him.

It had.

"It's easy for me to lose focus around you," Gabriel readily admitted, surprising her. Maybe surprising himself, too. "That can't happen. Because it could get one of us killed."

Jodi nodded. With that clarified, she should have looked away, probably should have just excused herself and gone back to the guest room to start making some calls to help with the investigation. But she stayed put.

Gabriel did, as well.

And, mercy, the heat came. She could feel it swirling between them. They'd never kissed, something she regretted simply because it made her want to do that now. Jodi wanted to know the feel of his mouth on hers. His taste. She was betting Gabriel was a good kisser, and there was the problem. With the heat and spent adrenaline already in play, it wouldn't stop with just a single kiss.

No, they'd land in bed.

At least, her body would want them to end up there, but Jodi was betting her mind wouldn't let things get that far. Heck, it was possible the kiss would even trigger a panic attack.

That reminder caused her to step back, though it wasn't necessary. Gabriel's phone rang, the sound slicing through the room—and the heat from the attraction—and he moved back as well to answer it. He didn't put the call on speaker, so she couldn't hear what the caller was saying, but whatever it was caused Gabriel's forehead to bunch up.

"Text them to me," Gabriel insisted, and he clicked the button to end the call. "The person who broke into your apartment left some pictures. Old ones from ten years ago."

Oh, God. "Not pictures of your parents' murders?"

He dragged in a long breath and nodded. "Brace yourself. Because the pictures are of you."

Chapter Eight

Gabriel was a thousand percent sure that it wasn't a good idea for Jodi to look at the pictures Jameson had just sent him. He was also equally certain that he wouldn't be able to stop her from seeing them. Not Jodi. She would insist on it.

From a law enforcement viewpoint, it was a good thing for her to study them. It might trigger some memories of the attack that would help them explain what was happening now. But it would also be an emotional nightmare for her. Something he wished he didn't have to put her through. Despite the thick wall Jodi had built around herself, Gabriel still wanted to protect her. Even when she wouldn't want him to do that.

He maximized the size of the first picture on his phone, but it still took Gabriel a few seconds to figure out exactly what he was seeing. It was a grainy shot, dark, but it soon became clear that it was of his front porch. The lights were on, and Jodi was in the doorway. She was wearing a familiar outfit—cutoff shorts and that red top.

Hell.

Someone had clicked a picture of them when Gabriel was turning her down, and while he didn't remember the exact words he'd said to her, the gist was for her to go back to his parents' house, where she was spending the night with Ivy.

"I didn't notice anyone," she said, her voice barely a whisper. She moved closer to him, arm to arm, and had another look.

He hadn't noticed anyone, either, but it could have been taken with a long-range lens. Still, if Gabriel had just glanced in that direction, he might have spotted the person and stopped what was about to happen.

But why would Travis have taken this?

The answer was—he wouldn't have. The man had been drunk, and it wasn't too likely he'd have been carrying a camera. Even if he'd used his phone for the shot, there was still no reason to do this. After all, Travis was well aware that Jodi often visited Ivy, and Gabriel.

Gabriel moved on to the next shot. This one was of Jodi walking away from his house. She was barely visible in the darkness, but she was already on the trail. Leaving. He was in the door, watching her go. He'd almost stopped her. Had almost run after her and kissed her. If he had, they wouldn't be standing here right now. Of course, his parents would likely still be dead since Gabriel had gotten the frantic call from Ivy less than five minutes after Jodi had left.

He cursed when he pulled up the third photo and tried to move his phone away so that Jodi wouldn't see it. Of course, she snatched it back and saw what had caused his profanity and had twisted his stomach into knots.

Jodi on the ground, bleeding out.

"The SOB took my picture while I was dying," she said.

Yeah, and that told him plenty that he hadn't known before. If Travis had indeed been the one to attack her because he'd thought she had witnessed the murders, he wouldn't have waited around to take a picture of her sliced up and on the ground. That applied to the other pictures, as well.

"You're right. Your father wouldn't have been the one to stab you," Gabriel admitted.

Jodi glanced at him and that's when Gabriel saw the tears in her eyes. She quickly blinked them away and turned her head.

"Yes." And that's all she said for several long seconds. "The person who took these photos was outside your house right about the time your parents were being killed." She paused. "My attack wasn't about them. It was about *me*."

The tears threatened again, and even though Gabriel figured it was a bad idea, he pulled her into his arms. He expected her to fight it or go stiff. But she didn't. Jodi melted against him.

That was what Gabriel wanted to protect her from seeing. Now, those images would stay with her just as they'd stayed with him. Because that's the way he'd seen her after he had found her just off the path.

"It wasn't my father," she whispered. Even through the emotion, he could hear the relief, and she looked up at him just as he looked down at her.

The air was already thick with emotion, but that eye-to-eye contact made it even worse. The attraction mixed with the old memories and the pain. Everything snowballed together until it felt as if he were being buried in an avalanche of heat. That's probably why he kissed her. Because it wasn't something he'd planned to do.

Definitely not a smart move.

His mouth barely touched hers before she scurried

back as if he'd scalded her. "I'm sorry," he said at the exact moment that Jodi said, "I can't."

He nodded and then put even more distance between them. Gabriel was ready to close down the pictures so he could look at them later when Jodi wasn't around, but before he could do that, he heard the sound of a car pulling up in front of his house. Normally, that wouldn't have been a reason for concern, but there was nothing normal about what had been going on.

Gabriel drew his gun and went to the window just in time to see their visitor pull to a stop. It was a black SUV, and since the windows were heavily tinted, he couldn't see who was inside.

"Recognize that vehicle?" he asked Jodi.

"No." She'd drawn her gun as well, and even though she still had to be shaken from those photos, she wasn't showing any traces of being upset now. Like him, she was focused on a possible new threat.

Gabriel could see the front license plate of the SUV, and he was about to phone it in when someone stepped out.

Russell.

That didn't make Gabriel holster his gun, but it was obvious that Jodi and he weren't the only ones on edge. Russell glanced around while staying behind the cover of the SUV door. They were the kinds of glances a person would make if they thought someone was following them.

"Why the heck is he here?" Jodi grumbled.

Gabriel didn't know, but he was about to find out. He disarmed the security system so that it wouldn't go off when he opened the door, opening it about halfway.

"I have to talk to you." Russell ran onto the porch while still firing glances all around him.

Gabriel didn't back up. He certainly didn't invite Russell inside, which earned him a puzzled look. "I'm in danger," the man added.

"Welcome to the club." But Gabriel knew he couldn't be flippant about this. He was a lawman. Danger came with the badge. Ditto for Jodi as a security specialist. But Russell was a businessman, a CPA, and this might be his first brush with some monster with a deadly agenda since he left the army.

Of course, in Gabriel's mind, Russell could be a suspect. Anyone with a personal connection to Jodi could be. Including Hector and August.

"Someone just tried to kill me," Russell spat out. He came closer as if ready to barge in, but Gabriel didn't let him.

Jodi, however, moved to Gabriel's side, which meant she was now in the possible line of fire if their bomber was still in the area. That was a good reason to put a quick end to this conversation so he could get her back inside.

Russell huffed. "Look, I just want you to put a stop to this. My wife and baby could be hurt."

Gabriel wanted to be unaffected by that, but he wasn't. He knew what it was like to have family members in danger. And what it was like to have that danger lead to their deaths.

"What happened?" Gabriel asked.

Russell looked around again and groaned softly. "I leave my car in the driveway overnight outside my house, and when I went to get in it early this morning, there were two rattlesnakes on the seats. Rattlesnakes!"

he repeated like profanity. "What if my wife had gone out there with me to kiss me goodbye for work? She could have been killed."

Possibly. But since it was Russell's car, the snakes had been meant for him. "You didn't see anyone suspicious in the area?" Gabriel pressed. "And did you report it to SAPD?"

"Of course I reported it. I called them right away. They came and took my statement. They asked if I saw anyone, too, and I didn't. This has to stop," he repeated after another groan.

While still keeping watch of Russell, Gabriel took out his phone and made a quick call to Cameron to have him request a copy of Russell's incident report from SAPD.

"Maybe you can make a public statement," Russell went on, looking at Jodi now. "Or visit your father and make sure he's not behind this. He could have put his brother up to all this in order to clear his name, but I can't have my family at risk because of you."

Gabriel felt Jodi tense. Probably because those words would have felt like a slap to the face. But it was a strange way of putting it. Yes, Russell was upset, but why had he dumped all of this on Jodi?

"We have reason to believe that Travis wasn't the one who attacked Jodi that night," Gabriel said, and he watched Russell's reaction.

And it was an interesting reaction all right. Russell's eyes widened, and he volleyed glances between Gabriel and her. "Then who the hell did it? Because that's probably the same SOB who put those snakes in my SUV."

Maybe. Probably, Gabriel amended. It was also likely the same person who'd blown up Jodi's car.

"You have to come up with a way to put an end

to this," Russell went on, his voice more frantic now. "Maybe set a trap for him or something."

Gabriel had no plans to do that, especially since it would require using Jodi as bait, but he figured Jodi was already thinking of doing just that.

"I'm scared of Hector," Russell added. "If he's the one doing this, then he's got the people and the resources to hurt me and my family."

Gabriel hoped he didn't look too surprised at Russell's comment against Jodi's boss. Hector was indeed a possible suspect, but Russell made it seem as if adding the man to Gabriel's suspect list was a done deal.

"Why would you think Hector's behind this?" Jodi asked, taking the question right out of Gabriel's mouth.

Russell lifted his shoulder. "I thought it was obvious. The guy's crazy in love with you. And he can't be happy that you're staying here with Gabriel. Something like that might send Hector off the deep end. Heck, it might send August off the deep end, too." He settled his attention on Gabriel. "August really hates you, and he wouldn't want his niece spending time with the man who helped put his brother in prison."

August did feel that way, but Gabriel decided not to confirm it. He just waited to see if Russell would say anything else. He didn't.

Russell checked his watch. "I need to be getting to work." He started to leave but then turned back. "I don't want you calling my home or going there. It'd only upset my wife even more." He wasn't talking to Gabriel but rather Jodi.

"No worries. I won't go there." Her voice was tight enough for Gabriel to know that she wasn't pleased with what was essentially a dig. It was long over between Jodi and Russell, and Gabriel doubted she had feelings for the man, but maybe Russell thought she did.

Gabriel stepped back so he could shut the door. He also made another call to Cameron, and the deputy answered on the first ring.

"I need you to bring in Hector and August for questioning again—" Gabriel started.

"August is already here," Cameron interrupted. "And he's demanding to speak to you."

"Put him on the phone." Gabriel still wanted to do a face-to-face interview with both men, but he could possibly clear up some things right now. Well, one thing anyway. "While I'm talking to him, see if you can pull up any financials on Hector, Russell and August. The FBI should have already done that because of the investigation into the email threats and the latest murder."

"Will do. Oh, and brace yourself because August is mad." There was sarcasm dripping from Cameron's voice, probably because August was usually angry about something.

"Where are you?" August snapped the moment he came on the line. "And where's my niece?"

"We're both safe," Gabriel answered. Even though August likely knew Jodi was at the ranch, he didn't want to confirm it. "I just got a visit from Russell. Any chance you put some snakes in his car?"

"What?" August howled. "Is that what he said?" He didn't pause long enough for Gabriel to respond. "Because he's a bald-faced liar. I hope you asked him if he's the one who killed your folks and knifed Jodi."

He hadn't, but Gabriel wasn't planning to accuse Russell of anything yet, especially since he didn't have any evidence.

"Russell had an alibi for the night of the attacks," Gabriel reminded him.

"Yeah, so what? It was a girl he'd met at a bar who admitted she'd been drinking. She could have passed out and not even known he'd gone out and done something like that."

Gabriel hadn't intended for the conversation to swing in this direction, but he went with it. "Okay, I'll bite. What motive would Russell have to kill my folks? He didn't even know them."

Of course, Gabriel had a theory that could work—that Russell could have killed them after going to the house to look for Jodi. Collateral damage.

"Russell didn't have to know them to kill them," August pointed out. "Maybe he was tanked up on drugs. Maybe he just wanted to kill something or somebody, and they were the ones who drew the short straw. I'm just saying, you need to take a hard look at that liar. If there were snakes in his car, he might have put them there himself."

Yes, and that's why Gabriel wanted to read the report from SAPD. There might be something suspicious that stood out. Also, Gabriel could start calling around to the local snake handlers to see if anyone had purchased any recently. Some people collected them for their venom and just because they liked having dangerous "pets." If any of them had recently sold a pair of snakes, it could lead them to Russell.

"Are you going to ask Hector if he put snakes in that idiot's car?" August went on.

"You bet I will. Now, wait there until I can get into the office and we can have a longer chat. For now, give the phone back to Cameron."

"He's on the other line, but I'll put the phone on his desk."

From the sound of it, August practically threw it there. He obviously wasn't happy about having to wait on Gabriel, but people often said more when they were riled, so he'd let August stew a while longer.

Then, he could figure out what to do about Jodi.

"I could go to the sheriff's office with you," she offered while he waited for Cameron. "If you give me access to a computer and a phone, I can start trying to take a better look at the photos that the intruder left at my apartment. I might see something I hadn't noticed before."

That was what Gabriel was afraid of. Still, the killer and she were likely the only ones at that particular time on the part of the trail where she'd been attacked that night. So Jodi might indeed see something new.

Along with having a panic attack.

But that was a bridge he'd cross if they got to it.

"Sorry about the wait," Cameron said when he came back. "I've got something to tell you, but I want to do that in your office. I'm walking there right now."

The deputy probably wanted some privacy because August was right there in his face, but it meant waiting a couple of seconds. "It's about Russell," Cameron said when he finally continued. "The FBI has been monitoring him along with Jodi, you and anyone else who might be connected to the recent threats, and they might have found something."

Jodi moved closer to him, clearly trying to hear what Cameron was saying, so Gabriel put the call on speaker. "Jodi's listening," Gabriel warned the deputy. That way,

Cameron could tone down anything that might be disturbing to her.

"Russell recently withdrew a rather large sum of money in cash. Nine grand. It came from an account he had before he got married. His wife's name isn't on the account. She might not even know it exists."

Not telling a spouse about an account wasn't unheard of, but that wasn't what caught Gabriel's attention. It was the amount of money. Just enough not to attract suspicion. At least it wouldn't have been if Russell weren't being monitored. Nine thousand was enough to pay off Billy and hire the guy who'd broken into Jodi's apartment. Maybe even enough to pay the man who'd blown up her car.

When Gabriel's eyes met Jodi's, he realized she'd come to the same conclusion.

"Does the FBI have any idea what Russell used the money for?" Gabriel asked Cameron.

"Not yet. He didn't deposit it into another account, didn't get a cashier's check with it, either. You want me to get him in here and question him?"

"No. Check with the FBI. It's possible they'll want to monitor him to see if this has anything to do with the murder or anything else."

"Yeah, about that," Cameron continued. "The lab got an ID on the dead guy. It's not good, Gabriel." He paused. "The guy was a cop."

Chapter Nine

Jodi's mind was whirling with everything Gabriel and she had learned. Whirling, too, because she'd been on edge the entire drive from his ranch to the sheriff's office. It wasn't far, less than ten miles, but each moment they'd been on the road had felt like an eternity.

Once Cameron had told Gabriel that their dead guy was a cop, Gabriel hadn't asked anything else. He'd just told the deputy that they were on their way there. Not just to read the reports on Russell but also so that Gabriel could reinterview August and Hector.

"I don't want you near the windows," Gabriel told her when he rushed her inside the building.

Cameron was right there to hand him some papers, but Gabriel paused only long enough to take them, and then he led her to his office. He lowered the blinds on the single window behind his desk and waited for Cameron to come in.

"That's a copy of the police report that Russell filed about those snakes," Cameron explained. "We're coming up empty on who might have gotten the snakes, but we'll keep looking. The next paper is about our dead guy. His name was Calvin Lasher, a small-town cop from Louisiana who'd recently been reported missing.

I don't know why his prints weren't in the system, but it could have been some kind of computer error."

Jodi repeated the man's name, but it didn't mean anything to her. "Why was he here in Blue River?" She went to Gabriel's side and started reading through the initial report that Cameron had done on the dead man.

"I don't have a clue," Cameron answered. "Lasher's boss and family don't know, either, but his boss said he'd been investigating Hector."

That caused both Gabriel and her to take their attention from the paper and look at Cameron. "Why?" they said in unison.

"An illegal wiretap. Lasher had arrested a pimp who wanted a plea deal. The pimp said Hector had set up an illegal tap on his phone."

Gabriel turned to her. "You know anything about that?"

"No. But we do have out-of-state clients. It's possible Hector knew one of this pimp's girls, and maybe she had complained to him."

"It's not as if Hector hasn't done something like this before," Gabriel grumbled.

She didn't miss the disdain in Gabriel's voice. "True, but it would have been stupid for him to do it when he's on probation. Something like this could land him in jail."

Of course, that might not have stopped Hector. His favorite saying was, never mistake the law for justice, so he was always bending rules to the point of breaking them.

"Hector doesn't live in Blue River, either," she added. "Seems a stretch that he could have lured a cop to the Beckett ranch in order to kill him."

"A stretch but not impossible," Gabriel pointed out. "This way he could eliminate someone who might be able to put him back behind bars."

Maybe. But that seemed extreme for what would have turned out to be a fairly short jail sentence, and it was a sentence that Hector could have perhaps beaten. He had a knack for escaping time behind bars.

"When did this wiretap supposedly happen?" she asked Cameron.

"About two weeks ago."

"Good, that's recent enough that the file won't be archived yet," Jodi explained. "If you let me use your computer, I'll see if I can access the info."

Gabriel motioned for her to use the laptop on his desk, and she was about to log on to the Sentry page when she heard footsteps in the hall. Cameron and Gabriel immediately reacted, both of them putting their hands over their weapons, but she saw them relax just as fast.

"Is my sister here?" someone demanded.

Theo.

Jodi hurried out from behind the desk to see her brother walking up the hall. It was the first time she'd seen him in a year, and she went to him, wanting to hug him but not sure how he would react.

Once Theo and she had been so close. But that had changed the night of her attack. In the aftermath, each of them had been dealing with their own pain. She, because she had nearly died, and Theo, because he'd been a suspect in the murders.

He'd changed a lot since she'd seen him. His hair was long, practically to his shoulders, and he was dressed more like a cowboy-biker than a federal agent. She didn't know if his leather vest and rodeo buckle were his own clothes or if this was something he'd been wearing undercover.

"Jodi," he greeted. He lifted his hand as if he might reach out for her, but he didn't. Maybe because he saw the unease in her eyes. Of course, there was plenty of unease in his eyes, as well. Probably because there was no love lost between Gabriel, Cameron and him.

She didn't ask him where he'd been. Jodi knew as a deep cover DEA agent Theo wouldn't be able to tell her anyway. Plus, she wasn't sure she wanted to know the kind of danger he was in on a daily basis. It was already hard enough to accept that he might never be a real part of her life.

Equally hard to accept that both of them wanted it that way.

"Are you okay?" Theo said to her.

She nodded. "You?"

He lifted his shoulder. "I got a threat just like all of you, but it's been sitting on my old server for days, so I just now got word of it." Theo turned his attention to Gabriel. "I'm guessing Ivy got one, too?"

It wasn't a surprise that Theo had asked about Gabriel's sister, Ivy. Theo and she been a couple of steps past just being close.

"Yeah, Ivy got one all right, but she's not here," Gabriel answered. Cameron and he shared a glance. "In fact, Ivy doesn't stay in touch with us."

Yet another casualty of the aftermath of that horrible night. Gabriel's family had been torn apart as well, and Jodi suspected that Ivy just hadn't been able to stay in Blue River with the god-awful memories of the place.

"I heard about the recent attack," Theo went on. "And the dead cop. I can't stay, but I wanted to let you know that I made some calls to a few criminal informants to see if there's any buzz about this. There isn't," he added a heartbeat later. "But I did turn up something that's been bothering me. It's about Russell."

Of course, Russell was on their suspect radar, but it was still a surprise to hear Theo bring up his name. "You talked to Russell?" she asked, ready to tell him about the rattlesnake incident. But Theo continued before she could do that.

"I didn't talk to him, but a CI happened to know one of his old friends. According to the guy, Russell was binge drinking after Jodi broke up with him. He possibly even used drugs. The friend said Russell kept going on and on about Jodi leaving him for some deputy."

Gabriel.

"I never mentioned Gabriel's name to Russell," she explained, "and I certainly never told Russell I was leaving him for Gabriel."

"The friend said Russell figured it out when he heard you talking with Ivy." Theo paused, rubbed his fingers over his left eyebrow. "From the part of the conversation he listened to, Russell decided that you were going to try to seduce Gabriel."

That had been the plan. No need to verify it because it was part of the statement she'd given the cops after the attack. Of course, Russell wouldn't have had access to the report to confirm his suspicions, but that sort of info tended to get out.

"Russell didn't say anything to you about eavesdropping on your conversation with Ivy?" Gabriel asked her.

"No. And he didn't say anything to the cops about it, either." Unlike Russell, she had managed to get her hands on the report and had read every word of Russell's statement.

"Who are you looking at for these latest attacks?" Theo asked Gabriel.

"We have someone, a schizophrenic teenager, in

lockup at a mental hospital." Gabriel made a sound of dismissal that Theo echoed. "That brings us to Hector March, your uncle August and Russell. We already know Russell had a thin alibi for that night. And he came here yesterday to Blue River, maybe hoping to see Jodi." A muscle flickered in Gabriel's jaw. "Jodi put out the word that she was remembering details of her attack."

Theo cursed. "Why the hell would you do that?"

She should have thought before she reacted, but Jodi lifted her T-shirt to remind him of the scars. Even though she only uncovered her stomach, there was plenty enough to see there.

Theo cursed again and glanced away. "Those scars are the very reason you shouldn't have put out a lure like that," he said. But he dismissed it with a shake of his head. "If I'd been in your position, I would have done the same thing. That's not a seal of approval, by the way, since most people think I'm crazy for doing what I do." He snapped toward Gabriel. "You can protect her?"

"I'll try."

"I'm trained to protect myself," she reminded both of them, but she might as well have been talking to the air because Gabriel and Theo stared at each other, some man-bond thing going on between them.

"Whoever attacked you outsized you by a good five inches," Gabriel said. "Outweighed you, too. We know that from the angle of your wounds and placement of your bruises. And all the training in the world won't stop him from trying to put a bullet in you."

Theo seemed pleased with Gabriel's stance. And the truth was—so was she. Even though it felt like this battle was hers and hers alone, it wasn't. In fact, her attacker could use Gabriel, Cameron or even Theo to get to her. That didn't make this easier to accept.

Especially not with this heat swirling between Gabriel and her.

The heat couldn't lead to anything, but her body was having trouble remembering that. And it was getting in the way of what she needed to be focusing on—the person who wanted her dead.

"If Hector's behind this," Theo went on, "things could get uglier than they already are. And as for August, well, he could just hire enough guns to finish whatever the hell he wants finished. Either way, be careful."

She would, but it sickened her to think that it might be any of those men. At various times in her life, she'd trusted each one of them. Of course, it could always be someone else. A nutjob whose name they didn't even know.

Not exactly a thought to ease her churning stomach.

"I have to go," Theo said, not sounding very pleased about that. "If anyone asks, I wasn't here. I can't give you a phone number, and you can't try to contact me," he added to Jodi, "but if I hear anything that'll help catch this piece of dirt, I'll find a way to get the info to you."

Jodi was about to thank Theo, but before she could do that, he brushed a kiss on her cheek, causing her to go board stiff. Theo noticed, too. He pulled back, making eye contact with her, and even though he didn't curse out loud again, she thought that might be what he was doing in his head.

"We'll talk soon," Theo whispered, and just like that she was a little kid again and he was her big brother. All the tension vanished. It wouldn't last, of course. Wounds this deep didn't heal, but for a moment it was good to have Theo back.

She stood there, watching him walk away until he disappeared out the door. Jodi turned to go to Gabriel's computer so she could do the search on the Sentry files, but Gabriel stepped in front of her as soon as she was back in his office. He shot Cameron a glance, and the deputy mumbled something about needing to check on a report.

Uh-oh.

That was not a good look in Gabriel's eyes, especially since his gaze kept drifting toward her stomach. "That's the first time I've seen your scars," he said.

"Sorry."

"Don't be." He put his fingers under her chin, barely touching her, but lifted it so they were staring at each other. "Please tell me you've let a man kiss you in the past ten years."

She shook her head, moving away from him. Not because his touch had sent her into a panic.

But because it *hadn't* done that.

No way did she want to talk about this with Gabriel, especially with all this energy and attraction zinging between them. While part of her desperately wanted a kiss from Gabriel, it would open wounds she didn't want reopened.

"The Sentry files," Jodi said once she'd gathered enough breath to speak. Somehow, she managed enough energy, too, to move away from him. Definitely not easy.

"You do know that by not answering," he grumbled, "that it was an answer."

Yes. She hadn't let a man kiss her since the attack. Hadn't even wanted a man to do that.

Until now.

Mercy, she was in trouble.

Jodi forced her attention on the laptop. Work had always gotten her mind off things, and she needed that to happen now. It did. The moment she accessed the files, she started going through them, looking for any of Hector's active cases. There were at least a dozen, and none of them had anything to do with their dead guy, Calvin Lasher. In fact, none of them were cases that involved pimps or eavesdropping devices.

She shook her head and was able to move to the archives when she spotted something. Not a case assigned to Hector but to her.

"I didn't work on this," Jodi mumbled, scrolling through it. "But it did involve a prostitute from the New Orleans area. Her name was Kitty Martin, and she wanted to hire Sentry for bodyguard duty."

"About how much would it have cost for that?" Gabriel asked after a long pause. Obviously, he'd been reading the file from over her shoulder.

"Hundreds at least. There's a start date of a month ago with no completion date. If she'd actually hired me for the full month, the cost would have been in the thousands." She shrugged. "Maybe Hector intended to assign the case to me but took it himself. Or else Ms. Martin changed her mind about wanting our services."

If either of those things had happened, then it should have been in the file and under Hector's name, not hers. Plus, there was the part about the dead cop who'd been investigating Hector's involvement with a pimp from New Orleans. Jodi doubted that was a coincidence.

And apparently Gabriel thought so, too. Mumbling some profanity, he took out his phone. "I'm putting out an APB on Hector. I want him brought in immediately."

Chapter Ten

Gabriel didn't like the way this investigation was going. Somehow, he needed to figure out who was behind the recent attack so he could stop another one. Because he doubted the danger was over.

Neither was the fallout.

Jodi was pacing again, something she'd been doing for the past three hours while they waited for SAPD to find Hector and bring him in. While it seemed as if seeing her brother had soothed her a bit, that soothing was long gone now. Probably because she dreaded the idea of Hector being guilty. It would mean the only man she'd completely trusted for the past ten years hadn't been someone she could trust after all.

There was a knock at his office door, causing Jodi to whirl in that direction. Gabriel could see her steeling herself up. But it wasn't necessary because it was only Cameron.

"It'll be another half hour or so before Hector gets here," Cameron told them right off, "but I finally got permission for an interview with Billy Coleman."

That was good news. Or at least it would be if Billy wasn't so drugged up that he couldn't talk to them. Still, it was a start.

"You want me to go see Billy, or should I stay here and do the interview with Hector?" Cameron asked.

If Gabriel could have been in two places, that would be ideal, but he needed to stay put with Jodi. "Since Jameson's already in San Antonio today at the Rangers' office, have him go see Billy," Gabriel instructed. "Jameson can probably be there in a matter of minutes. I also want him to record the interview if he can." Though he seriously doubted Billy's doctors were going to allow that.

Cameron nodded, looked at Jodi. "This probably won't come as a surprise, but Hector's not happy about having to come in."

"No. I wouldn't imagine he would be." Jodi paused. "Did he say anything about me?"

"Words that you probably don't want to hear. The man has a temper."

Great. Not a good combination, and when Hector aimed his temper and venom at Jodi, it would eat away at her.

"Anything else in the Sentry computer files?" Cameron asked, motioning to the computer that was still on Gabriel's desk.

Jodi shook her head. "And I've been through every one of them for the past year. Those the year of the attack, too."

Cameron's eyebrow lifted, and he shifted his attention back to Gabriel. "You don't think Hector's connected to your mom and dad?"

Gabriel blew out a weary breath. "If he is, he didn't surface as a suspect."

"And I didn't know him back then," Jodi added. She was no doubt thinking about how Hector just showed up out of the blue in her hospital room. "So, unless Hector's somehow linked to the late Hattie Osmond and that money she was seemingly paying out, then he wouldn't have had any part in the murder of Gabriel's parents."

But maybe he had a part now. Hector could have killed the cop and now could be so jealous of Jodi's return to Blue River that he could want her punished. Or worse.

"Would Hector have even been old enough to be swindling money from Hattie?" Cameron, again.

"He would have been in his early twenties," Gabriel supplied. "And he got his money to open Sentry from somewhere." Of course, it was a stretch to believe the money had come from Hattie, but Gabriel had to look at all the angles.

That angle included the most recent ones. The ones that included Jodi's uncle.

"Go ahead and call August and bring him back in for questioning, too. We know that Russell recently withdrew some money from his accounts, but maybe August did, as well."

Cameron nodded, turned to leave but then stopped. He eyed both Jodi and him. "If you want to take turns guarding Jodi, just let me know."

"What was that about?" Jodi asked the moment Cameron was out of the room.

Gabriel scowled and shut the door.

"Oh," she said, obviously picking up on the emotions behind his scowl. "He thinks we're getting together. Cameron clearly doesn't know me," she added in a mumble.

Gabriel hadn't needed a reminder of his earlier conversation with Jodi, the one about kissing, but her mumble brought it back to the surface anyway. He probably should just let it go, but it was hard to do. Plenty of things were hard when it came to Jodi.

He went to her, knowing it was a mistake but not able to stop himself, either. He cursed this attraction that seemed to be growing by leaps and bounds. The timing for it sucked, and plain and simple, it could be dangerous.

But this wasn't about common sense.

"You're feeling guilty," she said out of the blue. "If you'd kissed me that night, or had sex with me, then I wouldn't be like this."

Since it was true, Gabriel didn't deny it. But there was a flip side to this. "If you'd stayed and we'd had sex, it might not have turned out so well." Of course, almost anything would have been better than what Jodi had endured.

"Yeah. We're back to *sex is a commitment* when both of us know that for you it wasn't."

Gabriel tried to tamp down the slam of emotion that caused inside him. "Sex *with you* would have been a commitment."

As soon as he said the words, he knew it was a mistake. A mistake because it was the truth, and in this case he was pretty sure the truth wasn't going to help.

It didn't.

She looked at him, shook her head as if that couldn't possibly be right and then she cursed. Gabriel knew how she felt. He wanted to curse, too. But instead he made the mistake much, much worse by taking hold of her hand.

He didn't jump into a kiss. Though that's exactly what he wanted to do. Gabriel gave her a moment to adjust to his touching her. Gave her another moment while he eased her closer to him.

"I thought you hated me," she said.

"I wanted to hate you," he admitted. "But mostly I just wanted you. And you were too young. It wouldn't have taken you long to start resenting that you weren't out having those life experiences you should have been having."

The corner of her mouth quivered with a half smile, but it wasn't a smile of humor. "So much for life experiences."

Yeah. The attack had rid her of that chance. And even though it wasn't fair, now wasn't the time to go back and re-create the kiss he'd wanted to give her that night. This was the time to focus on the investigation so he could stop another attack.

But he didn't do that.

While he still had hold of her hand, he leaned in and brushed his mouth over hers. It barely qualified as a kiss, but it slammed into him like a Mack truck. It apparently did some slamming into Jodi, too, because she made a sound that was like a gasp.

Gabriel pulled back to make sure she wasn't on the verge of a panic attack. She wasn't. That wasn't panic he saw in her eyes. It was the fire from this blasted attraction.

She didn't move closer to him. Didn't touch him. Both cues that he should just back away, but again he didn't. Gabriel slid his arm around her waist, pulled her to him and kissed her.

Jodi went stiff. At first. Then, the stiffness vanished when she moved into the kiss. Of course, that meant her moving against him, too. Specifically, her breasts against his chest. Normally, it wouldn't have been a turn-on to be kissing a woman who was plenty unsure about this, but it fired every part of his body.

Especially one part that shouldn't be fired.

She tasted exactly how he thought she would. Like something special—a mixture of fire and innocence. He forced himself to remember that it wasn't a good combination. Of course, there was little about this that was good, other than the kiss itself. And that silky moan of pleasure that purred in her throat.

Kissing Jodi was one thing, but that was as far as it could go. Because that old rule still applied here. Sex with her would still be a commitment, and there was no way either of them was in a place for that to happen. That's why Gabriel moved back from her.

"Any feelings of a panic attack?" he asked.

She hesitated a moment, as if trying to figure that out, and shook her head. "Too bad, huh? Because a panic attack would have kept us away from each other."

Jodi was right about that. "It's still not a good idea for us to be kissing…or anything else."

No hesitation that time. She quickly nodded, but then ran her tongue on her bottom lip. She probably hadn't meant it to be sexual, but it certainly felt that way to his body, which was primed and ready to go. Gabriel had to remind his body that it wasn't going to get Jodi.

"But at least now I know," she said. She lifted her shoulder when he stared at her. "Before I was attacked, I thought a lot about kissing you. Now, I can tick that experience off my bucket list."

Yeah, but he was betting her bucket list didn't include dealing with the flames that kiss had fanned inside them.

"Sheriff Beckett?" someone called out. Except it was

more of a shout. And Gabriel knew that voice belonged to Hector.

Cameron had been right about Hector not being pleased because when Gabriel opened the door and spotted him, he could see Hector's eyes were narrowed to slits. The narrowing didn't ease up when Hector shifted his attention to Jodi.

"Why the hell did you let him do this?" Hector snarled to her.

Gabriel figured he was the *him* in that question. He also guessed that the guy in the suit next to Hector was his lawyer. The two uniformed SAPD officers behind them signed off on some paperwork that Cameron gave them and headed out—fast. No doubt because it had not been a pleasant ride with Hector to the sheriff's office, and they were eager to get away from him.

"We need you here to answer some questions," Jodi explained to her very riled boss.

"You didn't need the cops for that. I would have come. All you had to do was call and ask."

Gabriel was betting Hector wouldn't have been so cooperative if anyone but Jodi had made that call. And he wouldn't be so cooperative now, either. Clearly, Hector saw this as a betrayal on Jodi's part, and Gabriel hoped that didn't come back to haunt them.

"You have no grounds to hold my client," the suit snapped.

"Yes, I do." Gabriel motioned for them to follow him into an interview room. "He's connected to the man who was murdered. A cop named Calvin Lasher. Want to tell me about him?" he added once Hector, the lawyer and Gabriel were inside. Jodi stayed in the doorway. Maybe because she knew this was an official interview, and she didn't want to do anything to compromise it.

But it was Hector who waved her in. "You honestly believe I had something to do with a dead cop?"

"Lasher was investigating you," Jodi answered.

If looks could have killed, Hector would have finished Jodi off then and there. Yeah, he definitely saw this as a betrayal, so Gabriel tried to put the focus back on himself.

"Lasher thought you'd broken the law," Gabriel told him. "And since we know you've done that in the past—"

"Don't finish that," Hector warned him. "I didn't do anything wrong." He stopped, huffed, and it seemed to Gabriel that he was trying to rein in his temper. "About a month ago, I got a call from a woman, Kitty Martin. She thought maybe her pimp was bringing in underage girls that he was luring in with drugs. She wanted to go to the cops, but her pimp was violent, and she thought he might kill her."

That all meshed with what they'd learned, but there were still some gaps in the information. "Lasher thought you'd done an illegal wiretap on the pimp."

Hector was shaking his head before Gabriel even finished. "I had him under surveillance, but that was it. Then, I got a call from Kitty, and she told me to back off, that she didn't want to pursue the case. So, I stopped."

Gabriel couldn't tell if Hector was lying about that or not, and judging from the sound Jodi made, she was in the same boat. "Why put the file under my name?" she asked.

Hector's eyes widened for a moment. Either he was surprised or pretending to be. "Must have been a clerical error. I didn't do it," he added when Jodi and Gabriel just stared at him. He cursed. "If I'd wanted to cover up an involvement in this, why would I have left Kitty's file in the Sentry database?"

"Maybe an oversight on your part," Gabriel readily answered. That earned him a glare from both Hector and his attorney.

"I didn't do anything wrong," Hector repeated, turning that glare on Jodi. "I was just trying to help a woman, the same way I tried to help you ten years ago."

Jodi glanced away, and she said some profanity under her breath. "I will always be thankful for what you did for me," she added, "but Gabriel and I need answers."

"You mean you want to send me to jail," Hector snarled.

"No," Jodi readily argued. "I just want the danger to stop." She paused. "Is it possible that Kitty was setting you up in some way?" Jodi looked at Gabriel to finish that. "Maybe someone posing as a prostitute did this, so they could kill a cop and put the blame on Hector?"

It was a theory. Not necessarily a good one, but Gabriel thought about it for a moment. If this was a copycat killing to clear Travis's name, it didn't make sense to frame Hector. Especially since Hector didn't have an obvious connection to those decade-old crimes. A copycat would have stood a better chance of framing Russell or August.

Of course, maybe Russell or August were behind this. So, perhaps this was as Jodi had suggested and was simply about getting rid of a cop. Someone other than Hector could have had it out for Lasher. Someone who could have seen Hector as an easy target since he had a police record and maybe the wrong enemy who wanted to eliminate both Lasher and Hector. It was certainly something Hector's lawyer would argue.

And a judge would agree.

Now, Gabriel cursed because that meant he couldn't hold Hector. No way would the charges stick unless he had more evidence. Which he didn't.

Hector smiled as if he knew exactly what conclusion Gabriel had just reached.

"Jodi's in danger," Gabriel reminded the man. That caused Hector's smile to vanish. "I need you to go through all your files and figure out if someone is indeed setting you up. Find me anyone connected to Lasher and you."

Hector nodded, but he still looked riled to the core when he stood and faced Jodi. "So, you're helping Gabriel now?" he asked.

She shrugged. "He and I are in the same proverbial boat."

Hector shifted his gaze to Gabriel, and like before, it seemed as if the man could sense what was going on in Gabriel's head. And what was going on was the very recent memory of kissing Jodi.

"Do you know anything about rattlesnakes being put in Russell Laney's car?" Gabriel asked, and he watched the man's expression.

Surprise followed by annoyance went through Hector's eyes. "Trying to pin something else on me?"

"Just asking. And waiting for an answer."

"No, I didn't," Hector insisted. "That sounds like something a coward would do. I'm not a coward."

He probably wasn't, but that didn't mean Hector hadn't resorted to this low level of intimidation.

"Is my client free to go?" the lawyer asked.

Gabriel took his time nodding and wished that it didn't have to be this way. He wanted to get at least one of their suspects off the street, but apparently that wasn't going to happen today.

Jodi stepped back into the hall so that Hector could leave. The man walked out, shooting her a warning glance from over his shoulder, and his lawyer and he finally left the building. The moment they were outside, Cameron came to them.

"I didn't want to say anything with them here," Cameron started, "but I might have something. I called the prison to see who'd visited Jodi's father in the last month, and an interesting name popped up. Russell. He was there the day before we found Lasher's body."

Well, hell. This might be exactly the connection Gabriel had been looking for.

"I've already got approval from the warden if you want to visit Travis," Cameron added.

"I do," Jodi and Gabriel said in unison.

Since Gabriel doubted there was anything he could say or do to stop her from going with him on this visit, he just motioned for Cameron to follow them.

"Pull the cruiser to the front," he instructed Cameron, "so that Jodi won't have to be outside for very long."

Cameron nodded and headed out.

"You don't have to see your father if you don't want to," Gabriel offered her.

"No. I'm going."

That's exactly what he figured she would say. "How long has it been since you've seen him?"

"Shortly after his conviction eight and a half years ago." She paused. "The last visit didn't go well." Another pause. "He broke down, apologizing for nearly killing me."

That got his attention. "I thought he didn't remember anything about the attacks?"

She blew out a long, weary breath. "He didn't. But after sitting through all the court testimony, he had to consider that he could have possibly done it." She dismissed it with the wave of her hand. "My father is a broken man. I think he would have apologized for anything at that point, and he told me then not to come back. He didn't want me to see him behind bars."

Which would make this visit hard on Travis as well as Jodi. Of course, Gabriel didn't care a rat how Travis felt. He only hoped this wasn't a wasted trip.

The moment that Cameron pulled to a stop in front of the building, Gabriel got Jodi moving. He threw open the back door of the cruiser so she could climb inside, and he quickly followed behind her. However, the moment Cameron drove off, Gabriel's phone rang, and when he saw Jameson's name on the screen, he answered it right away. Since this was almost certainly about Billy, he put the call on speaker so that Jodi and Cameron could hear.

"It was no-go on recording the chat with Billy," Jameson said right off. "Our chat, if you can call it that, only lasted a few minutes. And his attorney and two doctors were there the whole time. Added to that, Billy was higher than a kite."

Gabriel didn't bother groaning since he hadn't expected much to come of it anyway. That's why Jameson surprised him with what he said next.

"Billy kept mentioning rattlesnakes," Jameson continued. "In fact, at first that's all he said while he rocked back and forth and asked for his mommy."

Jodi touched her fingers to her mouth, shook her head. They hadn't needed any other proof that they were dealing with a troubled teenager, but there it was.

"And then as I was leaving," Jameson went on, "Billy said a name. Not Russell. But August."

"Did he connect August to the snakes?" Jodi jumped to ask.

"No. But Billy did say I should watch out or that Uncle August would kill me. Then, he said "bye, Jodi.""

Jodi. Maybe he'd said that because August had mentioned her to Billy. Or it could simply be something Billy had overheard while he was at the sheriff's office.

"Please tell me you found some kind of link between Billy and August," Gabriel said while he kept watch around them. He didn't breathe easier until they were clear of all the buildings on Main Street.

"Not yet. But someone must have told Billy about those rattlesnakes because he was locked up when it happened."

Maybe he'd heard it from the person who'd killed, or who'd put him up to killing, Lasher. But that didn't mean the person was August. As much as it pained Gabriel to admit it, someone could have planted that name in Billy's sick mind. Heck, planted the idea of rattlesnakes, too.

"Jodi and I are going to the jail now to see Travis," Gabriel told his brother, "but when I get back, I'll question August again."

"I can do it. I'm heading back to Blue River right now, and I can call him on the way and have him meet me."

"Thanks." As much as Gabriel wanted to hear what Jodi's uncle had to say, he was already bone tired, and he had to face Travis. Besides, any confrontation with

August would include Jodi as well, and Gabriel doubted that she wanted to deal with him, either.

Gabriel ended the call and was putting his phone in his pocket when he glanced at the road ahead. They were still several miles from the interstate and were on a two-lane country road where there was usually little traffic. If this had been normal circumstances, the car ahead of them wouldn't have caught his eye. But since things lately had been far from normal, Gabriel had a closer look.

It was a dark blue four-door, and the driver turned on the right blinker before he pulled onto the shoulder. Such that it was. It was really just a narrow strip of gravel that divided the farm road from a ditch.

"You think that could be trouble?" Cameron asked.

"Maybe." And just in case it was, Gabriel added to Jodi, "Get down on the seat." Thankfully, she didn't argue, but she did draw her sidearm. So did Gabriel. "Don't stop or slow down," he added to Cameron.

Cameron didn't, but as soon as they got closer to the car, Gabriel saw that the driver's-side window was down.

And that the driver was wearing a ski mask.

Before Gabriel could even react, the ski-masked thug fired a shot directly into the cruiser.

Chapter Eleven

Jodi didn't see the gunman, but she instantly knew that someone had fired a shot. The sound of it blasted through the air and slammed into the window on the front passenger's side of the cruiser. The glass cracked, but it held, thank God.

She lifted her head to see what was going on, but Gabriel pushed her right back down. However, she did get a glimpse of a man behind the wheel of the car. Since he had a gun in his hand, he was almost certainly the one who'd shot at them.

When he fired two more rounds at them, Jodi had her answer.

"Get us out of here," Gabriel told Cameron.

Cameron did, but Jodi also heard another sound. The squeal of tires from the car that was now behind them. It was coming after them.

Gabriel cursed. "There are at least two of them." One to drive and one to shoot, and that's exactly what was happening.

The bullets continued to slam into the cruiser. So far, the metal and glass were holding, but eventually the shots could make it through. Worse, Cameron couldn't get away from the bullets by going on the interstate.

Because there'd be plenty of other vehicles, and an innocent bystander could be killed. Of course, the same could happen if one of the ranchers who lived out this way was on the road at the wrong time.

Gabriel took out his phone, and while she couldn't hear the other end of the conversation, he asked for backup and gave them their location. It wouldn't be long before one of the deputies arrived, and maybe another cruiser could come up behind the car, and they could sandwich in the shooters.

"I want at least one of these clowns alive," Gabriel said under his breath.

Jodi wanted the same thing. Because then they might find out who was behind this. Heck, they might even be able to confront the person directly since it could be any one of their three suspects in that car.

"Hell," Cameron said. He didn't hit the brakes, but he did slow down.

That caused Jodi to peer over the seat again. One look and Jodi was doing some cursing, too. Because straight ahead, sideways on the road, was another car.

Jodi doubted it was a coincidence. And it wasn't. Because almost immediately someone from inside that vehicle started shooting at them.

"I can't get around the car," Cameron said, slowing down even more.

Again, that wasn't a coincidence. So, they'd either have to stop and be sitting ducks caught in cross fire or crash into the car with the hopes of taking out that set of gunmen while not disabling the cruiser.

Not exactly stellar options.

Gabriel glanced at her. "There's not a ranch trail we can use," he let her know.

The gunmen probably knew that, too. And that meant Cameron, Gabriel and she were going to have to fight their way out of this. It wasn't the first time Jodi had been caught in gunfire. There'd been two cases where someone had tried to kill people she'd been assigned to protect. Like those other times, there was no feeling of panic. Strange, but in some ways this felt more comfortable than having someone touch her.

"I'll keep an eye on the guys behind us," she offered, and Gabriel didn't decline. Probably because he knew it would no longer do any good for her to stay down. The closer they got to the second car, the more bullets riddled the cruiser.

Cameron cursed when one of the shots tore through the front windshield. It was just a matter of time before more made it into the interior, and that meant they had to do something fast.

"Slow down enough to minimize the impact for us," Gabriel instructed. "But ram the cruiser right into the shooter."

The shooter wasn't hard to see because he was leaning out of the passenger's side of the second car. "I might be able to take him out," Jodi said. "I'm a good shot."

For a moment she thought Gabriel was about to agree to that, but two more shots tore through the glass, one in the front and one in the rear.

"Hit the second car!" Gabriel told Cameron. He pushed Jodi back down, but both knew she couldn't stay on the seat. Once they collided, all three of them would have to start firing.

"Hold on," Cameron warned them.

Jodi braced herself for the impact, and she didn't have to wait long. It was only a couple of seconds before she jolted forward, and she heard the slam of metal crashing into metal. Someone yelled out in pain. Probably the gunman in the second car. But that didn't stop the shots. They continued to come at them, shredding what was left of the front and back and windshields.

"Cameron, get down," Gabriel warned him.

Gabriel took aim at whoever was continuing to shoot at them from the second car. That made him an easy target for whoever was behind them. Jodi unbuckled her seat belt, came up on her knees and pivoted in that direction.

And fired.

She took out the shooter who was on the passenger's side. That didn't stop the driver, though.

"He's about to hit us," Jodi shouted, but the words had barely left her mouth when the first car slammed into them.

The jolt sent her flying into both Gabriel and the back of the seat. Her shoulder was hit so hard that it nearly knocked the breath out of her. Gabriel didn't fare much better. He landed partially over the front seat with his head just a few inches from Cameron. That wasn't good. Because the other shooter in the first car was clearly trying to kill him.

Gabriel fixed that.

Cursing, he emptied his clip into the driver of the second car.

The shots stopped then.

From that direction anyway. They continued behind them, and while Gabriel reloaded, both Cameron and she returned fire. She wasn't sure which of them managed to hit the driver, but she finally saw him slump forward onto the steering wheel.

Not dead, though.

He was groaning in pain.

Gabriel finished reloading and threw open the cruiser door. "Cover me," he said, the urgency not just in his voice but in his movements, as well. "I need to get to him before he dies."

GABRIEL CURSED HIMSELF for being too late. He couldn't go back and undo the attack, but in hindsight he should have never agreed to take Jodi to the jail. At least not without more backup. Now, they had four dead men on their hands, and he still didn't have any answers. Because the fourth one had died before Gabriel could question him.

"Anything?" Jodi asked when his phone dinged with a text.

He glanced at the text from Jameson and shook his head. "No ID on the gunmen, but they're running the prints now. Jameson is rescheduling our visit to see your father. We'll go in the morning."

With plenty of extra security. No way did Gabriel want a repeat of today. Judging from Jodi's shell-shocked expression, neither did she.

She was no longer pacing. Probably because the spent adrenaline had left her too tired to do much of anything. Still, she was searching through Sentry's archived files, trying to find anything that could help them with their investigation. She almost certainly didn't feel like doing that, but it was better than focusing on the fact that they'd come damn close to dying again.

"I nearly got Cameron and you killed," she said, glancing up at him. "I'm sorry."

So that was the reason for the look on her face. Not because she'd been in danger but because Cameron and he had been. Both of them were fine, literally not a scratch on them, but Jodi wasn't seeing that, only the possibility that it could have been much, much worse.

Gabriel sighed and sank down on the sofa beside her. His own legs were feeling the effects of the adrenaline, too, but he was afraid if he stopped moving, he'd crash. Still, he wanted to make something crystal clear, and it was best if he looked her straight in the eyes when he said it.

"Those men could have been after me," he reminded her. "We don't know why we're being attacked, but when the dust settles, I could be the one who owes you an apology."

She shook her head. "I'm the one who made myself bait, and in doing so, I put targets on all of us."

That theory only worked if their attacker was someone trying to cover up nearly killing Jodi ten years ago. But this might not have anything to do with that.

"Maybe your dad can give us some answers tomorrow," Gabriel added. Then, he paused. "Will it do me any good to ask you to stay at the sheriff's office while I go to the jail?"

"No," she immediately answered. "I'm going. Plus, if my father does know anything, he's far more likely to tell me than you. He still considers you the enemy."

No way could he argue with that. Because Gabriel considered Travis the enemy, as well.

"If anyone stays behind, it should be you," Jodi went on. "I can't imagine it'll be easy for you to see the man convicted of murdering your parents."

"It won't be. But I'd visit Travis a thousand times if it meant stopping another attack. Besides, it'll be just as hard for you since he was also convicted of attempting to kill you."

She made a sound of agreement and took a deep breath. "Being here brings it all back." Another deep breath. "But it's not all bad. I'd forgotten that."

Yeah. Easy to forget the good stuff after being knifed and left for dead on the very land where she'd played as a child.

"For as long as I can remember, I've had a crush on you," she said. She winced a little, probably because she hadn't meant to say that out loud.

"I know," he admitted, since she had been so honest. "You used to follow me around and talk to Ivy about me. Once you turned eighteen, she started trying to play matchmaker."

Jodi nodded. "But she didn't get to play it for long. Ivy and I left for college, and when I came back, you were dating that lawyer from over in Appaloosa Pass. When I finally caught you in between women, it was too late."

Because the attack had happened.

The timing had certainly sucked.

"I'm the one who found you," Gabriel admitted. "You didn't remember?"

"No." She stayed quiet a moment and repeated it.

Hell. He shouldn't have brought that up because she got that haunted look again, the one that was deep in her eyes.

"You did CPR on me," she whispered.

Gabriel wanted to drop this, but Jodi was staring at him, waiting for him to say something. "Do you remember that or did someone tell you?"

She moved the laptop to the table, motioned toward her head. "I get little flashes of memories. Pieces. Most of them I push away because of, well, just because. But I remember a little of the CPR. You saved my life."

Believing that had helped him get through some god-awful nightmares, but Gabriel wasn't sure it was true.

She smiled a little. "I thought you were kissing me, but you were giving me mouth-to-mouth. You were giving me your breath."

He was, all the while cursing himself and praying that the ambulance would get there in time. Now, Gabriel cursed himself again because he leaned in and kissed her. Much, much better than mouth-to-mouth and the memories of that.

Well, better for him anyway.

But as he'd done in his office, he pulled away to make sure Jodi was okay with this. Apparently, she was because she slipped her hand around the back of his neck and drew him to her.

No.

That was the thought that went through his mind. Jodi's hand slide was the same as a green light. One that could lead straight to sex. And that couldn't happen. This went back to the bad-timing thing again, but he certainly didn't push her away when she kissed him.

It was Jodi who deepened the kiss. Jodi who pulled him so close to her that they were touching in plenty of the wrong places. Or the right places, he amended, if they were going to have sex.

But they weren't.

She moved, angling herself so that her leg was on the outside of his thigh. Not fully in his lap but close. The kiss, which was already too hot, turned even hotter, and the heat slid right through him. Hard to think with that kind of fire going on inside him. And his body reacted all right.

He went rock hard.

Unlike Jodi. She seemed to be softening. Her silky skin, against his. Her moving in for the taking. Gabriel had to do something to stop this or at least cool it down to give her time to think. Because once she thought about it, Jodi would probably decide this just wasn't a good idea.

"You're a virgin, aren't you?" he said when she broke for air. She also stopped her hand, which was in the process of going to his stomach.

She didn't have to confirm it because he saw in her expression that the answer was yes. Of course, she was. This was a woman who had panic attacks when a man touched her. Well, most men anyway. She didn't seem to be having trouble with the touching now.

She studied his eyes as if trying to figure out what was going on in his head, and she cursed. "I missed my window of opportunity for sex. Because I wanted you to be my first. And then…afterward, because I didn't want to be with anyone."

He got that. "But if we have sex now, it's going to complicate things." That was not only stating the obvious but putting it mildly.

She nodded. "Plus, there's that whole commitment thing you don't want. But what if we take commitment off the table? What if this is only about sex for us?"

Gabriel gave her a flat look to let her know that wasn't possible. She must have believed it, too, because Jodi cursed again and moved off him.

"It would have been a bad idea anyway," she said, but it didn't sound as if she believed it.

Because he still had an erection, Gabriel didn't believe it, either.

Thankfully, his phone buzzed again, giving them a much-needed interruption, and since it was Jameson's name on the screen, it could turn out to be important.

"It didn't take long for us to get IDs on the dead guys," Jameson said the moment Gabriel answered. He put the call on speaker so Jodi could hear. "That's because all four had prints in the system. Kevin McKee, Scott Hartman, Walter Bronson and Barry Hiller."

She repeated the names and shook her head. "I don't recognize any of them."

"Neither do I," Gabriel agreed. "What do you know about them?"

"That they're not from here. McKee and Hiller are from Houston. The other two are from Laredo. There's something not quite right about this," Jameson added. "These guys were thugs. Long police records. Drug users. In and out of jail. Not the sort to hire out for an attack on two lawmen and a security specialist."

Gabriel thought about that for a moment. "You believe they were hired because they'd work cheap?"

"That's exactly what I'm thinking. I'm betting these clowns came after you for just a couple of thousand dollars."

Which would make it next to impossible to find a money trail. Any of their three suspects could have that kind of cash on hand. Still, it had to be a risk to hire someone who was underqualified and maybe even high.

And Gabriel thought that might point to Hector. Because Jodi's boss dealt with criminals like this.

"Did these thugs have cell phones?" Gabriel asked.

"No. No IDs on them, either. Nothing in their pockets and nothing in the cars. We might be able to get something on those, but they're late models, so it's possible the person behind this bought them used through someone online."

Again, hard to trace that.

"I'll keep looking," Jameson said. "We can't keep having this string of bad luck."

You'd think they would get a break. Gabriel just hoped it was sooner than later.

He was about to thank his brother, but Jameson spoke before Gabriel could say anything. "Hold on a second. I'm getting another call from Cameron."

Cameron was supposed to be home, having some downtime after the attack, but Gabriel suspected the deputy was already back at work. He certainly would be, but he didn't want to have to take Jodi out in the open. They'd already had one attack too many today.

The seconds crawled by with Jodi making uneasy glances at him and the phone. It seemed to take an eternity for Jameson to come back on the line, and when he did Gabriel knew it was bad because Jameson cursed.

"It's Billy," Jameson said. "Someone murdered him."

Chapter Twelve

Every muscle in Jodi's body seemed to be aching, and her head was throbbing. That probably had a lot to do with the fact that she hadn't slept and was using caffeine to help her stay alert.

It wasn't a good idea to go into a visit with her father when she couldn't think straight, but she had no choice. Now more than ever, they needed answers.

Because someone had murdered Billy.

The one person who could have possibly cleared all of this up.

It was hard to grieve for him. After all, Billy had likely murdered a cop, but he'd no doubt been manipulated into it. It was a sick, dangerous person who would do something like that to a mentally disturbed teenager.

A smart person, too.

According to the preliminary report, someone had injected Billy with a lethal dose of barbiturates. And the suspect? His high-priced lawyer, Mara Rayburn. The problem, though, was that Mara was missing.

"Are you okay?" Gabriel asked, pulling Jodi out of her thoughts. He was seated next to her in the prison visiting area where they were expecting her father to arrive at any minute. He wouldn't actually be in the room with them but rather on the other side of some thick Plexiglas.

"I'm okay about this visit," she said, choosing her words. The rest of her was pretty much spent. She was tired and confused. Confused not just about who wanted to kill them but also her feelings for Gabriel.

Until she'd come back to Blue River, Jodi had been so certain that what she'd once felt for him was long gone. She had also been sure that she would never again want a man to touch her.

Well, she'd been wrong about that.

She had certainly wanted Gabriel to touch her after the latest attack. Even after "sleeping" on it, she should have realized that would be a mistake. But it didn't feel as if it'd be one. And that was a problem. Because the last thing they needed right now was to have their thoughts straying in the wrong direction. She had a strong suspicion that handing Gabriel her virginity would drop them smack-dab in the "wrong direction" category.

"It'd be so much easier if I hated you," she admitted. That caused him to smile. Which, in turn, caused her to go all warm.

She so didn't have time for this.

"Part of you probably does hate me," he answered.

He was talking about the attack now, but somehow even it had changed in her mind. Not the attack itself but rather her blaming Gabriel. He'd saved her, and no part of her body or mind was going to let her forget that.

The side door finally opened, and Jodi felt herself go stiff when she spotted her father. The past eight years had obviously been hard on him, and he looked several decades older than he actually was. But his eyes seemed to be clearer than ever. Probably because he wasn't drinking.

Her father glanced at Gabriel, and she didn't see a trace of the bitterness that she'd expected. In fact, Travis nodded a friendly greeting to him, then to her as the guard ushered him to the chair behind the glass. He didn't move fast because both his hands and feet were chained, and those chains rattled as he sank down across from them.

"Thank you for coming," he said. His voice had aged, too. It cracked from the hoarseness. "It's good to see you, finally." He stopped, and it seemed as if he was trying to rein in his emotions. "God, I've missed you."

"I miss you, too. And it's good to see you, but it's not a social visit," Jodi clarified.

She hated that she had practically snapped it because it put some sadness in her father's eyes. Since he was a convicted killer, he didn't need anyone, especially her, to add sadness to the obvious miserable life he already had behind bars.

Travis nodded. "I suspected as much. Still, I'm glad you're here. I think about you all the time."

Jodi could say the same about him. In fact, she gave him too much thought, considering that remembering him only brought back the images of the night she'd nearly died.

Well, mostly that's what it brought back.

There were other memories of those times when he hadn't been so drunk that he had been a father to her. That didn't make this visit easier. Because part of her—the girl who hadn't been stabbed yet—wanted to hang on to those rare good times, and she couldn't. She didn't want that coming into play as she tried to get to the truth.

Travis shifted his attention to Gabriel. "This is about the attacks?"

"Yeah. How did you know about them?" Gabriel asked.

"August." A weary sigh left his mouth. Maybe his brother was wearing on his nerves the way he was wearing on everyone else's. "He visits me at least once a week. He thinks all this mess that's going on will help clear my name, but the only thing I want is for them to stop." He paused. "Were either of you hurt?"

Jodi shook her head. "But some gunmen were killed. Thugs. So was a teenage boy who got caught in the middle of this. Did August happen to mention that? Better yet, did he say anything about hiring them?"

Her father didn't seem surprised by the questions, and he certainly didn't jump to defend his brother. However, his mouth did tighten, the way it would when a person was going to have to talk about something unsettling.

"I told August that he'd better not do a single thing to harm you. Or you," he added to Gabriel. "You've both been through enough hell."

Yes, they had, but Jodi suspected the trip through Hades was far from being over. Until they had a name, the attacks would continue and wouldn't stop until someone else was dead.

"Did August say anything to implicate himself in these attacks?" Gabriel asked.

"No. He's too smart for that. Too loyal to me, as well." Travis groaned, shook his head. "God knows I don't deserve it."

Her father had definitely changed. This wasn't the defiant drunk who'd made so many people's lives miserable. Including hers. He'd never been physically abusive, but he'd had a razor-sharp tongue and an awful temper when the booze was in him. And the booze was often in him.

"I'm sorry," her father continued, still talking to Gabriel. "I'm scared for Jodi and you. Equally scared for your brother and sisters. For Theo. But I honestly don't know who's behind what's going on. If it's August, he hasn't given me any hint of it. And he won't. First, because he knows I absolutely wouldn't approve. Plus, he also knows our conversations are being recorded."

"What about Russell?" she asked. "He visited you. Did he mention anything about what's been going on?"

Travis nodded. "He did, but he didn't bring up the attacks. It's the second time he's come. He was here a few years back, not long after I was convicted."

This was the first she was hearing of that original visit. But then she hadn't exactly stayed in touch with either Russell or her father. Still, she had to wonder why Russell would have done that. It wasn't as if Russell and she had ever had a real relationship.

"What did Russell want?" Gabriel pressed.

"The first time he came, it was because he was mad about being a suspect in the murders and in Jodi's attack. He said it'd messed up his life, and he blamed me. Russell thought if I'd just confessed right off, that he wouldn't have been brought into it. But I couldn't confess to something I didn't remember."

Since Gabriel's arm was touching hers, she felt him tense. Probably because this was bringing back the mother lode of memories for him.

"I still don't remember," Travis added, "but I'm not whining about being innocent. Because I'm probably not. There was enough evidence to convict me, and I'll live with that. Die with it, too," he said under his breath.

She wasn't immune to hearing him spell everything out so clearly. No matter what he'd done, he was still her father, and she felt that biological connection tug at her. It was probably doing a lot more than just tugging at Gabriel, though. It was likely twisting him inside, and that's why she slid her hand over his.

Gabriel glanced at her, their gazes connecting for just a second. Since his mouth tensed, he was probably questioning what she was doing, but it didn't take long before he gripped her hand in his.

"Russell said you two were back together," Travis commented.

That caused both Jodi and Gabriel to snap toward him. "We're not," she assured him. "In fact, Gabriel and I have never been together."

Best not to mention that kiss and near-sex from the night before. Especially since there was something much more pressing to ask.

Jodi looked straight in her father's eyes. "Why did Russell come to visit you this second time?"

"He said it was because of an email threat he got. He thought maybe I was behind it, and he was worried about his wife and baby. Can't say I blame him, especially considering somebody murdered that cop and keeps trying to murder you."

Those emails definitely hadn't been empty threats, so Travis was right about Russell's concern. Two people were dead, along with some gunmen, and Gabriel, Cameron and she had come close to dying. No way did Jodi want an innocent baby to be caught up in another round of gunfire.

"I told Russell I had no idea who was doing all of this," her father went on. "I mean, I get *fan* letters, if you can call 'em that, but I don't answer them. Those people who write those letters are sick. And none of them have ever said anything about copycatting the crimes to set me free. The guards can verify that because they read everything before it comes to me." He paused again. "But I got the feeling Russell was here for more than just concerns about that email."

"What do you mean?" Gabriel snapped, taking the question right out of Jodi's mouth.

"Russell asked if I remember seeing anything that night. Specifically, he wanted to know if I remembered seeing Hector March around the Beckett ranch before or after the murders. I didn't know Hector, so Russell showed me a picture of him."

Maybe Russell was doing what Gabriel and she were—following the leads. But that wasn't a safe thing to be doing if he truly wanted to keep his wife and baby out of this. If Gabriel and she had found out Russell had visited the prison, then Hector or August could have learned it, too.

"And had you seen Hector?" Jodi pressed when her father didn't continue.

"He sort of looked familiar, but I couldn't be sure. Remember, I was drinking a lot in those days, and it's hard to sort it all out in my mind. It's possible, though, that I saw him at my trial."

Gabriel looked at her, no doubt wondering if that could have happened, and she had to nod. Hector had indeed come to the courthouse on the day she'd had to testify. He hadn't come into the courtroom itself, but he'd been in the hall, so there was a chance that her father had gotten a glimpse of him.

"August said you might be remembering more of what happened to you ten years ago," Travis said.

This was tricky territory. If she told the truth and admitted there were no new memories, it wouldn't stop the danger because her attacker might think she was lying. Besides, she wasn't sure she wanted to share any info like that with her father because he might just pass it along to August.

Plus, she *was* remembering.

When Gabriel had kissed her, her mind had slipped into a dreamy haze. Maybe it was because the kiss had caused her to relax, and she'd gotten some bit of the memories of him trying to revive her on that blood-spattered trail. If that had come back, maybe some of the other pieces would, too.

"I recalled the sound of his footsteps," she said. It was the truth. But that was a memory she'd had right from the start. "And grabbing the knife." That was a lie, but the prints proved she'd touched it.

"But you don't remember seeing his face?" her father pressed.

She studied his eyes, looking for any sign that he was worried about her recovering that particular memory, and she did see some concern. However, she didn't think it was for him but, rather, for her.

Jodi shook her head. "What about you? Have you remembered anything? Maybe dropping the knife? If you had done that, then someone else could have picked it up and used it on me."

Now, it was her father's turn to shake his head. "There are gaps in what went on that night, and some of that is just blank space. I remember arguing with Gabriel's dad about our cows that were breaking through his fences. After that, I got drunk, and I recall seeing Cameron. He took my truck keys 'cause I was trying to drive off from the bar, and he had somebody take me home. I kept drinking when I got there."

And she hadn't been at the house to stop him because she'd been at the Becketts. Of course, Cameron blamed himself, too, since he hadn't just arrested Travis and locked him up for the night. Jodi had given up on wondering "what might have been," but it was as if the fates had worked to bring about the murders and her attack.

"Other than the memories of drinking once I got home," her father went on, "there's nothing after that until the deputies found me by the river. I don't have a clue how I got there."

It was the same story her father had told after he'd been taken into custody, and it hadn't changed a bit over the years. She didn't know if that meant it was the truth or if he had made sure there were no variations to prove he was lying. Too bad she might never know which it was.

"Tell me about Hattie Osmond," Gabriel said, surprising her. Surprising her father, too, judging by the way his forehead bunched up. "Did you ever see her with August?"

"Probably. I mean, she lived not far from us. Why?"

Gabriel lifted his shoulder. "It might be nothing, but it's possible someone was milking money from her."

Travis stayed quiet a moment. "And you believe it could have been August?" He didn't wait for Gabriel to confirm that. "If it was him, then that would give him motive for murdering your father?"

Bingo. But she could tell from her dad's expression that it was a connection he wasn't going to make. Or else he didn't want to make.

Travis dragged in a weary breath. "August has been

good to me, and I talk to him a lot. Never once has he hinted that I'm here because of something he did."

That didn't mean it wasn't true. And it could explain why August was so hell-bent on clearing her father's name. What was missing, though, was any kind of proof. However, if they could connect August to the recent attacks, they might be able to get him to confess to things that happened a decade ago.

"Visiting time's up," one of the guards said to them. Both guards then went to Travis and helped him stand.

Travis made eye contact with her. "Thanks for coming." Then, he shifted his attention to Gabriel. "Don't let this SOB get to her again."

Gabriel nodded, but Jodi knew this was out of Gabriel's hands. He had already tied up three of his deputies just so they could make this trip to the prison. But he couldn't keep that kind of protection detail on her forever. That meant she either had to go into hiding or bring this monster out into the open.

She preferred doing the latter.

She'd lived enough of her life in the shadows, fearing another attack. Maybe it was time to face this head-on and, one way or another, bring it to an end.

Gabriel and she walked out after they ushered her father away. The moment they were back in the entry, Gabriel got back his weapon and phone, and he immediately called Cameron. Probably so the deputy could bring the cruiser to the front of the building.

"There's a problem," she heard Cameron say from the other end of the line.

Gabriel cursed and moved her to the side away from the door. "What happened?" he snapped.

"We found Billy's lawyer. And it's not good news."

Chapter Thirteen

Dead.

Gabriel wondered just how high this body count was going to go before he could finally arrest someone and put a stop to it. The latest casualty was Mara Rayburn, Billy's high-priced attorney, but in the end she hadn't fared any better than her client. Because now both of them had been murdered.

The moment Gabriel had Jodi in the back seat of the police cruiser, Cameron handed him his phone so that Gabriel could see what the SAPD officer had sent him about Mara. While Gabriel did that, Cameron started driving away from the prison. Fast. He was following Gabriel's orders since he didn't want Jodi on the roads any longer than necessary.

There was another cruiser directly behind them with two deputies inside. Jace Morrelli and Edwin Clary. All of them were prepared for a possible attack, but Gabriel hadn't braced himself nearly enough for the picture that was on Cameron's phone. One obviously taken from the most recent crime scene at the lawyer's condo.

The woman had been stabbed multiple times and had died in a pool of her own blood.

Jodi cursed, glanced away from the phone, and Gabriel cursed himself for not screening her from seeing the images. She already had enough nightmares without adding this.

"While you were inside talking to Travis, I've been getting a lot of updates," Cameron went on after he mumbled an apology to Jodi. An apology that she waved off, and she probably would have gone back for a second look at Mara if Gabriel hadn't handed Cameron the phone. "The ME doesn't have an exact time of death yet, but it appears she died shortly after Billy was killed."

So, if they went with their theory that Mara had murdered Billy, then someone had probably done this to make sure she stayed silent. That someone was no doubt the person behind the attacks.

"Mara's coworkers believe she was having an affair," Cameron went on, "and they said she seemed upset lately, like maybe the affair wasn't going so well. Of course, she could have been upset because she was plotting to murder her teenage client. That means if we can find her alleged lover, then perhaps we find the person who really did this."

"Her coworkers didn't know who her lover is...was?" Jodi corrected.

"No. They said she kept it secret. Who knows if that was her choice, or her lover's."

Yes, because if the killer's plan all along was to manipulate Billy and then have Mara off him, then no way would this snake want people to know who he was. It might not have started out that way, though. The affair could have started first, and then both Mara and, therefore, Billy could have been roped into committing murder. Then again, Mara could have agreed to all of this to please the man she "loved," and when the man was through with her, he killed her.

"There's more," Cameron continued. "Mara had a connection to our four dead thugs."

"I'm listening," Gabriel assured him. And so was Jodi. She'd moved to the edge of her seat.

"She once defended one of them, Walter Bronson, when she was doing pro bono work, and her coworkers said he recently showed up at her office. The thugs were friends, so it's possible she only had to convince Bronson to go after us yesterday, and he brought his buddies along to help."

That made sense, but Gabriel was betting that Mara hadn't been pleased about the gunman going to her office. "Is there a money trail that leads to Mara?" Gabriel asked.

"She withdrew about three grand yesterday morning. That could have been a partial payment or payment in full. I'm guessing the thugs worked cheap."

Jodi made a soft groan. "They were willing to kill us for what was probably pocket change to Mara."

Gabriel heard the disgust in her voice. The pain, too. All of this had to be clawing away at her, and there was nothing he could do to stop it.

Not yet anyway.

"SAPD thinks Mara knew her killer," Cameron explained. "There were no signs of forced entry into her condo, no signs of a struggle. Her attacker had simply gone in and started stabbing her. Her phone was in her pocket, and she hadn't even taken it out."

As she'd done to him, Gabriel slipped his hand over Jodi's. Yeah, definitely clawing away at her.

"The CSIs are still going through her condo," Cameron said a moment later. He, too, was checking Jodi's response in the rearview mirror. "Maybe they'll find something there to connect her to this secret lover. I told them to specifically look and see if there's anything to indicate if that lover could be Hector, Russell or August."

Jodi nodded. "That would be nice if it were all tied in a neat little package. But I doubt she left anything behind, and even if she had, the killer would have taken it." She paused. "What about surveillance cameras at her condo?"

"There weren't any, but SAPD said they'd check traffic cameras. If we have video proof that either Hector, August or Russell was near her condo, that might be enough to get an arrest warrant."

Coupled with the other circumstantial evidence they'd found, it should be, but they were still a long way from putting someone behind bars. Plus, SAPD would have jurisdiction in this, so Gabriel might not be able to interrogate a suspect even if the San Antonio cops did manage to take someone into custody.

"You want me to take you two back to the office or to your place?" Cameron asked.

One look at Jodi, and Gabriel knew the answer. She was exhausted and probably hungry. "To my house." Other than interviewing suspects, he could do pretty much everything else from his home office.

Jodi moved back, resting her head against the seat, and she closed her eyes. Gabriel doubted she was actually sleeping. More like trying to get rid of the images of seeing a butchered woman. No way for him to get rid of it. Because it had triggered the memories of how he'd found Jodi.

Since there was nothing he could say to her to help,

Gabriel decided to get some work done. He texted Jameson to find out if he'd learned anything new on any of the legs of the investigation. No updates with the exception that his brother had managed to get access to Hector's bank account. Since Hector was a security expert, Gabriel doubted he'd left a money trail, but if someone had used such a trail to try to set the man up, then that part of it might be traceable.

The miles and minutes crawled by with Gabriel checking his phone while he continued to keep watch around him. Cameron and the other deputies were no doubt doing the same, but there wasn't even a hint of trouble.

Not until Cameron arrived at the ranch. That's when Gabriel spotted someone he didn't want to see on the front porch of the old house, the one where his parents had been murdered.

August was waiting for them on the steps.

His car was parked on the side by some shrubs.

Jodi groaned, and that's when Gabriel realized her eyes were not only open but that she, too, had spotted her uncle. "What's he doing here?" she muttered.

Gabriel didn't know, but he intended to find out fast and then get rid of him. No way did he want one of their suspects hanging around Jodi or anywhere near the ranch.

Cameron pulled to a stop, and Gabriel threw open the door. "Wait in the cruiser," he told both of them. Cameron would, but he figured Jodi had no intention of doing that.

August stood, staggering a little, and that's when Gabriel noticed he had a bottle of whiskey on the steps where he'd been sitting. "You had Jameson haul me in like a common criminal," August snarled.

"Not common," Gabriel corrected. "You're a suspect in a murder investigation. That makes you far from common."

"Well, I didn't do it." His words were slurred, so he was clearly past the "having a drink or two" stage. He certainly wasn't in any shape to drive, so that meant two deputies would have to take him home. Gabriel didn't like to split his security detail like that, but he hadn't planned on them staying once he had Jodi inside his house.

"I didn't have anything to do with those snakes," August went on, "or with trying to hurt Jodi. I wouldn't do that. Do you know how pissed off Travis would be with me if he thought for one minute that I'd tried to hurt his little girl?"

"He wouldn't be happy," Jodi said, stepping from the car. "Now, what do you want?"

"I want you to tell everyone that I'm not guilty of all this bad stuff I'm getting accused of. I'm just doing what you should be doing—busting your butt to clear your daddy's name so he won't end up dying behind bars."

"You sound like a man with a guilty conscience," Gabriel remarked. He moved away from August so he could stand near Jodi. He also motioned for Cameron and the other deputies to keep watch. He didn't want Jodi gunned down while trying to get info from a drunk man.

August shot him a glare. It didn't last because August staggered again and had to catch on to the step railing to stop himself from falling.

"Russell's wife came to see me this morning," August went on. "Tracy. She's a pretty little thing, but she was boo-hooing about her husband. She's scared he's going to be hurt or killed because of Jodi."

"Was Russell with her?" Gabriel asked.

"No. And she said I wasn't to tell him, that he wouldn't like it if she stuck her nose in his business."

Interesting choice of words, but of course, Gabriel was hearing it secondhand, so there was no telling what she'd actually said. Still, it wouldn't hurt for someone to question the woman. While he was at it, he could arrange for Hector's employees to be interviewed, as well.

"Take August home," Gabriel instructed Cameron.

August didn't put up an argument. He started for the cruiser just as Gabriel went with Jodi to the second one.

"I told Hector about you and Jodi," August said, stopping in his tracks. Jodi quit walking, too.

"Told him what?" she asked.

"That you two were sleeping together." August smiled, and it wasn't a pleasant one. "Want to know what Hector said?" he continued before Gabriel or Jodi could say anything. "He called you an ungrateful bitch and said you'd be sorry."

JODI HAD CERTAINLY been called worse than the *B*-word. But never by Hector.

"August could be lying," Gabriel reminded her.

He could be. In fact, he probably was. But there was some truth in what he was saying. If Hector did indeed believe that Gabriel and she were lovers, then he wouldn't be happy about that. Jodi had seen how he'd behaved in the past couple of days, and plain and simple, he was jealous.

"I need to find a new job," she said as they made their way into Gabriel's house.

He immediately set the security system and moved her away from the windows. She was already heading away from them anyway since she wanted to sit down on the sofa. Her legs no longer felt steady.

"I could hire you as a deputy," Gabriel offered.

She looked at him and saw that he was already regretting that. "I doubt it would work out. Since you'd be my boss."

No need to say more, because it was clear that this attraction wasn't going away. Best not to bring that into the workplace. And if she worked for him, that would put them in constant contact each day. He wanted that contact but didn't especially want her to have a job where she could be required to put her life on the line.

Gabriel glanced out the window and gave a thumbs-up to Deputy Jace Morrelli, who'd be patrolling the grounds. There was a lot of ground to cover, which meant all of them were far from safe, but they couldn't keep everything fully guarded.

"Besides," she went on a moment later. "I have that badge-phobia thing." She was only half kidding, but the thought kept coming back to her—badges hadn't done a darn thing to keep his folks from dying or her from being attacked. "I need to find something that doesn't involve Hector."

Jodi cursed when her voice cracked. Cursed even more when the tears burned her eyes. "I'm not crying about Hector," she insisted. "I just hate knowing that I dragged you into this."

There was suddenly a lot of cursing going on, and it was coming from Gabriel. He sank down next to her. "Whatever you're thinking, the answer is no. You're not going to make yourself bait to protect me, and you're not going on the run to try to distance me from the danger."

Since those were the exact things she'd been thinking about doing, she just gave him a flat look. Well, as flat as she could manage, considering she was very close to tears again.

"I'm so tired of being afraid," she admitted. Of course, that wasn't the right thing to say to help with the tears or to steady her nerves. But Gabriel had something that worked.

He kissed her.

Even though he was already right there next to her, she hadn't seen the kiss coming, and despite the sizzle of heat she instantly felt, it didn't seem to be one generated by passion on his part. She figured that out when he pulled back, and she saw his eyes.

"You're distracting me," she said.

He certainly didn't deny it. "Did it work?"

It did. And there was no need for her to confirm that with words because the corner of his mouth kicked up. The smile didn't last, but he did brush his fingers on her cheek. Then, groaned.

"Eventually we're going to land in bed." His voice was a husky whisper. "I'm just trying for it not to be now. I don't think you could handle *now*."

Jodi wanted to assure him that she could, but that was attraction nudging her in his direction. The truth was, she could have a panic attack when they were only a few kisses in. She'd had attacks triggered by far less contact.

He didn't say anything for several moments, but she could see the debate he was having with himself. A debate he apparently lost.

Because he kissed her again.

This time she didn't feel the doubt or hesitation. And it didn't seem to be a distraction, either. Gabriel kissed her, sliding his hand around the back of her neck and pulling her to him.

Her stomach fluttered. Her heart began to race. It took her a moment to realize that it wasn't the beginnings of panic, but rather, it was pleasure.

Mercy, was it ever.

The heat from his kiss warmed her from head to toe, and she let that silky feeling wash over her. It both calmed and excited her, and it didn't take long before Jodi put her arms around him.

"You can stop this at any time," he assured her.

His voice only made her hotter. Of course, the kiss that followed his "stop" reminder probably had plenty to do with that increase in heat. The old feelings returned. Those days when she'd daydreamed about being with Gabriel just like this. Her, in his arms. Him, kissing her.

He lowered his hand from her neck to her back, all the while nudging her closer. Definitely no feelings of panic from this kind of contact. It felt natural.

Necessary.

As if she'd been starved for a very long time and was finally getting what she needed. And apparently what she needed was Gabriel.

He lowered the kisses to her neck, pausing between each one, no doubt to give her a chance to tell him to stop. But Jodi couldn't see herself saying that anytime soon.

She moved her hand, too. To his chest, and she slid her fingers over the muscles there. All toned and perfect, Gabriel had always had a great body. She got to see some of that body when she undid the buttons on his shirt. Then, she touched bare skin and got a nice reward when he grunted with pleasure.

So, she touched him again. While he took those wildfire kisses lower, to the tops of her breasts, she pushed open his shirt. He was still wearing a shoulder holster, so she couldn't get it all the way off, but she saw enough of him to kick up her pulse another notch.

"Remember, we don't have to keep doing this," he repeated. He slipped his hand under her shirt and did some touching of his own. Each stroke of his fingers created new fires and sent her soaring.

Jodi forgot how to breathe.

And didn't care if she ever remembered.

He didn't take off her top. Maybe because he knew it would bother her for him to see the scars, but Gabriel did lower his head, and he kissed them, one by one. But he didn't stop there. He kept kissing, going lower to the front of her jeans.

Oh, man.

That was what she wanted, and it didn't take much of that before Jodi was searching for his zipper. He stopped her by unzipping her first. The touches on her stomach were mild compared to what she felt when he slid his hand into her jeans. And then her panties. He pushed his fingers through the slick heat he found and nearly caused her to scream.

In a good way.

The pleasure soared, so intense that Jodi wasn't sure she could take it. But she did. And Gabriel clearly had plans to do more than touch.

"Should we stop?" he asked.

"No." She didn't have to think about that, either.

She wasn't sure if he was relieved, but he did start to

shimmy her jeans off her. Jodi helped, though she was trembling now. Not from fear or panic but because Gabriel kept adding some of those slick strokes in between the undressing.

By the time he had finally removed her jeans and panties, Jodi was more than ready to have him haul her off to bed. But he didn't do that. He hauled her onto his lap instead. She was about to protest, but then he kissed her again, and that rid her of any doubts that this was the right way to go.

She reached between them, finally locating his zipper, and she freed him from his boxers while he fumbled in his pocket. Then, his wallet. To take out a condom, she realized. Jodi had been so caught up in the heat of the moment that she'd forgotten all about safe sex. At least Gabriel had remembered.

There was just a jolt of panic when she saw him put on the condom, but again, that vanished when he kissed her. He also reminded her once again that they could stop. That's when Jodi took matters into her own hands. Literally. The moment Gabriel had gotten the condom on, she took hold of him and guided his erection inside her.

She got another jolt. Just a quick pinch of pain— that she ignored. Because there were much, much better feelings to focus on. Like this heat that was burning her from the inside out.

Gabriel didn't move. He gave her a moment, probably to adjust, but it wasn't a moment she wanted. Jodi started to move, and even though she didn't have a clue what she was doing, she went with what felt right.

He helped. Gabriel caught on to her hips with one hand, and he slid the other one between her legs. At first she had no idea why he'd done that. But she soon found out. He used those maddening touches in just the right place while the strokes inside her continued.

It didn't take long for her body to respond to that. In fact, it was too short. She wanted to hang on to this moment for a long, long time. But there was no way she could last. Gabriel made sure of that. He kept touching. Kept moving inside her. Until everything pinpointed to just him.

He pushed her right to the point where she could take no more. And then with one last touch, Gabriel sent her flying.

Chapter Fourteen

Gabriel hadn't remembered a mistake ever being this good. But despite the slack feeling he had from the great sex, he still had enough common sense to know that he shouldn't have done this.

This was a complication neither of them needed.

And it would be a complication all right. Not just because here he was holding her in bed but because he wanted to keep holding her.

He couldn't, and that's why Gabriel forced himself from the bed so he could pull on his jeans and go back into the living room to check his laptop. Even though it was already after regular duty hours, there could still be reports coming in. Updates. Hell, the world could have ended in the past couple of hours, and he wouldn't have even noticed it.

That's because he'd made another mistake by taking Jodi a second time.

She definitely hadn't said no, and he'd been counting on her doing just that. Because he certainly hadn't had the willpower to turn her away—as he'd done ten years ago.

He put on his shoulder holster—old habits—and grabbed a slice of leftover pizza from the fridge before he sat down to boot up his computer. Six emails from Jameson and all of them were about the dead lawyer. The first two weren't good news, either.

SAPD hadn't been able to find a security or traffic camera yet that had been at the right angle to see who'd gone into Mara's condo complex and knifed her to death. Jameson had managed a phone conversation with Russell's wife, Tracy, but it'd been a bust because Russell had told his wife to hang up—and she had. Russell might have just wanted to protect her, and he might not know that Tracy had paid August a visit.

Gabriel went to the next message. Photos of both Billy's and Mara's crime scenes. Photos that Jodi wouldn't be seeing. The next email was a lab report on the drugs Billy had been given, and which caused him to overdose.

And then Gabriel got to the last email.

Hell.

It was yet another picture, and according to Jameson, it was a note that the cops had found beneath Mara's body. It was just two words, scrawled on a piece of paper.

For Jodi.

If Gabriel had had any doubts that Billy's and Mara's deaths weren't connected to what'd happened a decade ago, that would have cleared them up. Because it was linked even if it was solely due to someone trying to cover their tracks.

He heard Jodi stirring in the bedroom and immediately closed the email. A moment later, she came in. She yawned, pushed her hair from her face and smiled at him.

She'd gotten dressed, but she still looked rumpled. Damn attractive, too. The woman certainly knew how to make his body notice her. He also noticed her weapons.

She had put them on, as well. Apparently, he wasn't the only one with some old habits. But despite the fact that they were behind locked doors and the security system was on, it still didn't feel safe.

Maybe no place would.

"Apparently, sex is the cure for panic attacks," she said. "Or maybe you're the cure. Either way, I'm hungry." She started toward the kitchen but then stopped. Probably because she'd noticed the worried expression on his face.

"What happened?" she asked.

It was a cheap, dirty trick, but he went to her and kissed her. He thought maybe she still had enough post-sex haze for it to work at distracting her. It didn't.

"Is someone else dead?" she pressed.

Since her mind was already leaping to a worst-case scenario, Gabriel knew he had to tell her the truth. Or rather, show her. He reopened the email and turned the laptop so she could see the message and Jameson's remark.

"Oh." That's all she said for several seconds, and then Jodi sat on the sofa. "I guess whoever's after me wants to rub salt in the wound."

It seemed that way to Gabriel, as well. And he was afraid the salt-rubbing would continue with another attack. That was probably why he went on full alert when he heard the movement in front of his house. Gabriel jumped to his feet, and in the same motion he drew his gun. Jodi drew her weapon as well, but he made sure he was in front of her when they went to the window to look out.

And he cursed.

"Hector," he said under his breath.

Jodi's boss was in the front yard. And he wasn't alone. Deputy Jace Morrelli was with him, and judging from Jace's expression, he wasn't any more pleased about this visit than Gabriel was. Not only was Hector a suspect, his car wasn't anywhere in sight, which meant he might have been trying to sneak up on them and that Jace had caught him.

Hector looked up at the window, making eye contact with Gabriel, and while the man didn't have a gun in his hand, Gabriel figured he was heavily armed. That's why Gabriel told Jodi to stay back. He disarmed the security system and opened the door just a fraction.

"What the hell are you doing here?" Gabriel demanded.

Hector spared him a glance. "Protecting Jodi. Something that I've been doing quite well for the past ten years. She comes back here, to you, and twice someone's tried to kill her."

"Because her attacker is afraid she's remembered his face. You think it's your face she'll remember?"

Now, Hector did more than glance at him. He turned, his hard stare drilling into Gabriel. Even though the sun was already setting, and there wasn't a lot of light, Gabriel had no trouble seeing the hatred in the man's eyes. Or the fact that Hector was armed to the hilt, along with wearing a bulletproof vest.

"I told him to leave," Jace said.

Good. Because it saved Gabriel from telling Hector that himself.

"I was just going back to my car," Hector insisted. "There's no law against a man sitting in his own car on the road." He made an uneasy glance around. "Someone's trying to set me up. Maybe August or Russell."

"They claim someone's trying to set them up, too," Jodi said. "And they believe you might be doing that."

She stepped to Gabriel's side. Well, as much of his side as she could manage since he was taking up most of the doorway, and he didn't intend to go out on the porch with Hector where the man could maybe try to gun him down.

Hector nodded, readily admitting that. "One of us is probably guilty, and it isn't me. That means someone is making himself look bad to get the limelight off him."

That was Gabriel's theory, too.

Hector shifted his gaze back to Jodi, and while she was fully clothed, Gabriel figured the man knew what had gone on tonight. What Gabriel couldn't tell was if Hector's tight expression was because he was jealous or just concerned about Jodi. Either way, he couldn't take the chance that it was the jealousy.

"Leave," Gabriel warned Hector.

For a couple of long moments, Gabriel thought he was going to have to arrest the man, but Hector finally turned and started walking away.

"Follow him to his car," Gabriel told Jace, and Gabriel intended to stand there and watch. If Hector was guilty and desperate, he might decide to try to shoot the deputy.

"Any chance Hector would have brought some of his security guys with him?" Gabriel asked while he glanced around the grounds.

"No. Hector works alone." She paused. "But if he's truly innocent, he could have come here with the hopes of trying to draw out the killer. Of course, that would only work if the killer was watching us."

Gabriel had the sickening feeling that he was. And no, he wasn't ruling out Hector. In fact, the man could have come here to set up cameras or listening devices, which meant Gabriel needed to get some backup out here.

While continuing to keep watch, he took out his phone to do that, but something flashed in the corner of his eye. It wasn't Jace or Hector because this came from the opposite direction.

From his parents' old house.

The electricity was off, but there was definitely a light in the window. Maybe either a candle or a flashlight.

"Someone's inside," Jodi said under her breath. "Could it be Jameson?"

"No. He wouldn't go there." They had had trouble over the years with thrill-seeking teens, but Gabriel figured with everything going on, this was much more serious.

"You see that?" Jace called out, tipping his head to the house.

"Yeah. Don't go there just yet." And Gabriel called the sheriff's office to round up every available deputy.

However, before he could even press the number, a shot cracked through the air.

THE SOUND OF the bullet had barely registered in Jodi's mind when she felt herself being shoved back. That was Gabriel's doing. He rammed his shoulder into her and sent her flying backward.

She caught on to him to keep from falling, but Jodi also did that to pull him back, too. He immediately shut the door but then went straight to the window. No doubt to check on Jace.

Jodi hurried to the side window in the living room, which would give her the best view of his parents' house. She didn't stand directly in front of the glass, though, since it would make her an easy target. She stayed to the side so she would not only have a view of the old house but also that stretch of the road. What she didn't have a good view of, however, was the trail in between the two houses. Too many shrubs and trees.

Too many places for someone to hide.

Just as they'd done the night she was attacked.

She tried not to think of that now because it wouldn't help. The only thing she could do was keep watch to make sure someone didn't get close enough to fire another shot.

The light was still on upstairs in the old house, and it was flickering. Maybe because someone was moving it, but if it was a candle, it was possible the wind was blowing it since the window seemed to be open a couple of inches. It definitely hadn't been open when she'd visited the place two days ago.

From the other side of the room, she heard Gabriel call the sheriff's office and ask for backup. It wouldn't take the deputies long to get out here, but she prayed they wouldn't be driving into the middle of a gunfight.

But there were no other shots.

In fact, there were no other sounds, period. The place had suddenly gotten so quiet that the only thing she could hear was her own heartbeat drumming in her ears. And she wasn't sure that silence was a good thing. At least if she could have heard footsteps or spotted movement of some kind, she would have known where the shooter was.

"Is Jace okay?" she asked Gabriel.

"Can't tell, but he doesn't appear to have been hit. Hector and he are behind some trees."

Not ideal, because if Hector was the one responsible

for the attacks, he could kill Jace. The deputy had to know that, of course, so maybe he was watching carefully to make sure that didn't happen.

"The shot couldn't have come from anywhere near my parents' house," she heard Gabriel say.

No, the angle was all wrong. Whoever had fired that shot was closer to where Hector's car was parked. Did that mean there were two attackers out there—one in the house and the other on the road?

Jodi glanced back at Gabriel, but he had his attention pinned to his side of the house. "Do you see anyone?"

"No. Maybe the person ran off after he fired." But Gabriel didn't sound very hopeful about that.

Part of Jodi didn't want this snake to run. She wanted to go ahead and have a showdown, one that would put an end to the danger once and for all, but with Jace out there, and the other deputies on their way, that wasn't a good idea. There had already been too many murders, and she didn't want anyone else dying tonight.

A sound shot through the room, causing her to gasp, but it was only Gabriel's phone. Without taking his attention off their surroundings, he hit the answer button and put the call on speaker.

"Sorry that I didn't see the guy before he took a shot at us," she heard Jace say from the other end of the line.

"I didn't see him, either," Gabriel answered. "He must have come on foot from up the road."

"Yeah, that's what I figured, too. But I did get a glimpse of him. Male, wearing a ski mask like the other guys who attacked us. He ran into the woods across from your folks' house. That was just a couple of seconds after Hector and me got behind these trees, and I haven't seen the guy since."

So, maybe he had run after getting off that single shot, but the knot in her stomach told her that there was another reason he wasn't firing. Like because maybe he was getting in a better position to do more damage. This way, too, Gabriel was separated from his deputy, so not only didn't he have immediate police backup in the house, Jace was out there without backup, as well.

"I'm going after him," someone said. Hector. She had no trouble hearing him, either. "I'm not just going to cower here while he picks us off one by one."

"You're staying put," Gabriel told him.

But neither Jace nor Hector answered. Jace did curse, though, and there seemed to be some kind of scuffle going on. Mercy, no. Hector couldn't be doing this.

However, he was.

"The SOB punched me," Jace said, "and then he started running. You want me to go after him?"

Before Gabriel could answer, there was another shot, then another. Both came from the same area where the first one had been fired.

"Stay put and take cover," Gabriel told Jace. There was a franticness in his voice. In his movements, too, because he threw open the door, took aim and fired.

Jodi couldn't see the person Gabriel had shot at, and she didn't want to leave the window in case someone came in or out of the old house.

"Get back!" she shouted to Gabriel when a bullet smacked into the door frame right where he was standing.

He did get back, but cursing, he hurried to the front window and threw it open. Like her, he stayed to the side, and he fired out through the screen.

"I think I might have hit him," Gabriel relayed to her.

Good. She hoped he'd killed him because this was probably a hired thug. Yes, they could possibly get answers from him, but the only way for that to happen was to get to him and arrest him. No way did she want Gabriel going out there.

"When Jameson gets here, I'll have him stay with you," Gabriel added. "Jace and I can go after this clown who shot at us. Hector, too."

Jodi shook her head. "The attacker will come to us, and when he gets close enough, we can kill him."

"Hector was right. This guy will try to pick us off, and he can sit out there and shoot at us until he gets us. We need to stop him."

She couldn't argue with that, but she didn't want Gabriel out there. He glanced at her, their eyes connecting, and even though he didn't say anything, the glance was a reminder that catching bad guys was his job. No way would he want to stay inside where it was safe while his deputies and heaven knew who else was in danger. But "safe" was where she wanted him to be.

This was about the sex.

It had indeed changed everything. And while even before tonight Jodi certainly hadn't wanted Gabriel hurt, now it cut her to the core to think of him being shot. Or worse.

Two more shots came at them, both of them smacking into the side of Gabriel's house. She doubted the bullets would be able to get through the walls, so maybe the gunman was doing this as a way of pinning them down.

But why?

She didn't like any of the answers that came to mind, but it was possible the shots were a distraction, meant to keep them occupied while someone sneaked closer to them. Jodi had already been keeping a close watch around them, but she tried even harder to pick through the near darkness and see someone.

And she did.

"Gabriel," she managed to say despite her breath having gone thin.

"Hell," Jace said only a few seconds later. Probably because the deputy had seen the same thing Jodi had.

Hector, coming out of the trees near the old house, and he wasn't alone.

The ski-masked thug was behind him and had a gun pointed right at Hector's head.

GABRIEL FELT A punch of dread and adrenaline. This was not what he wanted to happen, especially not without plenty of backup in place.

His first thought was this could be a ruse, one concocted by Hector to draw them out into the open. After all, Hector was a trained security specialist. But Gabriel knew firsthand that sometimes all the training and experience wasn't enough to keep thugs from getting to you.

Jodi moved away from the window, coming toward him. "You're not going out there," she said to him.

He was about to tell her the same thing, but if Hector was innocent, Gabriel didn't just want to stand by and watch an innocent man get killed. Especially since it appeared that the ski-masked guy had disarmed Hector.

"Call Hector right now," Gabriel instructed. "I need to see what this thug wants." And he also wanted to hear Hector's voice, to try to figure out what was really going on here.

Jodi nodded, and while she took out her phone and made the call, she also returned to the window to keep watch. Good. He hated having her near the glass where she could be shot, but Gabriel needed someone to keep an eye on that side of the house since it was essentially a blind spot for him.

Gabriel opened the front door, and while he didn't go onto the porch, he angled himself in the doorway so he could better see Hector. And also get a look at the guy in the ski mask. No way did Gabriel have a clean shot, but he wanted to be ready just in case.

Since he was watching Hector so closely, he saw when the man glanced down at Hector's pocket. Probably because his phone was ringing with the call from Jodi. His captor must have told him to answer it because a couple of seconds later, Hector reached in his pocket. Using just two fingers, he took out his phone, pressing the button on it and then lifting it in the air.

"Jodi," Hector answered. She put the call on speaker, so Gabriel had no trouble hearing the man.

Or the guy who had Hector at gunpoint.

"Do you want him dead?" the thug asked.

That was still to be determined, but for the moment Gabriel wanted both of these guys alive.

"I don't want Jodi coming out here," Hector said before Gabriel or she could answer.

"Neither do I," Gabriel assured him. "And it's not going to happen. She's staying inside, where she's safe." Hopefully.

"Then you're going to have to watch a man die," the gunman said.

Maybe it was a bluff, but every one of his lawman's instincts were yelling for him to stop this. If for no other reason than he didn't want Jodi to have to witness her boss and mentor being murdered in front of her.

"I might have a shot," Jodi mouthed, and she hit the mute button on her phone after she laid it on the window ledge. By doing that, she freed up both her hands. Probably to take that shot she'd just mentioned.

But Gabriel shook his head. "I don't want you that far out of cover. Besides, if you miss, you'll hit Hector."

Her mouth went flat, and she looked a little insulted that he'd even suggested she wouldn't be able to hit her intended target. "I'll aim for the goon's left leg. With the way he's standing, I can hit it, and when goes he down, Hector can get the gun away from him. Hector's probably already planning to elbow this guy in the gut or something."

Gabriel had figured that out. He just hoped it didn't get Hector killed. Because it was possible this guy wasn't alone. In fact, it was probable that he wasn't. Heaven knew how many *friends* he'd brought along with him. And if he wasn't holding his boss at fake gunpoint, then he could be out there, as well.

In the distance, Gabriel heard the sirens from the police cruisers, and that meant he had to make a decision now. He definitely didn't want his brother and deputies driving into a hostage situation.

"On the count of three, I'll fire over their heads," Gabriel finally told her. "You go ahead and try to hit the guy in the leg. If Hector moves out of the way, then one of us can take the kill shot."

She nodded, turned and didn't waste any time taking aim.

Gabriel wanted to count as fast as possible, so he could get her out of the line of fire. "One, two, three." And he pulled the trigger.

So did Jodi.

She didn't miss, either.

Her shot slammed into the thug's leg, and he howled in pain. The guy staggered back, and Hector went after him. If this was Hector's hired muscle, then Jodi's boss made the punch that he delivered look very convincing. Hector ripped the gun from the man's hand and took aim.

Just as another shot cracked through the air.

This one went right into Hector.

He fell, clutching his chest, but he didn't stay on the ground. Even though he was clearly struggling, Hector was trying to crawl toward the ditch.

"Oh, God." Jodi automatically turned as if ready to run out and help him.

"He's wearing a Kevlar vest," Gabriel reminded her.

But Kevlar wasn't going to help him if the wounded gunman shot him in the head. And that's what Gabriel thought he had in mind when the gunman whipped out another weapon from an ankle holster. When he took aim at Hector, Gabriel took aim at him.

And fired.

He went for the kill shot, two bullets to the head, since an injured hired gun could still do plenty of damage. The man fell back, his head smacking onto the ground. It gave Hector time to get into the ditch before the next shot came.

The second gunman was somewhere in the trees near the road. The very road where the cruiser would be arriving soon, so Gabriel fired off a quick text to let Jameson know to stay back until Jodi and he could figure a way to draw him out. Then, they could get an ambulance for Hector in case he was hurt.

"Watch out!" Gabriel heard Jace yell.

That's when Gabriel also heard something else. A car engine.

Gabriel pivoted, whipping around in Jace's direction, and saw a black car driving up the road. It was coming from the opposite direction of the cruiser, and the driver was speeding. He considered shooting into it, but it's possible this was someone who was merely in the wrong place at the wrong time.

It wasn't.

When the car reached the treed area where Jameson was, it veered off the road, and the driver, who was wearing a ski mask, jumped out. The car, however, continued to come right toward Gabriel.

"Run!" Gabriel shouted to Jodi. He hurried to her, caught on to her arm and got them moving toward the back of the house.

Not a second too soon.

The car rammed into the porch, and it wasn't just a simple crash. No.

The car exploded into a fireball.

Chapter Fifteen

Because of where she'd been standing, Jodi hadn't seen the car until she glanced back over her shoulder while Gabriel and she were running. It was an older model vehicle and obviously loaded with some kind of explosives for it to go up in flames like that.

Those flames could easily make it into the house.

Gabriel led her to the kitchen. No sign of any trouble here, but the smoke was already starting to make its way through the house. It reeked of gasoline, so maybe it hadn't actually been a real bomb. The person could have just filled the car with open containers of gas, and the impact could have triggered a spark.

"Who did this?" she asked, keeping her voice at a whisper.

What she wasn't able to do was tamp down all the fear and panic that was starting to roar through her. Gabriel's front porch was on fire. A fire that would no doubt spread—fast. And his brother, Jace and Hector were out there, maybe under attack right now. Since Gabriel and she could no longer see them, they couldn't help them. Not from the back of the house anyway.

"I don't know," Gabriel said, answering her question. He hooked his arm around her waist and moved her to the side of the fridge while he hurried to the back door to look out. "He was wearing a ski mask and jumped from the car."

Mercy. That meant the guy was still out there, and he had at least one hired gun to help him because there'd been the shot fired at Hector from the other end of the road. If Hector was innocent, she hoped he had managed to find some cover, because it was obvious things had gone from bad to worse.

"Keep watch behind us," Gabriel instructed. He opened the back door several inches.

Jodi did as he said, but she wouldn't be able to keep watch for long because of the smoke. It was getting thicker with every passing second, and soon they wouldn't be able to stay put. That meant going outside.

Where gunmen could be waiting for them.

What they needed was to get a better look at what was going on. Unfortunately, a better look came with risks. Because the moment they left the house, it could put them right in the line of fire.

"Call Jace," he said, passing her his phone. "Ask if he's got eyes on the driver of that car."

While she volleyed glances all around them, Jodi found his number and pressed it. She wasn't sure if the deputy would even be in a position to answer, but he did.

"Gabriel," Jace said. His voice was barely audible.

"It's me, Jodi. Are you okay?"

"For now." Jace whispered, as well. "The guy who was driving that car has to be nearby."

"Any idea where the other shooter or Hector is?" she asked.

"No. But you and Gabriel should get out of the house right now. The fire's spreading, and the fire department won't be able to get out here until we've rounded up these two thugs."

Jace was being optimistic that there were only two of them. There could be a dozen. She cursed the person who'd put all of this together.

"If Gabriel and you run out the back, I'll try to cover you," Jace said, ending the call.

There was no need for her to relay that to Gabriel since he'd been standing close enough to hear. He looked back at her, making eye contact, and he seemed to be saying he was sorry about all of this. Well, she was sorry, too, but only because she was probably the reason so many people were in danger right now.

Gabriel tipped his head to his truck that was parked out back. "That's where we're heading." And he pressed the remote on his keys to unlock the doors.

He didn't remind her to keep watch or be careful because he knew that she would be. As careful as she could be anyway.

Gabriel used his shoulder to open the door wider, and he stepped out onto the porch. He took a quick look around before he motioned for them to get moving. She did. Gabriel barreled down the porch steps, and Jodi was right behind him. They made a beeline for the truck.

But didn't get far.

Jace fired, his bullets going well over their heads. But one shot slammed into his truck, right into the engine. Judging from the angle, this bullet had almost certainly come from the driver of the car that was up in flames. She doubted that a single shot had disabled it, but the gunman fired again.

And again.

These didn't go into the truck, though.

They came right at Gabriel and her.

They immediately dropped to the ground, both of them rolling to the side of the porch. It wasn't much protection, especially considering this new position possibly put them in the direct sight of Hector and the other gunman, but at least the driver's shots were no longer an immediate threat. Not to them anyway. The goon could turn that gun on Jace.

"We can't stay here," Gabriel said, but it sounded as if he were talking more to himself than to her.

But Jodi agreed. Eventually, the fire would make it back here, and the flames and smoke could kill them. Running to the truck was out, too, since it was obvious the shooter had a good angle on that.

"The barn," Gabriel added.

It was to the side of the truck, and while it would indeed provide some cover, they still had to get to it. There were some trees and shrubs dotting the way, but it was possible Gabriel and she could get caught in the cross fire.

Gabriel's phone dinged with a text message, and since she still had his cell, she read Jameson's text aloud. "Approaching on foot. Don't fire in our direction."

However, the words had no sooner left her mouth when someone did fire. Not the driver or Jace this time. The shot had come from the area where she'd last spotted Hector. Of course, that was the same general direction as Jameson and the other shooter, so it could be one of them. She prayed that Jameson was all right.

She put Gabriel's phone back in her pocket, so her hands would be free when they ran. Which she didn't have to wait long for. Almost immediately, Gabriel got them moving, but they didn't make it far before the shots came. Not a single bullet, either. But a hail of them. They had no choice but to get back on the ground behind one of the trees.

Jodi automatically maneuvered into a position that would allow her to keep watch behind them, and she hated that her pulse kicked up when she realized her area to watch was the very trail where she'd nearly died.

The sun had fully set now, but there was enough illumination coming from the fire that she could see it. At least she could see the trail itself. However, it was impossible to tell if anyone was hiding in those tall shrubs. The very ones her attacker had used ten years ago.

"See anything?" Gabriel whispered.

Before she could answer, the phone dinged, but this time, it wasn't Gabriel's. It was hers. Keeping watch, Jodi took it from her pocket. Not a text but rather a call, and it wasn't from Jace.

It was from Hector.

Gabriel mumbled some profanity under his breath when she showed him the name on the screen. Jodi pressed the answer button, but she didn't say anything. That's because this might not be Hector. The gunman could have finished him off, taken Hector's phone and could be using this call to pinpoint her location by listening for the sound of her voice.

"Jodi?" someone said from the other end of the line. She couldn't tell if it was Hector or not because the voice was a hoarse whisper. "Please," he said. "I need your help."

It was Hector all right.

"What's wrong?" she asked as softly as she could manage.

"I've been shot, and I'm bleeding out fast." Hector cursed. "I'm pinned down."

And then Jodi heard something she didn't want to hear. Another gunshot. Followed by Hector's sharp sound of pain.

GABRIEL HEARD THE sound that Hector made. And he got a glimpse of the stark expression on Jodi's face, too. She was no doubt torn between getting to her boss but balancing that with the real possibility that this could be a trap that could get her killed.

Especially since it would mean going on that trail between his and his parents' houses.

"I can't go out there," she whispered. Maybe to herself. Maybe to Hector.

She then hit the End Call button so she could text for an ambulance. One was almost certainly on the way. Jameson would have called for it, but the medics wouldn't come closer as long as there was gunfire.

And there was plenty of that.

Shots came from Jace's direction. From Hector's, too, and Gabriel couldn't tell who was doing the shooting. It was possible that Jameson was in on this by now, since he would have had a chance to at least reach the area where Hector was. Maybe his brother had managed to take out the gunman. Gabriel didn't have to remind Jameson to be mindful of Hector, too, since his brother already knew Hector was a suspect.

Perhaps a dead one, though.

"Should we try to make it to the barn or truck again?" she asked.

It was tempting—especially the truck since they could possibly use it to escape. But Gabriel shook his head, and he tried to pick through the sounds to make sure no one was sneaking up on them. He could hear... something, but it was hard to tell what it was exactly, thanks to the fire now snapping and eating through his house.

His *home*, he mentally corrected.

It twisted at his gut to see it being damaged like this, but there was nothing he could do to save it. Right now, his priority had to be keeping everyone alive.

"I'm sorry," someone called out.

Jace.

Gabriel pivoted in that direction and saw something he didn't want to see. Jace being held at gunpoint. It was almost identical to what had happened to Hector just minutes earlier with a ski-masked thug behind him. The guy had jammed a gun to Jace's head.

"I didn't see him before it was too late," Jace added.

Gabriel hated that Jace felt the need to apologize for something like that, but it did put them in a really bad position. Because Gabriel figured he knew what was coming next, and he didn't have to wait long for it.

"Start running down the trail," the gunman said. "Or I'll shoot him where he stands."

Gabriel had obviously figured wrong. He'd expected the thug to tell Jodi and him to put down their guns. What kind of sick plan was this?

A bad answer immediately came to mind.

The same person who'd attacked Jodi ten years ago wanted a chance to finish her off in the same spot.

"And if we don't run?" Gabriel challenged.

The gunman fired a shot. Not into Jace's head. But rather his shoulder. At the same time, there was another shot—it came from Hector's direction—and Gabriel heard what was another loud groan of pain. Maybe Hector had been shot again. Maybe it was a ruse, but the ruse definitely didn't apply to Jace.

Jace dropped to his knees, the pain etched all over his face, and the gunman dropped with him, staying behind him so he could continue to use Jace as cover. Gabriel didn't have a clean shot, and he figured Jodi didn't, either.

"Run or I'll shoot him in his other shoulder," the gunman warned them. "The third shot will go in his gut. I'm thinking if you hadn't obeyed by the fourth shot, then your deputy will be a goner."

Hell, Jace might not survive the second, much less a third and fourth, shot. With the angle the clown was holding that gun, the bullet could go down Jace's shoulder and straight into his heart.

"Run!" the gunman shouted to them.

"We have no choice," Jodi said. Her voice was trembling a little, but that didn't stop her from turning in the direction of the trail.

Where someone was no doubt waiting to kill her.

"I can't let Jace die because of me," she added.

Gabriel couldn't let that happen, either, but he could take some precautions. "Stay low. I don't want this idiot gunning us down, and he might do that if we stand up. Crawl. And stay close to me."

Of course, that wouldn't stop anyone on that trail from shooting at them, too, but Gabriel figured the monster who was waiting there wanted to use a knife.

On Jodi.

Maybe that's why she pulled her own knife from her boot and clamped it between her teeth. The moment she did that, they started moving. Of course, there was no guarantee that the gunman holding Jace wouldn't just go ahead and shoot him, but at least this way, the deputy had a fighting chance. Plus, there was the possibility that Jameson would be able to help since the gunman was out in the open with Jace.

"I need to listen for footsteps," Jodi said under her breath. "I'll recognize the sound of his steps."

Maybe. But he wasn't sure how she would manage that. Her heart had to be beating a mile a minute right now, and added to that, there was still the occasional gunshot near Hector.

The very direction where they were going.

They crawled, stopping every few feet, and when they reached the first curve in the trail, Gabriel and she got to crouching positions. It still wasn't ideal, but it might give them a fighting chance.

Just ahead were the thickest shrubs. It was also the place where Jodi had been attacked. She knew that, of course, and it was probably why he heard her breath hitch in her throat. Yes, she was a trained security specialist, but she was also the woman who'd nearly died here. No way to erase that from her mind.

"If he gets his hands on me," she said, "kill him."

That was the plan, but Gabriel preferred to do the killing before this monster touched her.

They inched their way up the trail, and Gabriel heard another sound. One that caused him to curse. Not footsteps. Not gunshots. But it was something he instantly recognized.

A rattler.

Hell. They didn't need this now.

It wasn't unusual for rattlesnakes to be out among all the underbrush, but Gabriel figured it could be something that their attacker had planted. Something to get them moving so fast that it'd be easier to kill them.

"Freeze," Gabriel whispered to her.

In the darkness it was going to be pretty much impossible to see the snake, so he followed the sound of it. It was definitely agitated because the rattler was going practically nonstop. A warning to get them to back off. Gabriel wished they could do just that, but instead they had to crouch there and wait it out. That was the plan anyway.

But it didn't happen.

There was some movement to their left. Definitely footsteps this time, and Gabriel got just a glimpse of a hand that reached out from the shrub. The moonlight was just at the right angle for it to glint off the shiny blade.

As the knife plunged right into Jodi.

Chapter Sixteen

The pain shot through Jodi's shoulder. Familiar pain. It brought all the memories crashing back. The nightmare.

He was killing her again.

And she felt the warm blood start to slip down her back.

She took her own knife from her mouth and slashed it at him. Jodi thought maybe she connected with some part of him, but she couldn't tell for sure. That's because he was in the bushes, and she couldn't see him. However, she could see his knife, and he sliced it at her again. She ducked out of the way, barely in time.

If the rattler was still there, it had stopped making that god-awful sound. That was something at least, but it was also possible that it had been a recording. Her attacker probably wouldn't have wanted to risk being bitten by one of his "pets."

From the corner of her eye, she could see Gabriel. He lunged toward her, taking aim at her attacker, but he didn't get a chance to shoot. That's because the man latched onto her hair and dragged her into the shrubs with him. Gabriel wouldn't have risked shooting because he could have hit her.

She felt another cut from the knife. This time on her

arm, and he knocked her blade from her hand. More pain came. Not just from her physical wounds but because once again she was that nineteen-year-old girl. The one who this monster—or maybe the monster who'd hired him—had put in a shallow grave.

For a moment the fear froze her, but then she heard the shot. Heard Gabriel curse, too. And Jace shouted for him to watch out. The gunman who had Jace was no doubt on the trail, too, and he was trying to gun down Gabriel. Or else just keep him occupied while this goon stabbed her. Either way, that got her unfrozen, and Jodi remembered her training.

He still had hold of her hair. The knife, too, but she got to her feet, bashing her head into his chin. That stopped the next blow, but he made a feral sound and took another swing at her.

"Jodi!" Gabriel called out, and she heard him scramble toward her. Heard another shot fired, too. She only prayed they'd get out of this alive, but that might not happen if she didn't stop the knife.

Gabriel pushed through the shrubs, and she got just a glimpse of him before her attacker dragged her to her feet with her back against his chest. Like Jace, she was now a human shield. And she was bleeding. She could feel at least two stab wounds, but it was as if he'd cut her many more times.

Just like that night.

Her attacker motioned for Gabriel to drop his gun, and he put the tip of her knife right at her carotid artery. One jab of the blade, and she'd bleed out in no time at all.

"Let her go," Gabriel tried. "No way can you get out of here alive."

The man's silence let them know he didn't agree with

that. For a good reason. He had at least one healthy gunman and two hostages, Jace and her. That would get not only Gabriel but the deputies and Jameson to back off.

He started backing up, dragging her with him. The brushes scraped at her hands. Probably at him, too, but he didn't react. He was solely focused on getting her away from Gabriel. No doubt so he could finish her off.

This wasn't a hired thug. That feral sound he'd made had dripped with emotion. And she doubted it was a coincidence that he'd yet to say anything to them. This wasn't some hired gun. This was the *one*.

She heard it then. The sound that had been in her head for nearly ten years. His footsteps. Yes. They were identical to the ones that night. When he'd been dragging her nearly lifeless body into these very shrubs.

But who was it?

He was wearing a ski mask, so she couldn't see his face even if he would have allowed her to turn around. All of their suspects had similar builds, and she couldn't assume that Hector had truly been hurt. No. All of that could have been faked to bring them to this point.

Jodi let everything inside her go still. Just as Hector had taught her to do, and she gathered her energy. Her focus. And she pinpointed into the only weapon she had readily available to her.

Her own body.

It was a risk, but everything, and nothing, would be at this point. So, she made eye contact with Gabriel to try to give him some kind of heads-up that she was about to make her move. Whether he noticed her look or not she didn't know because he was volleying glances between her attacker and the approaching gunman.

Jodi dropped, her weight dragging her attacker down

with her, and in the same motion she rammed her elbow into his ribs. He staggered back, letting go of her and dropping the knife, but she soon realized the only reason he did that was so he could draw a gun and take aim.

He fired at Gabriel.

Thankfully, Gabriel must have realized what was happening because he was already moving to the side before the man pulled the trigger. The shot blasted into the ground.

Jodi fumbled around, looking for a knife or gun, but the man latched onto her again. He bashed the gun against her wounded shoulder, causing the pain to shoot through her. It was blinding and robbed her of her breath for a few precious seconds. Seconds that he used to drag her in front of him again. But Jodi did some grabbing of her own.

She caught on to the ski mask, dragging it from his face.

And she finally knew who wanted her dead.

Russell.

Even with only the watery moonlight, she saw him smile. A sickening smile that revealed the monster beneath. He'd been the bogeyman all this time.

"Why?" she managed to asked.

"You were a mistake," he said, surprising her with his answer. "I was mad, high and thinking like an idiot when I came here and saw you leave Gabriel's house. I lost my temper."

"You did all of that because you lost your temper?" she repeated, and Jodi didn't bother to take out the sarcasm. Nor the rage that was bubbling up inside her. "You stabbed me and tried to bury me."

"Like I said, it was a mistake. But your mistake was

remembering after all this time. I couldn't risk my wife finding out. I'd lose everything."

It twisted at her to hear that. It notched up the anger inside her, too. This sick excuse for a man was ready to murder heaven knew how many people to cover up his crimes.

Gabriel didn't move, but she could tell he was trying to figure out what to do. Once again, he couldn't risk shooting the man, so, like Jodi, he just had to wait and hope for some kind of opportunity.

"A lot of people are dead because of you," Gabriel said, his voice low and dangerous. "Why did you kill my parents?"

"I didn't," he said without hesitation. "They were already dead when I went to their house looking for Jodi. The blood was fresh, as if they'd just been killed. I figured the person who did that to them could still be around, so I ran out. I saw the knife in the yard, picked it up and then spotted Jodi at your house. I waited for her on the trail."

She wasn't sure about the timing of that. Jodi had always assumed that the Becketts had been murdered during a twenty minute or so window when she'd been at Gabriel's. But she'd thought that because of when Ivy had called Gabriel after discovering the bodies. Maybe, though, Ivy hadn't found her parents until minutes after they'd been killed. That would have given Russell time to find the knife, come after her and put her in that grave before Gabriel even started running up the trail to his parents' house.

Of course, Russell might be lying, too.

"That's when I lost my temper," Russell went on.

"When I saw her on the trail. I figured she'd just left your bed."

It wouldn't do any good to say that she hadn't done it, that Gabriel had rejected her that night. Even if Russell believed her, it wouldn't change anything that'd happened.

"Is Hector dead?" she asked.

"Maybe. If he's not, he should stay away from me because I'd have to kill him, too."

So, Hector hadn't been a part of this. That was something at least, though it might be too late for Jace and Hector.

"I'm tired of talking now," Russell said, dragging her even deeper into the shrubs just as he'd done ten years ago. "Jodi, I'm thinking you aren't going to cheat death this time—"

"Your wife is suspicious of you," Gabriel interrupted.

That stopped Russell in his tracks. Not Gabriel, though. He moved slightly to the right, and since he still had his gun in his hand, maybe he'd get in a position to shoot. Since the original attack, everything in her life had centered on killing the man who'd done those horrible things to her. But now, she just wanted him dead or at least locked up.

"What are you talking about?" Russell snapped.

"Your wife went to see August earlier today."

Judging from the way Russell's arm tightened, he hadn't known that. "What did that SOB tell her?"

"That he thought you were the one trying to kill Jodi and me."

Russell made another of those vicious sounds. "I'll kill him for doing that. He had no right. That fool has been interfering from day one, always digging, always sticking his nose where it doesn't belong."

"Ironic that you'd mention *rights* when you had a cop murdered so you could set up Hector. Billy and Mara, too. Plus, you might have let an innocent man spend a decade in jail for murders that he didn't commit. I'm guessing you and Mara were having an affair, and that's why she was so willing to help you." Gabriel paused, moved again. "By the way, your wife talked to August about your affair with Mara."

That was a lie, of course, but she understood why Gabriel had said it. It was to make Russell believe that this was all for nothing, that his marriage was going to fall apart after all. That way, he might let them go, so they could get an ambulance out for Jace, Hector and her.

"I'll fix things with Tracy when I'm finished here," Russell mumbled. He was getting more agitated with each passing second. "She's not like Jodi. She's loyal to me."

Jodi could have told him that she hadn't been loyal because they'd dated only a short period of time. It certainly hadn't been serious. Couldn't have been. Because she'd been in love with Gabriel.

Still was.

Too bad it was a tough time to remember that. Because it was also a reminder at how much she had at stake. She couldn't lose him.

She braced herself for Russell to shoot her. And there was a shot. It just hadn't come from him. It had come from the direction of Gabriel's house.

"It's me," Jameson called out. "We've got both gunmen in custody and an ambulance on the way for Hector and Jace. Where's Russell?"

Apparently, one or both the gunmen had decided to rat out their boss. So much for loyalty. Of course, if they were like the others Russell had hired, they were common thugs.

Thugs who could have easily killed them.

"Russell's here," Gabriel answered. "He's holding Jodi at gunpoint."

Before Gabriel had even finished what he was saying, Russell fired, the shot so loud that it blasted through her head. She couldn't hear, but Jodi could certainly feel, and she knew Russell was getting ready to run.

She dropped down before he could do that and grabbed the knife.

Jodi didn't have time to get back up and stab him in the heart, so she just slashed the blade at him, the knife gouging into his stomach.

Russell cursed at her, calling her a vile name, and he backhanded her with the gun. Again, the pain came and put her right back on her knees. Russell took advantage of that. He shoved her at Gabriel.

Gabriel and she collided, both of them falling to the ground.

Russell fired another shot and took off running. Jodi got up to go after him. But she stopped.

Because she saw the blood on Gabriel's chest.

Chapter Seventeen

Gabriel wished he had something to punch—hard. Preferably Russell. That might rid him of some of this lethal energy that was bubbling up inside him.

The pain didn't help with that energy, either. This was his first gunshot wound, and it thankfully hadn't been life-threatening. Russell's bullet had been a through and through into Gabriel's shoulder, but even after some meds, it was throbbing like an abscessed tooth. However, his pain was nothing compared to what he was feeling about Jodi.

Gabriel had refused to leave her side not only for the ambulance ride but while they were both getting examined and stitched up at the hospital. His staying close to her was partially because he was just plain worried about her.

But it was also because her would-be killer was still at large.

Somehow, Russell had managed to escape. Probably because he had a car stashed near the ranch, and he'd no doubt fled while Jameson was concerned with keeping Jace alive. The deputy and Hector were both going to be okay, but their injuries were more serious than Jodi's and his.

Of course, nothing was more serious to Gabriel than seeing the blood all over her. Hell. It was like that night all over again. He'd saved her then, but the cost of that attack had been sky-high, and he wasn't sure how long it would take Jodi to recover a second time. The images of this attack would now be piled on top of the nightmarish memories she already had.

Despite all the blood, Jodi had gotten lucky, too. There was a cut on her upper arm. Another near her left wrist. The doctor had taken off her T-shirt while he'd examined her, so Gabriel had no trouble seeing each wound. The camisole she'd had on beneath her shirt had blood on it, as well.

He wanted to punch something again, and that feeling got worse with every new bruise, cut and scrape he saw on her silky skin.

Jameson stepped into the treatment room, glancing at both of them and shaking his head. "I hope you know how to get bloodstains out of clothes."

It was a really bad joke, and Gabriel scowled at him. Jameson, however, went to Jodi and brushed a kiss on her forehead. She flinched a little, but that was possibly because she was reacting to the stitches that the nurse was just finishing applying to her wounds.

"Please tell me you caught Russell," she said.

"Not yet. But SAPD has officers at his house to protect his wife and baby. I had a Ranger go to August's place just in case, too."

Good idea. Russell had been pretty riled about his wife going to see August, and he might want to find out what the woman had told him. Of course, that was all water under the bridge now. They knew Russell was a killer, and soon his wife would know that, as well.

"I put two deputies at the hospital doors," Jameson went on, and he looked at Jodi's empty hip holster. Gabriel had managed to hold on to his own gun, but Jodi had lost hers in the scuffle. Jameson took out his backup from the slide holster in his jeans and gave it to her. "Just in case."

That put some alarm back in Jodi's eyes. Not that she'd exactly looked calm and serene before his comment, but this was a reminder that Russell could come charging in there and try to kill them. According to the hired guns Jameson had rounded up, there wasn't anybody else on Russell's dirty payroll, but Gabriel had seen the sick hatred in Russell's eyes.

If there was any humanly way he could get to Jodi, he would.

That's why Gabriel was thankful his brother had given her the gun. Now, he had to pray she didn't need it.

Gabriel stood from the table and reached for his shirt to put it back on. Before he could do that, though, Jameson snatched it away.

"No," Jameson said, "you're not going after Russell."

Since that's exactly what Gabriel had been planning to do, he couldn't deny it, but he could pull rank on a younger brother. He wasn't so sure, though, that he could do that with Jodi.

"You're not going after Russell," she echoed. "Not without me anyway." She stood, too, reaching for her shirt. Wincing and grunting in pain, she started to put it on.

"You're not leaving this hospital," Gabriel warned her.

"And neither are you." Jodi's chin came up, and he could have sworn she was fighting back a smile. Maybe because she'd just one-upped him. He didn't want her out there, so that meant he was staying put, too.

Gabriel went to her with the hopes of convincing her to stay seated. She did but only because he hovered over her and kissed her. He had intended for it to be just a peck, but it felt so good that he lingered a few seconds.

God, he could have lost her.

"I'll see if your rooms are ready," the nurse said, standing. She was fighting back a smile, as well. "And no, it won't do any good to tell Dr. Holliwell that you don't want to stay. He's already said he's keeping both of you for the night."

Yeah, that was an argument he didn't even want to try to win with the doc. Dr. Holliwell wanted Jodi in the hospital in case her injuries were worse than the original diagnosis, and Gabriel didn't want her alone. That meant both Gabriel and she were staying.

"I'll see if there are any updates," Jameson said. "You two look like you could use some alone time."

Gabriel gave him another scowl, but he did want some time with Jodi. There were things he had to tell her.

"I'm so sorry," he started. "I should have stopped this—"

She caught on to his neck, pulling him down to her, and kissed him. It hurt. Mainly because it tweaked the muscles in his throbbing shoulder. But he didn't care. Kissing her was worth the pain.

"I'm the one who should be saying I'm sorry," she insisted. "Russell was on the trail because he thought I would remember that he was the one who'd attacked me."

This called for another kiss to shut her up, but Gabriel got in something else he wanted to say first. "Neither one of us made Russell a killer. He did that all by himself."

And they'd both be cleaning up Russell's mess for a long, long time.

Now, he kissed her, and it wasn't to hush her. It was because he needed it. Judging from the sound she made in her throat, she needed it, as well. The kiss might have gone on a lot longer if his phone hadn't buzzed. Since it could be about Russell, he stepped back to take the call.

"It's August," he told her after seeing the name on the screen.

He considered letting it go to voice mail, but since August was in possible danger, he hit Answer and put it on speaker.

"Is it true?" August practically yelled. "Is that idiot Russell after me?"

"He could be. I told him that his wife had visited you."

August cursed him. And Gabriel let him go on for a while. In hindsight he probably should have figured out a different way to get Russell to confess to using Mara and then murdering her, but considering everything else that had been going on, it was the best he could do.

"I want you to stay in your house with the Rangers," Gabriel told him. "If Russell shows up, have the Rangers call me."

"Hell, no, I won't. I'll kill him on sight. And in the meantime, you'll get my brother out of jail. This proves he didn't—"

"Russell said he didn't kill my parents."

"And you believed him?" August howled.

"Yeah, I did. Because he didn't deny murdering Mara. Didn't deny attacking Jodi, either." Gabriel had to pause and gather his breath. It was hard to think of just how close Russell had come to ending her life—again. "If he had killed them, I believe Russell would have taken great pleasure in letting me know."

Jodi nodded in agreement. "It would have made things easier, for me anyway, if Russell had committed all the murders."

Yes, because it would mean her father was innocent. And with Russell's confession, Travis was clear of Jodi's attack. But clearing his name didn't extend to the deaths of Gabriel's parents. No. There wasn't enough evidence to overturn his conviction. However, it was something Gabriel would take a closer look at. Jodi would no doubt do the same.

Jodi took hold of his hand, gave it a gentle squeeze. Considering it was such a small gesture, it had a big effect. It didn't rid him of the ache in his heart, but it sure as heck helped.

"Don't think I'm just going to drop this," August went on. "As soon as you catch Russell, I'm finding a judge who'll set Travis free." With that, he ended the call.

"That won't happen," Gabriel assured Jodi.

She nodded. "I agree. If Russell had killed them, he would have said so." She paused. "But at least now I know my father wasn't the one who attacked me."

In all the chaos, Gabriel had forgotten just how important that was to her. Good. It might help with the nightmares and panic attacks. But she certainly wasn't panicking now.

She slipped right into his arms.

"I'm in love with you, you know," she said.

No. He hadn't known. And it left him speechless. Not the best time for that because she was clearly waiting for him to respond. Before he could get his mouth working, though, the nurse stepped in.

"Are you up to seeing Hector March?" The nurse directed her question to Jodi. "He's asking for you."

Gabriel wasn't sure it was a good idea, especially since Hector might verbally blast Jodi again for not sticking up for him, but he didn't stop her when she started to follow the nurse. Gabriel did go with her, though. For one thing, because she didn't look steady on her feet. For another, he didn't want her alone.

The hospital wasn't that large by anyone's standards, and it took them less than a minute to make it to the room where Hector was recovering. Unlike Jodi and him, Hector had required some surgery. Ditto for Jace, but both had come out of it just fine. Physically fine anyway.

The moment Jodi and Gabriel stepped into the room, Hector tried to sit up, but the nurse motioned for him to lie back down. He didn't listen. Instead, he winced and grunted until he got into the position he wanted. Probably so he'd be able to face them head-on.

Hector's mouth tightened when he looked at Jodi. "I would ask if you're okay, but I can see you're not." His attention lingered on the bloodstains on her shirt. "He knifed you?"

She nodded. "This time, though, he didn't hit any vital organs, and I did manage to cut him." Jodi tipped her head to the fresh bandage on his leg and chest. "How about you? Are you okay?"

"I'll be fine in no time. Just a few broken ribs."

"And two gunshot wounds," Jodi added. "The doctor mentioned it when he was examining Gabriel and me."

"Flesh wounds. I'll be back at work tomorrow."

"In a week if you're lucky," the nurse corrected, and she stepped out.

Gabriel was betting Hector wasn't going to stay in

that bed for a week. A night maybe, until the effects of the anesthesia wore off.

"It can't be easy for you to be here," Hector went on, and it surprised Gabriel that the man wasn't speaking to Jodi but to him. "You're probably blaming yourself for what happened to Jodi. I know I sure as hell am."

Jodi frowned. "It wasn't your fault." She looked at Gabriel and repeated it before she went to Hector and slid her hand over his.

Hector stared at her, clearly surprised. Maybe because Jodi wasn't the touching type. Ironic that she could manage to do it now when she'd just weathered another attack.

"Thank you for everything you did for me," she said.

Hector's stare continued. "But?"

Jodi drew in a long breath. "But I can't work for you any longer. And no, it doesn't have anything to do with what went on tonight."

"It has to do with Gabriel." Hector huffed, groaned softly and then scrubbed his hand over his face. "I'm guessing he's the reason I no longer see the panic in your eyes?"

She nodded. "He's the reason for a lot of things."

That got him a quick glare from Hector. Then, a nod. Hector and he would probably never be friendly to each other, but they could agree on one thing. They wanted what was best for Jodi. Because they both cared deeply for her.

"You're not going to become a cop, are you?" Hector asked, and it sounded as if he was only partially joking. Partially disgusted with the thought of that, too.

"No, but maybe a PI. That way, I can put all the training you gave me to good use. I can still help people.

Protect them, maybe. I could even set up an office right here in Blue River."

So, she was staying. Or least thinking of staying. Even though it wasn't a sure thing, it felt as if someone had lifted a weight off his shoulders.

Hector stayed quiet a moment while he continued to study Jodi's face. "Is this goodbye then?"

"Yes," she answered after a long pause. "Thanks again, Hector." She leaned down, dropped a kiss on his forehead.

Gabriel hated the punch of jealousy that went through him. Especially since it was obvious that Jodi didn't have any romantic feelings for her former boss, but Gabriel was just feeling possessive at the moment. That probably had something to do with what she'd said to him.

I'm in love with you, you know.

He was definitely still reeling from that. Because, no, he hadn't known.

The moment they were back in the hall, Gabriel eased her into his arms. He'd intended it to be just a hug since he figured she needed a little TLC after that chat. Of course, nothing ever stayed just a simple hug with them, so when she looked up at him, Gabriel kissed her. He would have also brought up that "I'm in love with you" if he hadn't heard the footsteps heading their way. He automatically stepped in front of Jodi and drew his gun.

But again, it was only Jameson.

However, unlike earlier when Jameson had come into the treatment room, his brother was now smiling. "The Rangers found Russell."

Gabriel still had his arm around Jodi, and he felt her practically sag against him in relief. "Where was he?" she asked.

"Not far from the ranch. He was on one of the old trails. He's dead," Jameson added a heartbeat later.

Gabriel's mind started to whirl with all sorts of bad scenarios—like a shoot-out where more law enforcement officers had been hurt, or worse. "Did Russell kill anyone else?"

Jameson shook his head. "He didn't get the chance. He bled out while sitting in his car. A knife wound to the stomach. Your doing?" he asked Gabriel.

"No. Jodi's."

So, she'd killed Russell after all.

Gabriel looked down at her to see how she was handling that. No tears. And she seemed a little stronger than she had been a couple of seconds earlier. Relieved, too.

"Good," she whispered.

Yeah, it was. Not only because they didn't have to worry about Russell coming after them, but because he also couldn't try to kill his wife or August. Of course, his wife's troubles were just beginning, because she'd have to live with the aftermath of what her husband had done.

"Are you okay?" Jameson asked her, but he waved it off. "Of course, you are. You're in good hands." He smiled, no doubt noticing that Gabriel and she were practically wrapped around each other, and he strolled off.

"Are you really okay?" Gabriel repeated to her.

She took a moment, as if trying to figure out how to answer him, and then nodded. "For years, I've dreamed about this happening. About getting back at my attacker. But now that I've managed it, it no longer seems important. *This* is what's important."

Gabriel hoped that she was talking about him. "Earlier you said you were in love with me."

She stared at him, maybe trying to figure out how he felt about that and how he felt about her. But Gabriel didn't want there to be any question in her mind.

"Right back at you," he said. He even managed a smile before he kissed her. And because he figured she needed the words as well, Gabriel added, "I'm in love with you, too."

Now, she smiled. Kissed him and slid as close to him as their injuries would allow.

She'd been right. This was what was important. And Gabriel now had everything he wanted right in his arms.

* * * * *

Look for the next book in USA TODAY
bestselling author Delores Fossen's
BLUE RIVER RANCH *series,*
available next month.

*And don't miss the most recent books
in her long-running series,*
THE LAWMEN OF SILVER CREEK RANCH*:*

*LANDON
HOLDEN
DRURY
LUCAS*

"I'm going to find out who did this," Harrison said. "I won't let anyone hurt you, Honey."

She started to say something but he stopped her. "Shh." He pressed his finger to her lips to quiet her. "I mean it. People in this town haven't been nice to you and it's not right. I should have stood up for you a long time ago, when we were kids."

A blush stained her face and she averted her eyes as if bad memories had assaulted her.

"I'm sorry. I didn't mean to remind you of the past."

"I can't ever forget the past," Honey said. "Not until we figure out if my father killed your sister."

Their gazes locked. Tension escalated. Emotions and desires flamed between them.

She shivered and Harrison realized he'd wanted to soothe and protect and touch her ever since he'd seen her at the morgue.

No longer able to resist, he stroked her cheek with the back of his thumb, then lowered his head and kissed her.

REDEMPTION AT HAWK'S LANDING

BY
RITA HERRON

MILLS & BOON

HarperCollins
PUBLISHERS
Since 1817

First Published in Great Britain 2017
By Mills & Boon, an imprint of HarperCollins*Publishers*
1 London Bridge Street, London, SE1 9GF

© 2017 Rita B. Herron

ISBN: 978-0-263-92938-6

46-1217

MIX
Paper from
responsible sources
FSC® C007454
FSC
www.fsc.org

This book is produced from independently certified FSC™ paper to ensure responsible forest management.

For more information visit: www.harpercollins.co.uk/green

Printed and bound in Spain
by CPI, Barcelona

USA TODAY bestselling author **Rita Herron** wrote her first book when she was twelve but didn't think real people grew up to be writers. Now she writes so she doesn't have to get a real job. A former kindergarten teacher and workshop leader, she traded storytelling to kids for writing romance, and now she writes romantic comedies and romantic suspense. Rita lives in Georgia with her family. She loves to hear from readers, so please visit her website, www.ritaherron.com.

Chapter One

The dead man lay sprawled on the mountain ridge at Dead Man's Bluff, his eyes blank, his arm twisted at an odd angle.

He'd probably broken it in the fall. Blood matted his graying hair from where he'd hit the rock as he'd gone over the edge of the ridge.

Sheriff Harrison Hawk cursed. Dammit, he'd recognized him immediately.

Waylon Granger.

The man his mother blamed for his sister's disappearance eighteen years ago. They'd never been able to prove he was at fault, though.

And now he was dead; they might never know the truth.

Curiosity over what had happened nagged at Harrison. Granger was a known drunk, and a mean one. Even his daughter, Honey, had left home after high school graduation to escape the bastard.

What was Granger doing here at Dead Man's Bluff?

This was the teenage hangout—just as years ago he and his friends had been drawn to the swimming hole and dark mines with the mysterious ghost stories that surrounded them, the local high schoolers still frequented it.

The two thirteen-year-old boys who'd called in the body sat hunched by Granger's rusty pickup, their young faces etched in horror.

The scent of death hit Harrison, the summer heat accentuating it.

Memories of the night his little sister, Chrissy, had gone missing bombarded him. The years since hadn't dulled the pain or trauma. It felt as if it had happened yesterday.

He was seventeen at the time and supposed to babysit his siblings that night while his parents attended a party. Instead, he'd sneaked out to meet his buddies at this very place.

He inhaled sharply. He'd thought Lucas, fifteen, would watch their thirteen-year-old brother, Dexter, eleven-year-old Brayden and their ten-year-old sister, Chrissy. But Lucas had a friend visiting and hadn't noticed when Chrissy and his youngest brother, Brayden, sneaked out. Dexter claimed he and Chrissy had argued because he was playing video games and she kept interrupting. Brayden and Chrissy rode their bikes to the bluff to see what Harrison was up to.

While they were exploring, Brayden tripped and sprained his ankle. Chrissy went to get help. Brayden thought she'd run to Honey Granger's, but Honey denied seeing her that night.

The sheriff organized a search party, and they'd searched the mines and town and dragged the swimming hole. But they hadn't found her.

Someone claimed they'd seen Granger's truck drive by, casting suspicion on him. Granger denied picking Chrissy up or having any contact with her.

Desperate for a big-sister role model, Chrissy had taken a shine to Granger's daughter, Honey. But Harrison's mother didn't like Honey and had forbidden her from hanging out with the teenager.

Honey's father didn't allow Honey friends or visitors, so Harrison's mother suggested that the man had caught Chrissy on their property, lost his temper and done something to her.

The boys' voices sounded from Granger's truck and dragged Harrison back to reality. The taller one stood and walked toward him, his eyes wide with fear. "C-can we go home now, Sheriff?"

Harrison felt for the boy. He and his friend were only

kids and had no business being out here by themselves. The mines and bluff were dangerous.

Hopefully they'd learned their lesson.

Unfortunately neither had seen anyone else at the bluff. They'd been horsing around, throwing rocks off the ridge when they noticed the vultures, then spotted Granger's body on the ledge below.

"Yeah, but be careful. If you think of anything else you saw, call me."

The boy nodded, then jogged over to his bicycle. His friend joined him, then the two of them began pedaling as fast as they could to get away. Tonight they'd probably be glad to go home to their parents.

A siren wailed in the distance, indicating the rescue team and crime team were approaching. Once they recovered Granger's body, they'd transport it to the morgue for an autopsy.

Although most likely Granger had been drunk and had simply slipped and fallen, Harrison had a job to do. Whether or not he liked the man didn't matter.

He had to verify that his death was accidental.

His stomach knotted. He also had to call Honey and deliver the news that her father was gone. It was one conversation he dreaded.

HONEY GRANGER WIPED perspiration from her forehead, the Austin summer heat stifling as she studied her latest project—a brick ranch built in 1960 that she was renovating.

The scent of dust and old weathered wood blended with the hint of new pine she'd bought to replace the rotting boards on the kitchen floor.

Adrenaline pumped through her. Taking dilapidated, run-down houses that had been left for dead and refurbishing them was challenging but stimulating. She loved transforming the ruins into something beautiful, and had built a successful business out of it.

She'd been trying to do the same for herself for years—take the battered girl who'd run from Tumbleweed, Texas, and make her into something to be proud of. Sometimes she thought she'd succeeded.

Other times she felt like the tainted teenager with the thrift store clothes and shady family, who'd run away when the gossip and rumors became too crushing.

Her contractor and business partner, Jared North, strode toward her, swinging his sledgehammer.

Today was his favorite part—demo day.

He tilted his hard hat. "You want that wall between the kitchen and living room knocked out?"

Honey nodded. "Everyone wants open concept these days, to be able to see their friends and family while they cook and entertain."

"Got it," Jared said. "It's load bearing, though, so we'll have to install a support beam."

"It'll be worth it." Honey stepped back, mentally picturing the reconfigured design of the kitchen. "With the wall gone, we can install upper and lower cabinets, and build a large center island, maybe from reclaimed wood, for more prep space and storage beneath." She walked over and examined the fireplace. "Remove the Sheetrock. My guess is there's shiplap below it. Exposing it will add character to the space."

"Yes, ma'am."

Honey laughed at his mock salute. The planning and design stage, she was in charge. But when it came to the actual construction details and labor, Jared took command and she saluted him.

"How about the bathrooms?" Jared asked.

"We're gutting them." The outdated tiles and flooring had to go. She just hoped they didn't find water damage or mold.

Her phone buzzed at her hip, and she checked the number. The area code wasn't Austin's, but it seemed familiar. It took her a moment to realize the location.

Tumbleweed.

Nerves fluttered in her belly. The sheriff's office.

Fear and anger resurfaced quickly. Good grief, she'd recognize that number anywhere. What had her father done now? He'd been arrested for public drunkenness, disorderly conduct and driving under the influence when she lived at home. And she'd had to bail him out.

But she'd cut off contact when she'd left town and told Sheriff Dunar not to bother calling her when he locked her father up again.

The phone buzzed again. Jared frowned. "Aren't you going to answer that?"

Honey shook her head. She didn't give a damn if her father was in trouble. He had shamed her enough in high school. She'd moved away years ago to escape the stigma.

She refused to let him taint her newfound life here in Austin.

The phone settled, and she and Jared walked through the rest of the house. She pointed out her plans—a new window here, French doors off the living room to open up to the patio they were resurfacing, removal of all the popcorn ceiling, bathroom remodel.

Her phone buzzed again just as they finished. The same number.

Damn.

"What's wrong, Honey?" Jared asked.

She bit the inside of her cheek. "Nothing." She snatched up the phone. "I guess I'd better take this." She'd tell Sheriff Dunar to lose her number and never bother her again.

Her lungs tightened as she hurried outside to the backyard for air. Just the thought of her father made her feel dirty.

Ready to get the call over with, she pressed Connect. "Hello."

A heartbeat of silence passed. "Is this Honey Granger?"

Honey heaved a breath. It didn't sound like Sheriff Dunar. "Yes, who is this?"

"Harrison Hawk... I'm sheriff now."

Honey swallowed hard. Harrison Hawk was sheriff of Tumbleweed?

Good God. She'd had such a crush on him when she was younger. But then his little sister went missing, and her hellish life became a real nightmare when her father became a suspect.

"Harrison?" Honey rubbed her damp forehead, wiping at the perspiration. "How did you get my number? Why—"

"Just listen, Honey. It's important."

She leaned her back against a sawtooth tree and waited, but her gaze homed in on the sagging porch and rotting awning of her renovation project.

"I have bad news," he said in a gruff voice. "It's about your father."

Was there any other kind of news where he was concerned? "What has he done now?"

Another tense moment passed, then Harrison cleared his throat. "I'm sorry, Honey. I hate to have to tell you this, but he's dead."

Honey's legs buckled, and she felt herself sliding to the ground just like the rotting exterior of her latest project.

SEVERAL TENSE SECONDS passed as Harrison gave Honey time to absorb the news.

A rescue team and the medical examiner sped up the winding road to the clearing at the top of the hill and screeched to a halt.

"Honey, are you still there?"

The rescue team climbed from their vehicle, followed by the ME. Harrison waved them over to the ridge and pointed out the body.

"Honey?"

"I'm here," she said in a strained voice.

"I'm sorry," he said again. "I just thought you'd want to know." Or maybe not. She hadn't returned to Tumbleweed in years. He didn't know if she'd spoken to her father recently or if they'd communicated at all since she'd left.

"How? His drinking?"

"I can't say for sure until the autopsy."

Another strained silence. She was obviously in shock.

"I'll transport the body to the morgue," he said, hating to sound callous but he didn't know what else to say. Better to just stick to business. "I didn't know if you wanted to come back and make arrangements—"

A heavy sigh. "I'll let you know when I get there."

"All right." He watched as the rescue team anchored a harness so they could climb down and bring up the body. "If there's anything I can do, just let me know."

Honey murmured, "Okay." A second later the phone went silent, leaving him wondering if she'd been alone or with someone. He should have asked before he dropped the bomb.

But he and Honey hadn't exactly been friends when she lived in Tumbleweed. Worse, his sister's disappearance had cast a dark cloud over both their families.

The rescue workers' voices jerked him from his thoughts, a reminder he needed to focus on the job. He strode to the edge of the bluff and looked down.

One of the workers was kneeling by Granger's body.

Harrison used his camera phone to take pictures before the men moved it. The ME stepped up beside him.

"What happened?" Dr. Weinberger asked.

Harrison shrugged. "Don't know. Looks like he fell. A couple of kids called it in. I took their statements and let them go home. They were pretty shaken."

The ME glanced around the area. "They see anyone else up here?"

Harrison shook his head. "No. They were throwing

rocks off the ridge when they saw vultures circling over Granger's body. See that blood on the back of his head?"

Harrison nodded. Granger lay facedown, arms at odd angles. "Looks like he broke his arms trying to brace his fall."

"Yes, it does," the ME said. "He fell face forward. So how did he get the gash on the back of his head?"

The air around Harrison stirred, bringing the scent of impending rain and the whisper of the ghosts the locals gossiped about. Some said it was the miners screaming when the mine had collapsed on top of them.

Others justified the eerie whistle of the wind as just that—the wind rolling off the mountain ridge.

The ME's words echoed in Harrison's ears. Granger fell face forward. The back of his head was one bloody mess.

His gaze met the doctor's as he realized the implication. "Damn. He didn't just fall, did he? He was murdered."

Chapter Two

Honey ignored the grief stabbing at her the rest of the day as she finalized plans for the house renovation. She left the project in her partner's hands, trusting him with implementing her design, then drove back to the small Craftsman-style bungalow she'd bought two years ago.

This was home sweet home. Her happy place.

Here she was safe from her past. From the rumors and gossip and the nastiness that had been her life.

She had no idea how long she'd be in Tumbleweed. Only as long as it took to address her father's will and handle his burial. She definitely would not give him a memorial service.

It wasn't like anyone would attend if she did.

Her father hadn't been a popular man in Tumbleweed when she lived there. She couldn't imagine he'd made friends since.

She took a deep breath as she entered her home, savoring the cozy interior she'd personally designed to her taste. She liked the farmhouse, shabby-chic look, but avoided anything reminiscent of her childhood home.

Memories bombarded her—sleeping in a room with no heat, with raggedy quilts piled so thickly on her that she couldn't turn over. The furnace in the den barely kept that room warm. The summers were hot and stale, the rooms reeking of smoke, rotting wood and booze.

She blinked back tears, walked to her bedroom and dragged out a suitcase. The earthy tones mingled with slate blue in the room to soothe her nerves after a long day.

But as she gathered jeans, shirts, boots and a couple of skirts, the memory of the wind jarring the windowpanes in her father's house taunted her as if she was standing in that old house.

She would be soon.

Scrubbing her hand over her eyes to blot out the tears and wipe her emotions away, she braced herself. She wouldn't let that place or her father's death get to her.

Not ever again.

In her mind, he'd died a long time ago. This visit was just a formality, then she could erase him, Tumbleweed and its residents from her life forever.

ANXIETY KNOTTED HARRISON'S shoulders as he parked at the morgue the next morning. Honey Granger was meeting him here.

He hadn't slept the night before for stewing over the fact that she was coming back to town. He didn't exactly know why that thought unnerved him, but it did.

His first instinct had been to call his family together and relay the news about Granger's death, but he'd kept the information between the ME, his deputy, Mitchell Bronson, and himself.

Telling his mother and brothers would dredge up all the pain again.

He also wanted to verify the cause of death. Everyone in town knew that his mother hated Granger, which would no doubt lay suspicion on her. Truthfully on his entire family.

He wasn't ready to deal with that suspicion or to throw his mother and siblings into the line of fire.

Sweat beaded on his forehead as he climbed from his SUV onto the hot asphalt and walked toward the hospital. The morgue and ME's office were located in the basement. Already the noonday sun was beating down full force and the temperature was climbing.

His phone buzzed. Dr. Weinberger. He punched Connect. "Sheriff Hawk."

"Harrison, Honey Granger is here."

"I'll be there in a couple of minutes. I just parked." He ended the call and took a deep breath as he entered the hospital. The image of Honey Granger at sixteen with her golden-blond hair, big brown eyes and long legs made his gut tighten.

As a teenager she'd been pretty but homely, with her ragged secondhand clothes. The popular girls had been mean to her, and the boys had joked about getting into her pants. Two football players had made a bet to see who could screw her first.

A foul taste settled in Harrison's mouth. She had definitely gotten a bad rap.

Oddly his little sister was the one who'd stood up for Honey instead of him. He wasn't proud of that.

Chrissy had liked Honey's flashy clothes, jewelry and makeup.

But their mother had forbidden her from hanging out with the girl, saying Honey was too old to be friends with Chrissy and that Honey looked like a tramp.

When Honey left town abruptly after high school, rumors surfaced that she'd gotten pregnant and had gone away to have the baby.

He'd hoped that wasn't true, that she'd found a better life.

The air-conditioning hit him as he entered the hospital, stark against the blazing summer heat. He strode to the elevator and rode down to the basement, the scent of cleaner and antiseptic was strong as he walked down the hall to the ME's office.

The receptionist waved him in. When he'd phoned Honey, she'd obviously been shocked at the news of her father's death and hadn't said much.

He had no idea what to expect today. Granger was her father and the only family she had left. He was surprised she hadn't asked for more details, but everyone reacted differently to bad news. She probably would be asking now.

And he needed to find out the answers.

He knocked then eased open the door to Weinberger's office. Dr. Weinberger stood and nodded in greeting, then Harrison's gaze fell on Honey.

The teenager with the too-flashy clothes had disappeared.

This woman wore jeans with a silky-looking deep blue top and strappy heels that made her legs look endlessly long. Her hair was just as blond and golden looking, her big brown eyes smoldering hot, sensual, like liquid pools a man could drown in.

His gut clenched. Dammit she was…beautiful. In a wholesome, almost-innocent way.

"Honey?" He offered his hand.

Her hand trembled as she placed her slender palm in his. Heat rippled through him at her touch.

A wary look flashed in her eyes, and she rubbed her palm on her jeans as if she'd felt it, too. Then her soft lips pressed into a thin line, and a frown darkened her face.

"We were waiting on you," Dr. Weinberger said. "I explained to Honey that she doesn't need to make an ID, that we recognized her father, and DNA confirms it's Waylon. But if she wants to see him, that's fine, too."

Harrison arched a brow, waiting on Honey's response. He needed time to get his reaction to her under control.

Their past was way too complicated for him to be attracted to her now.

HONEY QUICKLY AVERTED her gaze from Harrison.

Good heavens. She'd thought he was cute when he was seventeen, but he was so handsome now he could bring a woman to her knees.

He'd morphed into a mountain of a man with big, broad shoulders, a muscular body, the deepest amber eyes she'd ever seen and an all-gruff, masculine exterior. His tanned skin and dark hair accentuated his high cheekbones, square jaw and the cleft in his chin.

He had dimples, too, when he smiled, although that smile had disappeared after his sister went missing. It was still gone.

In fact, his frown suggested he found her lacking.

His mother's hateful words had been imprinted in her brain forever. "You're trash, Honey Granger. You're not welcome at Hawk's Landing. My daughter is *not* going to associate with the likes of you."

"Have you decided on arrangements?" Harrison asked, jarring her from the painful memories.

Honey shrugged. "According to Daddy's lawyer, Truitt Bennings, my father wanted to be cremated." She was surprised that her father had a will, but grateful he did. He'd left the house to her. Owning it outright would make it easier to sell.

She didn't intend to stay in this town any longer than necessary.

"I can call the crematory for you if you want," Dr. Weinberger offered.

"Thank you," Honey said. "I'd appreciate that."

Dr. Weinberger gave her a sympathetic smile. "Do you want to see him now?"

Did she? No. When she'd left town, she'd sworn never to see or speak to him again.

But some inner voice beckoned her to at least say goodbye. After all, he was her father. And he hadn't deserted her as her mother had, although some could argue that drinking himself into a stupor was his way of abandoning her and reality.

She stood, lifting her chin and putting on a brave face. "Yes. Let's get it over with."

Harrison and the doctor exchanged an odd look, but neither commented. She almost asked what was going on, but decided they'd probably discussed her before she'd arrived. Gossip in small towns was hard to overcome. For all she knew, everyone in Tumbleweed knew of her arrival.

She lifted her chin. Dammit, she didn't care what the people here thought of her anymore. She'd made herself a new life, and she was proud of who she'd become.

Still, their quiet looks made her uneasy and reminded her of the reason she hated Tumbleweed.

Dr. Weinberger led her from the office through a set of double doors past a room labeled Autopsy, then into a smaller space. She took a deep breath to brace herself, then followed him over to a steel gurney. The room was so cold that she shivered.

Her father lay beneath the draped cloth.

The ME stepped to the opposite side of the table. "Are you ready, Ms. Granger?"

She nodded.

He pulled the cloth away from her father's face, but she didn't react. It was as if she was looking at a stranger, someone she'd met years ago, someone who hadn't meant anything to her. Age had turned his hair gray, carved deep lines in his craggy face, and he'd lost weight. The yellow-ish-gray pallor of his skin coupled with the bruises on his face looked stark beneath the harsh lighting.

"What happened?" she asked. She'd assumed it was the liquor, but his face looked like he'd been in a bar fight.

The doctor shifted. Beside her, Harrison's breath puffed into the air. "I found him at Dead Man's Bluff."

Honey looked at him for confirmation. "Why was he there?"

"I don't know," Harrison said.

"How did he die?" Honey asked.

"Cause of death was head trauma," Dr. Weinberger said.

"So he was drunk and fell?" Honey said, disgusted.

A tense second passed. Harrison cleared his throat. "He didn't simply fall, Honey. It looks like he was struck by a rock then pushed over the edge."

Shock bolted through Honey. "You mean someone murdered him?"

"I'm sorry," Harrison said. "But yes, it looks that way."

Now she understood the odd looks between the men.

Her mind began to race. Her father hadn't had any friends in town. A lot of people didn't like him, but no one hated him enough to kill him.

Except…

Her gaze met Harrison's. Except for his family.

HARRISON SAW THE wheels in Honey's mind turning. She was jumping to the same conclusion that everyone else would—that one of his family members might be responsible.

"Do you know who pushed him?" she asked, tactfully avoiding an accusation.

He didn't have the answer to that question.

"Not yet."

He would find the truth, though. That was his damn job.

"Would you like a few minutes alone?" Dr. Weinberger asked.

Another tense heartbeat passed. Honey twisted her hands together, looking fragile for a moment, then she gave a slight nod.

"Let us know if you need anything," the ME said.

For some reason, Harrison was reluctant to leave her alone. She'd grown up in a house filled with turmoil. Had suffered at the hands of her mother and father. Had left nearly two decades ago.

And now she'd traveled back here alone to say goodbye to the man who'd failed her.

Compassion for her made him reach out and squeeze her arm. "Are you okay?"

A sad smile curved her mouth. "Of course. I'll just be a minute."

Harrison nodded, then followed the medical examiner into the hallway. Worried about her, he turned and watched her through the window in the door, unable to leave.

"She seems to be handling it okay," Dr. Weinberger said in a low voice.

Either that or she was good at acting. He had a feeling Honey Granger had done a lot of that over the years—pretending the rumors and gossip hadn't hurt her. But deep-seated pain colored her eyes.

He had the sudden need to make things right for her. To strip her of the anguish she was suffering.

But he didn't have a clue as to how to do that.

Besides, she would probably leave town as soon as she handled the details surrounding her father's death, the cremation and possibly the sale of his house. Unless she decided to move back and live in it.

A sardonic chuckle rumbled in his throat. He didn't see that happening. Ever.

"Did you find any forensics?" Harrison asked.

Weinberger crossed his arms. "Slivers of rock and dirt were embedded in the back of Granger's head where he was struck. My guess is that he was hit with a rock from the bluff."

Harrison shifted. "That would imply the murder wasn't premeditated, that something happened on that ledge that triggered the other party to attack."

He'd have to go back to the bluff, look for that rock, see if there were fingerprints on it.

"Anything else?" Harrison asked.

"Dirt under his fingernails and a short brown hair."

Harrison gave a nod. "Send it to the lab. That hair may belong to our killer."

Chapter Three

Her father had been murdered.

That fact echoed in Honey's head as if someone was pounding the words inside her skull.

Who had killed her father? And why?

Emotions welled in her chest as she studied his cold body. Eighteen years had aged him, but the alcohol had intensified the process, adding another ten years. The bruises and contusions on his face looked stark beneath the lights. His skin was a sallow yellow, lips a bluish purple, eyes closed as if…as if he was at peace.

Maybe he finally was. She'd never understood the reason he drank so heavily, why his moods changed erratically, and she'd blamed herself. He missed her mother… He hadn't wanted a child… He didn't know how to raise a daughter, especially alone… She'd been a bad kid.

On a more rational level, as an adult, she realized he'd battled inner demons that she knew nothing about; that alcoholism was a disease. But his behavior and his rejection had hurt.

Tears pricked at her eyes, and she ached with a sudden longing to go back in time. To a time when she was little, and he'd carried her fishing at the pond. He'd surprised her that day by packing a picnic and taking her on a canoe ride. For a couple of hours she'd felt like she had a real family. He'd taught her how to cast a fishing rod and laughed when she'd been squeamish over baiting her own hook with worms.

Yet that precious memory had been ruined when he'd pulled out a bottle of whiskey, consumed most of it and passed out in the sun. She'd fished alone and played at the edge of the water and pretended everything was okay. She'd gotten good at pretending.

But then night set in and the wilderness had seemed vast and lonely and…creepy. She'd been terrified as darkness encroached and the howl of coyotes had echoed around her. She'd shaken him to wake him up so they could go home, but he'd been belligerent, cursed her then backhanded her for crying.

He'd also been so inebriated that he'd woven all over the road and nearly crashed into another car head-on. He'd blamed that on her, as well.

She shivered. When they'd finally made it home, she ran into her bedroom, locked the door and hid there all night and half of the next day, too afraid to come out and face his wrath.

Honey straightened, banishing the memory to the attic of her mind with the other troubling ones that she'd packed away. No use dwelling on them. You had to play with the cards you'd been dealt.

She'd accepted her father for what he was long ago, but a sliver of hope had remained that one day he might change and she'd have the loving, caring father she'd always wanted.

Now any chance of that was lost forever.

Resigned and swallowing back tears, she placed her hand against his cheek. His skin felt leathery, rough, cold in death. She had an insane urge to kiss his cheek, but refrained.

Instead she whispered, "Goodbye, Daddy," and left the room, shutting out this image and the pain as the door closed behind her.

HARRISON CONTEMPLATED HIS conversation with the ME. If they identified Granger's killer, he could solve this case quickly. Then Honey could leave and take her tempting, pretty little butt with her.

Harrison phoned the crime scene investigator and spoke

with the lead CSI, Roger Watkins. "Did you find any forensics at the bluff where Waylon Granger's body was discovered?"

"Nothing on the ledge. No definitive footprints, either. We did collect a button. Looks like it came from a flannel shirt. Not Granger's and no print on it."

"Hell, it could have been there no telling how long."

But he had to revisit the crime scene. If Granger had been hit by a rock, the perp could have tossed it far enough away so CSI hadn't found it. That rock could be key evidence.

The door opened and Honey appeared. Harrison's gut tightened at the strain on her face.

"I should be finished with the autopsy by tomorrow, then I'll contact the crematorium," Dr. Weinberger said.

"Thanks." Honey folded her arms around her waist. "I'll be at my father's house for a couple of days. I'm going to see what needs to be done to get it on the market." She lifted her gaze to Harrison, a world of old hurts flashing in her big eyes, then directed her comment to the ME. "Harrison—the sheriff—has my number if you need me."

Dr. Weinberger gave a quick nod. "Yes, ma'am."

"I'll walk you out, Honey," Harrison said as she started toward the door.

She stiffened as he fell into step beside her, and they walked down the hall and rode the elevator in silence. Even though the heat was stifling, Harrison welcomed the fresh air as they stepped outside. Honey's shoulders relaxed, too.

He followed her to a white minivan emblazoned with a graphic of a house and a company name, Honey's Home Makeovers.

"You own your own business?" Harrison asked.

The anger on Honey's face dissipated slightly and a small smile titled her lips. "Yes. Don't sound so surprised."

Her defensive tone made him feel like a heel. "I didn't mean it like that." He shifted on the balls of his feet, hoping she'd elaborate but she didn't.

The familiar wary expression returned. "You said my

father was pushed over that ledge. Do you have any idea who did it?"

Her gaze met his, the past once again creating an impenetrable barrier between them.

"I'm investigating." He jammed his hands in his pockets.

She studied him for a moment, her lips pressed into a thin line. He wanted to see that smile again, and found himself wondering if she had someone special in her life, someone she graced with that smile all the time.

If she did, the guy was a lucky man.

She hit the key fob to unlock her van, and he closed his fingers around the handle to open the door. His arm brushed hers, and she startled, then stepped away from him as if he'd burned her.

"Sorry," he murmured.

She shrugged as if she realized she'd overreacted. Then she slid into the driver's seat.

He caught the door with his hand before she could close it. "Did you and your father stay in touch?"

She heaved a breath, filled with wary resignation, then shook her head. "No, I haven't spoken to him in years. Why? You don't think I had something to do with his death?"

He should consider that theory, but no, it hadn't occurred to him. "No," he said honestly.

"Good," she said sharply. "Because I have a life in Austin, Harrison. I have my own business and love what I do. When I left here, I left everything behind. That included my father." She clenched the steering wheel with a white-knuckle grip. "No matter how much I despised him, there's no way I would have jeopardized my career to get back at him, especially now." A sad expression washed over her face. "He wasn't worth it."

She started the engine, pressed the gas and sped from the parking lot.

Harrison stood for a moment, absorbing her statement.

Sad that she didn't feel more grief toward the old man. But then again, Granger didn't deserve it.

He glanced toward the mountain. Remembering that the murder weapon was most likely a rock, he walked to his SUV, climbed in and drove to Dead Man's Bluff. He parked, then scanned the area, tormented by the memory of that fateful night Chrissy went missing. The fact that her body hadn't been found should have given him hope that she was alive, but...he knew the odds.

Was her disappearance somehow tied to Waylon Granger's murder? He didn't see how it could be.

But he had to know.

He pulled on latex gloves and climbed from his SUV. The sun beat down on him as he combed the parking area and weeds beside it. He searched the overgrown bushes flanking the old mine, and the weeds jutting up by the swimming hole.

Nothing.

Of course the killer could have tossed the rock into the swimming hole and it could be under water. The wind whistled from the cave, that ghostly sound that stirred the rumors surrounding the place, and he retrieved his flashlight from the truck.

Determined to explore all possible avenues before diving into the swimming hole, he crept inside the entrance to the mine. It was dark as hell inside, cold, and smelled of wet moss, dirt and decay. The scent of urine was almost overpowering, suggesting that curiosity seekers not only ventured inside but used it as a bathroom, too.

Ignoring the stench, he raked the flashlight along the wall and searched the floor. The opening was clear. Cigarette butts, beer bottles and evidence of discarded drug paraphernalia.

He picked up a stick and raked away some of the trash then made his way to the corner where he found an old sleeping bag, two empty tin cans that had held beans and a metal coffee mug. Had someone been living inside?

He shone the light along the wall and spotted a small cluster of rocks in a circular pattern. Burned sticks lay in a pile of ashes in the middle.

His light illuminated the corner of the pile, and he noticed a rock shoved into the debris. He stooped down and raked away the ashes with a stick.

It definitely was a rock, a sharp, jagged one. He peered closer. Something red stained the side of the stone.

He pulled the rock from the pile and examined it. It was almost as large as his hand and could have been used as a weapon.

He sniffed the red substance. It was sticky and held a metallic odor—definitely blood.

Granger's? He'd have it tested.

Pulse jumping, he carried it from the cave, bagged it and stowed it in his truck. If there were prints on it, he might be able to nail the killer.

His gut tightened with dread.

He hadn't yet told his family about Granger's death. It was time he did.

He glanced at the rock on the seat of his truck with trepidation. He just hoped he didn't find one of their prints on that rock.

HONEY PASSED THE sheriff's office as she drove through Tumbleweed. She couldn't believe Harrison Hawk was sheriff. She'd expected him to leave this small town for something bigger and better. Harrison was smart, had been popular, had girls swooning over him.

His bad-boy sexy, flirty ways had been appealing. But after his sister disappeared, he'd become angry, moody and sullen.

His close-knit family had fallen apart.

Several mothers and their children played in the park at the edge of town where they'd added splash pads for the kids to cool off in the summer heat. Her heart squeezed as a little girl in pigtails with pink ribbons flying in the wind ran toward her mother and threw her arms around her.

Ribbons... Chrissy had loved ribbons in her hair and had collected a box of assorted colors.

Honey turned down the side street that led to Lower Tumbleweed, the street where her father lived. Technically the area was named Lower Tumbleweed because it sat in the lower valley. Although the name held another connotation, implying the families who lived there were lower-class. The families on the street were poor—the children received free lunches and free dental care, and they lived off food stamps.

Taunts from other kids about Lower Tumbleweed echoed in her head.

God, how she'd hated the cruel comments. Had hated that the kids at school knew so much about her. Worse, that the gossip about her mother being a tramp and her father a drunk were true.

At least her best friend at the time, Cora Zimmerman, had a mother who worked hard for a living. Not that Cora hadn't gotten teased, too, but at least her mother's job at the hair salon had been reputable.

She hadn't thought about Cora in a long time and wondered where she was now.

The street sign for her father's road had been run over and lay on the ground. Tire tracks marred the faded green metal. She knew the turn, though, and made it, her throat filling with disgust when she spotted the dilapidated, run-down houses and yards.

The houses had been small and worn eighteen years ago. Weather and lack of care had sent them downhill. Porches were sagging, boards rotting, paint peeling off, concrete driveways cracking, shutters dangling askew.

Weeds and dead bushes choked the yards, and debris from a recent storm littered what had once been grass. Most of the houses were vacant now, and a couple were boarded up as if they'd been condemned.

Her father's sat like an eyesore at the end of the street. The once-white wood had yellowed, and her father had substituted a lone brick to replace the broken steps to the porch. She sighed as she parked, and ran a hand through her hair.

She bought houses like this and completely renovated them, turning them into showcases. For a brief second an image of gorgeous little bungalows filled her vision. She could make this neighborhood into something to be proud of.

But every house needed to be gutted.

Sweat beaded on her neck as she climbed from the van.

No. She would not think about renovating the neighborhood. She didn't intend to stay here a minute longer than necessary. And she sure as hell didn't care if someone bulldozed every house on the street.

Tomorrow she'd talk to the local real estate agent and see if any investors were interested in the properties.

But tonight she had to stay here.

The thought sent dread through her. How was she going to sleep in this nasty place? It had been bad enough as a child before she'd known better.

She should have booked a room at the local inn, but she hadn't wanted to announce her arrival or come face-to-face with anyone else from her past.

Squaring her shoulders, she decided to check out the inside first. If it was unlivable, she'd try the inn.

Weeds clawed at her legs as she walked up to the porch. She climbed the makeshift brick step, then dodged holes in the floor as she crossed to the door. She jiggled it and it opened easily, then she stepped inside.

Nausea flooded her as her childhood rushed back. Images of her parents fighting hit her, along with the strong odor of cigarettes and booze.

It was a gut job. The threadbare sofa and chair her father had had when she lived here was falling apart. Cigarette ashes and empty liquor bottles testified to the fact that he hadn't changed his ways.

The kitchen was outdated, the cabinets sad looking, the Formica kitchen table and counters greasy and splattered with food stains.

Anger at her father for letting the place reach such disrepair railed inside her. She'd seen worse on jobs, but this had once been her home, albeit a dysfunctional one, but at least it hadn't been filthy. Because she had cleaned it.

She passed the kitchen, then stopped in the hallway in front of her father's bedroom. The faded chenille spread remained, stained and dotted with cigarette burns. The metal bed was rusty, the curtains dingy, her father's work boots and clothes piled on a chair in the corner.

She forced herself to go into her old room. He hadn't changed the pink-and-white-gingham bedspread or curtains. Her teddy bear and dolls still sat on the shelf on the wall. She spotted the jewelry box she'd gotten for Christmas the year before her mother left, picked it up and sank onto the bed.

The springs creaked beneath her weight. Her mother had loved costume jewelry and had given Honey some of her pieces when she'd grown tired of them. Honey had called them her treasures and had played dress up in them, pretending to be glamorous.

A bitter chuckle rumbled from her chest.

She'd never been glamorous. Instead her attempts at dressing up her homely clothes as a teenager had only made her look cheap. No wonder Harrison's mother hadn't wanted Chrissy around her.

Unable to resist, she opened the jewelry box to see what was left of the costume jewelry.

Instead her heart leaped.

On top of the pop beads and clunky gold-and-rhinestone pieces lay a yellow ribbon.

Nausea churned in her stomach.

Chrissy had been wearing yellow ribbons the night she'd disappeared.

Chapter Four

Honey draped the shiny bright yellow satin across her hand. An image of Chrissy's pigtails, tied with yellow ribbons, flashed behind her eyes.

Little Chrissy singing, "You are my sunshine, my only sunshine," as she skipped across the yard.

One day it would be yellow ribbons, the next day purple or red or blue.

Sometimes she wore ribbons of different colors and called them her rainbow hair.

She had been such a happy kid, all smiles and singing and curiosity. She had sneaked over to Honey's one day and asked Honey to show her how to wear makeup. Honey had thought it was sweet. Since the little girl only had brothers, she'd figured Chrissy needed a female in her life to teach her girl things.

In spite of Chrissy's pleas for layers of blush, eye shadow and lipstick, Honey had brushed her cheeks with a light powder, applied a pale pink gloss on her lips, then a very faint dusting of sparkly white eye shadow. Chrissy had thought she was beautiful.

But Chrissy's mother had stormed over to Honey's that night and ordered her to stay away from Chrissy. Mrs. Hawk finished by saying she didn't intend to allow Honey to make Chrissy look like a tramp.

Tears blurred Honey's eyes. She'd realized then that the gossip about her mother and father extended to her, and that she would never fit into the same social circle as people like Harrison Hawk and his family.

She'd also made up her mind to leave town as soon as she was old enough to get a job.

And she had.

She blinked to clear her vision and the memory. The yellow ribbon mocked her with questions, though.

How had it gotten in Honey's jewelry box?

If Chrissy was wearing this ribbon the night she disappeared, that meant whoever had killed her must have taken it. Which made it even more curious as to how it had gotten in her own jewelry box.

Rumors had spread that Chrissy had come to see Honey the night she went missing, and that Honey's father had done something to her. Honey had hated her father, but she didn't think he would have hurt Chrissy.

But this ribbon… What if her father *had* done something to Chrissy?

If so, why would he have kept the ribbon?

She'd never seen it before, and she'd used her jewelry box plenty of times after Chrissy went missing.

Maybe her father had hidden it, then after Honey moved out, he stashed it in the jewelry box, thinking that if anyone searched the premises and found it, they'd think it belonged to Honey.

Her hand trembled, the ribbon dangling between her fingers. If her father or Chrissy's abductor/killer had taken this ribbon, their fingerprints might be on it.

And she'd just contaminated it with her own.

Indecision warred in her mind. What should she do? She'd spent her childhood hiding her family's dirty little secrets. She could just stuff the ribbon back in the jewelry box and no one would ever know about it.

If she showed it to Harrison, he and everyone in town would assume, even believe, that her father was guilty of… murdering Chrissy.

Her stomach roiled. But could she keep quiet?

The Hawk family had been tormented for years, wondering what had happened to their little girl. They'd probably imagined a hundred different awful scenarios.

Although Mrs. Hawk hadn't liked Honey, Honey still had compassion for the woman and her family.

This ribbon might help them find the truth.

They deserved to have closure, didn't they?

HARRISON DREADED THE conversation with his family. Their dinners were meant to keep the family close, although Chrissy's disappearance had thrown a permanent kink in their relationships.

No dinner, holiday or amount of alcohol could smooth over the awkward tension between the brothers and their mother.

Still, he had to tell his family about Granger's death. Warn them that even if he didn't ask questions, others would.

Warn them that even though they might not have liked the man, it was Harrison's job to investigate his murder.

His phone buzzed just as he climbed inside his SUV. He checked the number. Honey Granger.

What did she want? Answers about her father's death?

Or maybe news about his body and what to do next?

The phone buzzed again, and he pressed Connect. "Sheriff Hawk."

Breathing rattled over the line. "Hello?"

"Harrison, it's me. Honey."

Her voice sounded shaky. Uncertain.

"Yes?"

"I…have to show you something. I don't know what it means or if it means anything, but, well, can you come out to my house? I mean, my father's house."

Harrison gritted his teeth. He had to deal with her, find her father's killer. But seeing her was difficult. It resurrected memories he'd tried to forget. And another kind of guilt—he should have stood up for Honey when his mother had judged her.

"Can you come?" Honey asked again.

"I'll be right there." Harrison's pulse clamored as he started the engine and drove toward the Granger's house. He phoned his deputy and asked him to do rounds around town.

Harrison had to be at his mother's house for dinner and drop the bombshell about Granger before she and his brothers heard the news from the local grapevine.

In a small town like Tumbleweed, word spread as quickly as butter melting on hot Texas pavement.

Night shadows hovered along the streets as he drove, the gray sky dark and desolate as he veered onto the road to Lower Tumbleweed. The yards were overgrown with weeds, the houses deserted, dilapidated and in need of repairs.

The neighborhood certainly didn't look welcoming or inviting to an outsider. The place probably held bad memories for Honey. An image of Honey, thin and wearing hand-me-downs two sizes too big for her, haunted him. She'd looked tiny and lost and lonely. She'd also been smart enough to understand the whispers and stares from the other kids.

No wonder she'd left town and never looked back.

He winced at the rotting porch with the brick for a makeshift step, then parked in the drive behind her van. Admiration for her for owning her own business mushroomed inside him. He didn't know how she'd done it, but he was proud of her for overcoming the obstacles her family had put in front of her. She'd made a success of herself in spite of adversity, an admirable accomplishment in his book.

He glanced around the unkempt yard and at the peeling paint on the weathered house and wondered what Honey planned to do with the place. Sell it as it was or fix it up then sell? Judging from the lack of curb appeal and rundown condition of the homes, the comps would be low.

Curiosity over Honey's call nagged at him as he walked up to the front door. He raised his fist and knocked. A second later, she opened the door. Anxiety and some other emotion he couldn't quite define streaked her face.

Alarm bells clanged in his head. "Honey, is everything all right?"

She shook her head. "I don't know, Harrison. I...honestly don't know."

He forced his expression to remain professional. "Let me come in and then you can explain."

She chewed on her bottom lip, then stepped aside and motioned for him to enter. He scanned the living area. A mess. Granger had let everything go. Judging from the number of empty liquor and beer bottles, drinking had been his priority just as it had been when Honey lived here.

When she reached the sofa, she picked up what looked like a child's jewelry box, and ran her fingers over the rosewood design.

"What's wrong?" he asked quietly.

She took a deep breath, then gestured toward the jewelry box. "This... I was looking through things after I got home, trying to sort out my father's stuff and what was left of mine. I have to decide what to do with it all."

He nodded. "And?"

Misery darkened her eyes. "I found this." She pushed the jewelry box into his hands.

He narrowed his eyes, confused.

"Open it," she said tightly.

An uneasy feeling rolled through him. Whatever she'd found had upset her.

"Go ahead," she said. "I'm not sure what it means, but I had to show it to you."

He frowned, but slowly lifted the lid to the jewelry box. A slip of bright yellow caught his eyes.

A yellow ribbon. Just like the one his sister was wearing the night she disappeared.

"It was hers, wasn't it?" Honey asked in a choked voice.

He lifted his gaze to meet hers. The turmoil in her eyes mirrored how he felt at the moment. "It looks like Chrissy's. My brother said she was wearing yellow ones the night she disappeared."

"I know." Honey bit down on her lower lip.

"Did she come to your house that night?" Harrison asked.

Honey's hand trembled as she rubbed her temple. "If she did, I didn't see her," she said in a raw whisper.

"Don't lie to me, Honey. I know you wouldn't have hurt Chrissy, but if you know something about your father..."

Tension escalated between them. "I don't. And if I did, I'd tell you. I want to know what happened to Chrissy, too."

The agony in her voice tore at him.

Of course the questions over Chrissy's disappearance had ripped her life inside and out, too.

"You really want the truth?" he asked gruffly.

She nodded. "We all deserve closure," she said softly.

That was one thing they agreed on.

"I'm sorry, but my fingerprints are on the ribbon," she said. "I wasn't thinking at first. But I'm sure you want to analyze it. If my dad's are there..."

Then that would mean that her father had touched the ribbon. That he'd either found it or taken it after he'd killed her.

He'd send it to the lab ASAP.

Two scenarios entered Harrison's mind. The first—Granger killed Chrissy and hid her body at the bluff. Then he'd returned to visit her.

But where had he hidden her? And why revisit her body now after all these years?

And if he had, who had killed him? Someone who'd discovered what he'd done?

Scenario two—Granger had been at the bluff and either stumbled on Chrissy's body or he stumbled on the killer, and the killer murdered him to keep him quiet.

HONEY COULD BARELY look at Harrison.

"Thank you for calling me, Honey," he said quietly. "I appreciate your honesty."

Honesty?

More guilt bombarded her. She hadn't mentioned that she'd been at the bluff that night, too. That if she'd been home, she'd know if Chrissy had come by. And she'd know if her father had done something to Chrissy or if he'd been passed out all evening.

His jaw tightened. "What if I find out that your father killed Chrissy?"

Honey sucked in a sharp breath. She and her father hadn't been close, but shame engulfed her. "Then we'll know."

The darkness in his eyes, a darkness filled with anger and pain, was a reminder that he and his family blamed her for his sister's disappearance.

If her father had killed Chrissy, he had a right to blame her.

Harrison shrugged. "The search parties never found anything belonging to my sister. Not her backpack or the pink jacket she was wearing or any clothing."

Honey thought back to the gossip after that night. "Some people thought that was a good sign. They thought she ran away and—"

"She didn't run away," Harrison said. "Chrissy may have argued with me and my brothers but she was afraid of the dark and wouldn't have gone out that night if Brayden hadn't convinced her to sneak out." He swallowed hard. "She was also attached to a stuffed doll that she won at a rodeo with my parents. She couldn't sleep without that rag doll." He paused, pain riddling his face. "If she was going to run away, she would have taken the doll."

Now that he mentioned it, Honey remembered the rag doll with the big blue painted eyes and red braided pigtails.

Honey had envied that doll because Chrissy had something Honey didn't—the innocence of childhood, which allowed her to play with dolls like a normal little girl.

Only Chrissy had lost her innocence—and maybe her life—that night.

"If you find any of those things, let me know."

"Of course," Honey said.

"Do you mind if I search the house?" Harrison asked.

Honey stiffened. "Go ahead. I'm not hiding anything."

His stormy gaze met hers, then he carried the ribbon to his SUV and returned with a flashlight.

Honey's phone buzzed just as he stepped back inside. Her business partner, Jared.

She couldn't stand to watch Harrison comb through her father's house and her own personal childhood belongings, so she stepped outside to answer the phone.

"I have to take this," she said as he started to search her father's dresser drawers. She said a prayer he wouldn't find anything else belonging to Chrissy as she rushed outside to the front porch.

"How are things?" Jared asked.

"Not good." Honey bowed her head and fought the panic setting in.

"What happened?"

She hadn't shared her past with Jared, and she didn't want to now. "I just don't like being in my father's house."

He murmured that he understood. "When will you be back?"

A heaviness weighed on her. She'd felt trapped here as a teenager. She felt trapped now.

She couldn't leave until she had answers, until she knew who'd murdered her father.

Until she knew if he was a killer.

Chapter Five

An hour later Harrison met Honey on the porch. "I'd like to come back during the day and look around the property."

Honey paled. "You think my father killed Chrissy and buried her here?"

Harrison shrugged. "I don't know what to think, Honey. But considering you found one of her ribbons, it's possible."

Honey clenched her hands together. She couldn't argue that point. "All right. Just let me know what time."

"I will." He studied her for another moment. He wanted to comfort her, but he had to do his job and it involved investigating her father. That was reality.

Just as reality meant that he had to talk to his family. Tonight.

For both their sakes, he hoped her father hadn't buried Chrissy on the Grangers' property.

He climbed into his SUV and cranked up the air as he drove toward the county lab. He dropped the ribbon off with instructions to send the results to his office ASAP.

Dark had set in as he drove through the entrance to Hawk's Landing. His father had first been drawn to the land because of the birds of prey that flocked to the south end. He claimed it was a sign that this land was meant to belong to him and that he was meant to build a family ranch on the property. He had insisted they keep a section as a natural habitat and sanctuary for the birds.

When he was a kid and needed time alone, Harrison used to ride his horse out to the corner of the property and watch the hawks soar. After Chrissy's disappearance, he'd found himself out there a lot.

His father had a huge wooden sign carved with the emblem of a hawk and had hung it over the gate to the ranch as a reminder of the birds.

Harrison checked his watch as he parked in the drive to his mother's Georgian home. He was half an hour late. His mother wouldn't be happy.

He wasn't happy, either.

Memories of playing on the property drifted back—fishing in the creek out back with his brothers, building the tree house with his father, playing horseshoes and baseball in the backyard.

So long ago.

All those fun times had ended abruptly when Chrissy disappeared. The house hadn't felt like a home but a tomb. The quiet had resounded with fear and grief. His mother had become a zombie. His father, angry all the time.

He'd shut down and his brothers had each retreated into their own rooms, silent and worried and alone.

Their vehicles were here now, though. When their father left, they'd formed an unspoken bond, knowing it was their job to take care of their mother. It hadn't been easy, but they'd survived.

Surviving was a long way from being whole, though.

Flowers filled the beds in front of the house, the roses climbing the trellis on the side a reminder that his mother loved gardening. It had become her therapy and filled her time.

He walked up the stone path to the door, his nerves on edge as he buzzed the doorbell. He didn't bother to wait for his mother to answer, though. He pushed open the door, slipped inside and removed his Stetson.

Voices sounded from the dining room, and he crossed the foyer, passed the living room and stepped into the dining room.

Lucas, Dexter and Brayden had gathered at the highboy, each with a drink in hand. Lucas had joined the FBI,

Dexter had opened his own detective agency and Brayden was a lawyer.

He might need their help on the case. Maybe he could explain before he talked to their mother.

She bustled in a second later, her arms laden with food, and gave him a pointed look. "It's about time you got here."

"I'm sorry," he said, "it's been a busy day."

She set a plate of roast on the table, then mashed potatoes and gravy, and wiped her hands on her apron. "I guess it has. I heard you found Waylon Granger dead at the bluff."

Surprise made him stiffen. He glanced at his brothers but they looked at him stoically.

"Where did you hear that?" he asked.

"It doesn't matter," his mother said. "I'm just glad that man is dead."

THE QUESTIONS AND worry needling Honey made her feel restless and on edge. She stared at her father's house with a knot in her stomach.

Even exhausted, there was no way she could sleep right now.

She dug into the cabinet, grabbed some garbage bags and dived into cleaning out the closets. She started in her room and made two piles—one for trash and the other for donations to the local church.

There were very few toys, except for a few stuffed animals and a couple of dolls, so she dusted them off and placed them in the donation bag. The clothes she'd worn as a teenager were plain but someone might be able to use the jeans and flannel shirts. Everything else was either ragged or so frayed that she put them in the trash.

She stripped the gingham bedspread and sheets, then the ratty curtains, and stuffed them into the donation bag. Washed, they could be reused. But if she did anything with this house, she would gut it and stage it with new things to make it look more appealing.

When her room was bare, she moved to her father's room and did the same. His clothing was old and worn and reeked of smoke. Unable to salvage anything, she shoved everything into trash bags. Work boots, overalls, jeans, socks, underwear, shirts, belts—she didn't bother to even look at them. No one would want the outdated, threadbare items.

The faded chenille bedspread was marked with cigarette burns and stains, as were his sheets. She rolled the items up and added them to the trash.

She collected all the soda cans, liquor bottles and other trash and carried it to the garbage can outside. The refrigerator reeked of soured milk and several containers of molded food. She cleaned everything out, including the condiments, which had probably been in the fridge for ages.

Thankfully she found a bottle of cleaner beneath the sink so she wiped out the refrigerator and counters, then scrubbed the Formica table.

The small bathroom came next. Shaving cream, used soap and other toiletries went into the trash, along with the nasty shower curtain. If she sold the place, the bathroom would be gutted, too.

But if she was going to stay here until her father's murder was settled, she had to make the place livable. Even though the bathroom tiles and flooring were outdated, she scrubbed the toilet, sink, tub and walls until they smelled like cleaner.

Her shoulders and muscles ached as she piled the donation bags into her van. She pushed the garbage can to the curb for pickup, then piled the other trash bags beside it.

Tired but needing to get rid of the donation bags, she grabbed her purse and drove to town. She dropped the bags off first, then stopped by the discount store and stocked up on more cleaning supplies, a cheap shower curtain, sheets and a pillow for her bed. She added some scented candles to help alleviate the smoky smell, picked up a case of bottled water, coffee, cereal and milk for breakfast, then headed to the café for dinner.

An older couple had owned it when she lived here, but now it was named Cora's Café so it had changed owners. Did her former friend Cora own it now?

She was surprised to see that the place had been renovated. It still sported a Western theme, but the oak tables looked new, as did the sky blue curtains. Bar stools jutted up to a counter for extra seating, and country music echoed through the room, a backdrop to the chatter and laughter. A chalkboard showcased a handwritten menu with the specials for the day.

Customers filled the booths and tables, evidenced by the number of cars outside. The scent of fried chicken and apple pie made her stomach growl.

A woman about her age with auburn hair in a pixie cut greeted her. "Honey, I heard you were back in town. I'm sorry about your father."

She smiled, grateful to see her old friend "Hi, Cora. I was thinking about you today. So you own the café now?"

Cora handed her a menu. "I bought it a couple of years ago and did a makeover. Guess cooking for the family all those years paid off."

"It looks good."

"Thanks." Cora blushed, and Honey smiled, grateful she seemed happy.

She noticed a booth to the far right and started toward it. Suddenly the room grew quiet, though, and an uneasy feeling prickled her spine.

She glanced around and noted several people looking at her.

She'd forgotten what it was like to live in a small town. Everyone knew everyone else. When a stranger visited, everyone knew that, too.

She offered them a tentative smile, but memories of being the hub of gossip made her want to run.

HARRISON GRITTED HIS teeth at the questioning looks from his brothers and his mother. Maybe he should have called and given them a heads-up.

"You didn't think to tell us before everyone in town knew?" Dexter asked.

Harrison took a deep breath before he responded. "I came here as soon as I could. I don't know how word leaked. It shouldn't have."

"Well, it did." His mother pushed her bangs off her forehead with a smile. The fact that the hair found at the crime scene was short and brown didn't escape him. His mother's hair was short and brown.

Lucas lifted his drink glass in a gesture of offering. "Fix you one and then we'll toast."

"What are we toasting?" Harrison asked gruffly.

"That Waylon Granger is dead," his mother said. "Tumbleweed is better off without him."

Harrison's patience was wearing thin. It had been a long damn day. "How can you say that, Mother? Granger was a crappy father, but we don't have proof he did anything else." Honey's face flashed in his mind. *She* didn't deserve any of this.

His mother patted his shoulder. "You always were the diplomat, Harrison. But we know, at least *I* know, that that damned man hurt our Chrissy."

Harrison glanced at his brothers to see if they were in agreement. Lucas sipped his drink, his expression neutral. Dexter slipped an arm around their mother as if to offer support. Brayden poured himself another drink, then fixed Harrison one and offered it to him.

Harrison took it, struggling to think of a way to defuse the situation. And how to subtly ask his family when they'd last seen Granger.

He sipped the whiskey, grateful for the warmth sliding down his throat. "Do any of you have evidence to prove that Granger did something to our sister?"

"Not yet," Lucas said.

Dexter cleared his throat. "I talked to Waylon's neighbors but no one remembered seeing Chrissy that night. They couldn't say he was at home all night, either."

"When did you talk to them?" Harrison asked.

"As soon as I got my PI license. But three of the families who lived in that neighborhood had already moved."

Brayden's look turned dark. "Have you found anything to incriminate him?"

Harrison bit his tongue. He didn't want to reveal what he'd found or learned; not yet. People would convict Granger—and he wanted the truth, not a vigilante situation.

But his family deserved answers.

"Let's sit down and eat before dinner gets cold." His mother ushered them to their usual chairs and for a few minutes, the discussion was put on hold as they served themselves from the platters of roast beef, potatoes and gravy and green beans.

Although Harrison wanted to gulp down his whiskey, he forced himself to eat instead. He still had work to do.

"How did Granger die?" Dexter asked as he forked up a bite of roast.

Harrison studied his family, searching for any sign that one of them already knew the truth. Emotions strained everyone's faces, as if just mentioning Granger's name stirred up the horrid memories of the night Chrissy disappeared.

His mother had been near hysterical when she and his father arrived home from their party and discovered Brayden and Chrissy weren't home.

Harrison had felt sick to his stomach—it was his fault they'd sneaked out. His fault they'd been at the bluff because they'd followed him.

Brayden had raced in on his bike with his ankle swollen, ready to fuss at Chrissy for not sending help, then realized she hadn't made it back to their house. Fear had ignited tempers, and a lot of screaming and yelling had ensued.

His parents had frantically called Chrissy's best friends but both of them had been home in bed and hadn't seen or talked to Chrissy.

His mother dropped her fork with a clatter. "What aren't you telling us, Harrison?"

His brothers stopped chewing and stared at him as if they, too, realized there was more to the story. Damn.

Harrison took another swig of his whiskey. "Granger didn't die of natural causes."

"What?" His mother gasped.

His brothers gave him questioning looks. "What's going on?" Dexter asked.

Harrison swallowed hard. "He was murdered."

His mother clamped her teeth over her bottom lip, then lifted her glass of wine. "Well, he got what he deserved."

Harrison agreed with her. But he still had to find out who killed the man. A silent prayer formed on his lips that his family had nothing to do with it.

HONEY SLIPPED INTO a booth, hoping to avoid attention. A teenager wearing tattered jeans and a denim shirt appeared, an order pad in her hands. Black square glasses framed a thin, pale face. A sadness radiated from the girl as if she had problems bigger than a teenager should.

Honey felt a kinship with her. At fifteen she'd worked at the Dairy Barn to make money so she could leave town. Did this girl have problems like she'd had? Did she have any family who cared about her?

Had Cora hired her because she wanted to help?

"What can I get you?"

Her name tag read Sonya. "A turkey sandwich and a bowl of that vegetable soup."

"Sure. What do you want to drink?"

Wine would be nice but the diner didn't serve it. "Just water. Oh, and a cup of coffee. Decaf, please." She didn't need caffeine to keep her awake tonight. It would be hard enough to sleep in her father's house anyway.

The girl nodded then made her way to the counter and dropped off Honey's order. She returned a minute later with the coffee and water.

Honey stirred sugar into her mug then sipped it, her gaze scanning the room. Two older couples sat having coffee and pie while a group of teens chowed on burgers and fries at a table near the door.

Three gray-haired women were huddled around a table beside her sipping tea.

"Did you hear that Waylon Granger died at the bluff?" the curly-haired woman with glasses said.

The other two women's faces expressed surprise.

The thin lady in a blue knit pantsuit leaned over the table, eyes wide. "Really?"

The curly-haired woman clinked her spoon on her teacup. "He sure did. My grandson was up there and found him. Waylon fell over that ridge."

The third lady clacked her teeth. "Wonder what he was doing up there?"

"Probably drunk," the thin lady said.

"He was always drunk," the curly-haired one whispered. "Such a sorry excuse for a man."

The third lady pushed her pie plate away, the pie half-eaten. "You know the Hawks always thought he killed their little girl, Chrissy?"

Honey averted her face so she didn't have to look at the women, but their voices reached her anyway.

"I heard that, too," the curly-haired one said. "He did have a temper."

"He sure did. I always felt sorry for that girl of his. No wonder she left town."

"I thought she left because she was pregnant."

"Could have been."

Honey sank down in the booth, hoping no one recognized her.

"I figured the Hawks ran her off," the woman continued. "I heard Ava saying that Granger's girl was white trash."

"If you ask me, Ava shouldn't have been pointing a finger."

"What do you mean?"

"Well, the night their little girl went missing, the Hawks were at a party for the mayor." She paused dramatically. "Steven accused Ava of having an affair."

The other women gasped. "What?"

"No."

"They were talking about Chrissy, too. Made me think that she wasn't Steven's baby."

"What did Ava say?"

"I don't know. They left in a huff."

Honey tensed. She despised gossip because she'd borne the brunt of it.

But what if the Hawks' marriage hadn't been perfect like everyone thought? What if Ava Hawk had had an affair?

What if Chrissy wasn't Steven Hawk's child?

Chapter Six

Honey's head reeled. Harrison's father had left the family and town a few months after the investigation into Chrissy's disappearance went cold.

Rumors surfaced then that he had something to do with his daughter's disappearance. Others whispered that he'd left because the tragedy of losing his daughter had broken his heart.

She drummed her fingers on the table. Now she wondered—had he left because his wife had cheated on him?

The waitress appeared with her soup and sandwich, and Honey thanked her, then dug in. She hadn't realized she was so hungry but hadn't eaten since breakfast and was starved.

The women stood, gathering their purses and hats, and Honey sank lower in the booth, angling her face away from them in case they recognized her. The woman in the blue knit pantsuit paused and peered at her, but Honey looked down at her phone to avoid eye contact.

The bell on the door tinkled as it opened and they left, then a tall woman with sharp features entered, a big guy with an awkward gait beside her holding her hand. One of his eyes looked blurry, his mouth twitched and he made an odd, high-pitched sound.

"Let's sit in that booth, Elden," the woman said.

Honey straightened. Elden?

She'd known him. Elden Lynch was three years older than she was and mentally challenged. She'd felt sorry for him because the kids at school made fun of him. Worse, some of the parents had been afraid of him and had warned their children away from him. Not that he was mean or violent.

In fact, he was sweet and childlike and just wanted to make friends.

He shuffled past, rocking his head back and forth. It was him, the boy she'd known.

Honey was tempted to say something, but his mother glared at her.

Mrs. Lynch ushered him into a chair. "Stay put, Elden."

The big woman stepped over to Honey's booth. "I heard you were back in town."

Honey tensed at the vehemence in her tone.

"I don't know if you're staying around here," Mrs. Lynch continued, "but if you are, keep away from my son. He doesn't need any trouble."

"I'm not here to cause trouble," Honey said, her voice firm. "I—"

"Then get your sorry daddy buried and leave town," Mrs. Lynch barked. "Tumbleweed is better off without any of you Grangers."

Hurt and anger bled through Honey. She wanted to defend her father and herself.

But an image of that yellow ribbon taunted her, and she kept her mouth shut.

When word about that surfaced, people would definitely condemn her father.

It shouldn't bother her. He had been a sorry drunk.

Elden's mother didn't have to worry about her staying. She'd leave as soon as possible.

"MOTHER," HARRISON SAID, measuring his words carefully, "I wouldn't go around telling everyone how glad you are that Waylon Granger is dead."

She gave him a sharp look. "Why not? I am glad he's dead."

"He was murdered," Harrison said, hoping to drive home his point. "That means there has to be an investigation."

Brayden's lawyer instincts quickly kicked in. "He's warning you not to incriminate yourself, Mother."

She finished her wine then set the glass on the table with an eyebrow raise. "And you're the sheriff so you're going to find out who killed him?"

Harrison nodded. "That's the way it works."

"How was he murdered?" Dexter asked.

Harrison wiped his mouth with his napkin. "I don't have an official statement from the ME, but it appears he was struck on the back of the head with a rock, then pushed over the edge of the ridge."

Other than his mother's eyes widening slightly, she showed no reaction.

"You find any forensics?" Lucas asked.

Harrison maintained a neutral expression. "I found a rock that might be the one that struck him. It's at the lab now, being tested."

"Anything else?" Brayden asked.

"CSI found a button in the bushes and a short brown hair that was caught on Granger."

"The teenagers still go up there," his mother said, ignoring the comment about the brown hair. "That button could be one of theirs."

Harrison narrowed his eyes. Was his mother trying to cover for herself? "True. But it was close to the ledge, so we'll test it for prints."

She tore a roll in half and buttered it.

"Mother, where were you last night?"

Brayden laid his hand over their mother's. "You don't have to answer that."

"Are you asking as my son or as the sheriff?" his mother said quietly.

Emotions clogged Harrison's throat at the hurt in his

mother's voice. Her screams the night Chrissy went missing echoed in his head, resurrecting guilt and anguish.

How could he interrogate his own mother after what he'd put her through?

She squeezed Brayden's hand. "It's all right, Brayden. Actually I don't mind answering. I was home all night."

Brayden's eyes went dark. "Was anyone here with you, Mother? Anyone who can corroborate your story?"

She stiffened. "It's not a story, it's the truth. And no one was here. I had one of my migraines so I took a pill and went to bed early."

"How about phone calls?" Harrison asked.

She sighed. "Like I said, I took a pill and went to bed early. If the phone rang, I didn't hear it."

Harrison raked a hand through his hair. Dammit, he wanted her to have a rock-solid alibi.

"I'm not the only one who disliked Waylon Granger," his mother said.

"But no one else had a motive to kill him," Harrison pointed out.

"Harrison," Lucas cut in, his voice hard. "You're not accusing Mom of murder, are you?"

Harrison folded his arms. "No, but it's my job to ask questions and find out the truth."

"The truth is that the town is better off without that low-life in it," his mother said curtly.

"We have no proof that he hurt anyone," Harrison said, testing the waters to see if one of his family members mentioned the ribbon.

"He hurt his own daughter," Dexter said. "Everyone in Tumbleweed knew that but no one did anything to help her."

Dexter was right. *Someone* should have stepped in and protected Honey.

"That girl wasn't worth saving," his mother said. "She was white trash just like her mama."

"She was only a kid." A trace of bitterness laced his voice. "She never did anything wrong."

"My God, you're defending her." His mother gave him a lethal look. "She probably lied about that night, Harrison. Chrissy always tried to sneak over and see that girl. I bet she did that night but Honey lied to protect her old man."

Harrison tossed his napkin on the table. "You were always unfair to her, Mother. And for your information, Honey hasn't held anything back. She hasn't defended her father or pointed the finger at anyone over his death." In fact, she'd given Harrison the ribbon she'd found at her father's house.

But he refused to share that information. His mother would convict Granger and Honey without any further questions.

His mother's hand slapped the table. "Oh, my God, she's back, isn't she?"

Harrison heaved a breath. "Yes, I had to inform her of her father's death."

"So you've seen her?" his mother asked, her disappointment palpable.

"Yes," Harrison said through gritted teeth. "At the morgue."

His mother frowned. "She's not going to stay around, is she?"

"I doubt it," Harrison said. Why would she want to? The people in Tumbleweed had been brutal to her. "But she has to bury her father."

"The next time you see her, make her tell you what he did with Chrissy," his mother said.

Disgust ate at Harrison. He'd felt sorry for his mother after Chrissy went missing and had blamed himself. He'd wanted to see her happy again.

But he didn't like her much at the moment.

He shoved away from the table. "Thanks for dinner, but I have to go."

"Ask her," his mother yelled as he stalked from the room. "Make her tell you, Harrison!"

He slammed the front door as he left. The sound of his mother's harsh, accusatory voice reverberated in his head, though, as he made it to his SUV.

THAT SAME SICK feeling she'd had years ago twisted Honey's stomach. She hadn't lived in Tumbleweed in nearly two decades, but Mrs. Lynch still remembered her and hated her.

Just because she'd been born on the wrong side of the tracks.

The young waitress stepped up to the Lynches' table. "Hey, Elden," the girl said sweetly. "How are you?"

Mrs. Lynch pulled her son closer to her as she glared at the waitress. "He's fine. Just take our order and leave us alone."

"Of course," the waitress said with a pained look. "What would you like?"

Elden made that odd sound again, then his mother ordered for both of them and the waitress disappeared.

Honey had little tolerance for bullies and judgmental people who discriminated against those different than themselves, whether it was race, ethnicity, gender, disabilities or social status.

Agitated, she finished her meal and paid the bill.

No use making a scene and drawing more attention to herself. She didn't intend to stay in this Podunk place and fight a battle she'd lost years ago.

She doubled the waitress's tip, then hurried outside to her van. The hair on the back of her neck prickled as she climbed in the driver's side. Was someone watching her?

She scanned the parking lot. Several teens were hanging out around a black pickup. Two older men huddled near the back door, heads bent, smoke curling from their cigarettes. A motor rumbled from somewhere in the parking lot. A horn honked. Directly across from her, a dark sedan with tinted windows was parked. Its lights flickered on, nearly blinding her.

Anxious to leave, she started the van, her pulse pounding when she pulled onto the road. The dark sedan followed. She wove through town, making several turns, hoping to lose the car, but it stayed behind her.

Heart drumming, she sped up and drove toward the sheriff's office. She slowed as she approached it. The sedan was still behind her.

Nerves on edge, she jerked her vehicle into the parking lot in front of the sheriff's office.

The sedan slowed and coasted by her. She tried to see the driver inside, but it was too dark outside and his windows were practically black.

The car finally went on, and she leaned her head into her hands and inhaled several deep breaths. She checked the parking lot for Harrison's police SUV. If he was inside, she'd tell him about the car.

But what could he do now? The sedan had already gone. And what if the driver hadn't been following her?

Why would anyone follow her anyway? No one but Harrison knew she was in town; well, except for Mrs. Lynch and the people who'd seen her at the café. But why would one of them want to scare her?

Shaking her head at herself for being paranoid, she pulled back onto the road and drove to Lower Tumbleweed. Her shoulders and muscles ached from fatigue and the stress of the day as she parked at her father's house.

The streetlights in the neighborhood had long ago burned out, casting an eerie darkness to the houses and overgrown properties.

Tomorrow she'd talk to her father's lawyer and finish cleaning out this place. Hell, if she had to, she could hire a crew to come in and empty it out.

So far, there was nothing she'd found inside that she wanted to keep.

Just as she climbed from the van and headed up the walkway to the porch, car lights flickered. She glanced back at the road, her pulse spiking.

That dark sedan was driving by her house.

Her hand trembled as she shoved the key into the lock. She fumbled with it, dropped the keys then picked them up. The sedan slowed, almost pausing in front of the house as if the driver was stalking her.

She jammed the key into the lock, twisted it and shoved the door open. The telephone inside was ringing as she fell into the foyer and slammed the door closed. She twisted the lock frantically and looked out the window. The sedan was still there.

The phone trilled again.

Nerves rattled, she darted to the table for her phone. Maybe it was Harrison calling to check on her. Praying it was so, she clenched the handset.

"Hello," she said shakily.

Heavy breathing rattled over the line.

She ran to the window and looked outside, the phone still in her hand.

More breathing.

Anger rallied inside her, blending with fear. "Who is this?"

Another heavy breath. Then a low, throaty voice. "Get out of Tumbleweed or you'll end up like your father."

Chapter Seven

"Harrison, wait up!"

Harrison paused by his car. He'd had to leave or he would have lost his temper with his mother.

Footsteps crunched gravel, the air charged as Lucas and Dexter joined him.

Harrison braced himself for a confrontation. "I know Mom's upset—"

"Brayden is trying to calm her down," Dexter said.

"Good. She may need a lawyer." He prayed it didn't come to that, but his cop instincts screamed that it might.

Lucas stared at him head-on. He was the same height as Harrison and they had similar builds. But even as the younger brother, Lucas could be intimidating. "What aren't you telling us?" Lucas asked.

"Yeah, spill it, brother," Dexter added. "We might be able to help."

Harrison clenched his jaw. That was true. Lucas was FBI and Dexter, a PI. "I told you all I know."

"Come on," Dexter said. "You're not talking to Mom. It's us."

"Yeah, we have as much interest in Granger as you do," Lucas said.

He doubted that. "I'm the one who was supposed to babysit that night," Harrison said gruffly. "It was my fault we lost our sister, and it's my job to find out what happened to her."

Dexter cursed. "Your fault? Hell, it was mine. I got mad at Chrissy that night because she kept following me around and I told her to get lost." His voice cracked. "Then she did."

Harrison studied Dexter with new eyes. He hadn't realized Dexter harbored guilt as he did.

"It's not either of your faults," Lucas said. "But it might be mine."

Harrison and Dexter both frowned at Lucas. "What are you talking about?" Harrison asked.

Lucas looked tortured as he glanced back at their childhood home. "I should have said something a long time ago."

Dexter cleared his throat. "About what?"

Lucas heaved a weary breath. "I was a jerk to Chrissy back then. You remember Geoffrey Williams?"

"He was that cool kid whose family had all that money, wasn't he?" Dexter said.

"He's on the town council now," Harrison said.

Lucas nodded. "He was the captain of the baseball team. I thought if I sucked up to him, he'd tell the coach to let me be assistant captain."

"What does this have to do with Chrissy?" Harrison asked.

Lucas rubbed the back of his neck. "Chrissy wanted to tag along with us to the fields, but Geoffrey didn't want a kid around. He told her to leave us alone, then he pushed her down. I…just stood there. I didn't do anything to defend her."

"You all were just kids," Dexter said.

Lucas shrugged. "Maybe. But later I realized how mean Geoffrey was. I saw him push some other little girl around, too. He was a bully. It made me wonder if he might have done something to Chrissy."

Harrison considered the information. "Was Geoffrey at the bluff that night?"

Lucas nodded. "Yes, I ran into him while we were out searching for Chrissy."

"Did you see him with Chrissy?" Dexter asked.

Lucas shook his head. "No. But he had dirt on his jacket. He said he skidded on the hill by the cave but…later, I wondered if he might have seen Chrissy. He could have shoved her again and she could have fallen over the edge or maybe he saw her in the cave…"

Harrison had no idea that Lucas blamed himself all these years or that he'd had his own theory about what happened to Chrissy.

"Why didn't you tell someone about this back then?" Dexter said.

Guilt and anguish darkened Lucas's eyes.

"Because you still wanted him to name you assistant captain," Harrison finished.

Lucas nodded. "I should have spoken up, said something."

Harrison and Dexter exchanged worried looks. "You're right. I can use the help. Talk to Williams."

Lucas shifted. "All right, I will."

"What can I do?" Dexter asked.

"Track down and question all of the kids who were at the bluff that night. Maybe someone lied or remembers something and is ready to talk."

Harrison's cell phone buzzed at his hip. He jerked it up and checked the caller ID. Honey Granger.

Aware his brothers were watching and listening, he answered the way he did on a business call. "Sheriff Hawk."

"Harrison, it's Honey." Her voice warbled. "Someone just called and threatened me."

Harrison tensed. "Are you all right?"

"Yes," Honey said. "But I'm scared."

Harrison cursed. "I'll be right there."

HONEY'S HAND TREMBLED as she ended the call. She rushed back to the window and peeked out. The sedan screeched away, disappearing into the night and leaving her with the eerie sensation that the threatening call had come from whoever was in that car.

She tried to read the license plate, but it was too dark.

Nerves raw, she clenched her phone and ran through the house to make sure no one was inside.

The rooms looked disheveled from her cleaning rampage, but nothing appeared to be missing and no one was inside.

Satisfied an intruder wasn't hiding in the house, she hurried back to the living room to wait for Harrison. Too antsy to sit or relax, she yanked another trash bag from the box and filled it with old magazines to take to recycling.

Several minutes later the sound of a motor rumbling startled her, and she rushed to the window. Harrison.

Relief filled her, and she opened the door and met him on the porch.

Harrison's dark gaze raked over her, concern in his eyes. "Are you all right?"

She nodded although tears pricked her eyes. She'd told herself she had to be strong and not lean on anyone, but she couldn't help herself. She threw herself against him and dropped her head forward, her breathing erratic.

He felt so big and strong, solid as a rock. A comfort in the wake of the night's unsettling events.

For a brief second his body tensed, muscles bunching, his breath puffing against her hair. But then he wrapped his arms around her and stroked her back.

"It's going to be okay, Honey," he murmured. "I'll make things right."

She leaned into him and closed her eyes. She wanted to believe him, but no one could change the past or make people think differently of her.

As soon as he murmured the promise, Harrison regretted it. Remembering his mother's reaction to Granger's death stirred fear that she had something to do with his murder.

But why would she have killed him now, after all the time that had passed?

Had she learned something incriminating against him then confronted him?

Honey's fingers dug into his chest, and he held her tighter, hating the fact that someone had frightened her.

Worse, what if his mother had called her to scare her off? She'd made no bones about the fact that she disliked Honey and didn't want her in Tumbleweed.

He rubbed Honey's back, his fingers brushing the long, silky strands of her golden hair. She felt small and fragile and so damn feminine that Harrison's body hardened in response.

He closed his eyes, hoping to rein in his libido. But she shifted against him, her belly brushed his sex and heat rippled through him.

His sex pulsed, thick and aching, and need hit him hard.

Dammit. It had been a long time since a woman had aroused him like this.

And Honey Granger was the last woman on earth he wanted to feel this way about. But she was vulnerable and had been hurt by his family and this town, and protective instincts surged through him.

Just as his brother felt bad for not standing up for Chrissy, he regretted not defending Honey years ago.

He wasn't an impressionable kid anymore. He would stand up for her this time if she needed it.

HE SLOWLY PULLED back until their bodies were no longer touching. He had to before he did something insane like kiss her or slide his hand lower to feel the curve of her breast or even lower to her hip.

He moved his hands to her arms and held her facing him. "Tell me exactly what happened."

She pushed a strand of hair from her face and blinked, then seemed to compose herself. "I dropped some of Dad's old clothes at the church, then stopped at the café to get something to eat." She hesitated as if debating what to say.

"Go on," Harrison said.

"I saw a guy there, Elden Lynch, who I remembered from childhood."

"I know Elden," Harrison said. "He was mentally disabled from birth, but he's harmless."

"I know. I was friendly to him when we were kids, but tonight his mother told me to leave him alone."

Harrison clenched his jaw again. "Mrs. Lynch is not always nice. She's very protective of her son."

Honey shrugged. "I guess I can't blame her. He was bullied terribly when he was young."

"People still stare at him and whisper behind his back," Harrison said grimly.

"Some things never change," Honey said.

Harrison nodded, although he didn't like it. "What happened next?"

Honey rubbed her arms in a nervous gesture. "I saw a dark sedan in the parking lot and it followed me."

"Did you see the driver?"

"No, it was dark and the windows were tinted."

That figured.

"I pulled up to your office to see if I could lose him and he went on," Honey continued. "But when I got home, the same car showed up in the street. I ran inside and locked the door, and it stopped in front of the house. That's when my phone rang."

"You think the person in the car was the caller?"

Honey nodded. "I don't know, maybe."

"What exactly did the caller say?"

"He said, 'Get out of Tumbleweed or you'll end up like your father.'"

Harrison sucked in a breath. "The voice was male?"

Honey's brow furrowed. "I'm not sure. It was low, muffled. It could have been a woman."

They were getting nowhere. "Did he—or she—say anything else?"

Honey shook her head. "I asked who it was, but the phone went dead."

"Did the call come in on your cell phone?"

"No, the landline in the house."

So the caller phoned Granger's house. "That could be good news. He or she doesn't have your cell phone."

"But whoever it is knows I'm staying here."

"True." And he didn't like that one little bit. "I'll stay here tonight to make sure you're safe," Harrison said.

Panic flashed in Honey's eyes. "No, I couldn't ask you to do that."

Harrison patted his badge. "I'm the sheriff, Honey. It's my job to protect the citizens and anyone visiting Tumbleweed."

"I am just visiting," Honey said.

"I figured as much."

"Although maybe I should leave town," Honey said. "I could hire someone to clear out the rest of my father's house."

"You could." For some reason, he didn't want Honey to leave. Not yet.

Honey straightened, lifting her chin. "No, I'm not going to let anyone run me off. Not ever again."

"Like you did when you were eighteen?"

Honey's gaze met his, emotions brimming in her beautiful eyes. Eyes that had seen pain and heartache. Eyes that flared with a determination that he admired.

"I want to know the truth about who killed my father and if he hurt Chrissy."

So did he. But they might not like the answers they found.

Still, he'd become sheriff to find justice for Chrissy. And nothing would stop him.

Chapter Eight

Harrison didn't like the fact that someone had threatened Honey. Granted, the call could be a prank or a meaningless threat, but her father had just been murdered and she was staying in the man's house.

Maybe whoever killed him was afraid Honey would find something inside the house or on the property.

"Thank you for offering to stay," Honey said. "But I'll be fine, Harrison. I'm accustomed to staying alone."

Did that mean she wasn't involved with anyone?

"I don't feel good about leaving you," Harrison admitted.

Honey lifted her chin. "Don't worry. I have protection."

He arched a brow. "You have a gun?"

She nodded. "I carry it when I look at properties. Sometimes I go into bad areas, and there've been a few times when someone was squatting inside one of the abandoned houses I was looking at to purchase."

Harrison crossed his arms. "So you know how to use the gun?"

"Yes." A look of defiance streaked her eyes. "I've been on my own since I left Tumbleweed."

He'd wondered about that. "You didn't go to live with other family?"

"I have no other family," Honey said.

Curiosity ate at Harrison. She had only been eighteen, a kid when she'd left. "How did you survive?"

Honey averted her eyes as if to avoid eye contact. "It's not important, Harrison. What's important is that I can take care of myself."

Only she'd been terrified and shaking earlier.

She didn't like being vulnerable, though; that was obvious. And she didn't want to need him or his help.

But she did need it.

"All right, but call me if you receive another threat or if that sedan shows up. I'll have my deputy check around to see if anyone in town drives a car like that."

She nodded and stepped back toward the door. "Thanks for coming out."

"That's my job," Harrison said, although even if he wasn't sheriff and he thought she was in danger, he would have driven over. No woman should have to be afraid in her own house.

"Right."

Her curt tone made him tense and reminded him that she and his family had been on opposite sides for years. That Honey had reason to dislike him and the Hawks.

"I'll be back in the morning with a warrant to search the property."

His comment brought pain back to her eyes, but also resignation.

He moved onto the brick step, scanning the yard and sides for trouble as he strode to his SUV. When he climbed inside, he glanced back at the shabby house and saw Honey at the window, watching him.

The idea of her alone at eighteen made his stomach knot. The idea of someone threatening her and possibly following through made that knot tighten even more.

She closed the blinds, and he pictured her undressing, slipping into pajamas and retrieving her gun to sleep with.

The image aroused him and stirred admiration for her independence.

It also made him want to go inside, crawl into bed and tell her she didn't need a gun, that he would take care of her.

Shaken by that thought, he started the engine. He phoned his deputy and asked him to check the databases to see if anyone in town owned a dark sedan. As he expected, a dozen or more popped up.

Geoffrey Williams was one. But, hell, so were the mayor and Cora Zimmerman and the local preacher.

Still, he spent the next hour driving from Honey's house to town and back, searching for the sedan.

No one would hurt Honey, not as long as he was sheriff.

HONEY LAY AWAKE for hours in her childhood bed, torn by memories of growing up.

As a child, she always locked her bedroom door.

Tonight she left it ajar so she could hear if an intruder broke in.

The day took its toll, though, and she finally fell into an exhausted sleep. Dreams of hiding in the closet when her father was in a drunken rage mixed with nightmares of showing up at school in mismatched, raggedy clothes and running from the mean girls who'd laughed at her and called her names.

She wanted to join in and had inched up to the circle of girls at the edge of the bleachers. But one of them spotted her and started laughing.

"Go away," one of the girls yelled. "We don't want you around."

She turned and ran. They chased her onto the football field where she fell face-first in a mud puddle. She pushed herself up, face and clothes covered in mud, and tried to stand, but she slipped and hit the wet ground again.

When she looked up through tear-soaked eyes, the football team was laughing. Harrison was standing at the edge of the field, stone-faced and disapproving as if she'd interrupted their game.

She scrambled up and ran from the field toward the woods. She wanted to get lost. Never go back again.

But where would she go? She was underage, would have

to live on the streets. Her house was dangerous, but she wasn't stupid.

The streets would be worse.

Still she ran into the woods. At least she could hide there until school was out. Then she'd run home and clean up the mud.

She tripped over a tree stump and hit the ground. Weeds clawed at her hands and she tasted dirt.

A NOISE SUDDENLY jarred her awake. Honey clenched the sheets and sat up to search the room. Cool air brushed her cheek, and she jerked her head to the side. The window was busted.

Moonlight shone in, illuminating a rock on the floor.

Another loud sound, glass shattering. She slid from bed, grabbed her robe and pulled it on, then slid her gun from the nightstand. Gripping it with both hands, she tiptoed to the bedroom door and looked around the living room and kitchen.

She didn't see anyone, but she went still and listened. The floor creaked. The wind whistled. The sheers in the living room billowed out as the wind blew through the shattered window.

Was someone inside?

Tense seconds dragged by. More glass breaking. The second window in the living room. Then another crash—the window in the kitchen.

The rock hit the floor, glass spraying.

She startled and bit back a gasp.

Someone was throwing rocks at her house. Why? To scare her off?

She inched toward the window and peered out but she didn't see anyone. The sound came again, this time from her father's room, then her room.

Someone was breaking all the windows. Was it the person who'd threatened her earlier?

She inched back toward the bedroom and grabbed her phone. She hated to call Harrison a second time in one night, but she was scared.

What if this was the same person who'd killed her father?

Another noise made her jerk her head toward the back door. She held her breath, straining to hear as she crept through the hall. Another loud noise. The rock hitting the door.

Heart racing, she punched Harrison's number.

HARRISON HAD JUST dozed off when the phone jarred him awake. He snatched it on the second ring.

"Harrison, it's Honey. I'm sorry to bother you but someone is throwing rocks through my windows."

What the hell? His feet hit the floor and he was dressed in seconds. "Lock the door and stay inside. I'll be right there."

He flipped his siren on as he got in his SUV, senses alert as he sped toward Lower Tumbleweed. The road was deserted, most houses dark, the citizens of Tumbleweed safely tucked in for the night.

Except for Honey.

Who the hell would throw rocks at her house this time of the night—or morning?

Dawn streaked the sky, the morning sun struggling to peek through the dark clouds. Dust blurred the horizon as the wind swept it from the abandoned farm. Desperate for rain, the grass was turning brown and the crops were hurting from thirst.

Deciding he didn't want to alert the culprit at Honey's with his siren, he flipped it off and slowed, cruising slowly down the street and searching for signs of trouble. The houses neighboring Honey's father's house were vacant, the run-down properties desolate and forgotten.

He should have stayed here tonight as he'd suggested to Honey.

What if she was hurt?

Images of her bloody and unconscious flashed behind his eyes. Then an image of her lying dead like her father.

If whoever had killed her father thought something in the house might incriminate him, he might try to frighten her off with a warning—or come after her.

He scanned both sides of the road and the woods backing up to the houses, but didn't see a car or a person. But the houses on both sides of Honey's had shattered windows, the panes broken out.

He cut his lights and veered into the Grangers' driveway. The lights in the den were on. The blinds slid open and Honey peered at him. Relief flooded her face.

He paused to listen for sounds of the culprit, but the whistling of the wind rattling the leaves on the trees was the only sound in the night.

He motioned to Honey that he was going to check the property, and she gave a nod. He pulled his flashlight from his pocket and shone it to the right of the house in search of the perp. Nothing but trees and a cat that darted from behind the neighboring house.

He flicked it across the front of the house. Both front windows were shattered. Turning in a wide arc, he scanned the ground for footprints. The grass looked marred, flattened in places from foot impressions.

But the rocks and dirt blended with the grass and he couldn't determine a definitive print. A partial near the sidewalk indicated the foot had been large, but he couldn't discern if the shoe was a sneaker or boot.

Damn.

He walked around the side of the house, searching the ground for more footprints or something the perp might have dropped. The side window had also been shattered. When he reached the back door, he spotted indentations in the wood from the impact of the rock. More than once. Wood had splintered to the point that the rotting board had a hole in it.

Anger surged through Harrison.

Honey hadn't done anything to deserve this.

He strode toward the woods, grass, leaves and brush crunching beneath his boots. A twig snapped. The sound of a coyote howled in the distance.

He spotted movement in the woods and shone his flashlight in the direction where he'd seen it. Seconds dragged by as he searched. Finally another movement deep in the woods.

An animal or the predator who'd terrorized Honey?

It was too damn far away to tell.

He glanced back at the house, tempted to give chase, but what if he was wrong and the movement was a damn deer and he left Honey alone and vulnerable?

Cursing again, he continued walking the back of the property, then veered left to the other side of the house. Another window shattered, this one in the laundry room.

No wonder Honey had been frightened. She'd been attacked from all sides. Had there been more than one perpetrator?

He shone the light toward the land connecting to the Grangers' place. The house was deserted and falling in. Rotting boards sagged on the exterior. The windows had also been shattered.

Irritated and worried about Honey, he conducted one more sweep of the property, circling the house. He stepped onto the makeshift step then jumped onto the porch.

Honey opened the door before he could even knock.

He swept his gaze over her, needing to know that she was okay. Safe. Unhurt.

"I'm sorry I called," she said, "but I thought if it was the person who killed my father…or Chrissy, you'd want to know."

Harrison ground his teeth. "You don't have to apologize, Honey. You did the right thing."

She bit down on her bottom lip and hugged her arms around herself, then nodded. She looked shaken and exhausted.

Harrison forgot that he shouldn't touch her or get involved or that they might be on the opposite sides of this case when it was over. Or that his mother would have a fit if he knew he actually cared about Honey Granger.

And he was starting to care for her.

That thought made his gut pinch with fear, but he ignored it and pulled her against him. "Are you okay?" he asked in a gruff voice.

Honey leaned her head against his chest, her breathing erratic. "Yes," she said so softly that he barely heard her.

But the courage in that voice and in the way she'd responded to everything that had gone wrong in her life aroused his admiration again. In his mind, he saw her as that skinny, frail, lonely little girl who was cast aside by her mother and classmates.

Saw her father raising his hand to her as he imagined he'd done a dozen or more times.

Saw her running from the football field that day she'd fallen in the mud.

He'd done nothing then.

He would make up for it now.

Guilt, need and fierce protective instincts surged through him, and he lifted her chin with his thumb and searched her face.

"You aren't hurt?"

She shook her head. "There's glass everywhere inside, but I'm fine."

Except she wasn't fine and they both knew it.

"I'm going to find out who did this," Harrison said. "I won't let anyone hurt you, Honey."

She started to say something but he stopped her. "Shh."

He pressed his finger to her lips to quiet her. "I mean it. People in this town haven't been nice to you and it's not right. I should have stood up for you a long time ago, when we were kids."

A blush stained her face and she averted her eyes as if bad memories had assaulted her.

"I'm sorry, I didn't mean to remind you of the past."

"I can't ever forget the past," Honey said. "Not until we figure out if my father killed your sister."

The mention of his sister twisted his insides, but he knew now without a shadow of a doubt that Honey had suffered because of Chrissy's disappearance. That she had cared about his sister and would never have covered up for her father if she'd known that he hurt her.

Their gazes locked. Tension escalated. Emotions and desires flamed between them.

She shivered and Harrison realized he'd wanted to soothe and protect and touch her ever since he'd seen her at the morgue.

No longer able to resist, he stroked her cheek with the back of his thumb, then lowered his head and kissed her.

Chapter Nine

Honey had wanted to kiss Harrison ever since she was sixteen.

His body felt hard and strong, his mouth hungry and eager but so gentle that tears pooled behind her eyelids.

She blinked them away and leaned into him. His hands stroked her back a second before he pulled her closer against him. She clutched his arms, suddenly dizzy, her world turning upside down as if she'd been swept up in a windstorm.

He deepened the kiss, his lips moving over hers. Her heart raced as he plunged his tongue deep inside her mouth.

Desire, need and hunger bolted through her, and she lost herself in the moment. She couldn't remember when she'd been kissed like this or when she'd even wanted to be kissed like this.

But Harrison's kiss made her feel alive. Her blood seemed hotter, her body achy, and need pulsed through her.

He lowered his hands, slid them over her hips and pulled her tighter. So tight she felt his hard length press against her belly.

But her common sense kicked in, whispering to her.

She couldn't—shouldn't—be kissing Harrison Hawk. He was the sheriff, for God's sake. He was trying to hang her father for murder.

His mother hated her.

And she hated Tumbleweed. She'd be leaving as soon as possible. Her life was in Austin.

The wind whistled around her, clearing her head, and she pulled away from Harrison. He gripped her waist, but she took a step back.

"Stop, Harrison, we can't do this."

His breath puffed out, erratic and unsteady. "I'm sorry. That was...out of line."

"Yes, it was," she said, regretting the words when he winced as if she'd slapped him. But she didn't apologize. It was better this way.

"I'm here to cremate my father and get rid of his house," she said, reminding them both that romance—or a one-night stand—didn't fit with her plans. Or his.

"I know," he said, his voice rough with what she assumed was regret. "It won't happen again."

"No, it won't," Honey said. "I'm not the person everyone made me out to be in high school. I don't sleep around." She wiped her sweaty palms on her robe, well aware that her nipples had tightened to hard buds beneath her gown. Had he felt it?

"I didn't—"

"Let's just drop it," she said, willing herself not to reach for him again. She felt safe in his arms. Safe and wanted and void of the shame and ridicule of the town.

Harrison Hawk was strong and protective and honest and handsome—everything she'd ever wanted in a man.

Everything she couldn't have, especially considering their pasts.

"I called you because someone was outside," she said, desperately trying to steer them back on track.

He shuffled, rubbed his chin and glanced toward the window. "I looked around but no one was out there. Did you see who it was?"

Honey shook her head. "It was too dark. And I was afraid to get too close to the window for fear of getting hit."

"That was smart," Harrison said.

Or cowardly, Honey thought.

"Some of the other houses out here have been vandalized," Harrison said. "Both houses next door had windows shattered, too. So it's possible that this was just some teenagers."

Honey nodded, although in light of the fact that her father was murdered and she'd already received one threat, it seemed too coincidental.

"You really believe that?" Honey asked.

Harrison shrugged. "I said it's possible. I'll collect the rocks and send them to the lab for analysis. If it's kids, we'll probably find prints."

"Thanks, Harrison."

He nodded, then hurried to his car and returned a minute later with a crime scene kit.

Honey went inside and started a pot of coffee. There was no way she could go back to sleep now. Not after being awakened by whoever had been out there.

And not when her body was still tingling from Harrison's kiss.

HARRISON CURSED HIMSELF for kissing Honey.

Just because he was drawn to her didn't mean she was attracted to him. For God's sake, he was supposed to be doing his job, not acting on impulses driven by his libido.

Honey had every reason to despise him and his family. They had treated her unfairly. And now here he was, getting warrants to search her property to find evidence to prove that her father was a murderer.

Even though Honey acted tough, labeling her father as a killer would hurt her.

He had to keep his distance. Besides, he did not push himself on any woman who didn't want him.

And Honey had made it clear she didn't.

Setting his jaw firmly, he phoned his deputy and asked him to pick up the search warrants for the Grangers' land, then strode up the step to the porch.

Dawn streaked the sky, the morning light illuminating the bleak condition of the house. The scent of strong coffee brewing and pine cleaner hit him as he entered. He scanned the living room area. It looked as if Honey had emptied shelves and cleaned, but shards of broken glass were scattered across the floor from the rock's impact. He took pictures of the windows, floor and glass shards.

Then he yanked on rubber gloves, opened his kit and removed evidence bags. He picked the first rock up and placed it in the bag, then put the second one in another bag.

Anger rolled through him at the sight of more glass in the laundry room and Granger's room. Glass was also scattered across the bed where Honey had been sleeping.

He knotted his hands into fists. Even if this was teenage vandals, they could have hurt Honey.

Furious, he photographed the damage.

By the time he finished, Honey was sipping coffee in the kitchen. She looked pensive as she gazed through the back window at the woods.

"My deputy should be here soon with the warrants."

Honey turned toward him, her slender face pale. But that spunky determination he'd seen in her eyes before, glimmered again, stronger than ever.

"Would you like some coffee?"

He did, but considering the tension between them, he didn't want to linger or be too friendly. "I'll pass."

She pushed a mug toward him. "Don't be silly, Harrison. I woke you up. The least I can do is give you coffee."

He accepted the mug with a muttered thanks, but didn't make eye contact. The more he looked at her, the more he wanted this mess to go away so he could kiss her again.

But she didn't want that.

So he took the mug outside with him and walked the property, searching for a clue to lead him to the person who'd terrified Honey tonight.

HONEY HAD TO distract herself from Harrison so she quickly changed into jeans and a T-shirt, then vigorously swept and cleaned up the glass. Her bed was more difficult so she stripped the bedding, rolled it up and took it outside to shake out the glass before putting it in the wash.

His deputy arrived a few minutes later, and Harrison introduced them. Mitchell Bronson was tall, dark and handsome.

But he didn't stir feelings inside her like Harrison did.

He shook her hand, his friendly smile putting her at ease. "Sorry about your trouble, ma'am. The sheriff and I will do everything we can to find out who did this."

"Thank you."

"We're going to search the property now," Harrison said.

Honey's heart thumped.

Harrison descended the step from the porch, followed by the deputy. She watched them comb the area in front of the house, then they moved to the left side.

Honey shoveled up more glass from the back hallway, praying he didn't find Chrissy.

For the past few years, she'd tried to forget everything about this town and this house and her father, but now she struggled to recall details about Chrissy.

How many times had she stopped by? One. Two. Maybe three?

The night she disappeared, Chrissy had sneaked out with her brother Brayden and followed Harrison to the bluff. Someone there said Chrissy left and came to Honey's.

But Honey didn't see Chrissy that night at her house because she'd also sneaked out to the bluff and hidden like a voyeur at the edge of the woods, watching the party. Watching Harrison.

Although she'd never told anyone that.

She'd felt lonely and too scared to join in because she'd known she didn't belong.

Just as she didn't belong now.

What if Chrissy had come to her house while she was

gone and her father had been so drunk he'd taken his anger out on Chrissy?

If she'd stayed home that night, she could have protected Chrissy.

HARRISON AND HIS deputy searched every corner of the woods, looked near tree stumps, checked uneven patches of ground in case Granger had buried her, and examined the yard and crawl space.

"She's not here," Deputy Bronson said.

Harrison heaved a sigh of relief. As much as he wanted to find Chrissy, he'd harbored hope that somehow she'd survived. Although that thought was terrifying in itself. Kidnap victims who were found after years of captivity often suffered from trauma, amnesia or Stockholm syndrome.

"Sheriff, you okay?"

His deputy's voice jarred him from his thoughts. "Yeah."

His phone buzzed, and he checked the number. The lab. "Let me get this, then we'll tell Honey that we're leaving."

"Honey?"

"Miss Granger," he said, realizing the way he'd said her name sounded personal. Harrison punched Connect and Bronson headed to his car while he walked toward the house. "Sheriff Hawk."

"It's Regan Willis from the lab. I have results on that ribbon you dropped off."

"Yeah?"

"The hair caught in the ribbon definitely matched your sister's, Harrison."

He sucked in a breath, grateful that the former sheriff had kept Chrissy's hairbrush so they could compare it for a match.

"There's more. I found traces of a chemical that is only found in the caves at the bluff."

"I know she was there," he said.

Which meant Granger had either been at the caves that

night and possibly killed Chrissy there, or she'd come to the Grangers' house and he'd killed her, then took her to another spot to bury her.

Or she could have come to the Grangers' house, lost the ribbon outside, then a stranger had picked her up and Granger later found the ribbon.

Dammit, he was grasping.

"What about the button?" Harrison asked.

"Some DNA but it doesn't match anyone in the system." She paused. "But I can tell you that it belonged to a female."

Hell, it could have been another teenage girl up at the bluff. Or…his mother…

No, his mother wouldn't have gone to the bluff. Unless she went looking for Chrissy after she'd learned Chrissy was missing.

He explained about the attack on Honey's house. "I'll drop the rocks off for you to analyze. But I'm heading to the bluff first to check those caves."

"Good luck, Sheriff. Let me know if I can do anything else."

He thanked her and hung up. By the time he reached Honey's house, she was coming outside.

"Did you find anything?" she asked.

He shook his head. "I'm going to the bluff to search the caves." He gestured toward the windows. "I'll come back later and board up the windows for you."

"I can take care of that myself," Honey said. "I need to go into town to meet the director of the crematorium anyway, so I'll pick up supplies."

He remembered the look of fear in her eyes when he'd first arrived. "I don't think whoever did this will come back during the day. But let me know if you need me."

Honey's withering look indicated that was the last thing she intended to do.

Resigned, he strode to his SUV and drove to the bluff.

The sooner he found answers, the sooner Honey could leave and return to Austin.

Did she have someone special waiting for her there?

He grunted and parked at the bluff, then climbed out to meet his deputy. It didn't matter if she did.

Nothing could happen between them.

"Where do we start?" Deputy Bronson asked.

Harrison noted a few kids hanging out at the swimming hole. Although it was only midday, the heat had already climbed, the sun blazing. Technically this area was a crime scene. He should shut it down to the students and others who liked to hike the trails into the mountain.

But they'd need serious manpower to keep people away.

If Chrissy was killed here, they'd also have to weed through eighteen years of locals and strangers on the grounds and in the caves. A near-impossible task.

In spite of the sunlight, the caves were dark inside, so he grabbed his flashlight. Bronson did the same and they started at the mouth of the cave.

"What are we looking for?" Bronson asked.

Harrison explained about the ribbon, and that he'd found the rock/murder weapon used on Granger. "We never found my sister's backpack or jacket or anything of hers," he said. "So keep an eye out for any clothing or items that may have belonged to a child."

"You know the teens like to camp out here," Bronson said. "And there are a couple of homeless men who use it for shelter in the winter."

"I know," Harrison said. "I found the rock used to kill Granger. Not sure if the other stuff belonged to the killer or if the killer just hid the murder weapon here." Harrison gestured to the section of burned wood, a water canteen, discarded blanket and cigarette stubs. "Bag all that stuff and send it to the lab."

Together they sorted through the stuff and bagged it, then Bronson took it to his car and locked it inside.

Back inside the tunnel, they parted, veering in different directions. The caves had once been mined and consisted of a maze of underground tunnels that spanned about three miles.

The air felt hot and stale, the scent of urine and a dead animal permeating the space. He shone his light along the walls, searching the corners and dirt. Cigarette stubs, discarded water bottles and a few liquor bottles and beer cans had been left throughout. He filled a trash bag with the items, then veered into the last area, a room at the end of the tunnel, which had once been mined.

He raked his flashlight across the wooden stakes marking areas where the workers had dug. Something shimmered beneath the beam of his flashlight. A streak of yellow.

His breath froze in his lungs.

Yellow. Another ribbon.

Fear seized him, and he stalked forward, knelt and zeroed in on the tip of the yellow.

It was a ribbon. Just like Chrissy's.

Only part of it was buried in the dirt.

Emotions flooded him and for a moment, he couldn't breathe. Couldn't move.

Had someone killed Chrissy and buried her here in this cave?

Chapter Ten

Harrison raked dirt away from where the strip of yellow poked through.

His lungs squeezed for air. After all this time, was he going to find Chrissy's body beneath the dirt and rocks?

It looked as if there had been a rockslide inside the cave in this area, so he moved several stones aside and tugged the ribbon free.

It definitely matched the one he'd found at Honey's.

Sweat beaded his neck, and he studied the rock pile. He had to dig deeper.

Nerves raw, he strode back through the cave, this time shining his light to see if there were any more sections on the ground that looked uneven, as if they might be burial spots, but he didn't find anything.

When he reached the mouth of the cave, he breathed in the fresh air, then rushed to his SUV and retrieved a shovel from the back. Gripping it with clammy hands, he hurried back inside the cave to the far end where he'd found the ribbon. He checked the area to make sure the walls wouldn't collapse when he dug, and decided it was safe. Wall supports had been built when the miners had worked the cave.

Then he began to dig.

Rocks, pebbles and dirt formed a small mound. Jaw set, he lifted one shovel full of debris, then another until he reached the ground beneath. He ran his hand over it and felt a small bump. God help him, he wanted answers.

But he didn't want to find his sister's body.

Resigned, he jammed the shovel into the ground and dug, moving dirt to create a hole. He continued digging two feet, then three, but the space was empty.

Relief flooded him. Chrissy wasn't here.

He stood, wiping dirt and sweat from his face with the back of his sleeve, then headed back outside.

His deputy was waiting at the mouth of the cave.

"Did you find anything?" Harrison asked.

"Afraid not," Bronson said. "You?"

Harrison removed the ribbon from his pocket. "This belonged to my sister."

"So she was here?"

Harrison rarely talked about that night, but he assumed Bronson had heard some version of it.

"We knew she came to the bluff," Harrison said. "Brayden and she sneaked out. They were exploring the caves when Brayden tripped and hurt his ankle. Chrissy was supposed to go get help, but was never seen again."

"I'm sorry, man," Bronson said. "That must have been rough."

Harrison gave a clipped nod, but his cell phone buzzed with a text, saving him from having to respond.

It was from Lucas.

Geoffrey Williams meeting us at your office. Half an hour.

Harrison sent a return text saying he'd be there. "Bronson, ride by the Grangers' place and make sure there's no more trouble there."

Bronson agreed, and Harrison hurried to his SUV. If Lucas had suspicions about Geoffrey Williams, Harrison had to interrogate the man.

Although he wasn't looking forward to it. Geoffrey Williams was well liked and served on the town council.

He wouldn't like any questions that remotely suggested he'd done something illegal.

HONEY HAD EXPERIENCE yielding a hammer. She found some plywood in the garage and boarded up the windows.

Stepping back to look at it, she realized that covering the windows meant the house was pitched in darkness inside.

A shiver rippled up her spine.

Boarding the window meant no one could look inside, but it also prevented her from looking out and made her feel claustrophobic.

The only way to solve the problem was to completely replace the windows, but to do that, she needed to repair rotting wood and casings, which meant committing to more improvements.

Even if she renovated her father's house, it would be a hard sell. One look at the surrounding yards and dilapidated houses in the neighborhood would scare away potential buyers.

She finished with the windows, then went to stow the hammer in the garage when she noticed a box of old junk. Yard tools and plant pots had been tossed into the box along with old work gloves and a broken picture frame.

Harrison had searched the garage, but when she moved the box to haul it toward the door to carry it to the junkyard, she spotted a small wooden box wedged in the back. She slid it from the shelf and set it on the workbench, then opened it.

An assortment of loose change filled the box.

Relief flooded her when she realized there was nothing of Chrissy's inside. But she scrounged through the coins and found an old photograph in the bottom of the box.

Her chest squeezed.

She'd forgotten what her mother looked like, but now she realized she looked a lot like her. Her mother had the same honey-blond hair and brown eyes, although she looked sickly thin and dark circles shadowed her eyes.

Pain rippled through her—her mother had left when she was seven.

Had her father turned his anger on her because she reminded him of his wife?

She traced a finger over her mother's face, aching for what she'd wanted and never had.

Why hadn't her mother taken her with her when she'd left? Was she that unlovable?

HARRISON MET LUCAS at the sheriff's office. Geoffrey Williams was waiting with him, his impeccable suit and designer shoes a sign he had money and wanted others to know it.

So opposite of Harrison and his brothers, who were focused on family and justice.

Williams buttoned his jacket as he stood, then extended his hand. "What can I do for you, Sheriff?"

Harrison shook his hand. "Lucas didn't tell you what this was about?"

Lucas kept a straight face. "I just explained that he might be able to help us with something."

Williams arched a brow. "I am your town councilman. Always happy to be of service."

The damn man was acting as if he hadn't attended school with Harrison and Lucas, as if his blue blood made him a class above the Hawks.

"Good, then have a seat," Harrison said. "We want to talk to you about the night my sister went missing."

Shock flashed in Williams's eyes. "What? Why? That was years ago."

"Yes, but her case has never been solved," Harrison said.

"I'm sorry about that," Williams said, "but I'm not sure how I can help." Williams's eyes narrowed. He was a thin man, his face long, his chin strong, his hands manicured.

"In fact, didn't I hear that Mr. Granger died?" Williams continued. "I thought your family believed he had something to do with your sister's disappearance."

"That was one theory," Harrison said.

Lucas folded his arms, adopting his federal agent demeanor. "Harrison and I have been reviewing everything that happened, Geoffrey. You were at the bluff that night."

A wary look snapped in Williams's gray eyes. "Yes, along with a dozen other teenagers. Are you talking to all of them?"

"Yes," Harrison said bluntly.

Williams squared his shoulders in a defensive gesture. "You know Sheriff Dunar questioned all of us. Why don't you read his report?"

"I have," Harrison said.

"So have I," Lucas added in a solemn voice. "But one thing is bothering me."

Williams's eyes darted back and forth between them as if he suspected they were trying to trap him. "What's that?"

Lucas cleared his throat. "You told the sheriff that you saw Chrissy but that you didn't speak to her."

Williams crossed his leg, chin lifted. "Yes. I was meeting Tina Fuller, not paying attention to your kid sister."

Harrison's jaw tightened. "What was she doing when you saw her?"

"Lurking around behind some rocks," Williams said. "Spying on us like she was a tattletale going to get us in trouble." He quickly realized how his comment sounded and added, "Not that we were doing anything wrong. Having a few beers, but it was the first day of summer break."

Memories of that long, hot summer bombarded Harrison. Days on end of searching the woods and posting fliers and…arguments between his parents.

"You're lying." Lucas's stone-cold expression was a sign of the tough interrogator and agent Harrison had suspected his brother was, although he'd yet to see him in action.

Anger replaced the coolness in Williams's eyes. "How dare you suggest that, Lucas. We were friends."

That was the problem. Harrison and Lucas both knew Williams. And didn't trust him.

"I've done everything I can to help this community,"

Williams continued, "and I've tried to bring revenue back to this fledgling hole in the wall—"

"You're forgetting that I knew you back then, Geoffrey," Lucas said. "You were always showing off, trying to impress everyone, especially the girls. You did meet up with Tina, then you saw my sister sneaking around and you went over and started making fun of her. You called her names, then you shoved her and told her to leave you alone."

The color faded from Williams's face. "We were just kids," he said. "If I pushed her, it was innocent. For God's sake, I didn't hurt her."

"Maybe, maybe not." Lucas leaned over, jamming his face into Williams's in an intimidating gesture. "Maybe she didn't listen and you and Tina sneaked off to make out and Chrissy followed. She was my sister and I loved her, but she could be annoying. Maybe she interrupted you and Tina, and you pushed her again, except this time she fell and hurt her head."

"It could have been an accident," Harrison cut in, following Lucas's lead. "She fell and was hurt or maybe worse, and you panicked." Although that wouldn't explain how Chrissy's ribbon ended up at Honey's. Unless she'd lost it that night, and Granger had found it and taken it home.

Still, something didn't fit.

Williams stood, rolled his shoulders then gave them both a cool look. "Listen to me. I did not kill your sister. Now, if you want to talk to me again, call my lawyer." He shoved a business card at Harrison.

Harrison met the man's gaze with a challenge, and Williams dropped the card on the desk, then strode out, carrying an air of authority with him.

"Damn," Lucas said.

"You think he's telling the truth?" Harrison asked.

"Hell if I know." Lucas stripped his tie and rubbed his neck. "But I'm going to talk with Tina Fuller. If Williams did something to Chrissy and Tina knows, maybe the guilt over keeping quiet is catching up with her."

QUESTIONS ABOUT HER mother needled Honey.

Had her father tried to convince her not to leave? Where had she gone? Had he tried to find her?

She hadn't.

She'd figured if her mother wanted to be with her, she wouldn't have abandoned her.

Unless her mother had been afraid of Honey's father— if so, why leave her child with the man?

The one person who might know was the former sheriff. He'd been called out to their house on numerous occasions.

She wanted to leave Tumbleweed but she couldn't do that without answers. And the only way to get them was to ask questions of her own.

She parked at Harrison's office, shoulders tense as she walked up to the door and went in. Harrison was standing at his desk as if ready to leave, another man beside him.

Lucas.

All of the Hawk men were handsome, although Harrison was always the most striking to her, but Lucas was good-looking. As a teen his smile and dimples had persuaded teachers to let him off the hook when he was in trouble.

Old insecurities nearly sent her running back to her van. But the logo on the outside reminded her that she was successful now. She didn't have to prove herself to anyone.

"Honey, what are you doing here?" Harrison asked.

"That's what I want to know."

Honey froze at the harsh sound of Mrs. Hawk's voice behind her. She braced herself by silently counting to ten.

"Mom." Harrison held up a warning hand. "Let me handle this."

Lucas's curious gaze fell on her. "Hello, Honey. I'm sorry about your father."

She breathed a little easier. Lucas hadn't lost his charm.

"Now that your father is dead, did you decide to tell the truth about what he did to our little Chrissy?" Mrs. Hawk asked.

Fury and hurt engulfed Honey. Mrs. Hawk hadn't lost her hatred for her. God help her, she was sick and tired of people in Tumbleweed judging her.

The gossip she'd heard at the diner echoed in her head.

She whirled around. "I told the truth—I didn't see Chrissy that night and I certainly never saw my father hurt her."

Mrs. Hawk took a step closer, her anger palpable. "You always were a little liar. You and your father tore our family apart. My husband left because of Chrissy—"

"Speaking of lying," Honey said, cutting her off. "Why don't you tell the truth about the real reason your husband left you?"

The woman paled. Harrison's boots pounded the floor as he crossed the room; Lucas followed.

Honey's gaze met Mrs. Hawk's. She had been vehement toward Honey, but now she'd clammed up.

"I don't know what you're talking about," Mrs. Hawk said in a brittle tone.

Honey arched a brow. "Really? Because I heard that the night Chrissy went missing, you and your husband had a fight at that party. A fight—"

Mrs. Hawk raised her hand and slapped Honey. The sharp sting made her jerk her head back.

Harrison grabbed his mother's arm and pulled her away. "Mother, what the hell?"

"Let's calm down," Lucas said in a low voice.

"Get out of here, Honey. You don't belong in Tumbleweed," Mrs. Hawk snarled.

"Don't worry. I hate this town as much as you hate me," Honey said. "But I'm not a liar. Tell your sons about the fight."

"What is she talking about?" Harrison asked.

"Nothing." Mrs. Hawk rubbed Harrison's arm.

He looked up at Honey with troubled eyes. "Honey?"

"You were always judging me," she said to his mother, her chest heaving. "So tell them about your affair."

Shock bolted across Harrison's and Lucas's faces.

"Mother?" Harrison and Lucas asked at the same time.

Mrs. Hawk squeezed her eyes shut for a moment as if struggling to decide how to respond.

Honey hated causing Harrison pain, but there was no turning back now. If they were going to get answers, they had to explore every angle. And they might have to face hard truths.

If Mrs. Hawk's affair had something to do with Chrissy's paternity, it might also have something to do with her disappearance.

Chapter Eleven

Harrison felt as if he'd been hit by a two-by-four.

"What are you talking about, Honey?"

Emotions darkened her eyes. "I'm sorry, Harrison. I shouldn't have said anything."

Except she *had* said something.

He turned to his mother, who looked shell-shocked. "Mother?"

Lucas cleared his throat and took his mother's arm. "Mom, what's going on?"

"I don't have to answer to *her*," his mother said vehemently.

An uneasy feeling clawed at Harrison's stomach. "But you do have to answer to us. We're your sons."

"I know that," his mother said. "But what happened between me and your father was our business."

"Not if it had something to do with the night Chrissy disappeared," Harrison said.

Lucas crossed his arms, his voice low, controlled. But filled with turmoil. "Or the reason he left us."

Harrison couldn't agree more. "That's right. What happened, Mother?"

She gestured toward Honey. "I don't intend to discuss my marriage or private life with her in the room."

Pain streaked Honey's eyes. "Fine. I'll leave. But I need to talk to you when you're finished, Harrison."

"Did you find something else at the house?" Harrison asked, then realized that he hadn't told his mother about the ribbon.

"No. But I still need to talk to you." She crossed the room and reached for the doorknob. "I'll wait outside."

He gave a quick nod, then glanced back at his mother. She was looking at the door as if she wanted to run.

"Mother," Lucas said. "Tell us the truth. What happened at that party?"

His mother fisted her hands by her sides. Her brows were pinched, her mouth tight. "Your father and I did argue. Married couples fight sometimes."

Harrison leaned against his desk, his gaze scrutinizing her. "You fought about the fact that you had an affair?"

A tense second stretched into an awkward moment, which Harrison took as a yes.

"Who was it with?" Lucas asked, his thoughts obviously on track with Harrison's.

"It doesn't matter. It happened a long time ago. It meant nothing."

"But Dad was upset about it," Harrison said. "When was the affair? Around the time Chrissy disappeared?"

She shoved a strand of hair behind her ear, her hand trembling. "No, it was long before that. Years before."

"Years before?" Harrison said, suspicion sneaking up on him. "How many years?"

Their mother fiddled with her purse strap, avoiding eye contact. "Eleven," she said so quietly that for a moment Harrison thought he'd imagined it.

"Eleven?" Lucas said in a low voice. "And Chrissy was ten…"

The truth dawned on Harrison in a sickening rush. "Chrissy… She wasn't Dad's child?"

A low sob rumbled from his mother's throat, and tears blurred her eyes as she looked at them. "No… I'm sorry… I never wanted you boys to find out."

"Is that why he left us?" Lucas pressed. "Because he discovered Chrissy wasn't his daughter?"

A wary resignation settled on their mother's face. "No, he left because he wanted to find Chrissy."

Harrison's investigative mind kicked in, the ramifications quickly adding up. "Did he suspect that Chrissy's biological father took her?"

"He wanted to talk to him," she said. "But I assured him that he wouldn't do such a thing. He wanted Steven to raise Chrissy as his own."

"Why would he want that?" Lucas asked.

"It's complicated," his mother whispered.

"What about Chrissy?" Harrison cut in. "Did she know?"

"No...at least I don't think so."

Harrison struggled to keep his temper in check. "What if she heard you and Dad talking and realized she had another father? Perhaps she decided to find him?"

"Maybe that's the reason she didn't come home," Lucas suggested. "She went to confront him."

"And things didn't go well," Harrison said. Anger railed inside him. All this time he'd blamed himself for his father leaving. For losing Chrissy to a possible predator.

"Did Dad talk to this man?" Harrison asked.

"No," his mother said. "He left in a rage and...he just never came back."

"You didn't hear from him again?" Lucas said. "No phone calls or a note?"

"Nothing," she cried. "I knew he was upset about the indiscretion, but it happened so long ago that I thought we'd already gotten past it. He loved Chrissy like she was his own daughter and she adored him."

"Who was the man?" Lucas asked.

"I don't intend to tell you," their mother said. "Like I said, it was over a long time ago."

"But what if he had something to do with Chrissy's disappearance? Perhaps she went to see him and he was afraid she'd tell everyone and ruin his life or marriage—"

"It wasn't like that at all." She raised a warning finger

to him then to Lucas. "I'm telling you—you boys need to drop it."

"Why should we?" Harrison asked. "You're quick to point the finger at Honey and her father when you're the one who's been keeping secrets all these years. A secret that might have led us to the truth about Chrissy."

His mother met Harrison's gaze with the stern look that had made him stop in his tracks as a kid. He'd never wanted to disappoint her or his father. And when he had, he'd mentally beaten himself up.

"I blamed myself because he left," Harrison admitted in a gruff voice.

Lucas grimaced. "And I blamed myself, Mom."

Regret wrenched her face. "I'm sorry, boys. I never meant for you to do that. But…you have to let this be."

"We need answers about Chrissy," Harrison said.

"So do I." She feathered her bangs away from her forehead with trembling fingers. "But Chrissy's biological father had nothing to do with her disappearance. Trust me, he's a good man and wanted her to be happy in our family."

"Did you ask him?" Lucas said.

She nodded. "Of course. He was upset that she was missing. But he hadn't seen or spoken with her."

With one last sharp look, she strode out the door.

Harrison's pulse pounded. Trust her?

How could they do that when she'd lied to them their whole lives?

HONEY CLENCHED HER hands together as she sat on the park bench outside the sheriff's office.

She shouldn't have confronted Harrison's mother. The hurt on Harrison's face…

The door swung open, and Mrs. Hawk appeared, clutching her purse as if it was a weapon. She stared at Honey, her condescending expression tearing at Honey.

"I'm sorry, Mrs. Hawk," she said softly. "I shouldn't

have said anything. I was angry and upset, but it doesn't excuse it."

The woman's eyes narrowed suspiciously as if she sensed Honey had some ulterior motive.

"I didn't mean to hurt your sons or you," Honey continued, determined not to let the woman turn her into a bitter person. She wanted to be strong, but not vindictive or mean or hurtful.

Lord knows she'd been on the receiving end of gossip and she understood how it could eat at a person's heart and soul.

"What do you want?" Mrs. Hawk asked.

Honey released a shaky breath. "Just the truth, like you do."

"No, I want my daughter back. Even the truth won't do that."

The anguish in the woman's voice wrenched Honey's heart. Losing her father was hard, but they hadn't been close. She couldn't imagine losing a child.

"I'm sorry," Honey said. "I can't imagine how painful it is to lose a daughter."

"No, you can't." Mrs. Hawk wiped at a tear seeping from her eye, then her frown returned.

"I won't let you take my son or sons from me," she said, the vehemence back. "So don't even try."

Honey opened her mouth to reassure her that she wasn't out to take one of her sons, but Harrison stepped outside and she bit back a response as the woman hurried to her vehicle.

Tires squealed as she sped down the street.

A muscle ticked in Harrison's jaw. Regret for hurting him made tears prick at her eyes. Harrison was a good man, a man full of passion and honor.

"I'm sorry," she said, standing to face him. "I shouldn't have confronted your mother. I...didn't mean to upset you, Harrison."

His stormy gaze met hers. The closeness she'd felt with him the night before was gone. The kiss seemed a million years ago.

"I'm going to talk to Sheriff Dunar," he said, ignoring her and her apology.

"I want to talk to him, too," Honey said.

His brows furrowed. "You need to stay out of this."

"I can't," Honey said. "Everyone in Tumbleweed thinks my father is a murderer. Even I'm questioning him and wondering about my mother's disappearance."

"What do you mean?"

Honey shrugged. "I thought she ran off, but if he was more violent than I realized, what if he did something to her?"

HARRISON'S HEAD WAS still spinning from the revelations about his mother's affair. He and Lucas planned to meet Dexter and Brayden for a beer later and fill them in.

He dreaded that conversation, but they had a right to know.

Dexter might be able to use his detective skills to find out the identity of their mother's lover. And they would find out, even if they had to follow her.

Most likely she would contact the man and give him a heads-up.

"Harrison?"

He jerked back to reality. Honey was talking. She'd apologized. She wanted to talk to the sheriff about her father and mother.

Under the circumstances, her questions seemed valid.

He admired the fact that she wanted the truth enough to face it, even if it was ugly.

"Let's go." He strode toward his SUV, not bothering to wait on Honey. She followed him silently, the mood tense as he drove toward the lake where the former sheriff had retired.

He clenched the steering wheel in a white-knuckle grip. He couldn't talk about the situation with Honey or his mother right now, not when his mother's reaction was too fresh in his mind.

She was definitely protecting the man she'd had an affair with. Why?

Because she still cared for him?

She said she'd talked to him after Chrissy went missing and he wasn't responsible. But she must have suspected that he had something to do with her disappearance or she wouldn't have asked him.

HONEY RUBBED HER cheek as they drove, her face still stinging from the slap she'd received.

"Are you okay?" Harrison asked in a gruff voice.

She twisted her head to look at him and dropped her hand to her lap. "Yes. I've had worse."

He winced. "I'm sorry. My mother had no right to hit you. I... I've never seen her like that."

"She didn't spank you when you were young?"

Harrison shook his head. "No, my father was the one with the temper."

"I seem to bring out the worst in her," Honey said in a low voice.

Harrison worked his mouth from side to side. "I know. I don't understand it."

She did—his mother thought she was protecting her sons from Honey, the bad girl.

But she knew nothing about Honey or the woman she'd become.

Harrison veered down a narrow dirt road that wove through the woods.

"Sheriff Dunar lives out here?"

He nodded. "When he retired, he and his wife wanted to live by the lake."

"It's pretty," Honey said. "I'd forgotten how close Tumbleweed is to the lake."

And to her father's house. If she decided to redo it and sell, the lake could be a marketing point.

The SUV rumbled over the rough terrain, and she noted a few rustic houses built along the way. If people wanted privacy and a retreat in the woods by the lake, this was the place.

They broke to a clearing where a small cabin sat, a black pickup parked in front. A gray-haired woman was tending a garden to the right.

Harrison parked and climbed out, and Honey followed.

"Mrs. Dunar," Harrison said. "Is your husband here?"

The woman shaded her eyes with one hand, a garden trowel in her other. "Sure is. Fishing on the dock out back."

"Thanks."

Honey followed Harrison around the side of the cabin. The sheriff had aged since she'd left town. His face was thin, but his belly had grown rounder. He pushed his hat back and peered at them.

"Well, well, Sheriff Hawk, I heard you found Waylon Granger dead. I figured you'd show up here sometime." He glanced at Honey with narrowed eyes, then a frown marred his face. "You're his kid, aren't you?"

Honey nodded. "Yes, I came back to handle funeral arrangements."

He set his fishing pole aside. "I'm sorry for your loss."

Honey murmured thanks, the moment awkward.

"So what can I help you with?" Sheriff Dunar asked.

"I have questions about when my mother left," Honey said.

"And I want to talk about my sister's disappearance." Harrison explained that Honey's father was murdered.

The older man pulled at his chin. "You got any theories about who killed Granger?" he asked Harrison.

"I think his murder may have something to do with

Chrissy," Harrison said. "Honey found one of my sister's hair ribbons in her father's house."

"So you think Granger killed Chrissy?"

"It's one theory. We searched his property but didn't find anything. Although I found her other hair ribbon in the mine."

The sheriff frowned. "We searched those mines and all around the bluff," he said, "and didn't find anything."

"The ribbon was half-buried in rubble inside the cave," Harrison said. "You questioned all the teenagers at the bluff that night, didn't you?"

"Yes, I made notes in my police report."

"Did anyone stand out to you or seem suspicious?" Harrison asked.

The sheriff folded his hands and laid them on his belly. "Well, there was one guy, a homeless drifter, who used to sleep in the park and at the bluff. I thought he might have seen something, but two weeks after I talked to him, he turned up dead."

The timing was interesting. "What was COD?"

"Liver failure," the sheriff said. "Poor guy died in his sleep."

"What about the teenagers?" Harrison asked.

"All the kids seemed nervous, but I assumed that was just because your sister disappeared. Something like that shakes up the whole town." He paused and worked the inside of his cheek with his tongue. "Honestly, I thought the incident might spook some of the teenagers enough to stay away from the bluff. I always thought that swimming hole and the ridge were dangerous."

Honey made a low sound in her throat. "Mrs. Hawk thought Chrissy came to my house. Did you question my father?"

He nodded, his thick brows meeting in the middle of his forehead. "Yeah, we talked."

"And?" Honey held her breath.

The sheriff sighed. "He was drunk as a skunk the next morning when I stopped by to talk to him. Said he didn't go anywhere the night before."

If only she'd stayed home, she'd know for sure if he'd left. Or if Chrissy had come by to see her.

The memory of that morning still disturbed Honey. She'd been terrified her father would catch her sneaking back in the house in the middle of the night, but he was passed out and hadn't stirred.

"Did he act suspicious when you talked to him?" Harrison asked.

"That's hard to say," Sheriff Dunar said. "When he was drunk, he got belligerent. But I didn't see signs of foul play at the house."

Honey swallowed hard. She had to summon the courage to ask him the question eating at her. "My mother left abruptly." She inhaled sharply. "Did you ever suspect that my father did something to her?"

Chapter Twelve

Honey held her breath while she waited on the sheriff's response.

"Your daddy was a mean drunk," the sheriff said. "When your mama left, I wondered if he'd hurt her, but Waylon showed me the note she left."

"She left a note?"

He picked up a twig and snapped it in two. "Yeah. She said she couldn't take it anymore, that she'd met someone else and was leaving town."

Her father could have forged the note. "Did you keep the note?"

"Naw, but I compared the handwriting against your mama's and it was hers. And I checked the bus station, and they verified that she boarded a bus headed toward San Antonio."

Honey wasn't sure if she was relieved or disappointed. She didn't want to believe that her father had killed her mother, but it hurt to know that her mother had abandoned her and never come back.

HARRISON GLANCED ACROSS the lake, giving Honey time to absorb the sheriff's words. Honey's mother had left without telling her goodbye. He understood—his father had done the same thing.

Agitation lined her face. "I'm going to take a walk."

"Honey?" Harrison glanced at her to see if she was okay.

"I'll be back." She avoided his gaze and walked from the dock to the path leading around the lake. The summer breeze blew gently, ruffling leaves, and water rippled beneath the sun.

She looked so lost and alone that he wanted to join her and comfort her.

But he was here for information and he had to get it.

"Sheriff," he said in a low voice. "I recently learned that Chrissy was not my father's birth child. My parents argued about it the night she disappeared. Did you know anything about that argument?"

The sheriff fiddled with the button on his overalls. "No. I sensed tension between your folks and thought they might be holding something back, but they didn't mention a fight or anything about Chrissy's paternity."

Then it was up to him and his brothers to find out the man's name and talk to him.

"My brother mentioned that Geoffrey Williams was one of the teens at the bluff that night," Harrison said. "When you questioned him, did he act strange or did any of the other teens mention seeing him with Chrissy?"

The sheriff pinched the bridge of his nose. "It was a long time ago, Harrison. Williams is on the town council. Most folks like him."

"But you don't?"

The sheriff shrugged. "He's always been too cocky for me. Back then he was a smart-ass. But if he said anything suspicious, I would have written it in my notes."

Harrison had reviewed them a dozen times, although he didn't recall anything specific about Geoffrey.

The sheriff snapped his fingers. "Although there was one thing that struck me odd. Happened a couple of years later."

"What was that?" Harrison asked.

"Another little girl went missing from Waco. She was about the same age as Chrissy."

Harrison's pulse jumped. "You think the two cases were related?"

The sheriff shrugged. "I called and talked to the detective working the case, and we didn't find any connection. But I always wondered…"

"Did they find that little girl?" Harrison asked.

The sheriff shook his head. "Afraid not."

"Were there any suspects?" Harrison asked.

"He looked at the immediate family, but they checked out."

Of course. Parents and families were always primary suspects.

"So you looked at my parents when Chrissy went missing?"

"I had to," he said. "Why, Harrison? Do you think one of them had something to do with her disappearance?"

Did he?

It had never occurred to him that that was a possibility. But knowing about the argument and his mother's affair shed a different light on the situation.

So did the fact that another little girl had disappeared from Waco.

HONEY LOST HERSELF in the beauty of the lake. She had to distract herself from her current situation.

Decisions had to be made about her father's house, but first she had to settle what to do with his remains.

She certainly didn't plan to take her father's ashes home with her to Austin.

Maybe she'd scatter them here in the lake.

Birds chirped from a tree overlooking the lake drawing her gaze to the water. The natural landscape and rustic cabins gave the property a serene, majestic look. There were also acres and acres of land that could hold lovely homes—or a retreat center—for travelers and guests visiting the area. A trail around the lake for horseback riding would be inviting and the wooded areas would offer great camping and picnic sites.

An investor could make a fortune if he developed the

property right. But someone else could ruin it if he or she chose to build condos or apartments.

The wooden dock creaked as she stepped back onto it. Not that she cared what happened here. This lake was part of Tumbleweed, a place she despised.

Harrison stood as she approached, his posture rigid. He looked troubled, as if disturbed by something the sheriff had said.

She'd wanted to hear their conversation but had to take a break. She'd also sensed Harrison wanted privacy to discuss his mother's affair.

Odd that the woman had judged her so harshly when she wasn't perfect herself.

"Are you ready to go?" Harrison asked.

She was ready to leave town, but she refrained from commenting and simply nodded.

"Thank you, Sheriff. If you think of anything else, call me."

The sheriff murmured he would, and Honey followed Harrison to his SUV. "Did you learn anything?" she asked as they drove away.

"Just that a little girl went missing in Waco a short time after Chrissy did. The sheriff doesn't think she was ever found."

Honey's mind spun. "You think that the same person who took Chrissy took that girl?"

"I don't know, but it's worth looking into."

Honey twisted her hands in her lap. If that was true, it might clear her father. He'd been drinking so much back then that he never left Tumbleweed.

HARRISON DROPPED HONEY back at her car at the sheriff's office, then drove to The Broken Spoke, the local bar, to meet his brothers.

Lucas looked antsy as he approached. Dexter and

Brayden were talking to the waitress as she set a pitcher of beer and a plate of wings and basket of fries on the table.

His stomach growled, reminding him that he hadn't eaten today, and he claimed a wooden chair at the table with his brothers.

Dexter poured them each a mug of beer, then pushed one toward Harrison. "So what's this family meeting about?"

He raised a brow at Lucas, who shook his head, indicating he hadn't explained.

"A couple of things," Harrison said. "But first, Lucas, tell them about Williams."

Lucas nodded. "He denied any wrongdoing and lawyered up. I talked to Tina Fuller. She said Chrissy followed her and Geoffrey to the creek but Geoffrey shoved her and told her to leave them alone, and she ran off."

"Which way did she go?" Brayden asked.

"Toward Honey's."

Damn, they were back to Granger.

Lucas gestured to Harrison. "You want to fill them in on the rest?"

He didn't, but he had to, so he explained about their mother's affair.

"You're kidding?" The color drained from Brayden's face.

"Mom cheated on Dad?" Dexter asked, his voice cracking.

"It gets worse," Lucas said.

Brayden and Dexter looked at Harrison as if begging him to say, "It's not so," but he refused to lie to them. "Chrissy was not Dad's biological child."

Shock bolted across his brothers' faces. He and Lucas sipped their beers while they gave Dexter and Brayden time to absorb the news.

"Dad knew this?" Dexter asked.

Harrison nodded. "Mom and Dad fought about it the night Chrissy disappeared."

Brayden swallowed hard. "Did Chrissy know?"

Harrison shrugged. "Mom said they didn't tell her, but it's possible that she overheard something at some point."

"Then she could have tried to find her birth father." Dexter gripped the table edge. "Who is the bastard?"

Harrison scraped a hand through his hair. "Mom wouldn't tell us."

"This is not exactly ethical," Lucas said, "but I could put a trace on Mom's phone to see if she calls him."

"I'll talk to her," Brayden said. "Maybe I can convince her to talk."

"She seemed pretty protective of the man's identity," Lucas said.

Harrison reached for a french fry. "She also said it had been over for a very long time and insisted the man wouldn't have hurt Chrissy."

"How can we believe her when she lied all these years?" A sense of betrayal laced Dexter's voice.

"I feel the same way," Harrison said. "So what do we do?"

"I'll watch her, maybe follow her," Brayden said. "She might try to see him."

A tense silence stretched between them, filled with guilt and indecision and the reality that none of them would be happy until they knew the man's name and confirmed that he wasn't involved in their sister's disappearance.

Finally they all agreed, then dug into the wings. But Harrison couldn't get the sheriff's words out of his head. "There's something else. It might be important."

Dexter released a weary sigh. "What else?"

Harrison snatched another wing, then relayed his conversation with the sheriff.

"Another girl went missing just like our sister," Lucas said. "Why didn't he mention this before?"

"He didn't find a connection."

Lucas grabbed a napkin. "I'll check the FBI's databases and see if there were other similar cases."

"I'll talk to the detective the sheriff dealt with," Harrison said. "If there's a connection, we might finally get a lead."

HONEY STOPPED BY the ME's office on the way back to her father's house.

"What have you decided to do?" Dr. Weinberger said.

"I haven't," Honey said. "There were no directives in Dad's will and he doesn't own a burial plot. I was thinking about scattering his ashes in the lake or the river."

"You'll have to get permission from the county to do that." Dr. Weinberger gave her the number of the contact person. "There's also a memorial center that has an area specifically designated for urns."

He handed her a couple of business cards from his desk. "How are you holding up?"

Honey offered him a tentative smile. "Fine. Hopefully I'll handle this quickly, then get out of town."

"I'm assuming you'll stay till the sheriff learns who killed your daddy."

Honey leaned against the door. "That depends on how long it takes. I…have jobs waiting on me back in Austin." And people who liked her work and cared about her.

Jared's face flashed through her mind. He was a good friend, trustworthy, and she enjoyed working with him. But she'd never been tempted to kiss him the way she had Harrison.

It would make life simpler if she did want Jared. They made a great team.

She and Harrison had nothing in common except their troubled pasts.

"I'll let you know what I decide to do with the urn," Honey said.

"All right. I'll send his body to the crematorium and they'll call you when it's done."

She thanked the ME then left, her stomach knotting as she passed through town and made her way to Lower

Tumbleweed. She parked in the drive, her designer instincts immediately imagining what this house would look like with her touch.

Don't go there, Honey. You are not taking on this mess.

The afternoon heat was sweltering and her clothes were sticking to her as she entered the house. She immediately froze, her senses alert as she spotted dishes broken and scattered all over the kitchen counter and floor. The couch cushions had been ripped with a knife, stuffing overflowing and falling out.

Spray paint marred the walls, with a message—Leave Town.

A noise outside startled her, and she gripped her purse, wishing she had her gun. Damn, she'd left it in her nightstand. She rushed down the hall to her room to get it, quickly noting other damage.

The mattress on her father's bed had been ripped, and something red that looked like blood was smeared on the dresser mirror.

Pulse hammering, she dashed into her room. Just as she reached the nightstand and grabbed her gun, the floor squeaked behind her. She started to spin around, but something hard smacked the back of her head.

Pain exploded in her skull, and she swayed. A second later stars swam in front of her eyes then the room blurred into black.

Chapter Thirteen

Harrison drove back to his office to make the call.

The detective who'd investigated the Waco case was named Jim Hudson. He'd retired five years before.

Harrison spoke with the man's wife, who promised to have him call Harrison. Frustrated, he used a legal pad to list everything he knew so far about Granger and his death.

Granger's murder. The only viable suspect he had at this point was his mother, who had no alibi. But she had no motive to kill Granger now, not after so many years had passed. Unless she'd learned that he had hurt Chrissy. Was it possible that somehow she'd discovered the truth?

If she had, she was so emotional she would have told him or one of his brothers instead of confronting him herself.

Next he wrote Chrissy's name and included everything he'd learned to date about her disappearance. Unfortunately, that wasn't much.

Granger topped the list of suspects, mainly because of the ribbon found at his house. Then Geoffrey Williams. Next he wrote *Chrissy's birth father* with a big question mark beside it.

He made a third column to list anything he learned about this other child so he could make comparisons.

His cell phone beeped. Jim Hudson was returning his call. He introduced himself then explained that he'd spoken to the former sheriff of Tumbleweed. "You worked a case where a little girl went missing two years later, didn't you?"

"Yeah, that case got to me. Never did find the child or figure out who took her."

Harrison rubbed his temple. "Tell me the circumstances."

"Her name was Cady Winters, eight years old. She lived

with a single mother who worked at a local hair salon. She left Cady with an elderly grandmother when she was at work."

"Go on."

"The grandmother took her to a local county fair. Said the little girl was there one minute, gone the next. Security searched the fairgrounds and canvassed the workers, but no one had seen her or knew what happened to her."

"The family check out?"

"Yeah, Mom was working. Grandmother's eyesight was failing and she moved slowly, but she adored Cady."

"The father?"

"Died in a car accident the year before. Mother had no boyfriends, no strange neighbors who expressed interest in Cady, no other relatives."

"What about someone at school or their church?"

"They didn't belong to church. I spoke to Cady's teachers and she said Cady was quiet, shy and had very few friends. No one at the school seemed suspicious, either."

"Did you have a theory?" Harrison asked.

Hudson's long-winded sigh rent the air. "I figured it had to be some stranger who saw her at the fair. As much fun as those events are, they're a hunting ground for pedophiles and predators."

"What about the workers?"

"Questioned them all, ran background checks, nothing popped." His voice cracked. "Poor little girl was in the wrong place at the wrong time. Someone lured her away and drove off with her." He paused. "Her name and information is still in the database for the National Center for Missing and Exploited Children"

"Sheriff Dunar told you about my sister?"

"Yes. I suppose the two could be related, but we had no leads to follow."

If Chrissy and this girl had been taken by the same person, they were dealing with a repeat offender.

Possibly a serial kidnapper or killer.

Neither Granger nor Williams fitted that profile.

He thanked the man and asked him to call if he remembered anything else. He hung up then logged on to the computer and ran a search for the girl's name in the NCMEC database.

He drummed his fingers on his desk while he waited. Finally a photo appeared. His stomach convulsed at the image—Cady was blonde and blue-eyed with a big smile that showcased a missing tooth. She looked innocent and sweet just as Chrissy had. She wore a pink flowered jacket, and pink and purple ribbons in her hair and was nuzzling an orange kitten to her cheek.

He was just about to phone Lucas and ask him if he'd found anything regarding the missing Waco girl when his phone buzzed.

He quickly glanced at it—Honey.

Reminding himself to keep it professional, he punched Connect. "Sheriff."

"Harrison…help…"

His heart thundered. "Honey?"

The sound of her labored breathing echoed over the line as he jogged outside to his SUV.

HONEY DRAGGED HERSELF to a sitting position, retrieved her gun and clenched it in her lap in case her attacker returned.

The room spun, and she leaned against her bedroom wall. Her head throbbed. Her fingers met sticky blood in her hair, and she tried to get up, but she had to close her eyes and concentrate to keep from sliding to the floor.

Harrison's voice echoed over the line. "Honey, talk to me. Are you all right?"

Was she? No. "I will be," she murmured.

"I'm on my way." The phone clicked silent, and she let it drop to her lap while she clenched her gun with her other hand. She wouldn't be caught off guard again.

The room blurred. She closed her eyes to stifle the dizziness and inhaled deep breaths. The sound of the wind whipping the trees outside made her tense. She opened her eyes and listened for footsteps. A low clattering sound—mice in the attic?

Seconds slipped into minutes.

Something banged against the house. More rocks? No…a shutter banging in the wind.

It had been windy the day her mother left. When her father told her that her mother was gone, she hadn't thought it would be forever.

Mothers didn't just go away. Even inept ones like hers.

That day Honey had cleaned the house, swept the floors and wiped down the kitchen. She tidied up the living room, made her bed and washed the sheets on her parents' bed. She'd even found an extra pillow in the closet, took a scrap of fabric and made a decorative pillow, thinking her mother would be excited to see things spruced up.

There hadn't been much food in the pantry, but she managed to pull together enough ingredients to make spaghetti and had set the table. She'd fantasized about her parents and her sitting down and having dinner together like a real family.

A tear trickled down her cheek. That hadn't happened.

She'd kept the spaghetti sauce warm for hours, even after her father had staggered in and passed out on the couch. Hating the rancid way he'd smelled, she'd stepped outside and waited on the porch. Every time a car had driven down the street, she'd hoped it was her mother.

But her mother hadn't come home that night. Or the next or the next.

After a month, she'd stopped listening or watching for her.

She hadn't eaten spaghetti since.

HARRISON ROLLED INTO the Grangers' driveway, senses alert as he scanned the property for trouble. Honey had been here a day and a half and already she'd been vandalized and threatened.

He wouldn't blame her if she packed her bags and left Tumbleweed tonight.

He parked, climbed out, made his way to the porch and knocked. The door wasn't locked, so he eased it open and peered inside.

The living room had obviously been ransacked, couch destroyed and a message painted on the living room wall.

"Honey, it's Harrison." He slowly inched into the hall, praying Honey was okay. The mattress on Waylon Granger's bed had been ripped with a knife, stuffing overflowing, the dresser mirror smeared with something that looked like blood.

"Honey?"

"In here," she called.

He stepped back into the hallway, then toward Honey's room. She staggered toward him and met him in the doorway. He grabbed her arms to steady her. She looked pale, and blood dotted her hair.

"Dammit, Honey, you need a doctor."

"No, just help me so I can wash this blood off."

He slid an arm around her waist and supported her as they walked to the bathroom. "What the hell happened?" he asked.

She sank onto the toilet seat, and he checked her eyes to see if they were clear.

"When I got home, someone had vandalized the place. Whoever it was must have still been here. I hurried to the bedroom to get my gun, but someone struck me from behind."

Just like her father had been hit from behind.

"Let me see where you were hit." Anger mushroomed inside him as she twisted on the seat. He brushed her hair away from the bloody mess. "Good God, Honey. You may need stitches."

"No, I'm fine. Just give me that hand towel."

He snatched one from the towel bar and pressed the towel to her injury to stem the bleeding.

"Did you see who hit you?" Harrison asked.

She shook her head. "No, it happened really quickly." She winced as he removed the towel and examined her wound again.

"You have a gash about an inch long but it's not too deep," Harrison said. "But you could have a concussion, Honey. We should go to the ER."

"I don't need a doctor," she said. "It's just a bump." She took the cloth from him and dabbed it over her injury, cleaning it and the blood from the strands of her golden hair.

"I'm going to call a crime team out here," Harrison said. "Maybe whoever did this left prints."

The message on the wall sounded personal, and in light of the threatening phone call she'd received, he couldn't dismiss the possibility that this person was serious.

And dangerous.

He knelt in front of Honey to check her eyes again. "Are you sure you're all right? Do you feel nauseous?"

"No, I told you I'm fine."

"Maybe you should leave town," Harrison suggested. "I can call you when I solve your father's case."

Honey squared her shoulders. "I'm not leaving, Harrison. I let people run me off when I was young. I won't do it again."

"But this is dangerous, Honey." He gently tucked a strand of her hair behind one ear. "I don't want to see you get hurt."

Her soft whispered sigh tore at him. "Then let's find the answers so we can both put this behind us."

"All right," he conceded. "But you aren't staying here alone. I'll either stay here or you can come to my place."

A sliver of awareness flared in her eyes, then disappeared quickly. Wariness followed.

"Just make the call."

He stood, determined that he would get his way on this.

He didn't intend to let anyone mistreat Honey, not ever
again.

HONEY'S FIRST INSTINCT was to clean up the mess her intruder
had made, but Harrison reminded her that cleaning would
destroy evidence. So she stepped onto the front porch and
waited while the crime scene team dusted her house for
prints, collected samples of the red smears on the walls
and combed the debris from the mattress and couch for a
hair or fiber, something that could help identify the culprit.

Needing a distraction from thinking about the attack,
she phoned the numbers Dr. Weinberger had given her to
discuss the disposal of her father's ashes. A warm breeze
blew through, bringing the scent of wildflowers somewhere
nearby, and she looked up to see the mountain slopes rising toward the skies at the bluff.

The houses on this street needed to be torn down or gutted, and she'd been so absorbed in the painful memories of
her past and her father's murder, that she'd forgotten how
beautiful the rugged mountain and terrain was.

Curious as to the status of the other properties, she
phoned a local real estate agent named Isla Fontaine and
asked her to find out.

"Most of the properties are owned by the bank," Isla
told her.

Harrison stepped outside with the lead crime scene investigator. "We'll analyze the forensics right away," the
CSI told Harrison.

"Good. I want to get to the bottom of this," Harrison said.

The crime team left and Honey pocketed her phone.
"Thanks for coming, Harrison. I'm going to clean up now."

"I've called a crime scene cleanup team," Harrison said.

"There's no need for that," Honey said. "I can take care of
it myself." She started inside but Harrison caught her arm.

"No, you've been through enough today. You need rest."

"I need to have this mess go away," Honey said.

"I understand." Harrison offered her a sympathetic smile. "And it will. But tonight you're coming to my place so you can sleep."

Honey glanced back at the house. The ugly writing on the living room wall mocked her through the screen door.

Harrison was right. She wouldn't be able to sleep in this house tonight.

But staying with Harrison caused anxiety of another kind. It had felt so heavenly when he'd kissed her. She'd felt safe.

And more alive than she'd ever felt in her life.

She wanted that feeling again. To be held in his arms. To have his lips touch hers.

But she was terrified that if he kissed her again, she wouldn't tell him to stop.

Chapter Fourteen

Harrison's phone buzzed and he quickly connected.

"Harrison," Brayden said, "I talked to Mom about Chrissy's birth father, but she got upset and clammed up."

"Did she tell you the man's name?"

"No, and I don't think she will. She's protecting him for some reason."

Did his mother love the man? If so, why hadn't they gotten together after his father left?

"He may be married, or an affair could mess up his personal life in another way."

Brayden hissed. "Either way, she's not talking. She's adamant that he loved Chrissy and that he would never have hurt her or anyone in our family."

Without knowing the man's identity, Harrison couldn't take his mother's word for it.

Another possibility struck Harrison.

If Chrissy's biological father thought Granger had killed Chrissy, would he have killed Granger to get revenge?

If so, why would he have done so now?

Brayden cleared his throat. "I followed Mom. She's at Reverend Langley's house."

Reverend Langley?

Brayden made a low sound in his throat. "I guess she needed someone to talk to."

Harrison paced the front porch, his heart squeezing at the turmoil on Honey's face. "Maybe."

"What do you want me to do?" Brayden asked.

"Let me handle it. I'm at Honey Granger's right now. Someone broke in, vandalized the place and threatened Honey. I need to get to the bottom of who's doing this."

"You think it has to do with Chrissy?"

"Yes. Either the perp knows Granger did something to Chrissy and killed Granger, or the intruder is afraid Honey is going to find something in her father's house to clear her father and point the finger toward him."

"Let me know if I can do anything else," Brayden said. "I'm going back to the ranch to take care of the horses for the night."

They didn't have livestock at this point, but his mother kept horses so they could ride whenever they wanted.

"Thanks. I'll keep you posted."

Harrison ended the call and pocketed his phone. "Are you ready to go?"

Honey shook her head. "I told you I'm okay to stay alone."

"You are not staying here, Honey, so stop arguing," Harrison said.

A van rolled up, and a man and woman climbed out.

"There's the cleanup crew." Harrison gestured toward the house. "Go pack a bag while I run an errand. I'll come back to get you. You should be safe with them here."

Harrison hurried down the step from the porch, introduced himself to the cleanup crew, then headed to his SUV.

If his mother was talking to the preacher about what had happened, maybe he'd convince her to tell the truth.

Night had fallen, the heat still sweltering. He veered through town then took the side street by the library that led to the church on the outskirts of town. His parents had attended the church together before his father left, then his mother had taken him and his brothers. He searched his memory for any hint of another man his mother had been friendly with, but couldn't recall anyone in particular.

He passed a few cars on the road, but the town seemed quiet tonight. Farmland stretched between the town and the bluff, and the little church sat on a small hill surrounded by open land with the mountains as a backdrop.

The parsonage, a rustic ranch, had been built beside the church for convenience and sat nestled in the woods. The black sedan in the drive belonged to the reverend.

The dark gray SUV was his mother's.

He swallowed hard. She wouldn't be happy to see him or know that Brayden had followed her.

But he didn't intend to let secrets keep him from the truth.

Eighteen years was long enough to live with the lies.

He pulled up the drive and parked, then settled his Stetson on his head as he made his way to the front door.

He raised his fist and knocked, pulse hammering. A minute later the door opened and Reverend Langley greeted him. Silver tipped the reverend's hair, and crow's-feet around his eyes testified to his age.

"Hello, Harrison, I figured you'd show up sometime."

Harrison frowned at his comment. "Can I come in?"

"Of course." He gestured for Harrison to enter, and Harrison stepped inside, then followed the reverend to the den, a cozy room with dark leather furniture and wood floors. A Doberman lay on a braided rug in front of the fireplace.

His mother was perched on the sofa, hands twisting frantically in her lap. "Harrison, what are you doing here?"

"We have to talk," Harrison said.

She stood, arms folded across her chest, her anger a palpable force. For a small-framed woman, she'd never backed down from disciplining her sons, who all stood a foot taller than her. "How did you know where I was?"

Harrison gritted his teeth. "Brayden said you were upset when you left."

"He followed me?" she asked in an incredulous voice.

Harrison shrugged. "He was worried about you."

"I can't believe you and Brayden would follow your own mother," she snapped as if he and Brayden had betrayed her.

"You're the one who lied to us all these years," Harrison said. "And you're still refusing to tell us the truth."

Reverend Langley held up a hand. "Let's all calm down." He gestured to Harrison. "Sit down."

Harrison strode into the living room but leaned against one of the wing chairs that flanked the fireplace. "I'm sorry to intrude on you, Reverend. But I thought my mother might have come to you for advice." He glanced at his mother. "Does he know?"

His mother and the reverend traded an odd look. "Yes," Reverend Langley said.

"Then you know why I'm asking questions about Chrissy's biological father," Harrison said. "He may have something to do with Chrissy's disappearance."

"I told you he didn't," his mother said sharply. "You need to trust me on this, Harrison."

"It's hard to trust someone when you find out they've kept secrets for years, and that they betrayed your father."

"That's enough," Reverend Langley said in a tone that brooked no argument.

His mother started toward the door. "I'm sorry, Ross. I'd better go."

"No." The reverend caught his mother's arm. "It's time to be honest with your boys."

Harrison narrowed his eyes. "He's right, Mother. I'm trying to find out who took Chrissy."

"It wasn't her biological father," the reverend said.

Harrison's look shot to the reverend. "Then you know who took her?"

The man shook his head, his gray eyes serious. "No, but I do know that it wasn't Chrissy's father."

"How do you know that?"

Harrison's mother squeezed the reverend's arm. "Ross, no—"

"It's all right, Ava." Reverend Langley patted his mother's hand then turned to Harrison. "I know Chrissy's birth father didn't hurt her because Chrissy is my daughter and I loved her with all my heart."

HONEY BLINKED BACK tears and hurried to her bedroom as the crime scene team processed the house.

It didn't take Honey five minutes to pack her clothes back in her rolling bag to go to Harrison's. She hadn't exactly unpacked.

Because this house wasn't home.

It was a physical structure where the unhappiness between her parents had affected her. Where love hadn't thrived as it would in a real home, where forgiveness wasn't common, and anger ruled the roost.

If she ever had a family, she would do things differently. Her husband and children would know that she loved them unconditionally.

She froze, one hand gripping the picture of her mother that she'd found. She tried to see her features in her mother, to have some connection, but she felt none.

She stared out at the woods from the porch while the crime scene team worked, a chill washing over her. At five, she'd stood in this same place, gazed out at the woods, and she'd wanted to run away.

Back then she'd been afraid of the dark and spiders and snakes and other creatures that lived in the woods.

Now…she'd renovated so many abandoned, dilapidated houses that critters didn't faze her. She'd grown accustomed to going into a dark house alone at night.

Living alone and sleeping alone meant she didn't have to please anyone or answer to anyone or…be disappointed when they didn't love her back.

She heaved a wary breath.

The only thing that really frightened her now was her crazy attraction to Harrison Hawk.

HARRISON STARED AT the reverend in stunned silence. A quick look at his mother, and guilt streaked her face.

Damn. It had never occurred to him that the man his mother had an affair with was the pastor he'd heard preaching when he was a little boy. The man who'd counseled him on drugs, sex and respecting girls when Harrison was a teenager. The very man who'd taught him to believe in God and to have faith that good prevailed in the end.

Betrayal cut through him. How could he ever look at his mother and this man the same way again?

He held up his hands in disbelief, or maybe it was just that he couldn't handle any more shocking news. He wasn't a kid anymore. He couldn't run from things he didn't want to face or hear.

This was too important.

He wanted, he *needed* to know more.

"I'm sorry, Harrison," Reverend Langley said in the voice he used to soothe agitated parishioners. "It happened a long time ago, right before I decided to give my life to the Lord. In fact, our indiscretion was one reason I decided to serve God."

"You have to understand, Harrison," his mother said in a pleading tone. "We never meant for it to happen. Your father and I were having a difficult time with the ranch, with money, and your father was—"

"Don't make excuses," Harrison said, cutting her off.

"He's right." Reverend Langley patted Harrison's mother's shoulder. "But please know that your mother loved your father dearly, and I respected that. I envied it but I also admired her devotion."

Harrison gave his mother a cutting look. "Devotion would have meant being faithful."

The reverend had the decency to wince. "It was wrong of both of us to betray your father."

"You're damn right it was," Harrison snapped.

"I regretted it the moment it happened," his mother said. "But, Harrison, I never regretted having Chrissy. I loved you boys and I still do. But she was my little girl."

"You're sure she's yours?" he asked the reverend.

The reverend murmured, "Yes. I loved her too much to

let her grow up shamed by what we'd done in a moment of weakness." A sad smile settled in his eyes. "I thought she'd be better off raised as a Hawk."

"Are you sure she didn't find out the truth?" Harrison said. "Maybe she heard you and Dad arguing and came to see you that night."

"She didn't hear us," his mother said. "We argued at that stupid party. By the time we got home, we had settled things. Steven knew I loved him and he loved Chrissy and we didn't want to tear her world apart."

"You were okay to stand back and let another man raise your daughter?" Harrison asked the reverend.

"Yes, I told you I loved Chrissy. I wanted what was best for her." Reverend Langley patted the Bible. "I asked for forgiveness and made peace with God and myself a long time ago."

Harrison shifted. The man sounded sincere, like the preacher who'd doled out advice on life to him and his siblings.

Still, the sheriff in him had to ask, "Where were you the night Chrissy disappeared?"

His mother gasped. "Harrison, you can't possibly think—"

Reverend Langley gestured for her to remain calm. "I was attending a private meeting with a pastor in El Paso who offered to mentor me through the seminary. You can check if you need to." He snatched a memo pad from the sofa table, scribbled a name and number, then handed Harrison the paper.

The paper crinkled in Harrison's hand as he stuck it in his pocket. Dammit. He didn't need to call. In spite of his anger, he believed the man.

"My heart has ached every day since Chrissy disappeared," Reverend Langley added softly. "I've prayed you'd find her alive and safe."

Tears blurred Harrison's mother's eyes, and she released

a small sob. "When she vanished, I was certain it was God's way of punishing me."

Harrison didn't think God worked like that, but he didn't know what to say. His emotions were all over the place.

His phone buzzed. Lucas.

"I have to go." His mother reached for him, but Harrison wasn't ready to hug and forgive and forget.

"I'll continue to pray you find Chrissy," Reverend Langley said.

Harrison gave him a quick nod, then strode toward the door. He connected the call from Lucas as soon as he stepped outside.

"Yeah?"

"Harrison, I looked into that case you sent me, then checked the FBI databases and there were two other little girls in Texas around the same age who disappeared and were never found."

Harrison's blood ran cold. "You think they're connected?"

A heartbeat passed. "I think it's possible and that we should look into it."

Harrison wiped perspiration from his forehead. If that was true, they were dealing with a serial criminal—perhaps a serial kidnapper/killer.

Chapter Fifteen

"I'll fax the information on both cases to your office," Lucas said. "Look them over, then we'll interview the families."

"Sounds like a plan." Harrison started his SUV. "I'm just leaving Reverend Langley's house."

"What were you doing there?"

"Brayden followed Mom to the reverend's house. I thought he might convince her to divulge the name of Chrissy's biological father."

"Did he?" Lucas asked.

Harrison silently cursed. "Oh, yeah."

"What does that mean?"

"Chrissy's biological father is the reverend," Harrison said, disgust still eating at him.

"What?" Lucas sounded incredulous. "That can't be right."

"It's not right, but it's the truth," Harrison said. "They both admitted that they slept together when Dad and Mom were having a rough patch."

"My God, I can't believe this," Lucas said with equal parts denial and disapproval.

"According to them," Harrison continued, "they decided Chrissy should grow up in our family as a Hawk."

"Dad knew about this?" Lucas asked.

"Yes, but Mom said she thought they'd gotten past it. For some reason he brought it up that night at the party, and they argued. I thought Chrissy might have overheard and run off to find her biological father, but Mom insists that Chrissy didn't know she wasn't Dad's."

"Have you told Brayden or Dexter?" Lucas asked.

"Not yet."

"What a mess," Lucas said.

Harrison headed back toward Honey's. "Yeah." It sure was messing with his head.

"I'll talk to Brayden tonight if you'll let Dexter know," Lucas said.

"No problem."

"Just remind Dexter to keep his cool. You know he can be a hothead sometimes."

He rubbed his jaw where he'd borne the brunt of his brother's temper in the past. "I remember," Harrison said. Dexter had been angry when their father left and took that anger out on everyone. Rebellion had fueled his temper, and acting out had been his norm. Their mother had been at her wit's end until a local cowboy/rodeo star had taken Dexter under his wing and taught him to break horses.

But no one had broken Dexter. Even now, instead of conforming to a job where he worked for someone else and had to play by the rules, he'd opened his own detective agency so he didn't have to answer to anyone.

Brayden had been the calm, methodical one, although Harrison always wondered if that tight control wasn't a cover for the anger and hurt beneath the surface.

"Tomorrow let's concentrate on investigating those other two cases. If they're connected," Harrison said, "we might learn something to help solve our own."

Lucas agreed. "It'll go faster if we split up the work. Why don't I talk to the family of the victim from Corpus Christi, and you take the one in Austin?"

"That works for me," Harrison said. "The sooner we question them, the sooner we can get answers."

Although it was past dinnertime and the day was wearing on him, Harrison called Dexter.

Dexter answered on the third ring. "You got news, brother?"

Harrison veered down the street toward Lower Tumbleweed. "I know who fathered Chrissy."

"You mean who Mom cheated on Dad with," Dexter said in a growl.

Harrison gritted his teeth. "Yes. But before I tell you, you have to swear you won't go half-cocked and do something stupid."

"Like what? Pound the bastard's head in?"

"Dexter," Harrison said in a warning voice.

Dexter's dark chuckle rumbled over the line. "I won't do anything you wouldn't do," he said. "Now, spill it. Who is he?"

"Reverend Langley."

His brother took a minute to absorb the information, then Dexter cursed. "Is this some kind of joke?"

"Nope." Harrison paused. "I talked to Mom and him. They confirmed that they were together years ago, but the affair didn't last. Reverend Langley chose to go to the seminary and Mom chose Dad. Dad found out after Chrissy was born."

"But he stayed with Mom after that," Dexter said, confusion lacing his tone.

"Yes. Apparently they agreed not to tell Chrissy and for Dad to raise her as his own."

"Unbelievable."

Harrison silently agreed and parked in the Grangers' drive. The crime scene cleanup crew was still working. "Lucas discovered two cases similar to Chrissy's. We're going to talk to those families tomorrow and compare notes."

An expletive erupted from Dexter. "What can I do to help?"

"Have you been following up with everyone at the bluff that night?" Harrison asked.

"Yeah, but so far nothing. I have a few more names to cross off the list."

"Okay, keep working that angle. Something is bound to break sometime."

Honey stepped onto the porch, and his heart jumped to his throat. She looked so damn beautiful he wanted to haul her in his arms and kiss her.

She was also in danger.

Like it or not, she was stuck with him. There was no way in hell he'd let anyone get to her.

HONEY FORCED A brave smile as Harrison parked.

But the image of those threatening words and the violence in the destruction made her skin crawl. She'd never felt welcome or loved in Tumbleweed, but this intruder was dangerous.

"Just lock up when you leave," Honey told the woman in charge of the cleaning crew. Not that locking up mattered. There was nothing valuable inside, and the vandal had easily broken in.

Harrison stepped from his SUV and she rolled her suitcase to the edge of the porch and handed it to him. He grabbed it while she climbed down the brick step.

She rubbed the back of her head where it was throbbing. Her muscles ached from fatigue and the stress of the day.

"Let's stop and get something to eat on the way to my place."

She sank into the seat, and he drove toward town. His body was stiff, his jaw set tight.

"How did it go with your mother?" she asked softly.

He mumbled something beneath his breath, then explained that he'd met Chrissy's biological father. Then he relayed his conversation with his mother.

"I'm sorry, Harrison. That must have come as a shock."

"Yeah." He turned into the parking lot for the Pie in the Sky, a pizza place that had been built since she'd left town. An outdoor patio offered a view of the mountains and bluff in the distance.

The decor was more eclectic and modern than any place in Tumbleweed, and probably drew the younger crowd as well as families.

Voices and laughter echoed through the open dining area, which was painted blue and silver and boasted scenes of constellations. Country music flowed from an old-fashioned jukebox, and the bar area was packed.

Several teenagers were laughing and hanging out in the back room. The front room held couples, families, and a few truckers occupied a booth to the left. A little boy with dark hair banged his spoon on the table, a mischievous look in his eyes. He reminded Honey of Harrison and what his child might look like.

She froze, wondering where that thought had come from. Then the question—was Harrison involved with anyone? Why wasn't he married?

"It smells good," she commented as the scent of freshly baked pizza wafted toward her from the brick oven.

"Food's good, beer's good," Harrison said as he led her to a booth.

A tall, broad-shouldered man with dark, wavy hair and sparkling green eyes approached them, wiping his hands on an apron. "Nice to have you back, Harrison." The man turned a curious look her way.

"Danny, you remember Honey Granger?" Harrison asked.

"Sure thing. Hey, Honey, I heard you were back." He offered her a big smile. "So sorry about your daddy."

"Thanks."

Harrison angled his head toward her. "Honey, you remember Danny, don't you?"

Her eyes widened. Danny Busby had been a skinny geek in high school with big black square glasses and he'd stuttered. He and Harrison hadn't exactly been friends.

He'd bulked up, the glasses were gone and so was his stutter.

"Of course," she said, finally gathering her wits. "This place looks nice."

He shrugged. "I was a biology major, then decided, what the hell, I always liked to cook so I figured I'd open my own place."

"It's done well," Harrison said. "Just what the town needed."

Danny blushed.

Honey relaxed slightly. The atmosphere was friendlier than the diner where the people had recognized her and hadn't been welcoming.

"What can I get you?" Danny asked.

Harrison ordered a beer and Honey asked for a glass of wine. She needed something to ease the tension from the day. For a moment they discussed what kind of toppings they wanted on their pizza. It seemed surreal, yet normal, almost as if they were on a date.

But this was not a date, and she couldn't harbor false fantasies.

Honey folded the menu and placed it back in the holder on the wall. Harrison did the same, then gripped the beer the waitress delivered and took a sip. His weighted sigh reeked of exhaustion.

But he was still taking care of her.

Emotions welled in her throat. No one had ever done that before.

"How'd it go with the cleaners?" he asked.

She ran a finger along the stem of her wineglass. "Fine. They should be finished soon."

"I'll check with the lab tomorrow to see if they found any forensics." He removed his hat and laid it on the bench seat beside him, then raked a hand through his thick, dark hair. His beard stubble and coppery skin made him look so sexy that she had to tear her gaze away.

"Lucas called," Harrison said in a gruff voice. "There were two other girls around Chrissy's age who went missing after she did."

Honey gasped softly as the implications set in. "You think the same person took them?"

"I don't know, but Lucas and I are investigating the possibility."

He fell silent as the pizza arrived, and Honey contemplated the implications of his discovery.

If he was right, that meant a serial kidnapper/killer had been preying on little girls. A serial criminal who might live in Tumbleweed.

Chapter Sixteen

Honey felt as if everyone in the restaurant was looking at her, but when she glanced around, she realized she was being paranoid.

Old habits died hard.

Not everyone in Tumbleweed remembered her, especially the younger generation.

She offered to help pay the bill, but Harrison insisted on taking care of it. Tension knotted her shoulders as they climbed into his SUV.

It hadn't occurred to her that staying at Harrison's might mean his family ranch. "Do you still live at Hawk's Landing?" she asked. If he did, she'd insist on a motel.

"Not at the main house," he said. "We had some cabins built on the property for workers when my dad used to raise cattle, so I moved into one of them for more privacy. Since I became sheriff and my brothers have their own lives and jobs, we got out of the cattle business. We keep a few horses for riding."

"Do your brothers still live at home?"

He shook his head. "Like me, they wanted their own places, so each of us took a cabin. Although Lucas is with the FBI and has a place in San Antonio. Brayden works for a law firm in Austin and has a loft downtown."

"And Dexter?"

"He has a PI office in Tumbleweed and an apartment in Austin, as well."

She relaxed slightly, grateful she didn't have to face Harrison's family tonight. He turned onto the oak-lined drive into Hawk's Landing, and Honey's heart stuttered. She had heard things in town about how beautiful the ranch was but the descriptions didn't do it justice.

Acres and acres of plush green grass spread before her. The land was flat at first but gave way to rolling hills leading into the mountains. He drove past the main farmhouse, a sprawling white two-story, showcasing wraparound porches complete with rocking chairs and a porch swing. A stable and riding pen sat adjacent to the house, and several horses galloped freely on a hill in the distance.

"I heard your ranch was beautiful, but this is amazing," she said in awe. "Do you miss ranching?"

Harrison shrugged, his jaw tight. "Sometimes. I loved it as a kid when my dad was here, but it's hard work. And after Chrissy disappeared, all I did was think about finding her killer."

"That's the reason you went into law enforcement," Honey said more as a statement than a question.

He nodded. "Yeah."

"And your brothers followed suit?"

"I guess they were driven for the same reasons I was." He shrugged, the SUV bouncing over the graveled drive. "My mother was disappointed that we didn't keep up the cattle business, but she understood. She wanted answers, too."

"Of course you all did."

His gaze met hers as he parked in front of a small log cabin, which backed up to the creek. For a moment, tension lingered between them then she followed him inside.

The rustic furnishings were masculine but homey. On the mantel, a family picture caught her eye and made her feel totally out of place.

She didn't belong here in Tumbleweed, especially at Harrison Hawk's house. Another photo of Chrissy that must have been taken shortly before she went missing sat beside the family picture. In the photo, she was wearing the yellow ribbons. He paused to look at it and Honey couldn't resist. She took his hand in hers. His was big, strong, wide with long fingers while her hand seemed tiny next to his.

Unlike most women he probably dated, her nails were filed short and blunt, her hands rough from refurbishing houses.

His eyes darkened as he looked at her hand. He licked his lips.

Dear heavens, she wanted to kiss him.

"We're getting close," she said softly. "I can feel it."

Another hesitation, and she realized she was talking as much about them as she was about finding out the truth about Chrissy.

She wanted to be closer.

A dark, primal hunger radiated from his eyes, and she sensed he wanted more, too. That he was hurting and confused and needed comfort as much as she did.

She squeezed his hand and leaned toward him. He took her face in his and stared deep into her eyes.

Hunger and desire spiraled in her belly, and she sighed softly, letting him know that she wanted him.

His gaze raked over her, but he resisted. For a fraction of a second.

Then he drew her into his arms and closed his mouth over hers. She gave in to the moment and the heat simmering between them and slipped her hands around his neck. He felt warm and strong and hungry, a potent combination that stirred her own primal desires.

He plunged his tongue into her mouth, and she opened and welcomed him, meeting his urgency with her own as she dragged her hands across his back. She wanted to touch him and taste him, to feel him naked and hot, bare skin to bare skin.

She'd never wanted a man like that.

It scared her to think that she did now.

His family hated her. Or at least his mother did.

His hands trailed down her back to her hips, and she

moaned as he deepened the kiss. Her body hummed with desire, overruling her common sense, and she pulled at his shirt and opened the top two buttons so she could slip her hands inside and touch his bare skin.

Heaven. It was pure heaven feeling the heat emanating from him, and knowing that he wanted her.

That touching her was exciting him.

She groaned and he yanked her closer, pressing his thick length against her belly so his erection pulsed between her legs. Raw need pummeled her.

She'd only been with a couple of men in the past, and no one who rivaled Harrison in the sex appeal department. No one she'd liked and admired and felt such a connection to.

No one she'd loved…

Her heart hammered. Her pulse stopped. She froze, cold fear gripping her in a vise.

Loved?

She'd never loved a man in her life. Had never even wanted to be in a long-term relationship.

She'd only meant to survive.

First as a child with her parents' dysfunction and then the stigma of the gossip in Tumbleweed. The past few years she'd poured herself into her job, building a career and a name for herself.

She'd been on her own.

She didn't know how to be anything else.

Harrison groaned and planted kisses along her neck, and she clung to him, wanting him to take her to bed.

But if he did that, she'd be lost to him forever.

And she could not lose herself.

She was the only person she could count on. For God's sake, she'd learned that at a young age. She was simply feeling weak because she was back in Tumbleweed.

He kissed her again, and she kissed him back, but slowly ended the kiss and pulled away.

"We can't do this," she whispered, remembering his mother's animosity.

He lowered his head, tilted his forehead against hers, his breathing ragged as they held each other and the heat slowly cooled between them.

"I should go to bed," she whispered.

He nodded but instead of releasing her, one hand brushed her breast as he lifted it to her chin. "I'll show you the way."

God, she wanted that.

She barely bit back a moan and fought her instincts to drag him to bed with her. It would feel so good to be naked in his arms, to have him inside her, to hear him calling her name in the throes of passion.

A weary breath escaped her. That could never be. Girls like her didn't end up with men like Harrison Hawk.

She gave him a gentle push, silently telling him they had to stop this craziness, and he stepped back.

Turmoil darkened his eyes, desire and regret blending, then he raked a hand through his hair and released her. "The guest room's this way."

She couldn't bring herself to speak so she simply nodded, then followed him to a second bedroom, which thankfully had its own bath. A log cabin quilt draped a four-poster bed with a painting of Hawk's Landing centered above the bed.

The painting was a reminder of where she was and the family who owned the land and this cabin. Of the son who had gone into law enforcement to solve his sister's case.

"What's going to happen tomorrow?" she asked.

He paused, his shoulders rigid. When he turned back to face her, he wore his sheriff's expression.

"I'm going to Austin to interview the family of one of the victims," he said gruffly. "I won't rest until the bastard who took Chrissy is behind bars."

Or dead, she thought, sensing his underlying meaning as he stalked to his bedroom and closed the door.

Body still humming with unspent passion, she stripped her clothes and dragged on pajamas.

But as she climbed into bed, she closed her eyes and imagined Harrison crawling in beside her, naked and hot with need.

Her body tingled with desire as she envisioned him above her, his arms braced as he thrust inside her, his eyes hooded with passion meant for her.

One touch of his lips and they'd forget the reasons they shouldn't be together, and they'd make love until dawn.

WHAT THE HELL was wrong with him?

Why couldn't he keep his hands off Honey?

Harrison retreated to his bedroom, disgusted with himself. Thank God she'd had the good sense to stop things or right now he'd be naked in the bed with her, feasting on her body and tasting every inch of her.

He flipped the shower water to cold, stripped and dived beneath the spray, desperately needing to wrangle his libido under control.

He hadn't felt like this with a woman in ages. Maybe never.

Truthfully, though, he hadn't dated much. He'd been too focused on his family and his sister's case to pursue a relationship with anyone.

Why Honey, though? And why now?

Because their emotions were running high from the threats against her and the connection between their families?

He closed his eyes and willed away images of Honey's golden hair spread across his pillow. Of her lips on his. Of her body joining his in blissful pleasure.

Despite the cold water, his traitorous body wanted her. Dammit.

He finally shut off the shower, dried off, dragged on boxers and padded his way to the bed.

But when he lay down, more images of Honey came to him.

She was in the next room, probably curled up in his guest bed asleep. Was she wearing some skimpy nightgown? Or was she naked?

Was she still thinking of him?

He punched his pillow and rolled to his stomach. It didn't matter. He couldn't have her. Not even once.

If he did, he'd want her again. And again.

Her big, sad eyes haunted him.

Tomorrow he had work to do. She was right—they were uncovering the truth about his sister.

Trouble was, he was getting closer to Honey, too.

But he had to stay focused.

He closed his eyes, and this time he pictured his little sister in his mind. If she'd lived, she might be married by now. Might have a family.

Hell, all of their lives would be different. His parents might have stayed together.

And he…he didn't know what he'd be doing. If he would have become sheriff or if he might have taken over the ranch.

But it did no good to think of "what if."

He was mired in reality. His family had lived in the dark for years. Guessing and imagining the worst. Hoping and praying for the best.

Struggling through each Christmas and birthday with a hole in their hearts.

And nothing could change that.

Chapter Seventeen

Harrison barely slept. Keeping his body in his own bed had consumed all his energy.

He took another shower to wake himself up, then dressed and brewed a pot of coffee. By the time Honey emerged from the bedroom dressed and showered, he'd cooked bacon, eggs and toast.

She looked surprised to see food on the table. "You didn't have to make breakfast."

"I needed food," he said. He'd had to stay busy to distract himself from joining her in the damn shower.

She looked wary but sank into a chair and sipped the coffee he poured for her. He claimed the chair across from her and wolfed down his food, anxious to get on the road. Being in close quarters with Honey was too damn tempting.

She buttered her toast then added jelly and took small bites in silence.

"Did you sleep okay?" he finally asked.

Her gaze met his. "Yes. Thanks for letting me stay here. I'm sure I got more sleep than I would have at my dad's."

He wiped his mouth. "Have you decided what you're going to do with his house?"

She sipped her coffee. "I've spoken to the local real estate agent about the neighborhood. Some of the houses already belong to the bank so an investor could pick them up for a good price and build a nice group of homes."

"That would be good for the town," Harrison said as he grabbed another piece of toast.

"The trouble is people need jobs, and Tumbleweed doesn't look as if it's grown since I left."

"True. We need something to draw people," he said, although he had no answers for the economy. His job was to protect the citizens.

He carried his plate to the sink, rinsed it and put it in the dishwasher. "I'm going to Austin this morning to talk to the family of one of the girls who went missing. You're welcome to stay here or I can give you a ride back to your father's house to retrieve your car."

"Let me go with you to Austin," Honey said. "I need to check on a project I have there."

"Can't you handle that over the phone?"

"I could, but it would be nice to get away from Tumbleweed for a little while."

He understood. Things had been intense.

"I like to review the details of the design myself, too." She cleaned her plate and rinsed her coffee cup while he strapped on his gun and holster. Being in his kitchen and sharing breakfast with her felt too intimate and made him wonder what it would be like if they had made love and then shared breakfast.

Dangerous thoughts.

He stepped outside for air while she grabbed her purse and phone. They drove to Austin in silence, the miles ticking away as the ranches and farmland grew more sparse and the city slipped into view.

He'd already phoned the family to ask if he could stop by so he drove to their house first.

"Tell me about these people," Honey said as he parked.

He killed the engine. "Their names are Irene and Karl Armond. Their daughter Yvonne disappeared about six months after Chrissy did. No one has heard from her or seen her since."

"My father never drove as far as Austin," Honey said. "And if these two cases are connected that means someone was preying on young girls back then."

Harrison nodded. "Exactly. We might be dealing with a serial predator."

Honey fidgeted as she got out of the SUV.

If that was true, they might prove her father was innocent. But it also meant that Sheriff Dunar had missed something.

"You said there were two girls?" Honey said as they walked up the drive.

Harrison nodded. "Lucas is going to talk to the other family."

The Armonds lived in an overgrown ranch house outside Austin in a small neighborhood that looked family friendly. A blue sedan sat in the drive, a pickup behind it.

Harrison knocked on the door, and footsteps sounded inside, then a female voice yelled to hold on.

"Did they have other children?" Honey asked.

Harrison nodded. "An older daughter. I'm not sure what happened to her."

The door opened, and a fiftysomething woman with a thick, silver-streaked bob answered the door. A tall thin man with hunched shoulders stood behind her, puffing on a cigarette.

Harrison identified himself, then Honey. "May we come in?"

"I don't know how we can help you," Mr. Armond said.

"I just need a few minutes." Harrison brushed past the woman, and Honey followed.

The house was outdated with worn linoleum, yellowing tile, and smelled of dog. She spotted food and water bowls at the edge of the laundry room, then saw a big, furry animal sprawled on a towel in the kitchen.

"You want coffee?" Mrs. Armond asked.

Harrison declined, and Honey thanked her but shook her head. The woman led them to the den, where a plaid couch and recliner flanked the fireplace.

They took seats and Mr. Armond stubbed his cigarette out in the ashtray. "Do you have new information about Yvonne?"

Harrison's jaw tightened. "I'm afraid not," he said. "But my sister disappeared from the small town of Tumbleweed a few months before your daughter went missing. I'm still working her case. It's possible the two are connected."

Mrs. Armond's eyes widened. "You think the same person kidnapped them?"

"I'm not sure, but answering my questions could help us both."

Mr. Armond rubbed the back of his neck with a groan. "Do we have to drag this up again?" Pain underscored his tone. "Every time we do, Irene doesn't sleep for weeks. We get our hopes up and then get all disappointed again. We can't take it anymore."

"I'm so sorry," Harrison said. "I understand how you feel. My family and I have suffered the same way."

Mrs. Armond twisted her hands in her lap. Honey stroked one freckled hand to calm her twitching. "Trust me, he wants to help."

Mr. Armond started to speak again, but his wife pressed her hand over his. "Let's talk to him. Maybe this time we'll get some answers. If we find our baby, we can finally put her to rest and she'll be at peace."

"WHAT DO YOU want to know?" Mrs. Armond asked.

Harrison knew damn well how difficult it was sitting in this couple's shoes, being questioned by the police, at the same time wondering if the people were trying to pin the crime on you.

"Tell us about the day your daughter went missing, and the days before. Sometimes we remember things after time passes that can help." He gave the couple an understanding smile. "Even if my sister's disappearance isn't related, fresh eyes and ears can pick up things that others missed."

She nodded, and she and her husband grasped hands. Comforting to see that even though they'd lost a child, it hadn't completely broken them apart as it had his parents.

Then again…his mother's affair and Chrissy's paternity had been a double-edged sword.

Mr. Armond removed another cigarette and rolled it between his fingers. "Yvonne was ten years old," he said in a voice that sounded far away, as if he was literally traveling back in time. "She liked softball, climbing trees and animals."

Harrison smiled, his heart aching. "My sister was a tomboy, too. Of course, she had to be. She had four brothers."

The couple shared a soft laugh. "I imagine so," Mrs. Armond said. "Our other daughter, Hazel, is the opposite. Such a girlie girl."

"Did they get along?" Honey asked.

Mrs. Armond fidgeted again. "Most of the time. Hazel tried to get Yvonne interested in girlie things like pretty clothes and lipstick and hair ribbons."

"Ribbons?" Harrison said, the memory of Chrissy playing with the ribbons in her treasure box taunting him.

Mrs. Armond nodded. "Hazel spent her allowance at the sale rack, buying ribbon by the yard. She tied them around her ponytail, and she learned how to make bows and hot glued them to barrettes."

Mr. Armond leaned forward, then dropped the cigarette onto the coffee table. "Is that important?"

Harrison exhaled slowly. "It might be." He paused. "Go on."

"Yvonne had a lot of friends in school," Mrs. Armond continued. "She played soccer and liked mystery books, and she loved animals, especially horses. We used to have an old mare that she rode. She loved rodeos so much that for her birthday, we got tickets…"

"God, I regret that," Mr. Armond said.

Honey stiffened, but Harrison forced himself not to react. "She disappeared at the rodeo?"

Yvonne's mother clung to her husband's hand. "Yes."

"If we'd stayed home that day, Yvonne might still be with us," Mr. Armond choked out.

"I'm so sorry," Honey said softly. "But it's not your fault. You loved her and wanted to make her happy."

Anguish wrenched the woman's face as she wiped at fresh tears.

"Tell me about that day," Harrison said. "Did your other daughter go with you?"

Mrs. Armond nodded. "Yes. She wanted to stay home with her boyfriend, but we insisted it was a family event and we were celebrating Yvonne's birthday." She paused, sweat beading her forehead.

"Her boyfriend showed up," Mr. Armond continued. "Hazel slipped off to meet him and left Yvonne alone at the concession stand."

Harrison's stomach churned. "That's when she went missing?" he asked softly.

The couple both nodded, grief emanating from them.

Harrison forced his voice to remain calm, nonjudgmental. "Did Hazel see anyone watching Yvonne or paying attention to her?"

"No," Mr. Armond said with a slight tinge of bitterness. "She said Yvonne went to get a snow cone. She was infatuated with the balloons. Hazel figured she just wandered off. So she went to make out with this guy while her sister was taken."

Harrison gritted his teeth. The scenario could have fitted a hundred child abductions.

If a predator was hunting, watching for an opportunity, he pounced when given one.

"How old was Hazel at the time?" he asked.

Mrs. Armond wiped at her eyes again. "Fourteen."

"She blamed herself," Mr. Armond said. "She went into a depression, and for a while we thought we'd lost her, too."

"We were so distraught ourselves that we were rough on her at first," Mr. Armond added grimly.

"But we went to counseling," Mrs. Armond added. "We realized that Hazel was just a kid and we forgave her."

"Did she forgive herself?" Harrison asked.

The woman shook her head sadly. "I don't think so. She works with troubled kids now through a YMCA."

Harrison felt a kinship with Hazel. "Is there anything else you can think of about that day? Did you see strangers, perhaps a vendor or rodeo worker watching your daughter?"

They both looked lost, as if they were struggling for details.

"There was a group of mentally challenged and handicapped children there." Mrs. Armond stroked the chain of her necklace, then rubbed her fingers over a chip attached to the end. A sobriety chip from AA. "She talked to all of those kids."

"She talked to a teenager mucking the stalls, too," Mr. Armond said. "But the sheriff questioned him and he was cleared."

Frustration gnawed at Harrison. He'd hoped to get a concrete suspect, but just as the sheriff's report stated, they hadn't narrowed down one.

Still, their conversation confirmed that the cases might be connected. That a serial predator had been hunting in Texas for years.

It was high time someone stopped him.

Chapter Eighteen

"Did detectives question people at the rodeo?" Harrison asked.

"Yes," Mr. Armond said. "One lady saw Yvonne talking to a rodeo clown. A teenager claimed she saw her at the cotton candy stand."

"Were there security cameras?"

Mr. Armond shook his head. "Not back then."

Damn, that would have helped.

"You never received a ransom note or message of any kind?" Harrison asked.

"No." Mrs. Armond's voice broke. "Not that we had any money, but we would have done everything possible to raise some if we'd received a note."

Harrison cleared his throat. "Did Yvonne have anything with her when she was taken?"

"What do you mean?" Mr. Armond asked.

"Like a backpack or toy?"

"She liked real horses but she was obsessed with unicorns," Mrs. Armond said. "We gave her a stuffed one for her birthday. She had it with her that day."

"Was it recovered after she disappeared?" Harrison asked.

"No." Mrs. Armond picked up a photo book from the coffee table, flipped through the pages and showed them a picture of Yvonne wearing a birthday hat and hugging the colorful unicorn.

One of Mrs. Armond's teardrops fell on the picture book. "Before we went to the rodeo, she braided the unicorn's mane and tied it with ribbons."

Mr. Armond curved his arm around his wife and pulled her against him in a comforting gesture.

"I hoped we'd find it and it would lead us to Yvonne, but the longer she was gone, I just prayed she had it with her. It would have given her comfort."

Harrison hissed a breath. "Could I see her room?"

Mrs. Armond stood slowly. Her husband snatched the cigarette and lit it.

He and Honey followed Mrs. Armond down the hall past the master bedroom to the room on the end. "I haven't changed a thing since we lost her. I kept hoping she'd come back and…"

Pick up where they'd left off.

"My mother kept my sister's room just as she'd left it, too," he said, his throat thickening.

Mrs. Armond gave him a knowing smile, obviously grateful he understood. Like his family, so many people told them they needed to move on. Pack up Chrissy's things and give them away. Turn her room into a guest room or a media room or office.

But doing that meant forgetting about her, erasing her from their lives as if she never existed.

That was something he and his family could never do.

HONEY'S HEART ACHED for this couple. Just like the Hawks, their lives had been torn apart by the loss of a child.

How did one overcome such a tragedy? Parents weren't supposed to bury their children. It should be the other way around.

Harrison looked solemn as they entered Yvonne's room. A pink ruffled bedspread with matching curtains added a feminine touch, although the bookcase held plastic toy ponies and a framed photograph of Yvonne playing T-ball.

Children's books lined the shelves as well, and a jewelry box took center stage. Harrison tugged on latex gloves and opened the box, revealing an assortment of plastic necklaces, beads and rings. A wooden doll with braids made of yarn held an assortment of colorful bows.

Harrison used his phone to snap pictures of the room and items inside. True to Mrs. Armond's words, the little girl's clothes still hung in the closet. A bright pink jacket hung next to a pink cowboy hat. Cowboy boots, sneakers and black patent leather shoes lined the shoe shelf.

Tears blurred Honey's eyes. The furniture looked polished as if the Armonds kept it clean, just waiting for Yvonne's return.

Harrison rifled through school notebooks on the child's desk. Honey spotted a diary, picked it up and skimmed several entries. Typical ten-year-old comments about her friends at school, the horse she wanted her parents to buy for her at the stable where she rode, and a boy at the stables who annoyed her because he pulled her pigtails.

Honey smiled. Two years later and she probably would have had a crush on the kid.

"I don't see anything helpful," Harrison said. "I'm going to request a copy of the file on the investigation. Maybe the detective mentioned a similarity to Chrissy's case."

"Maybe." Although so far, nothing had stuck out.

The Armonds were standing at the door waiting, a wistful sadness emanating from them.

"Please let us know if you learn anything," Mr. Armond said.

Harrison promised he would, then Honey followed him outside.

"What do you think?" Honey asked as they got in the SUV.

"The only commonality so far is the age of the girls and that they both liked ribbons in their hair. But most little girls do."

"That's true," Honey agreed.

"Yvonne disappeared from a public event, the rodeo,

where strangers as well as numerous workers and cowboys were in attendance."

"Still, no one saw anything," Honey said. "If someone wanted to kidnap her, he could have lured her away with a toy, balloons, even a rodeo animal."

"But Chrissy disappeared from the bluff where a bunch of teenagers were hanging out. Unless one of them also attended the rodeo, I don't see how we're dealing with the same perp."

"Did you suspect anyone at the bluff?" Honey asked.

Harrison drummed his fingers on the steering wheel as he pulled from the drive. "My brother mentioned that one of his friends shoved Chrissy that night. Geoffrey Williams."

Harrison snatched his phone and punched a number. "Lucas, I just talked to the Armonds. Their daughter disappeared from a rodeo. Check and see if Geoffrey Williams attended that rodeo."

A hesitation. "Okay, thanks. Let me know what you learn from the Ritter family."

He ended the call and rolled his shoulders. "You wanted to check on one of your projects. Which way?"

Honey directed him toward the neighborhood south of Austin where her latest renovation was underway.

She wondered what Harrison would think of her work. For some reason, she wanted to show him that she'd risen above her white trash roots and made something of herself.

HARRISON WOVE THROUGH the streets of Austin, his heart hammering. He sensed he was onto something with the case, but he wasn't sure what it was.

Traffic sounds, cars honking, people bustling on the sidewalk, everyone in a hurry… City life. It was quitting time already, and happy hour had begun.

The restaurants were crowded, music blaring from bars, city lights twinkling, the sidewalks packed with residents and tourists.

So different from Tumbleweed and the quiet country-side, the slower pace, the ranches and farm animals, the friendly faces.

Except someone in Tumbleweed might have been hiding behind a friendly face for years. His sister's kidnapper/killer could have been living in town laughing at him as sheriff because he hadn't put together the pieces of the puzzle to unearth the truth.

"It's the neighborhood on Silver Spurs Drive," Honey said. "Turn left at that next light and take it about five miles."

He made the turn, grateful to be leaving the heart of the city and driving into the less crowded neighborhoods that fanned out from Austin. He passed a new condo development complete with offices, businesses and restaurants then an apartment community and another business development.

Three miles later Honey pointed to another turn. Although they were within ten miles of the city, it felt as if he was driving into the wilderness.

"This is an older development," Honey said. "Most of the houses are in disrepair, but I bought a couple to flip."

"How did you get into the business?"

Honey's face seemed to change as she entered the neighborhood. Her eyes looked brighter, hopeful, void of the pain and emptiness that haunted her in Tumbleweed.

"It's kind of a long story," she said.

"We've got time."

Honey squared her shoulders. "After I left Tumbleweed, I got a job as a waitress and rented a room from this lady. Her house was falling apart, so in my spare time, I helped fix it up. It took a couple of years, but the house came alive."

"Sounds like you found your calling," Harrison said.

Honey shrugged. "I enjoyed taking something that was in ruins and fixing it. The woman and her family liked the changes. When she died, her son, a general contractor, was so impressed with the improvements, that he offered me a job as his designer. I took some classes on the side and we've done okay."

"We're working on that ranch right now," she said as they bypassed two other houses that looked as if they needed her touch. Work crews were all over the yard and ranch house.

He pulled in the driveway and parked, and Honey slid from the SUV. "I won't be long, but if you have something else you need to do, I can get a ride and meet you."

His pulse jumped as a tall dark-haired guy in jeans and a work shirt loped out, a tool belt around his hips. The man swept Honey into a big bear hug.

No wonder she'd put the brakes on the night before when he'd kissed her. She obviously had someone waiting on her here in Austin.

HONEY GAVE JARED a hug, grateful for his support and for picking up the slack in her absence.

"You okay?" he asked.

She nodded, puzzled by the scowl on Harrison's face. "I should have things tied up soon and be back."

Harrison's jaw tightened, and she introduced him to Jared.

"Jared is the contractor I told you about," she said. "He's been manning the crew while I was gone." She motioned to the house. "Let me take a quick look around, then we'll go."

"Are you going to give me the tour?" Harrison asked.

If there was one thing Honey enjoyed, it was showing off her reno projects. "Sure." She turned to Jared. "Anything I need to know about?"

He shrugged. "We had a delay with the cabinets, but we're back on track now. We'll be cutting it close to the deadline, but we should make it."

"Great." Her heart stuttered as she led Harrison into the

house. "We replaced old linoleum with hardwood floors throughout," she said to give him an idea of just how much the house had changed. "Luckily we found shiplap in the den and dining room so we restored that and rebricked the fireplace." She paused at the kitchen. "The house was cut into choppy rooms, but we took out walls and reconfigured the space to create an open concept between the kitchen, dining and living areas. A local woodworker custom built a farm table and bench to fit the house."

From the kitchen, she showed him a powder room that had been redesigned, then the master bedroom with a vaulted ceiling and a massive bathroom. The tile work in the shower was intricate, the cabinets and counter were reflective of the farmhouse style she'd chosen in the other room.

Harrison scanned each room, a smile twitching at his face. "The house is stunning," he said. "You're obviously good at what you do."

Honey's throat closed. Jared had praised her work and so had a few Realtors and clients, but hearing the admiration in Harrison's voice touched her deeply.

The people in Austin didn't know about her past or her family or the names the kids had called her. She'd left that behind when she'd run from Tumbleweed.

Although returning to the small town had resurrected those memories. But she wouldn't be staying there.

Her life was here.

And Harrison's was back in the town near his family. With his mother, the woman who hated her.

HARRISON WAS IMPRESSED with Honey's work. She changed when she spoke of the house and design.

But on the way back to Tumbleweed, she lapsed into a tense silence. They stopped at a barbecue restaurant and ate, the tension still thick between them.

She was probably thinking about Jared, maybe missing

him. Counting the days until she would be with him again, back doing the work she loved.

It was where she belonged.

Clouds rolled in, darkening the sky as he headed along the interstate. He hoped to hear back from Lucas, but the miles stretched out without a call. By the time they made it to Tumbleweed, Honey was fidgeting, agitated.

"Why don't you drop me off at my father's? I can stay there tonight."

Harrison chewed the inside of his cheek. "It's not safe," he said. "You're staying at my place."

She bit her bottom lip and glanced ahead, and he wondered if she was nervous.

"Listen, Honey, I promise I'll leave you alone. I won't kiss you or push myself on you again."

Her eyes widened, and she opened her mouth to speak, but looked down at her hands then ahead again.

Harrison spotted a bright light ahead. A light coming from lower Tumbleweed. "Good God, Honey." He accelerated and flipped on his siren. "Call 911."

Honey fumbled as she punched the numbers on her cell phone. "It's my father's neighborhood," she cried. "Hurry, Harrison. There's a fire!"

Chapter Nineteen

Honey gave the address to the 911 operator. "Please hurry," she said as Harrison rounded the corner and turned onto her street. Flames shot into the sky, smoke billowing in a thick cloud.

The back side of her father's house was engulfed. Flames ate at the dry grass, spreading to the two neighboring houses. The wind picked up, blowing smoke so thick that as Harrison parked and she threw the door open, she could hardly see the driveway.

Her feet crunched gravel, though, as she dropped to the ground.

"Stay in the SUV!" Harrison shouted.

But panic seized Honey and his words sounded as if they'd come from far away. She had to get her mother's picture.

Heart hammering, she ran toward the front of the house and darted inside. Heat seared her and smoke clogged her lungs.

"Honey, stop!" Harrison yelled behind her.

But Honey plunged on. There wasn't much inside she wanted to save, but the picture she'd found was the only one she had of her mother. She coughed, feeling her way through the smoke until she found it, then dashed down the hall to her room to retrieve the jewelry box. If she ever had a little girl, she wanted to pass it on.

Fire snapped and wood crackled and popped as flames engulfed the back walls and room. The flames had inched into her room and were climbing the wall, quickly feeding on the battered wood and rotting boards. The jewelry box was sitting atop her old dresser, which had started to catch fire.

She grabbed a bathroom towel, then wrapped it around her hand as she reached for the jewelry box.

"What the hell are you doing?" Harrison yanked her back toward the door.

"Let me go!" she shouted.

"The roof is going to give any second!"

She pushed at his hands. "Let me go. I want my jewelry box."

He cursed. "Dammit, Honey, it's not worth it!"

"It's all I've got left." Tears blurred her eyes. She hadn't realized how important it was that she keep something from her childhood, but now she did.

She started back into the bedroom, but he caught her arm. "I'll get it. Stay here!"

He took the towel, pushed ahead of her and darted through the rising flames. The wall in the back collapsed with a crash, the ceiling raining down flaming boards. Sparks flew and heat seared her.

A crashing sound echoed through the house, roaring with the noise of wood cracking, and she shouted Harrison's name.

If he got hurt, she'd never forgive herself.

She stepped toward her bedroom, but flames engulfed her old bed. "Harrison!"

Panic nearly crippled her as she searched the smoky haze for him.

It seemed like an eternity, but finally he grabbed her hand. "We have to get out of here now!" He tucked the jewelry box under one arm, and the two of them ran through the house. Wood splintered and windows shattered. They dodged fiery debris and jumped over patches of flames eating the rotting floor.

She coughed and clung to Harrison's hand as they ducked to avoid a falling board. She shouldn't have let Harrison risk his life to save her childhood jewelry box. There wasn't anything valuable inside, no precious gems or antiques or family heirlooms.

Just cheap beads and bracelets she'd played with as a kid, ones that had belonged to her mother.

A loud boom sounded and the roof collapsed. Sparks flew and pummeled them as they ran onto the porch, then jumped to the ground and raced to safety.

HARRISON COVERED HONEY'S head to protect her from being hit by flying embers as they dived beneath a live oak. The sound of glass shattering and wood crashing down splintered the air.

Granger's house was totally engulfed in flames, the two houses nearest it smoking and burning, as well.

A siren wailed. Brakes squealed as the fire engine careened into the drive.

He quickly searched Honey's face. "Are you okay?"

She nodded. "Thanks for saving my jewelry box."

"You're welcome." He pushed himself up. He had no idea what was so valuable inside, but it had been important to Honey, so he'd had to retrieve it.

"Let me talk to the firefighters." Harrison jogged to the fire engine to meet the rescue workers. A big, burly man named Wes Comber introduced himself as the fire chief.

"The first house is a goner," Harrison said to the chief, referring to the Grangers' home. "I doubt you can save the other two, but we need to contain the fire so it doesn't spread to the woods."

The chief shouted orders to his team and they quickly began to work, unrolling the hoses and aiming the spray on the ground by the other houses, then the houses themselves to keep the fire contained.

"What happened?" the chief asked.

Harrison shrugged. "I don't know." He pointed toward Honey. "Miss Granger's father owned the house that was engulfed when you arrived. We were in Austin today. When we got here, everything was ablaze."

"These houses are old," the chief said. "You think she lit a candle and left it, or used the stove and there was faulty wiring?"

"I think there's foul play. Miss Granger's father was

murdered a few days ago, and since she returned to Tumbleweed, she's been threatened and attacked."

Deep frown lines marred the man's face as he studied the blaze. "I'll have my men look for point of origin and evidence of arson."

"Thanks." Cold fear seized Harrison. What if the perpetrator had set the fire while Honey was inside?

She could have been hurt or...worse. Killed.

The thought of something happening to her made anger churn in his gut. It wouldn't happen...not on his watch.

HONEY WIPED SWEAT and soot from her forehead as her childhood home crumbled to the ground.

If there had been any happy memories in that house, they'd died years ago, destroyed by the misery of living with her father and knowing her mother hadn't loved her enough to stay around.

The embers burned bright against the brittle grass, orange and yellow glowing in the dark. Thankfully the homes were vacant so no one was inside or hurt.

The firemen worked diligently to extinguish the blaze over the next two hours. Wildfires could be dangerous and run rampant, destroying miles of woods and homes if left untended in these dry conditions. Just last year fourteen people had died in a wildfire accidentally set by teenagers when their campfire got out of control.

Harrison coordinated with the firefighters and walked the property edges, searching for the cause of the fire.

A black sedan rolled up, windows tinted, and Honey hugged her arms around her middle, wondering who it was. Lucas Hawk emerged from the vehicle in a dark suit, his gaze hooded as he scrutinized the scene.

Harrison strode around the side of the house, his gloved hand wrapped around the handle of a gas can. He met the fire chief and Lucas on the lawn near Lucas's car.

"I found this at the edge of the woods. Someone used it to set the blaze," Harrison said.

"The point of origin was the laundry room," the fire chief said. "I found signs of matches and smelled the gas there."

"Dammit, I hope he left prints on the can," Harrison said.

"Do you know who did this?" the fire chief asked.

Harrison shook his head. "Not yet. But I'll catch the son of a bitch. He didn't hurt anyone this time, but he could have."

"You think it was kids or vandals?" Lucas asked. "Or someone who owned one of these houses wanting to collect on insurance."

Harrison shifted. "No." He explained to Lucas about the threats against Honey.

"I'm sorry someone is trying to scare you off," Lucas said. "You don't deserve this."

Honey offered a small smile. "I'm just glad no one else was around or hurt."

The fire chief tilted his hat. "When things cool, we'll process the scene."

Harrison nodded and thanked him, and she followed him back to Lucas's sedan. "Did you talk to the Ritters?" Harrison asked.

Lucas pulled a photo from his car and handed it to Harrison. Honey's heart melted at the sight of the little red-haired girl with braids.

"Her name was Trish," he said. "She was eight years old and infatuated with cats. Parents took her to a town fall festival. There were games and a cakewalk and pony rides. The mom went to get popcorn and drinks while the little girl rode, but the lady manning the ponies said Trish ran off, chasing a kitty. They searched the festival and town, put up fliers, did everything they could think of, but never saw or heard from her again."

"She looks so innocent," Honey said, her emotions on her sleeve.

"This is beginning to sound like a pattern," Harrison said. "I can't believe no one saw it before."

"Information sharing and access to information across territories, especially in small towns, wasn't as easy back then as it is now," Lucas said.

Harrison heaved a disgusted breath. "I know. But somehow this creep got away with kidnapping children for nearly two decades and no one saw the pattern."

"Maybe because he traveled from one place to another," Lucas pointed out.

Honey's gut tightened. What if Chrissy and/or these other little girls had been kidnapped by someone who'd taken them out of the country?

She closed her eyes and said a silent prayer that they hadn't fallen prey to one of those soulless child-theft rings.

Or to a sexual predator or a captor who'd done unspeakable things to them.

HARRISON READ THE fear on Honey's face and wanted to comfort her. Lucas stepped away to answer the phone.

"I'm sorry about the house," he said to Honey.

"The house doesn't matter," Honey said. "Finding out what happened to these little girls and to Chrissy does."

How could he ever have wondered if Honey had lied to protect her father? She'd been almost as traumatized as he and his family by what had happened.

Lucas pocketed his phone as he approached. "Bad news. Dexter has been searching for other cases that might be connected to this one. Campers found a little girl's body in the mountains. It could be related."

Or it could be Chrissy. Harrison felt as if he'd been hit in the belly. "We should go."

Lucas nodded. "Get in. I'll drive."

Harrison glanced at Honey. "We can drop you off at my place."

Honey shook her head. "No, I'll go with you. There's no way I could sleep right now."

He climbed in the front seat and Honey in the back, and they settled in for the drive.

"Did they identify the girl?" he asked Lucas as Lucas veered onto the highway leading toward the mountains.

"Not yet," Lucas said, his voice on edge. "They think she's been there for a while, though."

Harrison swallowed bile.

Lucas's hands closed around the steering wheel in a white-knuckle grip as he drove. Farmland gave way to desertlike terrain, the thick boulders and rocks a testament they were getting close.

Harrison's mind raced with questions as they crossed the miles. If this body was Chrissy, whoever had taken her had a car...

"I checked on Williams," Lucas said. "He was nowhere near Austin or Corpus Christi when the other girls disappeared."

Damn, if the cases were connected, Williams wasn't their guy.

The sedan bounced over the ridges and rough terrain as Lucas sped toward the flashing lights. He wove around a curve and then they were there.

Dread clenched Harrison's stomach as they climbed from the car and met the detective.

He gestured toward an old mine. "Hikers ducked in to seek shelter and found the body. No ID on her and she's pretty decomposed. But a pair of pink socks were half-buried in the dirt, still attached to the skeletal feet."

Harrison pinched the bridge of his nose as sorrow overcame him.

Lucas looked pale and leaned against a boulder for a moment, and Harrison felt Honey's hand go to his back. He breathed in and out deeply to stem the nausea.

This could be it. The day they'd finally found their sister.

But if it was her, there wouldn't be much left.

Chapter Twenty

Honey's stomach rolled as she glanced toward the cave.

Whether the girl was Chrissy or another child, she hadn't deserved to be left dead—or to die—in a cave alone in the middle of nowhere. In a place where animals roamed freely at night, hunting for food.

A shiver rippled up her spine, and Honey caught Harrison's arm. "You don't have to go inside. Why don't you let the medical examiner handle it?"

Harrison stepped away from her. "This is my job, Honey. And that girl may be my sister. You can't possibly understand what that means."

Hurt swamped Honey at his tone, and she dropped her hand.

His gaze met hers, his pain so intense it pulsed through her own body.

The detective gestured toward the cave. "Let's go."

Lucas and Harrison followed the man up the incline where they met two other law enforcement officers. They handed Harrison and Lucas flashlights, and the men ducked inside the opening and disappeared into the darkness.

HARRISON STRUGGLED TO mentally remove himself from the possibility that the skeleton they were looking at might be Chrissy.

He wanted to remember her the way she was, with chubby cheeks, a gap-toothed smile and pigtails. With an infectious laugh and an annoying way of tagging after him and his brothers. With ice cream smeared on her face as she licked her cone.

The detective introduced them to the medical examiner, a middle-aged man named Dr. Thoreau. "Was there anything about your sister that would help identify her?"

Harrison and Lucas exchanged questioning looks.

"Had she broken any bones?" the doctor clarified. "Had any injuries?"

"She sprained an ankle once jumping from the swing at the playground," Harrison said. "But I don't recall her breaking any bones."

"Me, neither," Lucas said.

"Well, this girl did," the doctor said. "It looks like her femur was completely shattered."

"Did the killer do it?" Harrison asked.

The ME shrugged. "I don't think so. I think it happened when she was much younger. Judging from her bones, it looks like it healed but not properly."

Which meant this probably wasn't Chrissy. Although they still needed to wait on the autopsy.

"How long has the body been here?" Lucas asked.

The doctor shrugged. "Years. I'll call in a forensic specialist to help us narrow down the time frame and cause of death."

Lucas jammed his hands into the pockets of his slacks. "Let me know what you find so we can compare to the FBI's database and NCMEC. We also have a forensic artist who does facial reconstruction."

"Have you searched the mine?" Harrison asked.

The detective rubbed his temple. "We did a preliminary search in case there were more bodies, but didn't find one. We'll process again for forensics."

"Lucas and I want to look around," Harrison said.

The detective nodded agreement, and Harrison and Lucas tugged on gloves, then used their flashlights to illuminate the interior as they examined the area where the body lay.

Harrison stooped to study a clump of dirt and found a book of matches that were half-rotted along with kindling as if someone had built a fire inside. Kids or hiker/campers, although they weren't very smart. There could be gas pockets inside and the place could have exploded.

The tunnel led to a section that had once been excavated, then parted in two directions. Lucas took one and Harrison inched into the other. The space was small, ceiling low, dark and dank, and somewhere ahead water trickled.

His foot hit something, and he shone the flashlight on it and realized he'd stepped on a beer can. Moving deeper, he scanned the floor and walls, then something shiny glinted in the darkness.

He inched toward it, then dropped to his knees and aimed his light on it. Something was almost buried in the dirt. He dug the dirt away with his fingers, his breathing puffing into the enclosed space as he struggled for air.

The dirt gave way to a silver chain. Frowning, he dug more dirt away until he freed the chain.

He held it up, studying it. It was an old-fashioned pocket watch. Not one a little girl would have, but a man.

Had it belonged to the girl's killer?

HONEY RUBBED HER arms to chase the chill away as she watched medics bring the body out and load it to transport to the morgue.

Harrison and Lucas finally emerged, both ashen faced and grim. She joined them with the detective by the ME's vehicle.

Harrison lifted a silver pocket watch and showed it to the detective. "I found this inside. It could belong to one of the miners or someone exploring the cave. But it's possible it was the killer's."

Lucas bagged it. "I'll get it to the FBI's lab right away."

Dr. Thoreau opened the driver's side of his vehicle. "I'll let you know as soon as I finish the autopsy and the forensic artist does her thing. I'll also send those samples to the lab as you requested and fax you the results."

The men shook hands and the ME climbed in his vehicle and took off.

Harrison and Lucas headed toward Lucas's sedan and she climbed in the back seat.

But the image of that pocket watch nagged at Honey as Lucas drove away.

Someone she'd known as a kid had a pocket watch.

Her father?

She racked her brain but couldn't remember him owning one.

Fatigue pulled at her, but every time she closed her eyes, she saw the girl's skeleton. Vacant pockets where her eyes had been. Bones brittle and decayed.

Lucas and Harrison had lapsed into a strained silence, the tension thick with unanswered questions.

"Do you think we should talk to Mother?" Lucas asked as he made the turn to Lower Tumbleweed.

"Not until we know something for certain," Harrison said.

Lucas agreed, then pulled up to the ruins of her father's house. The scent of burned wood, grass and leaves permeated the area, smoke clogging the air. A few embers still sparkled in the debris, but a fire worker remained to monitor the area in case the sparks reignited and started to spread.

They all climbed from the sedan and the Hawk men stepped near Harrison's SUV and conferred for a moment while Honey retrieved her keys and unlocked her van.

"What about Honey?" she heard Lucas murmur to Harrison. "Is she in a hotel?"

"She's going to stay at my place," Harrison said in a low voice.

A breeze stirred the smoke again, reminding her of the fact that someone burned down her house tonight.

"What's going on with you two?" Lucas asked.

Harrison muttered something beneath his breath. "Nothing. I'm the sheriff and she's in danger. I'm just doing my damn job."

Honey opened her van door and slid inside. Harrison was right. Nothing was happening between them.

It couldn't.

Even though she wanted him with every breath of her being.

HARRISON WAITED FOR Honey to park at his cabin before he went inside. He'd lied through his teeth to Lucas.

Well, maybe not lied...

There was nothing really between him and Honey, except...this tension. Sexual tension he had to resist.

Hell, after seeing her work in Austin, his admiration for her had risen even more.

Liking her and wanting her was messing with his mind.

"I need to shower," he said as they entered his cabin. He desperately had to wash the stench of the mine and what he'd seen off him. The acrid odor of smoke and sweat also permeated his skin.

"I need a shower, too," Honey said.

She slipped into the guest room, and he gritted his teeth as the shower water kicked on. Dammit, he wanted to strip and join her. Work off some of his nerves and anxiety and hunger for her by pounding himself inside her body.

He wanted to wipe the pain and fear off her face and make her smile and whisper his name in the throes of passion.

Anything to erase the memory of that skeleton from his mind.

He ducked into his room, removed his clothes and stepped into the shower. The hot water soothed the knots in his shoulders, and he soaped and scrubbed his skin and hair, washing away the odors of the night.

He wished he could wash away the ugliness in his soul,

the pure bitterness and hate he had for the person who'd taken Chrissy and destroyed his family.

The water grew cold, and he stepped from the shower and dried off, then slipped on clean jeans and threw on a T-shirt. The cabin felt warm from the Texas heat, and outside the trees stood motionless with the lack of a breeze.

He ran a towel over his wet hair then shoved it back off his forehead with one hand and strode into the den. He went straight to the bar and poured himself a whiskey.

The guest bedroom door opened, and Honey appeared, wearing a tank top and pair of thin cotton pajama bottoms. His mouth watered as he looked her over.

Her long golden hair hung in damp strands around her shoulders, framing her beautiful face. Void of makeup, she looked impossibly young and innocent. Her rose-colored lips accentuated her pale skin and triggered wicked thoughts of kissing her again.

"I understand today was hard for you," she said in a low voice.

HE TOSSED THE drink down, then poured another. Honey walked toward him then picked up a second highball glass.

"Mind if I have one?"

He shook his head. "Sorry, I should have asked. I—"

"You don't have to explain," she said softly.

He averted her gaze and focused on pouring her whiskey to keep from touching her. But when he turned to hand the glass to her, and their fingers brushed, a current of need shot through him.

Her eyes widened as if she felt it, too. As if she shared that same need.

He hastily walked away, stood in front of the French doors leading to the back porch and stared at the view of Hawk's Landing that stretched behind his cabin. This ranch was beautiful, but he hadn't enjoyed it in years for dwelling on his family's sorrow.

Behind him, he heard Honey approach. Then he felt her stroke his shoulder, and he groaned.

"I'm sorry, Harrison. It's been a rough day."

He nodded. "For you, too."

"Like I told you, that house means nothing."

But it was her childhood home. It held bad memories of a life when she'd felt unwanted.

Yet she'd come so far since. In spite of the cold way his mother and the people in Tumbleweed had treated her, she'd grown into a loving, caring woman and made a success out of herself. Here, today, she'd been threatened and her house had burned down in front of her eyes, yet she seemed more concerned about him than herself.

He tossed the second drink down, then faced her. The compassion and yearning in her eyes shredded his last bits of composure.

He set the glass on the side table, then took a step closer to her. Her eyes darkened. Her lips parted on a breathy sigh.

He slipped her empty glass from her hand and set it beside his own. Then he yanked her into his arms and closed his mouth over hers.

HONEY DIDN'T KNOW what to think. She'd heard Harrison say there was nothing between them, yet all she *could* think at the moment was how much she wanted him and that he wanted her.

And after all they'd been through, there was no way she would deny him. Or herself.

Pleasure rarely came to her and she wanted it now. Wanted this time with him. Wanted to feel what it was like to be naked with Harrison, to be held in his arms and loved by him.

Even if it only lasted tonight.

He plunged his tongue inside her mouth and she met him thrust for thrust. Her arms slid around his neck, her body fitted hot and close against his as he drew her hips into the V of his thighs.

Hunger, need and desire exploded inside her, and she murmured his name, silently begging him not to stop. Not ever.

He cupped her hips with his hands and thrust his hard length against her belly and she moaned his name.

The clothes were too much.

They had to go.

She was emboldened by the passion in his touch as he raked kisses along her neck and jaw and trailed one hand over her breast. Gently he stroked her ripe nipple until it ached for his mouth, and she pushed his shirt off his shoulders.

He hadn't bothered to button it, thank God, or she would be ripping buttons in her haste.

With one quick flick of her hand, she dropped the garment to the floor and drank in his bare chest. Bronzed, wide shoulders led to taut muscles in his arms and chest that hardened and flexed beneath her gaze. She traced her fingers down his chest to the waistband of his jeans.

His breath hissed out. "Honey..."

"Yes," she breathed against his chest as she teased his nipple with her tongue.

He threw his head back and moaned, allowing her access, and she kissed and stroked his chest and abdomen, tasting the salty skin of his washboard abs and lower to his belt line where she yanked the snap on his jeans free and slid her hands inside to stroke his waist and hips.

He groaned again, then pushed her away, swung her up in his arms and carried her to his bedroom. He closed the door with his foot and laid her on his massive oak bed, then stopped and stared at her with hooded eyes.

She was afraid he'd change his mind, but instead he released a guttural groan, half pain, half pleasure. "Honey, I wish I didn't want you but I do."

Hurt wavered with the heat his words evoked. She started to get off the bed and run, to try to save herself from the memory of his touch so later she wouldn't be tormented by it, but he growled and shook his head, then leaned close to her and kissed her again.

This time a fever broke loose in her body, the throbbing need so intense, she forgot everything except that she had to have him.

She raked her nails down his bare back as he climbed on the bed on top of her, then she shoved at his jeans. He pushed at her pajama bottoms just as frantically, and she kicked them away, leaving her wearing a tiny white lace thong and tank top. He lowered his mouth and kissed her neck and throat, his fingers toying with her nipples through the thin fabric. His hot breath bathed her neck and breasts as he lifted her top over her head and tossed it to the floor. She heaved a breath and closed her eyes, savoring the sensations spiraling through her as he tugged one nipple between his teeth.

She clawed at him, wanting him closer. But he took his time, suckling one nipple then the next, triggering erotic sensations to stir in her womb and rise to a crescendo.

His lips found her belly button next, and he licked and teased his way along the lace line of her panties, then tugged them away and fused his mouth to her center.

She cried out as he lifted her hips, tossed the panties aside and took her sweet nub into his mouth.

Her body quivered in ecstasy and she groaned his name, losing herself in the moment as he brought her to the brink of release.

When he pulled away, leaving her aching, she whispered his name in a plea. He smiled through eyes glazed with passion, then snatched a condom from the bedside table, rolled it on and shoved her legs apart.

Wet, slick and needy, she opened for him, clinging to him as his sex teased her opening. He moved against her, stroking her inner thighs with his fingers until she practically begged him to join his body with hers.

And he did.

One quick hard thrust, and his thick manhood filled the emptiness inside her. She cried his name as sensations overcame her and her body exploded in a frenzy of mindless heat and pleasure. He stroked and rubbed her with his sex, pulling out and thrusting again, tormenting her with the force of his hunger.

Her body shook and quivered, and she wrapped her legs around him, pulling him deeper inside her until she felt him stiffen, then tense.

She sucked at his neck and raked her hands over his butt, thrusting her hips upward. He buried his head in her neck and moaned as he came apart inside her.

Chapter Twenty-One

Harrison's body shook with the force of his release.

He breathed against Honey's neck, savoring the feel of her soft skin and body beneath his.

Unexpected emotions pummeled him, and he held her tighter, willing himself to maintain control. He'd had sex with plenty of women before, but he'd never made love.

Love?

He couldn't love Honey Granger.

She whispered his name against his chest, and he stilled and looked into her eyes. He feared he'd see regret and she'd shove him away, but instead passion glazed her expression and a soft smile lit her normally sad eyes.

God, she was beautiful when she smiled.

He wanted to erase the sadness forever.

Fear nearly choked him. How could he do that?

She rubbed his back, planted a kiss on his chest, then cupped his face between her hands and drew him closer for another long, heated, mind-blowing kiss.

He forgot all reason and kissed her again, loving the way their bodies fitted together and the way she clung to him.

He rolled her sideways, then slowly extricated himself, dropped a kiss into her hair, then slipped from bed and padded to the bathroom to dispose of the condom. A quick look in the mirror and he didn't recognize himself.

Hunger and raw desire darkened his eyes and made him look primitive and rough.

He washed up, then glanced at Honey through the crack in the door. She lay naked, tangled in the sheets, and she'd turned to her side, facing him. Her hair draped one sexy bare shoulder and spilled across the pillow, the pale moonlight streaming through the window creating a soft glow. She looked like a cross between an angel and a sex goddess.

Desperate need burned through him. He didn't stop to analyze it. There would be time for that when she left Tumbleweed.

Right now she was here, in his bed, naked and hot from his loving. He wanted to keep her there a little longer.

Heart hammering, he strode back to the bed. One knee hit the mattress, then the other. He tilted Honey's chin up with his thumb. Her lips parted, her breath puffed out. Her gorgeous breasts rose and fell, her nipples' stiff buds begging for his touch.

He complied. First with his hands, and then with his mouth.

She gave in return, kissing and suckling his neck, raking her fingers across his back, then his butt, then guiding his sex to her. He paused long enough to roll on another condom, then he parted her legs and stroked her sensitive nub.

She braced her hands on each side of him, rotating her hips in sensual decadence as she coaxed him deep inside her. He gripped her waist and thrust hard and fast, plunging in and out of her warm chamber, driving her to a frenzy of need that sent them both over the edge.

She cried out his name as her body quivered in release. Then she rotated her hips again, pumping his hard length until his body gave in to another orgasm. Sweet, blissful release overcame him, and he dragged her mouth to his, telling her with his moan and with his body how much she meant to him.

HONEY CLENCHED THE covers and willed this euphoria to last as Harrison disappeared into the bathroom again. She half expected to hear an apology, but instead he climbed back in bed, wrapped his arms around her and pulled her next to his hard body.

She smiled, pure bliss enveloping her, as she snuggled into him.

She'd been alone all her life. But tonight she'd made love

to the man she'd fantasized about for years. It was even more wonderful than she'd imagined.

Harrison brushed her arm with his thumb, and she closed her eyes, content in his arms.

Fatigue dragged her into a deep sleep, and she dreamed that she and Harrison had made a life and a home together. They'd built a house on his ranch and they had horses and…a baby on the way.

She jerked awake, certain he'd be gone, but his arms were still wrapped around her and his breathing was shallow in sleep. She pressed her hand against his firm jaw. His beard stubble was rough, his lips parted, his face a picture of masculinity.

She planted a soft kiss on his cheek and closed her eyes again, treasuring the night as she fell asleep again.

Sometime later, a loud banging sound jarred her awake. Harrison bolted upright, then scrubbed his hand over his face as if he was disoriented.

The pounding continued. Someone was at the front door.

"Dammit." Harrison threw the covers aside, treating her to the sight of his hard, muscular body.

She silently groaned. She wanted to tell him to ignore the door and come back to bed. But the reality of the day before interceded, and she wrapped the sheet around her and ducked into the guest room while he yanked on clothes and hurried to the door.

In the guest room, she retrieved underwear, jeans and a T-shirt from her bag, and hurriedly dressed. It was probably Lucas with news from the lab, or maybe the fire chief…

She splashed cold water on her face, a tingle spreading through her at the sight of her red cheeks. Harrison's scruffy beard stubble had abraded her skin. Her hair was tousled, so she dragged a brush through it. Unable to tame the wild, wavy strands, she pulled it into a ponytail and secured it with a clasp.

Her body still smelled of Harrison, though. But if this was news about the case, they might need to act quickly.

Taking a deep breath, she walked into the den, which adjoined the kitchen. She veered toward it, hoping to brew a pot of coffee.

A loud gasp punctuated the air, and Honey froze.

"I heard there are other girls who disappeared like Chrissy, Harrison."

"Yes, Mother, I'm working on it—"

Honey bit her bottom lip, wishing she'd stayed in the bedroom.

Mrs. Hawk stalked into the room, arms folded, her eyes blazing with anger. She shot daggers at Harrison with her eyes. "My God, you're not working. You're shacking up with this whore instead."

ANGER AND HURT boomeranged inside Harrison. The pain of his mother's words on Honey's face shook him to the core.

"Mother," he said, not bothering to hide his disdain. "You have no right to speak to Honey like that. She has done nothing to hurt you or Chrissy and doesn't deserve the way you've treated her."

"She's that awful Granger man's daughter. And you know what his wife was—"

"Children are not a reflection of their parents, just as parents aren't a reflection of their children," Harrison snapped. He gave Honey an imploring look, hoping she understood the double meaning.

Honey folded her arms. "I'm sorry you feel that way, but more than that, I'm sorry for your loss," she said softly. "For the record, Harrison spent all day yesterday investigating Chrissy's case and the other girls' disappearances."

His mother started to speak but Honey cut her off.

"Also, someone burned my house down last night and your son was a complete gentleman. As the sheriff, he allowed me to stay in his guest room for my protection."

Harrison's pulse clamored. "You don't have to justify anything to my mother."

His mother spun toward him. "You're defending her over me."

"Do not go there, Mother," Harrison said. Because at this moment he would defend Honey. "And if you weren't so nasty to Honey, you'd realize that she is not to blame for Chrissy being gone. She left this town because of the ugly way you and others treated her. You should see the business she's built for herself. It's impressive, and she did it all on her own."

Honey arched a brow, seemingly surprised at his praise. But it was well earned.

His mother huffed. "All I want to know is if that body those detectives found was my little girl."

The raw agony in those words softened his anger. "How did you know about that?"

"I overheard Dexter and Brayden talking. You boys must be conspiring to leave me in the dark."

"Mother, stop it," he said, the chastising note back in his voice. "We will tell you something when we have answers. Actually this girl had suffered a broken femur at a young age, so we don't think it was Chrissy, but are waiting on confirmation."

He hadn't meant to sound harsh, but his mother staggered slightly as if she might faint.

Honey rushed forward to steady her. "Mrs. Hawk, why don't you sit down? I'll get you some coffee or tea—"

"I don't want anything to drink," his mother snapped. "I want my daughter back."

Honey nodded, sympathy in her eyes then started a pot of coffee.

Harrison pulled his mother into a hug. "I know, Mother. So do I."

But they both knew that was not likely. And he refused to promise his mother that he could make it happen.

His cell phone buzzed, and Harrison strode to the bedroom to retrieve it then answered. "Sheriff Hawk."

"It's Luke. Dammit, Harrison, another girl has disappeared."

Harrison's breath stalled in his chest. "Same age?"

"Yes. From Leadfoot Hollow about fifty miles from here. Nine-year-old girl named Kitty Walker. She and her big brother, George, were at a rodeo last night when the girl disappeared."

"Where are you?"

"On my way to get you."

"I'll be ready." He hung up and hurried to the den. He had to get his mother to leave. Honey could go with them.

He didn't intend to leave her in Tumbleweed alone. No telling what might happen to her while he was gone.

HONEY REMAINED SILENT as Harrison walked his mother to the door. "Mother, I promise, we'll call you when we know something."

His mother looked pale but nodded then gave Honey a sideways glance. Honey held her gaze. She refused to be intimidated.

Besides, it was obvious that Harrison's mother was suffering the deep-seated kind of pain only a mother who'd loved and lost her child could feel.

Not like Honey's own mother, who'd deserted her without ever looking back. She probably hadn't even shed a tear.

As soon as the door closed, Harrison snatched his keys. "We have to go. Another little girl is missing, not too far from here."

Honey gasped. "Oh, my God, what happened?"

"She and her big brother were at a rodeo last night."

Honey grabbed her purse while Harrison poured them both coffee in to-go mugs.

A minute later Lucas pulled into the drive and honked.

They raced to his sedan and Honey sipped her coffee as he peeled from the driveway.

"The local sheriff has had a search party looking for the girl all night," Lucas said. "Her mother does marketing for the rodeo. She knows a lot of the workers there and so do her kids, so she felt comfortable with the two of them hanging out until she finished last night."

"I assume they canvassed the workers and participants as well as attendees."

Lucas shrugged. "They did their best. Got all the employees for sure, but it was a late night and started raining so some of the ticket holders left early. Brother said he left the girl at the concession stand while he went to the bathroom. When he returned, he couldn't find her. That was close to eleven o'clock."

"Then he panicked, I guess," Harrison said.

"Not at first. He figured she went to the manager's office to see their mom, but she wasn't there. The mom paged the daughter, but she never showed." Lucas paused, voice troubled. "That's when they panicked. The staff checked the bathrooms, stalls, tents. It was a good hour before they called the sheriff."

He swung into a driveway for an older ranch home sitting on a hill in a neighborhood that had probably been built in the 1950s. A deputy sheriff's car was in the drive along with two other vehicles.

Lucas parked and the three of them walked up the drive to the house. Harrison knocked, and an older woman with a gray ponytail answered the door. "I'm a neighbor, Birdie Samson," the woman said. "I came to stay with Melody and George last night. They're not doing too well."

She stepped aside, and a thin woman in jeans and a T-shirt with black hair, crying into a handkerchief, sat hunched on the couch. A teenage boy with black hair sat beside her, his head bowed, body shaking.

Lucas and Harrison followed Birdie inside and introduced themselves to the deputy. Honey hung back, her heart aching as she scanned the wall of photographs in the entry.

Photos of the boy and his sister riding horses. They looked young and happy and as if they were best friends.

She zeroed in on the little girl's face and her stomach twisted. She reminded her of Chrissy. Same age. Same innocent look.

Braided pigtails. Bright ribbons in her hair.

Just like Chrissy and the other victims.

Chapter Twenty-Two

Harrison cleared his throat. "Mrs. Walker, tell us what happened last night."

She twisted her hands around the handkerchief. "We went to the rodeo like usual. The people there are like a family, so I let George and Kitty be on their own a little. I…guess I shouldn't have."

"It's understandable that you feel comfortable there," Harrison said. "I know the sheriff issued an Amber Alert and you gave him a photograph of Kitty. Is there anyone at the rodeo who paid a particular interest in Kitty?"

"She loves everyone," Mrs. Walker said. "The cowboys treat her like a kid sister, and the vendors like she's their daughter."

"I'm compiling a list of all the employees and rodeo riders and will run background checks," Lucas said. "Was there anyone new working last night?"

The woman fidgeted. "Not that I know of. Larry, the owner, usually vets everyone before he hires them."

"Can you give me his number, ma'am?" Lucas asked. "I want to get on that right away."

She grabbed a sticky note pad on the table and scribbled down a name and number, then handed it to Lucas. He excused himself and stepped into the other room to make the call.

George pinched the bridge of his nose, and Harrison's chest squeezed. "George, did you notice anyone paying attention to your sister?"

His brown eyes looked tortured as he looked up at Harrison. "Not really. She was talking to the clowns before they took to the ring. Then she wanted snacks, so she went to the concession stand while I went to take a leak."

"George," his mother admonished.

"It's fine, Mrs. Walker," Harrison said. "Let him tell things his way." He gave George a sympathetic look. "So you left her at the stand and when you got back, she wasn't there."

"No," George's voice cracked. "I was…mad at first. I figured she went back to the stands where we were sitting or to the stables to see the horses, but I checked both places and she wasn't there."

"Was she shy around strangers?" Harrison asked.

"No. She talked to everybody," George said. "A couple of times she wandered off and joined a bunch of kids who'd come for a birthday party. She wanted some cake and ice cream." He wiped at his eyes. "She loved balloons and was always sneaking over to play with them during the show."

"She liked the souvenir stands, too," Mrs. Walker said. "She collected the little stuffed ponies."

"You checked those stands?" Harrison asked.

"Yeah," George said. "She stopped at Benny's booth and talked to some other kids. Benny said this big guy, older, about your age, was right in the middle of them." He blushed as if he hadn't meant to imply that Harrison was old.

"A big guy? You mean a father?" Harrison asked.

"No," George said. "This guy was mentally challenged. He talked like a kid."

Harrison swallowed. Something about the story rang a bell.

A PICTURE OF what had happened flashed in Honey's mind.

"Tell me more about the man," Honey said.

George bounced his knee up and down. "He didn't talk very plain, sort of made a weird noise. He was intrigued with the colored streamers at the booth. He touched one of my sister's ribbons and told her how pretty it was."

A sense of déjà vu swept over Honey, stirring a memory of Chrissy twirling her hair ribbons around her finger one day at the park in town. Then Elden ran up and talked to Chrissy. He wanted to touch Chrissy's ribbons.

Honey had felt sorry for Elden because the other kids made fun of him. He had no friends, so she'd encouraged Chrissy to be nice to him. That day he'd followed them all over the park...

"What was this guy's name?" she asked, her throat thick with fear.

George shrugged. "I don't know. But some lady stormed up and took his hand and told him to come with her. She sounded mad."

Elden's mother?

Honey's stomach clenched.

Oh, God...

She covered her mouth to stifle a gasp and stood.

Harrison's hand brushed over hers. "What is it, Honey?"

She glanced at George, then at his parents, and suddenly felt sick. "I need some air."

Harrison's brows arched, but he nodded, and she raced from the room. Seconds later he joined her outside. She was leaning against his SUV, perspiration beading her forehead and neck as she fought nausea.

Harrison's boots crunched the gravel as he approached. "Honey, what's wrong?"

She inhaled a deep breath. "The mentally challenged guy the little girl was talking to... I think it was Elden."

He took her arm and forced her to face him. "Elden?"

She pushed her hair behind one ear. "In Yvonne's diary, she mentioned a boy teasing her. Something about that pocket watch seemed familiar, and I remember now that Elden had one. He tied a ribbon to it and was mesmerized by it as he swung it back and forth."

Harrison's eyes widened as he considered her theory. "But we found the ribbon at your dad's house."

"He or his mother could have put it there," Honey said. "At the park one day, Elden was intrigued with Chrissy's ribbons and... Oh, God, it's all my fault."

Harrison's jaw tightened. "What do you mean?"

"I told Chrissy he was harmless, to be nice to him, and she let him touch her hair ribbons." She'd thought Elden was harmless, but what if she was wrong?

The color drained from Harrison's face. "I wonder if he was at the bluff that night."

Honey strained to recall the faces she'd seen, but she'd been so disappointed that Harrison was meeting another girl that she hadn't stayed long. "I don't know." She wiped at her forehead. "Although if the same person hurt all these girls, that means he was in different places. Elden doesn't drive—"

"His mother could have taken him to the rodeo and the carnival. Those are all places kids like to go," Harrison said between gritted teeth.

Horror engulfed Honey. If that was true, and Elden was guilty, his mother had known and covered for him.

Lucas strode toward them. "Larry wasn't any help. No new employees that stuck out as suspicious. What's going on?"

Harrison quickly explained Honey's theory.

Lucas jangled his keys. "I'll drop you at your car and do some checking on Elden and his mother while you drive out to the Lynches' house."

They quickly climbed in Lucas's car and Harrison phoned a local judge for a warrant. If Honey was right, Elden might have Kitty now.

She closed her eyes and prayed they found the little girl in time.

HARRISON'S STOMACH CHURNED as Lucas dropped him and Honey at his SUV. He had phoned his deputy to fill him in on the drive, and Mitchell was supposed to be canvassing the town in case Elden and his mother were at the diner or shopping.

He flipped on the siren and pressed the accelerator. Honey fidgeted nervously. "I never thought he was dangerous."

"Me, neither," Harrison admitted. "And his mother always kept him on a short leash."

"What if that's the reason she did?" Honey asked. "Maybe he was different when he was alone. Maybe he had a bad temper and snapped?"

Harrison raked a hand through his hair, weaving around traffic. Sadly, he'd never thought Elden completely understood what was going on. But maybe he had. Still, why hurt little girls?

He stopped at the judge's house to pick up the warrant, then hurried back to the car and raced away. He rounded a curve, tires squealing, and bounced over a rut in the road as he flew toward Lower Tumbleweed. Elden and his mother lived in a mobile home not far from the Grangers' house.

He turned into the drive for the mobile home park, slowing in case children were outside. A swing set and jungle gym had been added to a central area, creating a park for the kids. He scanned it to see if anyone was there. If Elden was a child predator, he had the perfect hunting ground.

Although none of the victims had lived in his neighborhood.

He screeched to a stop in the drive, then jumped out. Honey started behind him, but he gestured for her to wait. If Elden was guilty and his mother was protecting him, she might be dangerous.

He strode up the three steps to the door and knocked. "Mrs. Lynch, open up, please, it's Sheriff Hawk."

Nothing.

He banged harder and shouted again, but no one answered, so he jiggled the doorknob. It was locked. Dammit.

He had a warrant but that didn't give him a right to break in. But a little girl's life was in danger...

He jammed his lock-picking tool into the lock, then twisted it until the door popped open.

The car door slammed behind him, and Honey got out. He motioned that it was okay for her to join him, and she ran up the steps. He pushed the door open and inched inside. "Anyone home?"

No answer.

Only the sound of a fan whirring.

He scanned the small living area with a frown. Elden's mother cleaned at the local inn and for others in the town. Her own place was sparsely furnished, the furniture old, but the room looked tidy and the kitchen was clean.

One corner of the den held a bookcase full of toys—building blocks, crayons and paper, toy cars and plastic animals—a sign of Elden's mental age.

"Look for anything that might belong to a little girl," he murmured.

Honey searched the bookcase while he walked down the narrow hall and glanced in the first bedroom. Elden's.

Blue-painted walls, a comforter with a farm animal theme, and posters of various rodeos and rodeo stars. He checked the desk and found art paper and crayons, then several drawings of little girls.

His gut tightened.

In each drawing, he'd sketched colored ribbons in the little girl's hair.

Anger and sorrow engulfed him.

He opened the closet door and dug through the man's clothes and shoes, his pulse jumping when he found a toy chest inside.

He lifted the lid and his heart stopped. All toys little girls would play with.

And other items—a pink backpack, a purple hair ribbon, a child's pink purse...

Had the items belonged to the missing girls?

Then a little beaded bracelet. Tears flooded his eyes. It was Chrissy's.

HONEY FOUND NOTHING in the kitchen or den and rushed to help Harrison in the bedroom. "Did you find anything?"

He was standing at the closet with his back to her, but he was so still she knew something was wrong. Then he slowly turned and she saw a child's bracelet in his hand.

"It was Chrissy's," he said in a tortured voice. "There are other things in there, too, from other girls."

Her breath caught at the implication. "Oh, Harrison. I'm sorry…"

His phone buzzed, and he whipped his head around as if physically jerking himself back to reality. "Sheriff Hawk." A pause. "No, they're not at the house, Lucas. But I found some things that belong to the little girls. Elden is our guy." Another pause. "Okay, let me know if you find something."

He hung up and wiped a hand over his eyes. "He's going to put a trace on the Lynches' phones."

Honey's skin prickled as she studied the drawings on Elden's desk. The little girls, the ribbons…then a sketch of the bluff and the swimming hole and the caves…then a second entrance, one she'd never been in.

Inside the cave, though, was a clump of rocks. A flower was sticking up between them.

Her heart hammered. "Harrison, look at this. This could be the place where he left the girls."

Harrison snatched the picture then took her hand. "Come on, we need to hurry. If he has Kitty, maybe we can save her."

Chapter Twenty-Three

Harrison's pulse raced as he drove toward the bluff. He called Lucas and left him a message about the sketch.

Honey sat stone still in the seat beside him, except for her hands, which she kept twisting in her lap.

"I should have remembered about Elden and the pocket watch and his fascination with the ribbons earlier," Honey said in a strained voice.

"That would have been helpful."

Pain flashed in her eyes, and he regretted the bite to his voice, but he couldn't retract the words.

Neither could he forgive himself for not staying home and watching Chrissy that night. If he had, she'd be alive.

Although traffic was minimal, the minutes dragged as he drove over the terrain. Dark clouds hovered above the sky. They rarely got rain this time of year, but today's clouds looked dismal and threatening.

Honey stared out the window, her face ashen. He swung up the dirt road to the bluff, bypassing the scenic overhang, and barreled into the clearing where the teens usually parked.

A rusty black pickup sat sideways in front of a cluster of rocks. Elden's mother's truck.

"They're here."

Honey gripped the door handle as she scanned the area. "Look, Harrison, over there!"

He jerked his head to the left near the mouth of the cave and his blood ran cold. Elden was hunched low on the ground, his mother pacing beside him.

"Wait here!" he told Honey as he eased open his car door. She shook her head and slid from the SUV. He motioned for her to stay by the car then laid his hand over his gun and stepped forward. Rocks crunched beneath his boots as he slowly walked toward them.

A low, wailing sound echoed from Elden, teeth jarring in its shrill intensity.

A coldness washed over Harrison. Elden was holding the little girl, Kitty, in his arms, rocking her back and forth, his body shaking with sobs.

Elden's mother swung around, eyes wild with terror and desperation. She aimed a gun at them.

Harrison halted, and Honey froze beside him.

"Stop, Sheriff," she growled. "Don't come any closer."

Harrison held up a warning hand. "Please, Mrs. Lynch. You don't want to shoot me or anyone else. This has to stop."

Her hand trembled as she waved the gun around. Somewhere in the distance a wild dog howled. Or maybe it was a coyote. "I have to protect my baby. That's what mamas do."

"That's true," Harrison said, his voice low, controlled. "But they don't murder for them."

"I haven't murdered anyone," she shouted.

"But Elden has, and if you're covering for him and letting him continue, then you are as much to blame as he is."

"He didn't mean to hurt them!" she cried. "He wanted to play with them."

Honey eased up beside him. "He likes the ribbons in their hair, doesn't he?" Honey said softly.

Mrs. Lynch's face crumbled. "He wanted to make friends. Kids laughed and teased him all his life, but he just wanted to play like they did."

"Only he was bigger and got rough," Harrison guessed.

Sorrow streaked her face as she glanced down at her son, who was wailing like an injured animal. "He tried to tell them how pretty they were, but they got scared and ran from him."

Harrison envisioned the scene she described, and felt like his heart had been shredded with a sharp knife. "Is that what happened with my sister?"

Tears leaked from the older woman's eyes and she nodded miserably. "I'm sorry. He didn't mean to hurt her. But she ran and he chased her like it was a game."

"It wasn't a damn game," Harrison bit out.

"No, but he thought it was. When he caught her, he tried to hug her, but…he hugged her too hard."

The breath whooshed from his lungs in an excruciating rush. "He smothered her?"

Misery emanated from the woman as she laid a hand on her son's back. The gun bobbed in her trembling hand. "It was an accident."

"Then you should have done the right thing and reported it." Harrison forced his voice to remain calm as he inched closer to the woman.

"But the state would have taken him away from me," she said on a sob. "Then he would have been stuck in some home and treated like an animal or a criminal. Poor Elden didn't deserve that."

"My sister didn't deserve to have her life snuffed out when she was ten," Harrison said bitterly. "Neither did the other little girls. And their families didn't deserve to lose their children."

"I know, and Elden and I are both sorry," Mrs. Lynch mumbled.

Harrison spoke through clenched teeth. "He was dangerous and should have been locked away so he couldn't hurt anyone else."

Honey eased toward Elden and spoke softly. "It's okay, Elden, do you remember me? I'm Honey."

"Stay back!" Elden's mother warned.

But Honey crept closer. "I just want to comfort him. Elden and I were friends. Weren't we, Elden?"

Mrs. Lynch looked rattled by Honey's tone, and Harrison took advantage of her distraction and jumped her. She screamed and swung the gun toward him, but he knocked her arm upward and the gunshot blasted the air.

She lost the grip on the weapon and it sailed through the air toward the cave and landed in the dirt.

"Mama!" Elden cried.

The woman pummeled Harrison with her fists, but he overpowered her, grabbed her arms and yanked them behind her.

"I just wanted to protect him!" she screamed as tears rained down her cheeks.

"What about those little girls?" Harrison growled next to her ear. "What about protecting them from your son?"

"He didn't mean to hurt them!" she cried again.

"But he did hurt them," Harrison said as he snapped handcuffs around her wrists. "And you stood by and let him."

HONEY'S HEART ACHED as she knelt beside Elden. He was hysterical, sobbing, rocking back and forth, his head buried against the little girl.

"It's me, Honey," she said softly. "I know you wanted to play with her, Elden." In spite of her terror for Kitty, she rubbed his back to calm him. "But you can let her go now. She needs to rest."

Tears blurred her eyes as she imagined him holding Chrissy this way, of his shock and frustration when he realized he'd hurt her.

He made a low, mewling sound, and she gently rubbed his arms. "Just lay her down gently," she said in a low murmur.

She continued to whisper soft words of encouragement until he eased the child to the ground. He spread her hair around her face and kissed her cheek, sobs racking his body.

Honey pressed her hand to the little girl's chest and suddenly realized she was still breathing. "Harrison, she's alive. Call 911!"

Elden sank back on the ground, wrapped his arms around himself and continued crying and rocking. Harrison quickly phoned an ambulance.

Honey cradled the little girl in her lap and gently

smoothed the hair from her cheek. Seconds later Harrison joined her and checked the child's pulse. Relief filled his face when he realized she might make it.

Elden's mother rushed to her son, her arms still cuffed behind her back, and sank down beside him.

Harrison ordered her to stay beside him. "Where is my sister?"

"In the cave near that back entrance," the woman murmured. "Behind the rocks. I…put her there so she could rest."

Honey's chest heaved at the anguish in Harrison's expression. "And the other little girls?"

"They're all together," Elden's mother choked out. "I didn't want them to be alone."

"Except we found a child in the mountains."

"I didn't want to leave her, but I didn't have time to bring her back here."

"What about Honey's father?" Harrison bellowed. "Did you kill him?"

Her body shook with her sobs. "He started coming up here drinking and snooping around," she shouted. "I saw him in the cave. He found that damn ribbon."

Honey swallowed hard. "So you were afraid he'd find Chrissy and you killed him?"

"I couldn't let anyone take my baby away from me," she cried again. "He's just a kid…"

"You put the ribbon in my father's house to frame him," Honey said through clenched teeth.

Elden's mother nodded miserably again. "Your daddy was worthless. I figured the Hawks would believe it."

"And they did," Honey said. "But you could have saved these other children if you'd gotten Elden help."

"Did you threaten Honey and burn down the Grangers' house?" Harrison asked.

"I couldn't let her find the truth," Elden's mother cried. "Those houses needed to be torn down anyway."

"Let me call my brothers." Harrison stepped to the side

and made a phone call. Honey heard him tell Lucas where they were and what had happened. "Bring shovels," he said. "We have to dig those rocks away to get to Chrissy."

A siren wailed, the shrill sound drowning out the woman and her son's cries. Honey understood the need to protect a child, but not at the cost of other children's lives.

Nothing justified that.

EMOTIONS PUMMELED HARRISON as the paramedics and his brothers arrived. Time seemed to stand still as they waited to see if the little girl was all right. The medics gave her oxygen and she immediately stirred. She looked frightened and confused, but she was going to be fine.

He called the parents and told them to meet her at the hospital.

He forced Elden and his mother into the back of his SUV, both cuffed and restrained so they couldn't escape. Honey wanted to help, but he insisted it was dangerous and ordered her to remain outside while he and his brothers hurried into the cave with shovels and flashlights.

It took him no time to find the rocks as he'd noticed them earlier but had thought they'd fallen in a mining landslide. They eased away the rocks, stacking them to the side, and Harrison crawled through the opening.

A wave of sorrow and pain engulfed him when he saw the skeletal remains of his sister and three other girls lying side by side. Elden's mother had covered each of them with a blanket. Chrissy's rag doll was tucked beside her.

A strangled sound caught in his throat. His brothers' faces were etched in grief and horror.

Finding Chrissy and learning the truth about what happened to her should have given him peace.

But anguish filled him. And now they had to break the news to their mother.

Chapter Twenty-Four

An hour later guilt still weighed on Honey as she watched Harrison and his brothers exit the cave with the ME. They had called in a team to remove the bodies and transport them to the morgue.

The identity of the girls had to be verified, families called, then the process of funeral arrangements made.

Harrison's mother was going to be devastated. But at least now she could give her daughter a proper burial and Chrissy could rest in peace.

And now Honey knew who'd killed her father, she could return to Austin and leave Tumbleweed behind.

Sun slanted off Harrison's strong jaw as he glanced up at her. The pain emanating from him made her want to go to him and soothe his anguish. But only time could do that.

The fact that she'd encouraged Chrissy to be nice to Elden meant she'd put Harrison's sister in danger. Granted, she'd been trying to do the right thing, but in doing so, she was responsible for Chrissy's death.

How could Harrison ever forgive her?

How could she forgive herself?

HARRISON COULD BARELY look at Honey. His family had blamed her and her father for his little sister's disappearance when all along they weren't responsible.

Elden was.

No one had ever thought to suspect him.

Honey had been nice to Elden, which might have contributed to the problem, but she'd been bullied and teased herself, and she'd simply been trying to be nice to a mentally challenged child.

How could he fault her for being a kindhearted, good person?

His deputy arrived, and Harrison turned Elden and his mother over to him. Mitchell would take care of locking them up and booking them.

The transport team drove away with the girls' remains, and grief and dread welled in his chest.

"We should talk to Mother," Dexter said.

Harrison nodded. They'd wait to notify the other families until they'd verified the girls' identities.

"I'll drop Honey off and meet you at the ranch."

His brothers agreed and they separated to go to their individual vehicles. Honey was waiting by the SUV, her sympathetic look mixed with other emotions he couldn't define.

"We're going to go see my mother and break the news," he said, his voice dark. "I'll drop you at my place. That is, unless you're ready to go back to Austin."

Honey's phone buzzed and she gave it a quick glance, but didn't answer. Instead she climbed in the passenger side in silence.

"I'm sorry, Harrison. If I hadn't encouraged Chrissy to be friends with Elden, she'd be alive."

The guilt in her voice triggered his own. It wasn't her fault. He should have been watching his sister that night.

But he was too emotional to speak. All he could think of now was the expression on his mother's face when he and his brothers delivered the news they'd found Chrissy and that she'd been dead all these years. That her body had been left to rot in a cold cave.

Honey turned to look out the window, and he sped toward his cabin, his body tight with anxiety.

He parked and turned to her, his heart hammering. "Now you know what happened to your father, what are you going to do?"

"I guess I'll get Dad's property cleaned up and put it on the market," Honey said.

"Then you're going back to Austin?"

"That's where my life is," she said quietly.

That was true.

The thought of her leaving made his throat thicken. But she had reason to hate Tumbleweed and as she said, she had a life in Austin. That guy she worked with was probably waiting on her.

She climbed out, and he started to ask her to stay, but that wouldn't be fair.

He had a rough time ahead at his mother's, too, and he needed to get going. Anything that had happened between him and Honey was due to the stress of the past few days.

She had given him no indication that she cared about him or wanted to stay. That she might even love him.

So he gritted his teeth and let her climb from the SUV and head inside his cabin. With a heavy heart, he drove toward the farmhouse on Hawk's Landing to meet his brothers.

As HONEY WALKED through Harrison's cabin, the memory of making love to him made her heart ache with love. She wanted to stay, to comfort him when he returned, to tell him how much she cared for him.

But she didn't belong here. Not with a Hawk.

She had to tie things up and go back to Austin where no one knew the girl she'd been and the family she'd come from.

Where they only knew her as Honey Granger, the fixer-upper, the renovator/designer who turned crumbling properties into beautiful homes for families.

She repacked her suitcase, then drove to her old neighborhood. The devastation was stark, the scent of smoke and burned rubble so strong she had to inhale deep breaths to calm the queasiness in her stomach.

Queasiness from the destruction but also from the fact that the people who'd lived here had suffered, lost their homes to the bank and, now, to fire. And that other kids like her would grow up homeless, in shelters or on the streets because they had no good place to go.

Kids who'd be bullied and teased like she was.

Elden's face flashed in her mind, and as much as she regretted what he'd done, she couldn't have been mean to him years ago.

That would have been wrong, too.

Sympathy for him also filled her. He hadn't meant to hurt the girls. He'd simply wanted love and hadn't realized his own strength.

She hugged her arms around herself and turned in a wide arc to study the property. The neighborhood could hold at least ten to fifteen homes. Although three had completely burned down due to Elden's mother, ten others still stood in poor condition. Abandoned and left for dead.

A vision of what the houses could look like hit her, and adrenaline surged through her just as it did at the beginning of any new project.

She hadn't always believed in fate, but perhaps everything that had happened in her past and this past week was for a reason. She couldn't change anything in that past, but she could do something about the future.

She could give other children the kind of hope that she'd craved. And if she found some investors and financial assistance, she could give them an affordable home and prove to the people in Tumbleweed that she'd made something of her life.

Decision made, she retrieved her cell phone and called Jared to tell him her plans. Together they could put together a deal and make this burned-down, run-down neighborhood into something to be proud of.

HARRISON AND HIS brothers gathered around their mother in the den and delivered the news. Her face crumpled, but she seemed to accept the fact that Chrissy was gone as if in her heart she'd known it all along.

She knotted a tissue in her hands. "So Waylon Granger and his daughter had nothing to do with it?"

Harrison shook his head. "No, Mother. Elden was infatuated with little girls and drawn to the pretty ribbons in their hair. He's mentally challenged and didn't realize how big or strong he is and tried to hold them when they ran from him."

"He smothered them," Lucas said quietly.

A choked sob came from their mother. "Our poor little Chrissy lying up there all alone all these years."

Harrison's stomach twisted. The thought of Chrissy lying in that cold cave made him feel ill inside, as well. They had searched it so many times but never moved those damn rocks aside.

Brayden squeezed their mother's hand. "Elden's mother said she put the other girls there so they wouldn't be alone."

His mother gave him a sharp look as if that comment didn't offer any comfort. "What's going to happen to the Lynches?"

Harrison glanced at Dexter. Technically Elden was a serial killer although the circumstances were a consideration. "Elden will be charged, but considering his mental impairment, he'll go into a special facility where he'll be monitored. But he won't be able to go free and hurt anyone else."

"And his mother?"

"She'll be charged as an accomplice for covering up the crimes," Harrison said.

"The judge may be sympathetic to her," Dexter said. "But if she'd come forward and institutionalized Elden after he killed Chrissy, those other little girls would still be alive."

Harrison nodded. "I'm sorry, Mother. No one suspected Elden or noticed signs that he was violent. It really was more accident than intention. He…loved the girls."

Tears streamed down his mother's face. "It doesn't bring our little girl back, though."

"No," Harrison said softly. "But at least we know that she wasn't killed by a deviant who tortured her or inflicted unnecessary pain on her."

"We can give her a nice burial," Brayden added. "And now we'll have a place to visit her."

Their mother nodded and wiped at her tears. Dexter moved to the kitchen to make some tea while his mother retrieved the photo album she'd kept of Chrissy's childhood. They spent the next two hours looking at pictures and sharing memories of Chrissy.

She had been lost long ago, but at least they had her back now, and they would always remember her in their hearts.

THREE HOURS LATER Harrison left the ranch house. His mother had already started making arrangements for a service for Chrissy and was going to try to get some rest. Brayden offered to stay at the house with her that night while he and Dexter and Lucas left.

As they'd reminisced over Chrissy, he couldn't help but think about Honey. She had the answers she needed about her father. What was she going to do now?

His lungs squeezed for air as he remembered making love to her. And he had made love to her—it hadn't simply been sex.

He cared about Honey.

A pain ripped through him. His family had found closure, finally. But sometime during the last few days while he was looking for Chrissy and trying to find Waylon Granger's murderer, he'd fallen in love with Honey.

He pulled up to his cabin and instantly noticed that Honey's car was missing. Disappointment bombarded him. She couldn't have gone back to her father's. There wasn't enough house left to stay in.

He ran a hand through his hair as he parked and walked

up to the door. The house was dark when he entered, a lone lamp illuminating the den.

The floors creaked as he walked into the entryway, the emptiness accentuating the loneliness engulfing him.

She was gone.

Dammit.

He flipped on a light and strode into the kitchen, then spotted a note lying on the table. Hope budded inside him.

Maybe she'd gone to the inn for the night and he would see her in the morning.

But emotions pummeled as he read the note.

Dear Harrison,

My heart aches for you and your family. I'm so sorry about Chrissy. I wish I could go back and change things, but I can't.

I can leave town, though, so your family can honor your sister the way Chrissy deserves without having me as a reminder of the past.

Take care of yourself, Harrison.

Goodbye,

Honey

Harrison crushed the note in his hands. He didn't want Honey to leave, but he couldn't blame her for hating this town after the way they'd treated her.

But dammit, he'd lost Chrissy a long time ago.

And now he'd just found Honey, and he'd lost her, too.

Chapter Twenty-Five

The next week was hell.

Harrison tried to focus on his family's needs and his mother during the memorial service and his sister's burial, but all he could think about was Honey and why she hadn't stayed around to say goodbye to him in person. He'd called her numerous times, but she hadn't returned his call.

She obviously didn't love him.

She'd walked away without looking back, just as she'd left Tumbleweed years ago and lost touch.

Except she'd built a life for herself and a good reputation and business. And just this afternoon Geoffrey Williams had told him that she'd bought the land/lots in her father's neighborhood and planned to transform the area into affordable, nice homes for low-income families. How she planned to pull it off, he didn't know. But he trusted that Honey would do what she'd said.

She had integrity.

"She's back," Cora said as Harrison sipped his coffee.

"What?" For a moment, he was disoriented. "Who's back?"

"Honey Granger," Cora said. "They've already started bulldozing that land where her daddy lived. Leroy Pirkle and Betty Sumner saw the plans for the development and it's quite impressive."

Leroy and Betty were on the town council.

"Honey is here herself or did she send her coworker?" He'd heard that her partner, Jared, had met with Leroy and Betty.

"I saw her van myself," Cora said. "Not sure how long she's staying, but she booked a room at the inn for two weeks."

Harrison's pulse jumped, but he forced himself to remain passive. He hadn't yet told anyone, including his family, how he felt about Honey.

But he missed her like crazy. And he wanted her back in his life.

She left you without saying goodbye.

That had hurt.

Except he'd reread her note a hundred times and sensed she thought she didn't belong in this town.

She was wrong.

He stood and tossed some cash on the table to pay for his lunch. "Thanks. I gotta go."

Cora smiled, took the money along with his empty coffee cup and dish and sauntered toward the kitchen.

Heat suffused him, nearly robbing his breath, as he stepped outside. Three buildings down, his gaze zeroed in on the jewelry store.

He had no idea how Honey felt about him, but he knew how he felt about her. And it was damn time he told her.

She might laugh in his face or tell him to get lost, but this time if Honey Granger left Tumbleweed, she'd know that she was loved and that at least one person wanted her to stay forever.

ADRENALINE SURGED THROUGH Honey as she watched the bulldozer clear the burned rubble from her father's house and the neighboring properties. She had worked with Jared and an architect to design a street lined with Craftsman and ranch homes that would provide comfortable, affordable homes and add value to the town of Tumbleweed.

She'd spent the last week working on the plans, drawing designs and soliciting financial assistance. She was also using local building companies, suppliers and workers, which would feed money back into the community.

She couldn't wait to see the houses popping up and families moving in.

"This is going to be fabulous," Jared said. "But you know this project will take time."

Honey nodded. She wanted to be here every step of the process, but that would mean she'd be close to Harrison.

Too close.

She couldn't stay here and not want him.

"Are you interested in overseeing it?" Honey asked.

Jared's eyes widened in surprise. "I thought you'd do that. I know this was your hometown."

"It was, but I have mixed memories here and—"

Harrison's SUV rolled down the street, cutting off the rest of her statement. Her breathing turned choppy, a blend of nervous anticipation and sadness.

The owner of the bulldozer shouted that he needed to talk to them, and she gestured for Jared to handle him.

Harrison parked on the side of the street, his big body taut with tension as he strode toward her.

She told herself to run. To get in her car and drive away before she did something stupid like admit that she was in love with him.

"I heard what you're doing," he said in a gruff voice.

She nodded. "It's a good business move." Although business really had nothing to do with it. Her heart was in this project because like it or not, part of her heart was still here.

With Harrison.

His dark gaze met hers as if he recognized the lie. She averted her gaze, determined to keep her emotions at bay, but she could smell his masculine scent and the aftershave that had lingered on her skin after they'd made love, and tears burned the backs of her eyelids.

He took her hand and pulled her beneath a sawtooth tree away from the work crew and Jared.

"Honey," he said on a deep breath. "I had to see you."

"What's wrong?" she said. "Did Elden or his mother get out?"

"No, they're both locked away now, and all the families have been notified." He scrubbed a hand over his face. "The people, little girls, in town are safe."

She breathed out in relief. "Good. I know it hasn't been easy on your family and your mother."

He released a weary breath. "No, but she's holding up. But that's not what I wanted to talk to you about."

Heat seared her skin where he was still holding her hand. She should let go. Put some distance between them. But she couldn't bring herself to break the moment.

He lifted her hand and kissed her palm and her heart melted. "I'm glad you came back," he said in a low voice. "I...missed you."

"Harrison, don't—"

"Why not?" His voice grew stronger, and he cupped her face between his hands. "When you left, I realized how much I missed you, how much you meant to me." His eyes darkened, and he slid one hand into his pocket.

Her breath caught as he opened his palm to reveal a stunning diamond in an antique setting. "I love you, Honey. I want you to marry me."

Oh, God, she wanted that, too. She loved him with all her heart. She probably always had.

She always would.

But his mother hated her.

And there was no way she could come between them.

"I'm sorry, Harrison, it would never work."

Pain flashed in his eyes. "Because you don't feel the same way."

"Because I'm Honey Granger, the girl your mother has always despised. She thinks I'm a tramp and that I'm not good enough for you."

"I don't give a damn about what she thinks," he said. "Besides, she's wrong."

"Well, I care what she thinks," Honey said. "She's your mother and you love her. Your family has been through enough. I certainly won't be the reason for more tension and unhappiness between you."

"But Honey—"

She pressed her finger to his lips. "No, Harrison." She closed his fingers around the ring and kissed his cheek.

"Thank you, but no, I can't marry you. I'm leaving my partner in charge of the project and I'm leaving town tonight."

She hadn't planned that, but now that he'd proposed she had to. If she stayed another minute, she'd back down, confess her love and throw herself at him.

Her chest burned with the pressure of holding back her tears, and she rushed to her van, climbed inside and sped away from the curb. She glanced in the rearview mirror and wished she hadn't. He stood ramrod still, his handsome face etched in hurt, staring after her.

But she didn't turn back. She told herself to keep driving until she reached Austin.

HARRISON MET HIS brothers at the Broken Spoke for a beer to drown his sorrows.

"You look like someone shot you," Lucas said.

Dexter elbowed him as he poured himself a beer from the pitcher. "Or run over you."

Brayden took a mug for himself. "Yeah, what gives?"

Honey had turned him down, that was what was wrong. She must not love him.

"If you're worried about Mom, I think she's okay," Brayden said.

"Yeah, except she hates Honey," Harrison muttered in frustration.

"What does that matter?" Dexter asked.

Harrison stared into his beer, sullen and brooding.

"Uh-oh," Lucas said. "I know what's wrong. You fell for Honey, didn't you?"

Harrison cut his eyes toward Lucas. "She's nothing like what Mom thought."

"I know," Brayden said. "Hell, have you seen the houses she's renovated in Austin? They're amazing."

"And she's doing that here in Lower Tumbleweed," Dexter said, a hint of awe in his voice.

Misery clawed at Harrison. "She's pretty amazing."

Lucas chuckled. "So what are you going to do about it?"

Harrison grunted and took a sip of his beer. "I asked her to marry me."

"Whoa," Brayden said. "That's serious."

"When's the wedding?" Dexter asked.

Harrison cursed. "She turned me down."

"Damn," Lucas said.

"Why?" Dexter asked.

"I thought she was crushing on you in high school," Brayden added.

"Mother hasn't made any bones about the way she feels about Honey," Harrison said, his throat rough with emotions. "Honey said she wouldn't come between me and my family."

"Good God, she does love you," Brayden said.

Harrison looked at them in confusion. "Did you hear me? I said she turned me down."

"She wouldn't care so much about your family if she didn't love you," Dexter said.

Harrison rubbed his hand over his eyes. Were his brothers right? Did Honey love him?

If so, how could he convince her to marry him?

He shoved his beer away. "I have to talk to Mother." Then he hurried from the bar. He just hoped he could persuade his mother that she was wrong about Honey.

He didn't want to have to choose between them...

HONEY HAD CRIED herself sick all the way back to Austin. She slipped into her house, the empty walls echoing with loneliness, a reminder of what she'd left behind.

All her life she'd wanted Harrison. Had fantasized about having him touch her, hold her, make love to her.

Had dreamed about being his wife.

Although she thought she'd cried all her tears out, another sob escaped her and the flood began again.

She showered, purging her emotions and praying one day she'd get past the pain of losing Harrison.

But he was the only man she'd ever loved.

And she would never get over him.

Chapter Twenty-Six

Two days later

Honey hung the last of the sketches for Lower Tumbleweed on the wall of the showroom in her home office. The houses were going to be beautiful.

The developer she was working with, a man named Tanner Baldwin, was almost as excited about the project as she was.

Fatigue pulled at her muscles, and she stood and stretched. Everything was going well in her business.

But at night, the empty rooms of her house haunted her.

She missed Harrison so much that her heart literally throbbed.

A knock sounded on the door, and she rushed to answer it. Surprise tightened her chest. Harrison's mother, Mrs. Hawk, entered, her gaze wary as she glanced around the interior of the showroom.

Uncertain what to expect from the woman, Honey simply folded her arms and greeted her. She'd seen the notice for the memorial service for Chrissy and knew the past week had been difficult for the Hawks.

"Hello, Honey," Mrs. Hawk said.

She offered the woman a tentative smile. "Mrs. Hawk."

Mrs. Hawk feathered her hair behind one ear. "We need to talk."

Honey frowned. Was she going to try to stop her from developing that neighborhood? "If this is about the housing development—"

"It is and it's not," Mrs. Hawk said, cutting her off.

"I don't understand," Honey said.

Mrs. Hawk walked over and studied the sketches on the wall. "I saw your plans."

Honey swallowed hard. "What is it you don't approve of, the plans or the fact that I'm developing the neighborhood?"

Mrs. Hawk winced. "I guess I deserve that, but truthfully I think the plans are phenomenal."

Shock slammed into Honey. "Really?"

"Yes, I'm impressed with what you're doing for our town, especially considering how some of the people treated you."

"Some of the people?" Honey said, hurt lacing her voice.

Mrs. Hawk nodded. "Yes, some of them. And I'm aware that includes me."

An awkward silence stretched between them. Honey wanted to fill it, but her emotions got in the way. Besides, she still didn't know the woman's agenda.

And she was certain Mrs. Hawk had one.

"I came to apologize." Mrs. Hawk's voice cracked. "I… I misjudged you."

Honey arched a brow, speechless.

Mrs. Hawk fiddled with the cuff of her satin blouse, obviously nervous. Tense seconds passed.

Honey remained silent, waiting on the other shoe to drop. "What is it you want?"

The woman winced again. "Like I said, I came to apologize. I was harsh toward you when you lived in Lower Tumbleweed." She paused and fidgeted. "But I had my reasons."

She'd driven all the way to Austin to justify her behavior. "I know, I wasn't good enough for your family." Honey sighed. "You didn't need to come here to tell me that again."

"That's not exactly it." Mrs. Hawk dropped her purse onto the conference table where Honey usually met with clients.

"Then what is it?"

Mrs. Hawk inhaled sharply. "When you were a teenager, you reminded me of myself."

Honey stared at her in shock. She certainly hadn't expected the woman to say that.

"I had a wild streak in me before I met Steven, the boys' father. In fact, I didn't exactly come from a very nice family myself."

"You didn't?"

Mrs. Hawk shook her head. "No, my mother was the alcoholic, though. She also slept around. And then when Steven and I had trouble, and I had that affair, I was terrified I was going to be like her. So I broke it off with the other man, and Steven and I made amends, and I swore I would make it up to him the rest of our lives."

Honey had never imagined Harrison's mother as anything but the imposing, judgmental woman who'd hated her.

"Anyway, it doesn't make my behavior right, but I wanted my kids to grow up and have everything. Then Chrissy became infatuated with you and I was terrified she'd end up like me or my mother, and I...took it out on you."

"I would never have hurt her," Honey said. "I think she just wanted a big sister."

"I know." Mrs. Hawk's voice cracked. "I've blamed myself for years for her disappearance. I thought that perhaps she'd run off because I was too harsh on her and that's why she was taken from me."

Sympathy for the woman filled Honey. "Chrissy loved you," she said simply. "She wasn't running away from you."

Tears trickled down her cheeks. She wiped them away with trembling hands. "I was wrong and cruel to you. You deserved kindness and understanding, not my judgmental attitude."

Honey bit her bottom lip. She didn't know how to respond.

"Anyway, I don't know if you can ever forgive me, but I realize now that I lost a daughter and have a void in my heart from missing her, and you lost a mother and you might have a void, too."

Honey swallowed hard.

Mrs. Hawk continued, "I admire what you've done here in Austin and what you're doing in Tumbleweed, and I wanted you to know that if you and Harrison want to be together, that you have my approval."

Honey's heart squeezed. "Mrs. Hawk, I care about your son, but—"

"No buts," Mrs. Hawk said. "My son has been miserable the past few days. He loves you, and he's blamed himself long enough for what happened to Chrissy. He deserves to be happy, and if that means marrying you, then that's what I want for him." She gestured toward herself then to Honey. "I just hope that you can find some way to forgive me and we could perhaps even be friends."

The woman held out her hands in an offering, and Honey read the sincerity in her eyes and voice. How could she say no?

"You do love him, don't you?" Mrs. Hawk asked.

Tears blurred Honey's eyes. "Yes."

A smile broadened the woman's face. "Then let's go tell him."

Harrison dreaded another family dinner. Dammit, he was tired of trying to put on a happy face. He missed Honey like crazy.

His brothers had guessed the reason for his sour mood and his mother had interrogated him, but he'd refused to talk about it.

How could he tell her that she'd run off the love of his life? Although part of him wondered if Honey just didn't love him.

If she did, why hadn't she fought to be with him?

You know why. She hates Tumbleweed and the people in it.

Although if she truly hated the town, why was she spending money and time developing that neighborhood for other families to move into? If she hated it, why wouldn't she have simply sold off her father's land and be done with the community?

Did she think she had something to prove to everyone?

He wiped his feet on the mat and went inside the house, surprised that his mother didn't greet him at the door. The funeral had been heart wrenching, but afterward, it almost seemed as if a weight had been lifted from her shoulders.

The burden of not knowing had taken its toll on all of the Hawks.

Brayden, Dexter and Lucas met him in the dining room, and greeted him with a drink. The scent of something cooking—maybe her Crock-Pot chicken stew—wafted to him.

"Where's Mom?"

His brothers shrugged and looked around with vague expressions. Before they could discuss it further, the door opened and his mother's heels clicked on the foyer floor. When she rounded the corner into the dining room, he was surprised to see Honey with her.

He froze, drink midair, mouth agape.

Honey's gaze met his, uncertainty glinting in her eyes.

"We have company tonight," his mother said.

He and his brothers traded confused looks, then his mother waved her hand toward the bar. "Well, where are your manners, boys? Someone get Honey a drink."

A tiny smile tugged at the corner of Honey's mouth. Lucas rushed to the bar. "Wine? Scotch?"

"White wine would be nice," Honey said softly.

Lucas poured her a glass while Harrison stood gaping at her like a lovesick fool. He wanted to swing her up in his arms and carry her upstairs, but she had turned down his proposal, and his pride and heart still ached.

"It will take me a few minutes to get dinner on the table," his mother said. "Harrison, why don't you take Honey outside for some fresh air? I think she has something to say to you."

Honey shrugged. "Maybe this is a bad time."

"This is a fine time," his mother said firmly.

Lucas nudged him. Dexter chuckled and Brayden raised a brow in challenge. He felt like an idiot.

Honey dampened her lips with her tongue, drawing his hungry gaze to her mouth. "Harrison?"

He gathered his wits and gestured toward the front door. "Yes, let's step onto the porch."

Her sweet scent teased at his senses as he followed her to the front porch like a dog in heat.

"If you want me to leave, just say so," she said as she faced him on the porch.

"I don't want you to leave," he said gruffly. "I just wasn't expecting you. Is something wrong?"

She bit down on her lower lip then shook her head slightly. "Your mother came to see me."

Shock slithered through him. "God, Honey, I'm sorry. I had no idea she was going to do that. What in the world did she say to you now?"

A slow smile spread on her beautiful face. "Actually we had a nice talk. She apologized for the way she treated me."

"My mother apologized?"

Honey nodded. "We came to an understanding."

He rubbed his forehead, confused. "What kind of understanding?"

Honey sipped her wine, her gaze hooded as she stepped closer to him. Then she lifted her chin with that stubborn glint that he recognized from childhood. And from their discussions about her father and the investigation.

"An understanding that we both care about you," she said.

His heart picked up a beat.

"In spite of everything, I know my mother loves me," he said, uncertain of her meaning.

She raised one hand and pressed it against his cheek. "So do I, Harrison."

His breath stalled in his chest. Did she mean that?

"Am I too late?" Honey asked. "Have you changed your mind about wanting me?"

A deep laugh rumbled from him, pure surprise, joy and hope, and he swung her up into his arms. "Not a chance."

She fused her mouth with his, and he kissed her so deeply that every cell his body screamed with hunger. "I have to know this is forever, though," he murmured against her ear as they broke the kiss. "I know you hate this town and I don't want you to be unhappy." He pulled away and gazed into her eyes, pouring his love and heart into the words. "I want us to be a family, to get married and have a home and babies. And if that means leaving Tumbleweed, we will."

Honey looped her arms around his neck. "Home is wherever you are, Harrison."

"God, I love you," he growled.

"I love you, too."

He wrapped his arms around her and kissed her again. "And you'll marry me?" he murmured.

Moonlight played off her eyes, which sparkled with affection. "Yes, Harrison, I'll marry you."

He reached inside his pocket and retrieved the ring that he'd bought her. He'd considered returning it, but had held on to it just as he'd held on to hope that one day she'd change her mind and have him.

He knelt on one knee, took her hand in his and slid the diamond onto her finger.

Tears slipped down her cheeks, but her radiant smile told him they were tears of happiness.

The front door swung open then, and his brothers appeared. "What's going on?" Brayden asked.

Harrison scooped Honey into his arms, swung her around, joy overflowing from both of them.

"I'm marrying Honey Granger," he shouted.

His mother appeared then, a smile on her face. "It's about time we had a wedding at Hawk's Landing."

He looked at Honey for confirmation, and she kissed him and murmured, "Yes." His brothers cheered and congratulated them, and Harrison hugged his mother.

Finally the dark days were over for the Hawks. A new chapter was starting, and he and Honey would make their own family and create new, happy memories together.

Memories that would bring Hawk's Landing back to life again just the way Honey had brought new life back to him.

Memories that would last forever.

* * * * *

Look for more books in USA TODAY
bestselling author Rita Herron's new series,
BADGE OF JUSTICE,
in 2018.

And don't miss the titles in her previous series,
THE HEROES OF HORSESHOE CREEK:

LOCK, STOCK AND McCULLEN
McCULLEN'S SECRET SON
ROPING RAY McCULLEN
WARRIOR SON
THE MISSING McCULLEN
THE LAST McCULLEN

Available from Mills & Boon Intrigue!

Sheriff Flint Cahill can and will endure elements far worse than the coming winter storm to hunt down Maggie Thompson and her abductor.

Read on for a sneak preview of
COWBOY'S LEGACY,
a CAHILL RANCH *novel from*
New York Times *bestselling author*
B.J. Daniels!

SHE WAS IN so fast that she didn't have a chance to scream. The icy cold water stole her breath away. Her eyes flew open as she hit. Because of the way she fell, she had no sense of up or down for a few moments.

Panicked, she flailed in the water until a light flickered above her. She tried to swim toward it, but something was holding her down. The harder she fought, the more it seemed to push her deeper and deeper, the light fading.

Her lungs burned. She had to breathe. The dim light wavered above her through the rippling water. She clawed at it as her breath gave out. She could see the surface just inches above her. Air! She needed oxygen. Now!

The rippling water distorted the face that suddenly appeared above her. The mouth twisted in a grotesque smile. She screamed, only to have her throat fill with the putrid, dark water. She choked, sucking in even more water. She was drowning, and the person who'd done this to her was watching her die and smiling.

Maggie Thompson shot upright in bed, gasping for air and swinging her arms frantically toward the faint light coming through the window. Panic had her perspiration-soaked nightgown sticking to her skin. Trembling, she clutched the bedcovers as she gasped for breath.

The nightmare had been so real this time that she thought she was going to drown before she could come out of it. Her chest ached, her throat feeling raw as tears burned her eyes. It had been too real. She couldn't shake the feeling that she'd almost died this time. Next time...

She snapped on the bedside lamp to chase away the dark shadows hunkered in the corners of the room. If only Flint had been here instead of on an all-night stakeout. She needed Sheriff Flint Cahill's strong arms around her. Not that he stayed most nights. They hadn't been intimate that long.

Often, he had to work or was called out in the middle of the night. He'd asked her to move in with him months ago, but she'd declined. He'd asked her after one of his ex-wife's nasty tricks. Maggie hadn't wanted to make a decision like that based on Flint's ex.

While his ex hadn't done anything in months to keep them apart, Maggie couldn't rest easy. Flint was hoping Celeste had grown tired of her tricks. Maggie wasn't that naive. Celeste Duma was one of those women who played on every man's weakness to get what she wanted—and she wanted not just the rich, powerful man she'd left Flint for. She wanted to keep her ex on the string, as well.

Maggie's breathing slowed a little. She pulled the covers up to her chin, still shivering, but she didn't turn off the light. Sleep was out of the question for a while. She told herself that she wasn't going to let Celeste scare her. She wasn't going to give the woman the satisfaction.

Unfortunately, it was just bravado. Flint's ex was obsessed with him. Obsessed with keeping them apart. And since the woman had nothing else to do...

As the images of the nightmare faded, she reminded herself that the dream made no sense. It never had. She was a good swimmer. Loved water. Had never nearly drowned. Nor had anyone ever tried to drown her.

Shuddering, she thought of the face she'd seen through the rippling water. Not Celeste's. More like a Halloween mask. A distorted smiling face, neither male nor female. Just the memory sent her heart racing again.

What bothered her most was that dream kept reoccurring. After the first time, she'd mentioned it to her friend Belle Delaney.

"A drowning dream?" Belle had asked with an arch of her eyebrow. "Do you feel that in waking life you're being 'sucked into' something you'd rather not be a part of?"

Maggie had groaned inwardly. Belle had never kept it a secret that she thought Maggie was making a mistake when it came to Flint. Too much baggage, she always said of the sheriff. His "baggage" came in the shape of his spoiled, probably psychopathic, petite, green-eyed, blonde ex.

"I have my own skeletons." Maggie had laughed, although she'd never shared her past—even with Belle— before moving to Gilt Edge, Montana, and opening her beauty shop, Just Hair. She feared it was her own baggage that scared her the most.

"If you're holding anything back," Belle had said, eyeing her closely, "you need to let it out. Men hate surprises after they tie the knot."

"Guess I don't have to worry about that because Flint hasn't said anything about marriage." But she knew Belle was right. She'd even come close to telling him several times about her past. Something had always stopped her. The truth was, she feared if he found out her reasons for coming to Gilt Edge he wouldn't want her anymore.

"The dream isn't about Flint," she'd argued that day with Belle, but she couldn't shake the feeling that it was a warning.

"Well, from what I know about dreams," Belle had said, "if in the dream you survive the drowning, it means that a waking relationship will ultimately survive the turmoil. At least, that is one interpretation. But I'd say the nightmare definitely indicates that you are going into unknown waters and something is making you leery of where you're headed." She'd cocked an eyebrow at her. "If you have the dream again, I'd suggest that you ask yourself what it is you're so afraid of."

"I'm sure it's just about his ex, Celeste," she'd lied. Or was she afraid that she wasn't good enough for Flint—just as his ex had warned her. Just as she feared in her heart.

THE WIND LAY over the tall dried grass and kicked up dust as Sheriff Flint Cahill stood on the hillside. He shoved his Stetson down on his head of thick dark hair, squinting in the distance at the clouds to the west. Sure as the devil, it was going to snow before the day was out.

In the distance, he could see a large star made out of red and green lights on the side of a barn, a reminder that Christmas was coming. Flint thought he might even get a tree this year, go up in the mountains and cut it himself. He hadn't had a tree at Christmas in years. Not since…

At the sound of a pickup horn, he turned, shielding his eyes from the low winter sun. He could smell snow in the air, feel it deep in his bones. This storm was going to dump a good foot on them, according to the latest news. They were going to have a white Christmas.

Most years he wasn't ready for the holiday season any more than he was ready for a snow that wouldn't melt until spring. But this year was different. He felt energized. This was the year his life would change. He thought of the small velvet box in his jacket pocket. He'd been carrying it around for months. Just the thought of it made him smile to himself. He was in love and he was finally going to do something about it.

The pickup rumbled to a stop a few yards from him. He took a deep breath of the mountain air and, telling himself he was ready for whatever Mother Nature wanted to throw at him, he headed for the truck.

"Are you all right?" his sister asked as he slid into the passenger seat. In the cab, out of the wind, it was nice and warm. He rubbed his bare hands together, wishing he hadn't forgotten his gloves earlier. But when he'd headed out, he'd had too much on his mind. He still did.

Lillie looked out at the dull brown of the landscape and the chain-link fence that surrounded the missile silo. "What were you doing out here?"

He chuckled. "Looking for aliens. What else?" This was the spot that their father swore aliens hadn't just landed on one night back in 1967. Nope, according to Ely Cahill, the aliens had abducted him, taken him aboard their spaceship and done experiments on him. Not that anyone believed it in the county. Everyone just assumed that Ely had a screw loose. Or two.

It didn't help that their father spent most of the year up in the mountains as a recluse trapping and panning for gold.

"Aliens. Funny," Lillie said, making a face at him.

He smiled over at her. "Actually, I was on an all-night stakeout. The cattle rustlers didn't show up." He shrugged.

She glanced around. "Where's your patrol SUV?"

"Axle deep in a muddy creek back toward Grass Range. I'll have to get it pulled out. After I called you, I started walking and I ended up here. Wish I'd grabbed my gloves, though."

"You're scaring me," she said, studying him openly. "You're starting to act like Dad."

He laughed at that, wondering how far from the truth it was. "At least I didn't see any aliens near the missile silo."

She groaned. Being the butt of jokes in the county because of their father got old for all of them.

Flint glanced at the fenced-in area. There was nothing visible behind the chain link but tumbleweeds. He turned back to her. "I didn't pull you away from anything important, I hope? Since you were close by, I thought you wouldn't mind giving me a ride. I've had enough walking for one day. Or thinking, for that matter."

She shook her head. "What's going on, Flint?"

He looked out at the country that ran to the mountains. Cahill Ranch. His grandfather had started it, his father had worked it and now two of his brothers ran the cattle part of it to keep the place going while he and his sister, Lillie, and brother Darby had taken other paths. Not to mention their oldest brother, Tucker, who'd struck out at seventeen and hadn't been seen or heard from since.

Flint had been scared after his marriage and divorce. But Maggie was nothing like Celeste, who was small, blonde, green-eyed and crazy. Maggie was tall with big brown eyes and long auburn hair. His heart beat faster at the thought of her smile, at her laugh.

"I'm going to ask Maggie to marry me," Flint said and nodded as if reassuring himself.

When Lillie didn't reply, he glanced over at her. It wasn't like her not to have something to say. "Well?"

"What has taken you so long?"

He sighed. "Well, you know after Celeste…"

"Say no more," his sister said, raising a hand to stop him. "Anyone would be gun-shy after being married to her."

"I'm hoping she won't be a problem."

Lillie laughed. "Short of killing your ex-wife, she is always going to be a problem. You just have to decide if you're going to let her run your life. Or if you're going to live it—in spite of her."

So easy for her to say. He smiled, though. "You're right. Anyway, Maggie and I have been dating for a while now and there haven't been any…incidents in months."

Lillie shook her head. "You know Celeste was the one who vandalized Maggie's beauty shop—just as you know she started that fire at Maggie's house."

"Too bad there wasn't any proof so I could have arrested her. But since there wasn't and no one was hurt and it was months ago…"

"I'd love to see Celeste behind bars, though I think prison is too good for her. I can understand why you would be worried about what she will do next. She's psychopathic."

He feared that that maybe was close to the case. "Do you want to see the ring?" He knew she did, so he fished it out of his pocket. He'd been carrying it around for quite a while now. Getting up his courage? He knew what was holding him back. Celeste. He couldn't be sure how she would take it—or what she might do. His ex-wife seemed determined that he and Maggie shouldn't be together, even though she was apparently happily married to local wealthy businessman Wayne Duma.

Handing his sister the small black velvet box, he waited as she slowly opened it.

A small gasp escaped her lips. "It's beautiful. *Really* beautiful." She shot him a look. "I thought sheriffs didn't make much money?"

"I've been saving for a long while now. Unlike my sister, I live pretty simply."

She laughed. "Simply? Prisoners have more in their cells than you do. You aren't thinking of living in that small house of yours after you're married, are you?"

"For a while. It's not that bad. Not all of us have huge new houses like you and Trask."

"We need the room for all the kids we're going to have," she said. "But it is wonderful, isn't it? Trask is determined that I have everything I ever wanted." Her gaze softened as the newlywed thought of her husband.

"I keep thinking of your wedding." There'd been a double wedding, with both Lillie and her twin, Darby, getting married to the loves of their lives only months ago. "It's great to see you and Trask so happy. And Darby and Mariah... I don't think Darby is ever going to come off that cloud he's on."

Lillie smiled. "I'm so happy for him. And I'm happy for you. You know I really like Maggie. So do it. Don't worry about Celeste. Once you're married, there's nothing she can do."

He told himself she was right, and yet in the back of his mind, he feared that his ex-wife would do something to ruin it—just as she had done to some of his dates with Maggie.

"I don't understand Celeste," Lillie was saying as she shifted into Drive and started toward the small Western town of Gilt Edge. "She's the one who dumped you for Wayne Duma. So what is her problem?"

"I'm worried that she is having second thoughts about her marriage to Duma. Or maybe she's bored and has nothing better to do than concern herself with my life. Maybe she just doesn't want me to be happy."

"Or she is just plain malicious," Lillie said. "If she isn't happy, she doesn't want you to be, either."

A shaft of sunlight came through the cab window, warming him against the chill that came with even talking about Celeste. He leaned back, content as Lillie drove.

He was going to ask Maggie to marry him. He was going to do it this weekend. He'd already made a dinner reservation at the local steak house. He had the ring in his pocket. Now it was just a matter of popping the question and hoping she said yes. If she did…well, then, this was going to be the best Christmas ever, he thought and smiled.

* * * * *

*COWBOY'S LEGACY, available
wherever Mills & Boon Books and
ebooks are sold.*

www.millsandboon.co.uk

MILLS & BOON®

INTRIGUE
Romantic Suspense

A SEDUCTIVE COMBINATION OF DANGER AND DESIRE

A sneak peek at next month's titles...

In stores from 14th December 2017:

- **Gunfire on the Ranch** – Delores Fossen *and* **Safe at Hawk's Landing** – Rita Herron
- **Ranger Protector** – Angi Morgan *and* **Whispering Springs** – Amanda Stevens
- **Soldier's Promise** – Cindi Myers *and* **Forgotten Pieces** – Tyler Anne Snell

Romantic Suspense

- **Colton Baby Rescue** – Marie Ferrarella
- **In the Bodyguard's Arms** – Lisa Childs

Just can't wait?
Buy our books online before they hit the shops!
www.millsandboon.co.uk

Also available as eBooks.